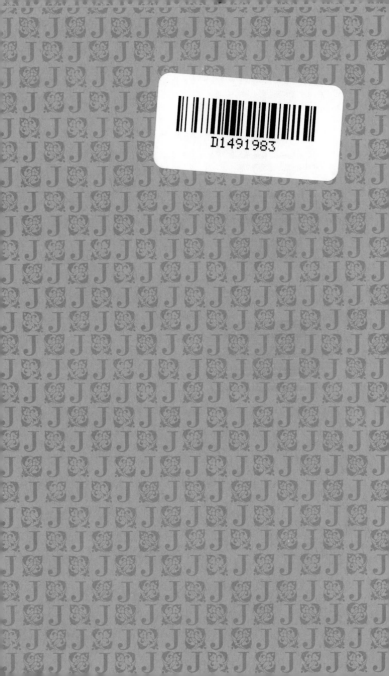

A Publication Distributed by Heron Books

RODERICK HUDSON

HENRY JAMES

1843–1916

RODERICK HUDSON

BY

HENRY JAMES

DISTRIBUTED BY HERON BOOKS

I.S.B.N. for complete set of ten volumes:
0 86225 187 7
I.S.B.N. for this title:
0 86225 189 3

RODERICK HUDSON.

I.

ROWLAND MALLET had made his arrangements to sail for Europe on the 1st of September, and having in the interval a fortnight to spare, he determined to spend it with his cousin Cecilia, the widow of a nephew of his father. He was urged by the reflection that an affectionate farewell might help to exonerate him from the charge of neglect frequently preferred by this lady. It was not that the young man disliked her; on the contrary he regarded her with a tender admiration, and he had not forgotten how when his cousin brought her home on her marriage he seemed to feel the upward sweep of the empty bough from which the golden fruit had been plucked, and then and there accepted the prospect of bachelorhood. The truth was that, as it will be part of the entertainment of this narrative to exhibit, Rowland Mallet had an uncomfortably sensitive conscience, and that, in spite of the seeming paradox, his visits to Cecilia were rare because she and her misfortunes were often uppermost in it. Her misfortunes were three in number: first she had lost her husband; second she had lost her money (or the greater part of it); and third she lived at Northampton, Massachusetts. Mallet's compassion was really wasted, because Cecilia was a very clever woman and a skilful counterplotter to adversity. She had made herself a charming home, her economies were not obtrusive, and there was always a cheerful flutter in the folds of her crape. It was

the consciousness of all this that puzzled Mallet whenever
he felt tempted to put in his oar.   He had money and he
had time, but he never could decide just how to place these
gifts gracefully at Cecilia's service.   He no longer felt
like marrying her ; in these eight years that fancy had died
a natural death.   And yet her extreme cleverness seemed
somehow to make charity difficult and patronage impossible.   He would rather chop off his hand than offer
her a cheque, a piece of useful furniture, or a black silk
dress ; and yet there was much sadness in seeing such a
bright proud woman living in such a small dull way.
Cecilia had moreover a turn for sarcasm, and her smile,
which was her pretty feature, was never so pretty as when
her sprightly phrase had a lurking scratch in it.   Rowland
remembered that for him she was all smiles, and suspected awkwardly that he ministered not a little to her
sense of the irony of things.   And in truth, with his
means, his leisure and his opportunities, what had he
done ?   He had a lively suspicion of his uselessness.
Cecilia meanwhile cut out her own dresses, and was
personally giving her little girl the education of a
princess.

This time however he presented himself bravely enough ;
for in the way of activity it was something definite at
least to be going to Europe and to be meaning to spend
the winter in Rome.   Cecilia met him in the early dusk at
the gate of her little garden, amid a studied combination
of horticultural odours.   A rosy widow of twenty-eight,
half-cousin, half-hostess, doing the honours of a fragrant
cottage on a midsummer evening, was a phenomenon to
which the young man's imagination was able to do ample
justice.   Cecilia was always gracious, but this evening she
was almost joyous.   She was in a happy mood, and Mallet
imagined there was a private reason for it—a reason quite
distinct from her pleasure in receiving her honoured kinsman.   The next day he flattered himself he was on the
way to discover it.

For the present, after tea, as they sat on the rose-framed
porch, while Rowland held his younger cousin between his
knees, and she, enjoying her situation, listened timorously
for the stroke of bedtime, Cecilia insisted on talking more
about her visitor than about herself.

"What is it you mean to do in Europe?" she asked lightly, giving a turn to the frill of her sleeve—just such a turn as seemed to Mallet to bring out all the latent difficulties of the question.

"Why, very much what I do here," he answered. "No great harm!"

"Is it true," Cecilia asked, "that here you do no great harm? Is not a man like you doing harm when he is not doing positive good?"

"Your compliment is ambiguous," said Rowland.

"No," answered the widow, "you know what I think of you. You have a turn for doing nice things and behaving yourself properly. You have it in the first place in your character. You are an amiable creature. Ask Bessie if you don't hold her more gently and comfortably than any of her other admirers."

"He holds me more comfortably than Mr. Hudson," Bessie declared roundly.

Rowland, not knowing Mr. Hudson, could but half appreciate the eulogy, and Cecilia went on to develop her idea. "Your circumstances in the second place suggest the idea of some sort of social usefulness. You are intelligent, you are well-informed, and your benevolence, if one may call it benevolence, would be discriminating. You are rich and unoccupied, so that it might be abundant. Therefore I say you are a man to do something on a large scale. Bestir yourself, dear Rowland, or we may be taught to think that virtue herself is setting a bad example."

"Heaven forbid," cried Rowland, "that I should set the examples of virtue! I am quite willing to follow them however, and if I don't do something on the grand scale it is that my genius is altogether imitative and that I have not recently encountered any very striking models of grandeur. Pray what shall I do? Found an orphan asylum or build a dormitory for Harvard College? I am not rich enough to do either in an ideally handsome way, and I confess that yet a while I feel too young to strike my *grand coup*. I am holding myself ready for inspiration. I am waiting till something takes my fancy irresistibly. If inspiration comes at forty, it will be a hundred pities to have tied up my money-bag at thirty."

"Well, I give you till forty," said Cecilia. "It's only a word to the wise—a notification that you are expected not to run your course without having done something handsome for your fellow-men."

Nine o'clock sounded, and Bessie with each stroke courted a closer embrace. But a single winged word from her mother overleaped her successive intrenchments. She turned and kissed her cousin and deposited an irrepressible tear on his moustache. Then she went and said her prayers to her mother; it was evident she was being admirably brought up. Rowland with the permission of his hostess lighted a cigar and puffed it a while in silence. Cecilia's interest in his career seemed very agreeable. That Mallet was without vanity I by no means intend to affirm; but there had been times when, seeing him accept hardly less deferentially advice even more peremptory than the widow's, you might have asked yourself what had become of his vanity. Now, in the sweet-smelling starlight he felt gently wooed to egotism. There was a project connected with his going abroad which it was on his tongue's end to communicate. It had no relation to hospitals or dormitories, and yet it would have sounded very generous. But it was not because it would have sounded generous that poor Mallet at last puffed it away in the fumes of his cigar. Useful though it might be, it expressed most imperfectly the young man's own personal conception of usefulness. He was extremely fond of all the arts, and he had an almost passionate enjoyment of pictures. He had seen a great many, and he judged them sagaciously. It had occurred to him some time before that it would be the work of a good citizen to go abroad and with all expedition and secrecy purchase certain valuable specimens of the Dutch and Italian schools as to which he had received private proposals, and then present his treasures out of hand to an American city, not unknown to æsthetic fame, in which at that time there prevailed a good deal of fruitless aspiration toward an art-museum. He had seen himself in imagination, more than once, in some mouldy old saloon of a Florentine palace, turning toward the deep embrasure of the window some scarcely-faded Ghirlandaio or Botticelli, while a host in reduced circumstances pointed out the lovely drawing of a hand.

But he imparted none of these visions to Cecilia, and he suddenly swept them away with the declaration that he was of course an idle useless creature, and that he should probably be even more so in Europe than at home. "The only thing is," he said, "that there I shall *seem* to be doing something. I shall be better entertained and shall be therefore, I suppose, in a better humour with life. You may say that that is just the humour a useless man should keep out of. He should cultivate discontent. I did a good many things when I was in Europe before, but I did not spend a winter in Rome. Every one assures me that this is a peculiar refinement of bliss ; most people talk about Rome in the same way. It is evidently only a sort of idealized form of loafing : a passive life in Rome, thanks to the number and the quality of one's impressions, takes on a very respectable likness to activity. It is still lotus-eating, only you sit down at table and the lotuses are served up on rococo china. It's all very well, but I have a distinct prevision of this—that if Roman life doesn't do something substantial to make you happier, it increases tenfold your liability to moral misery. It seems to me a rash thing for a sensitive soul deliberately to cultivate its sensibilities by rambling too often among the ruins of the Palatine or riding too often in the shadow of the crumbling aqueducts. In such recreations the chords of feeling grow tense, and after-life, to spare your intellectual nerves, must play upon them with a touch as dainty as the tread of Mignon when she danced her egg-dance."

"I should have said, my dear Rowland," said Cecilia, with a laugh, "that your nerves were tough—that your eggs were hard ! "

"That being stupid, you mean, I might be happy ? Upon my word I am not happy ! I am clever enough to want more than I have got. I am tired of myself, my own thoughts, my own affairs, my own eternal company. True happiness, we are told, consists in getting out of one's self ; but the point is not only to get out—you must stay out ; and to stay out you must have some absorbing errand. Unfortunately I have no errand, and nobody will trust me with one. I want to care for something or for somebody. And I want to care with a certain ardour ; even, if you can believe it, with a certain passion. I can't just now feel ardent and passionate about a hospital or a dormitory. Do you know I sometimes think that I am a man of genius, half finished? The genius has been left out, the faculty of expression is wanting; but the need for expression remains, and I spend my days groping for the latch of a closed door."

"What an immense number of words," said Cecilia after a pause, "to say you want to fall in love! I have no doubt you have as good a genius for that as any one, if you would only trust it."

"Of course I have thought of that, and I assure you I hold myself ready. But evidently I am not inflammable. Is there in Northampton some perfect epitome of the graces?"

"Of the graces?" said Cecilia, raising her eyebrows and suppressing too distinct a consciousness of being herself a rosy embodiment of several. "The household virtues are better represented. There are some excellent girls, and there are two or three very pretty ones. I will have them here one by one to tea, if you like."

"I should particularly like it; especially as I should give you a chance to see by the profundity of my attention that if I am not happy it's not for want of taking pains."

Cecilia was silent a moment; and then, "On the whole," she resumed, "I don't think there are any worth asking. There are none so very pretty, none so very pleasing."

"Are you very sure?" asked the young man, rising and throwing away his cigar-end.

"Upon my word," cried Cecilia, "one would suppose I wished to keep you for myself! Of course I am sure! But as the penalty of your insinuations, I shall invite the plainest and prosiest damsel that can be found and leave you alone with her."

Rowland smiled. "Even against her," he said, "I should be sorry to conclude until I had given her my respectful attention."

This little profession of ideal chivalry (which closed the conversation) was not quite so fanciful on Mallet's lips as it would have been on those of many another man; as a rapid glance at his antecedents may help to make the reader perceive. His life had been a singular mixture of

the rough and the smooth. He had sprung from a rigid
Puritan stock, and had been brought up to think much more
intently of the duties of this life than of its privileges and
pleasures. His progenitors had submitted in the matter of
dogmatic theology to the relaxing influences of recent years ;
but if Rowland's youthful consciousness was not chilled
by the menace of long punishment for brief transgression,
he had at least been made to feel that there ran through
all things a strain of right and of wrong as different after
all in their complexion as the texture to the spiritual sense
of Sundays and week-days. His father was a chip of the
primal Puritan block, a man with an icy smile and a stony
frown. He had always bestowed on his son, on principle,
more frowns than smiles, and if the lad had not been turned
to stone himself it was because nature had blessed him
inwardly with a well of vivifying waters. Mrs. Mallet had
been a Miss Rowland, the daughter of a retired sea-captain
once famous on the ships that sailed from Salem and New-
buryport. He had brought to port many a cargo which
crowned the edifice of fortunes already almost colossal,
but he had also done a little sagacious trading on his own
account, and he was able to retire, prematurely for so
seaworthy a maritime organism, upon a pension of his
own providing. He was to be seen for a year on the
Salem wharves, smoking the best tobacco and contemplating
the seaward horizon with an inveteracy which superficial
minds interpreted as a sign of repentance. At last, one
evening, he disappeared beneath it, as he had often done
before ; this time however not as a commissioned navigator,
but simply as an amateur of an observing turn likely to
prove oppressive to the officer in command of the vessel.
Five months later his place at home knew him again, and
made the acquaintance also of a handsome, light-coloured
young woman, of redundant contour, speaking a foreign
tongue. The foreign tongue proved after much conflicting
research to be the idiom of Amsterdam, and the young
woman, which was stranger still, to be Captain Rowland's
wife. Why he had gone forth so suddenly across the seas
to marry her, what had happened between them before,
and whether—though it was of questionable propriety for
a good citizen to espouse a young person of mysterious
origin who did her hair in fantastically elaborate plaits

and in whose appearance "figure" enjoyed such striking predominance—he would not have had a heavy weight on his conscience if he had remained an irresponsible bachelor; these questions and many others bearing with varying degrees of immediacy on the subject were much propounded but scantily answered, and this history need not be charged with resolving them. Mrs. Rowland, for so handsome a woman, proved a tranquil neighbour and an excellent housewife. Her extremely fresh complexion however was always suffused with an air of apathetic homesickness, and she played her part in American society chiefly by having the little squares of brick pavement in front of her dwelling scoured and polished as nearly as possible into the likeness of Dutch tiles. Rowland Mallet remembered having seen her as a child—an immensely stout white-faced lady, wearing a high cap of very stiff tulle, speaking English with a formidable accent and suffering from dropsy. Captain Rowland was a little bronzed and wizened man, with eccentric opinions. He advocated the creation of a public promenade along the sea, with arbours and little green tables for the consumption of beer, and a platform, surrounded by Chinese lanterns, for dancing. He especially desired the town Library to be opened on Sundays; though as he never entered it on week-days it was easy to turn the proposition into ridicule. Therefore if Mrs. Mallet was a woman of an exquisite moral tone it was not that she had inherited her temper from an ancestry with a turn for casuistry. Jonas Mallet at the time of his marriage was conducting with silent shrewdness a small unpromising business. Both his shrewdness and his silence increased with his years, and at the close of his life he was an extremely well-dressed, well-brushed gentleman with a frigid grey eye, who said little to anybody, but of whom everybody said that he had a very handsome fortune. He was not a sentimental father, and the roughness I just now spoke of in Rowland's life dated from his early boyhood. Mr. Mallet whenever he looked at his son felt extreme compunction at having made a fortune. He remembered that the fruit had not dropped ripe from the tree into his own mouth, and he determined it should be no fault of his if the boy were corrupted by luxury. Rowland therefore, except for a good deal of expensive instruc-

tion in foreign tongues and abstruse sciences, received the
education of a poor man's son. His fare was plain, his
temper familiar with the discipline of patched trousers,
and his habits marked by an exaggerated simplicity which
was kept up really at great expense. He was banished to
the country for months together, in the midst of servants
who had strict injunctions to see that he suffered no serious
harm, but were as strictly forbidden to wait upon him. As
no school could be found conducted on principles sufficiently
rigorous, he was attended at home by a master who set a
high price on the understanding that he was to illustrate
the beauty of abstinence, not only by precept but by
example. Rowland passed for a child of ordinary parts,
and certainly, during his younger years, was an excellent
imitation of a boy who had inherited nothing whatever
that was to make life easy. He was passive, pliable, frank,
extremely slow at his books, and inordinately fond of trout-
fishing. His hair, a memento of his Dutch ancestry, was
of the fairest shade of yellow, his complexion absurdly
rosy, and the measurement of the waist, when he was about
ten years old, quite alarmingly large. This however was
but an episode in his growth; he became afterwards a
fresh-coloured, yellow-bearded man, but he was never
accused of anything more awkward than a manly round-
ness. He emerged from childhood a simple, wholesome,
round-eyed lad, with no suspicion that a less roundabout
course might have been taken to make him happy, but with
a vague sense that his young experience was not a fair
sample of human freedom, and that he was to make a great
many discoveries. When he was about fifteen he achieved
a momentous one. He ascertained that his mother was
a saint. She had always been a very vivid presence in his
life, but so intensely gentle a one that his sense was fully
opened to it only by the danger of losing her. She had
an illness which for many months was liable at any
moment to terminate fatally, and during her long-arrested
convalescence she removed the mask which she had worn
for years by her husband's order. Rowland spent his days
at her side and felt before long as if he had made a new
friend. All his impressions at this period were commented
upon and interpreted at leisure in the future, and it was
only then that he understood that his mother had been for

fifteen years a singularly unhappy woman. Her marriage
had been an immitigable error which she had spent her life
in trying to look in the face. She found nothing to oppose
to her husband's rigid and consistent will but the appearance of absolute compliance ; her courage sank, and
she lived for a while in a sort of spiritual torpor. But at
last, as her child emerged from babyhood, she began to
feel a certain charm in patience, to discover the uses of
ingenuity and to learn that somehow or other one can
always arrange one's life. She cultivated from this time
forward a little private plot of sentiment, and it was of
this secluded precinct that before her death she gave her
son the key. Rowland's allowance at college was barely
sufficient to maintain him decently, and as soon as he
graduated he was taken into his father's counting-house
to do small drudgery on a proportionate salary. For three
years he earned his living as regularly as the obscure func-
tionary in fustian who swept out the place. Mr. Mallet
was consistent, but the perfection of his consistency was
known only on his death. He left but a third of his
property to his son, and devoted the remainder to various
public institutions and local charities. Rowland's third
was a very easy competence, and he never felt a moment's
jealousy of his fellow-pensioners ; but when one of the
establishments which had figured most advantageously in
his father's will bethought itself to affirm the existence of a
later instrument in which it had been still more handsomely
treated, the young man felt a sudden passionate need to
repel the claim by process of law. There was a lively
tussle, but he gained his case ; immediately after which he
made in another quarter a donation of the contested sum.
He cared nothing for the money, but he had felt an angry
desire to protest against a destiny which seemed determined
to be exclusively salutary. It seemed to him that he
should bear a little spoiling. And yet he treated himself
to a very modest quantity, and submitted without reserve
to the great national discipline which began in 1861. When
the Civil War broke out he immediately obtained a commission, and he did his duty for three long years as a citizen
soldier. His duty was obscure, but he never lost a certain
private satisfaction in remembering that on two or three
occasions it had been performed with something of an ideal

precision. He had disentangled himself from business, and after the war he felt a profound disinclination to tie the knot again. He had no desire to make money, he had money enough; and although he knew, and was frequently reminded, that a young man is the better for a fixed occupation, he could discover no moral advantage in driving a lucrative trade. Yet few young men of means and leisure ever made less of a parade of idleness, and indeed idleness in any degree could hardly be laid at the door of a young man who took life in the serious, attentive, reasoning fashion of our friend. It often seemed to Mallet that he wholly lacked the prime requisite of a graceful *flâneur*—the simple, sensuous, confident relish of pleasure. He had frequent fits of extreme melancholy, in which he declared that he was neither fish nor flesh nor good red herring. His was neither an irresponsibly contemplative nature nor a sturdily practical one, and he was for ever looking in vain for the uses of the things that please and the charm of the things that sustain. He was an awkward mixture of moral and æsthetic curiosity, and yet he would have made an ineffective reformer and an indifferent artist. It seemed to him that the glow of happiness must be found either in action of some immensely solid kind on behalf of an idea, or in producing a masterpiece in one of the arts. Oftenest perhaps he wished he were a vigorous young man of genius without a penny. As it was, he could only buy pictures and not paint them; and in the way of action he had to content himself with making a rule to render scrupulous justice to fine strokes of behaviour in others. On the whole, he had an incorruptible modesty. With his blooming complexion and his quiet grey eye, he felt the friction of existence more than was suspected; but he asked no allowance on grounds of temper, he assumed that fate had treated him inordinately well and that he had no excuse for taking an ill-natured view of life, and he undertook to believe that all women were fair, all men were brave, and the world was a delightful place of sojourn, until the contrary should be distinctly proved.

Cecilia's blooming garden and shady porch had seemed so friendly to repose and a cigar that she reproached him the next morning with indifference to her little parlour, not less in its way a monument to her ingenious taste.

"And by the way," she added as he followed her in, "if I refused last night to show you a pretty girl, I can at least show you a pretty boy."

She threw open a window and pointed to a statuette which occupied a place of honour among the ornaments of the room. Rowland looked at it a moment and then turned to her with an exclamation of surprise. She gave him a rapid glance, perceived that her statuette was of altogether exceptional merit, and then smiled knowingly, as if this were a familiar idea.

"Who did it? where did you get it?" Rowland demanded.

"Oh," said Cecilia, adjusting the light, "it's a little thing of Mr. Hudson's."

"And who the deuce is Mr. Hudson?" asked Rowland. But he was absorbed; he lost her immediate reply. The statuette, in bronze, something more than two feet high, represented a naked youth drinking from a gourd. The attitude was perfectly simple. The lad was squarely planted on his feet, with his legs a little apart; his back was slightly hollowed, his head thrown back; his hands were raised to support the rustic cup. There was a loosened fillet of wild flowers about his head, and his eyes, under their dropped lids, looked straight into the cup. On the base was scratched the Greek word $\Delta i\psi a$, Thirst. The figure might have been some beautiful youth of ancient fable—Hylas or Narcissus, Paris or Endymion. Its beauty was the beauty of natural movement; nothing had been sought to be represented but the perfection of an attitude. This had been attentively studied—it was exquisitely rendered. Rowland demanded more light, dropped his head on this side and that, uttered vague exclamations. He said to himself, as he had said more than once in the Louvre and the Vatican, "We ugly mortals, what beautiful creatures we are!" Nothing in a long time had given him so much pleasure. "Hudson—Hudson," he asked again; "who is Hudson?"

"A young man of this place," said Cecilia.

"A young man? How old?"

"I suppose he is three or four and twenty."

"Of this place, you say—of Northampton, Massachusetts?"

" He lives here, but he comes from Virginia."

" Is he a sculptor by profession ? "

" He is a law-student."

Rowland burst out laughing. " He has found something in Blackstone that I never did. He makes statues then simply for his pleasure ? "

Cecilia, with a smile, gave a little toss of her head. " For mine ! "

" I congratulate you," said Rowland, " I wonder whether he could be induced to do anything for me ? "

" This was a matter of friendship. I saw the figure when he had modelled it in clay, and of course I greatly admired it. He said nothing at the time, but a week ago, on my birthday, he arrived in a buggy, with this affair. He had had it cast at the foundry at Chicopee ; I believe it's a beautiful piece of bronze. He begged me to accept."

" Upon my word," said Mallet, " he does things handsomely ! " and he fell to admiring the statue again.

" So then," said Cecilia, " it's very remarkable ? "

" Why, my dear cousin," Rowland answered, " Mr. Hudson of Virginia is an extraordinary—" Then suddenly stopping—" Is he a great friend of yours ? " he asked.

" A great friend ? " and Cecilia hesitated. " I regard him as a child ! "

" Well," said Rowland, " he's a very clever child ! Tell me something about him ; I should like to see him."

Cecilia was obliged to go to her daughter's music-lesson, but she assured Rowland that she would arrange for him a meeting with the young sculptor. He was a frequent visitor, and as he had not called for some days it was likely he would come that evening. Rowland, left alone, examined the statuette at his leisure and returned more than once during the day to take another look at it. He discovered its weak points, but it wore well. It had the stamp of genius. Rowland envied the happy youth who, in a New England village, without aid or encouragement, without models or examples, had found it so easy to produce a lovely work.

II.

In the evening, as he was smoking his cigar on the verandah, a light quick step pressed the gravel of the garden path, and in a moment a young man made his bow to Cecilia. It was rather a nod than a bow, and indicated either that he was an old friend or that he was scantily versed in the usual social forms. Cecilia, who was sitting near the steps, pointed to a neighbouring chair, but the young man seated himself abruptly on a step at her feet and began to fan himself vigorously with his hat, breaking out into a lively objurgation upon the hot weather. "I'm dripping wet!" he said, without ceremony.

"You walk too fast," said Cecilia. "You do everything too fast."

"I know it, I know it!" he cried, passing his hand through his abundant dark hair and making it stand out in a picturesque shock. "I can't be slow if I try. There's something inside of me that drives me. A restless fiend!"

Cecilia gave a light laugh, and Rowland leaned forward in his hammock. He had placed himself in it at Bessie's request, and was playing that he was her baby and that she was rocking him to sleep. She sat beside him, swinging the hammock to and fro and singing a lullaby. When he raised himself she pushed him back and said that the baby must finish its nap. "But I want to see the gentleman with the fiend inside of him," said Rowland.

"What is a fiend?" Bessie demanded. "It's only Mr. Hudson."

"Very well, I want to see him."

"Oh, never mind him!" said Bessie, with the brevity of contempt.

"You speak as if you didn't like him."

"I don't!" Bessie affirmed, putting Rowland to bed again.

The hammock was swung at the end of the verandah, in the thickest shade of the climbing plants, and this fragment of dialogue had passed unnoticed. Rowland submitted a while longer to be cradled, and contented himself with listening to Mr. Hudson's voice. It was a soft and not altogether masculine organ, and was pitched on this occasion in a somewhat plaintive and pettish key. The young man's mood seemed fretful; he complained of the heat, of the dust, of a shoe that hurt him, of having gone on an errand a mile to the other side of the town and found the person he was in search of had left Northampton an hour before.

"Won't you have a cup of tea?" Cecilia asked. "Perhaps that will restore your equanimity."

"Ay, by keeping me awake all night!" said Hudson. "At the best, to go down to the office is like getting into a bath with the water frozen. With my nerves set on edge by a sleepless night I should sit and shiver at home. That's always charming for my mother."

"Your mother is well, I hope?"

"Oh, she's as usual."

"And Miss Garland?"

"She's as usual too. Every one, everything, is as usual. Nothing ever happens in this benighted town."

"I beg your pardon; things do happen sometimes," said Cecilia. "Here is a dear cousin of mine arrived on purpose to congratulate you on your statuette." And she called to Rowland to come and be introduced to Mr. Hudson. The young man sprang up with alacrity, and Rowland, coming forward to shake hands, had a good look at him in the light projected from the parlour window. Something seemed to shine out of Hudson's face as a warning against a "compliment" of the idle unpondered sort.

"Your statuette seems to me very good," Rowland said gravely. "It has given me extreme pleasure."

"And my cousin knows what is good," said Cecilia. "He is a connoisseur."

Hudson smiled and stared. "A connoisseur?" he cried, laughing. "He is the first I have ever seen! Let me see what they look like;" and he drew Rowland nearer to the light. "Have they all such good heads as that? I should like to model yours."

"Pray do," said Cecilia. "It will keep him a while. He is running off to Europe."

" Ah, to Europe ! " Hudson exclaimed with a melancholy cadence as they sat down. " Happy man ! "

But the note seemed to Rowland to be struck rather at random, for he perceived no echo of it in the boyish garrulity of his later talk. Hudson was a tall slender young fellow, with a singularly mobile and intelligent face. Rowland was struck at first only with its responsive vivacity, but in a short time he perceived it was remarkably handsome. The features were admirably chiselled and finished, and a frank smile played over them as gracefully as a breeze among flowers. The fault of the young man's whole structure was an excessive want of breadth. The forehead, though it was high and rounded, was narrow ; the jaw and the shoulders were narrow, and the result was an air of insufficient physical substance. But Mallet afterwards learned that this fair slim youth could draw indefinitely upon a fund of nervous force which outlasted and outwearied the endurance of many a sturdier temperament. And certainly there was life enough in his eye to furnish an immortality ! It was a generous dark grey eye, in which there came and went a sort of kindling glow which would have made a ruder visage striking, and which gave at times to Hudson's harmonious face an altogether extraordinary beauty. There was to Rowland's sympathetic sense a slightly pitiful disparity between the young sculptor's delicate countenance and the shabby gentility of his costume. He was dressed for a rural visit—a visit to a pretty woman. He was clad from head to foot in a white linen suit, which had never been remarkable for the felicity of its cut and had now quite lost its vivifying and redeeming crispness. He wore a bright red cravat, passed through a ring altogether too splendid to be valuable ; he pulled and twisted, as he sat, a pair of yellow kid gloves ; he emphasized his conversation with great dashes and flourishes of a light silver-tipped walking-stick, and he kept constantly taking off and putting on one of those slouched sombreros which are the traditional property of the Virginian or Carolinian of romance. When his hat was on he was very picturesque, in spite of his mock elegance ; and when it was off and he sat nursing it and turning it about and not knowing what to do with it, he could hardly be said to be awkward   He evidently had a natural relish for brilliant accessories and he appropriated what came to his hand. This was visible in his talk, which abounded in the florid and sonorous. In conversation he was a colourist.

Rowland, who was but a moderate talker, sat by in silence, while Cecilia, who had told him that she desired his opinion upon her friend, used a good deal of characteristic finesse in leading the young man to disclose himself. She perfectly succeeded, and Hudson rattled away for an hour with a volubility in which boyish unconsciousness and manly shrewdness were singularly combined. He gave his opinion on twenty topics, he opened up an endless budget of local gossip, he described his repulsive routine at the office of Messrs. Striker and Spooner, counsellors at law, and he gave with great felicity and gusto an account of the annual boat-race between Harvard and Yale, which he had lately witnessed at Worcester. He had looked at the straining oarsmen and the swaying crowd with the eye of the sculptor. Rowland was a good deal amused and not a little interested. Whenever Hudson uttered some peculiarly striking piece of youthful grandiloquence, Cecilia broke into a long, light, familiar laugh.

"What are you laughing at?" the young man then demanded. "Have I said anything so ridiculous?"

"Go on, go on," Cecilia replied. "You are too delicious! Show Mr. Mallet how Mr. Striker read the Declaration of Independence on the 4th of July."

Hudson, like most men with a turn for the plastic arts, was an excellent mimic, and he represented with a great deal of humour the accent and attitude of a pompous country lawyer sustaining the burden of this glorious episode of our national festival. The sonorous twang, the see-saw gestures, the patriotic pronunciation, were vividly reproduced. But Cecilia's manner and the young man's quick response ruffled a little poor Rowland's paternal conscience. He wondered whether his cousin were not sacrificing the faculty of reverence in her clever *protégé* to her need for amusement. Hudson made no serious rejoinder to Rowland's compliment on his statuette until he rose to go. Rowland wondered whether he had forgotten it, and supposed that the oversight was a sign of the natural self-sufficiency of genius. But Hudson stood a moment before he said good

night, twirled his sombrero and hesitated for the first
time. He gave Rowland a clear penetrating glance, and
then, with a wonderfully frank appealing smile—" You
really meant," he asked, " what you said a while ago about
that thing of mine? It is good—essentially good?"

" I really meant it," said Rowland, laying a kindly
hand on his shoulder. "It is very good indeed. It
is, as you say, essentially good. That is the beauty
of it."

Hudson's eyes glowed and expanded; he looked at
Rowland for some time in silence. " I have a notion you
really know," he said at last. "But if you don't, it
doesn't much matter."

" My cousin asked me to-day," said Cecilia, "whether I
supposed you knew yourself how good it is."

Hudson stared, blushing a little. " Perhaps not ! " he
cried.

"Very likely," said Mallet. "I read in a book the
other day that great talent in action—in fact the book said
genius—is a kind of somnambulism. The artist performs
great feats in a dream. We must not wake him up lest he
should lose his balance."

" Oh, when he's back in bed again ! " Hudson answered
with a laugh. "Yes, call it a dream. It was a very
happy one ! "

"Tell me this," said Rowland. "Did you mean anything by your young Water-drinker? Does he represent
an idea? Is he a symbol?"

Hudson raised his eyebrows and gently stroked his
hair. " Why, he's youth, you know; he's innocence, he's
health, he's strength, he's curiosity. Yes, he's a good
many things."

" And is the cup also a symbol?"

"The cup is knowledge, pleasure, experience. Anything
of that kind ! "

" Well, he's guzzling in earnest," said Rowland.

Hudson gave a vigorous nod. "Aye, poor fellow, he's
thirsty ! " And on this he cried good night, and bounded
down the garden path.

" Well, what do you make of him?" asked Cecilia, returning a short time afterwards from a visit of investigation
as to the sufficiency of Bessie's bedclothes.

"I confess I like him," said Rowland. "He's crude and immature—but there's stuff in him."

"He's a strange being," said Cecilia musingly.

"Who are his people? what has been his education?" Rowland asked.

"He has had no education, beyond what he has picked up with little trouble for himself. His mother is a widow, of a Massachusetts country family, a little timid tremulous woman who is always on pins and needles about her son. She had some property herself and married a Virginia gentleman—an owner of lands and slaves. He turned out, I believe, a dreadful rake, and made great havoc in their fortune. Everything, or almost everything, melted away, including Mr. Hudson himself. This is literally true, for he drank himself to death. Ten years ago his wife was left a widow, with scanty means and a couple of growing boys. She paid her husband's debts as best she could, and came to establish herself here, where by the death of a charitable relative she had inherited an old-fashioned ruinous house. Roderick, our friend, was her pride and joy; but Stephen, the elder, was her comfort and support. I remember him later; he was a plain-faced, sturdy, practical lad, very different from his brother and in his way I imagine a very fine fellow. When the war broke out he found that the New England blood ran thicker in his veins than the Virginian and immediately obtained a commission. He fell in some Western battle and left his mother inconsolable. Roderick however has given her plenty to think about, and she has induced him by some mysterious art to take up a profession that he abhors and for which he is about as fit as I am to drive a locomotive. He grew up à la grâce de Dieu; he was horribly spoiled. Three or four years ago he graduated at a small college in this neighbourhood, where I am afraid he had given a good deal more attention to novels and billiards than to mathematics and Greek. Since then he has been reading law at the rate of a page a day. If he is ever admitted to practice I am afraid my friendship will not avail to make me give him my business. Good, bad, or indifferent, the boy is an artist—an artist to his fingers' ends."

"Why, then," asked Rowland, "doesn't he deliberately take up the chisel?"

" For several reasons. In the first place, I don't think he more than half suspects his talent. The flame is smouldering, but it is never fanned by the breath of criticism. He sees nothing, hears nothing, to help him to self-knowledge. He is hopelessly discontented, but he doesn't know where to look for help. Then his mother, as she one day confessed to me, has a holy horror of a profession which consists exclusively as she supposes in making figures of people without their clothes on. Sculpture to her mind is an insidious form of immorality, and for a young man of a passionate disposition she considers the law a much safer speculation. Her father was a judge, she has two brothers at the bar, and her elder son had made a very promising beginning in the same line. She wishes the tradition to be kept up. I am pretty sure the law won't make Roderick's fortune, and I am afraid it will spoil his temper."

" What sort of a temper is it ? "

" One to be trusted, on the whole. It is quick, but it is generous. I have known it to breathe flame and fury at ten o'clock in the evening, and soft sweet music early on the morrow. It's a very entertaining temper to observe. Fortunately I can observe it dispassionately, for I am the only person in the place he has not quarrelled with."

" Has he then no society ? Who is Miss Garland whom you asked about ? "

" A young girl staying with his mother, a sort of far-away cousin ; a good plain girl, but not a person to delight a sculptor's eye. Roderick has a good share of the old Southern arrogance ; he has the aristocratic temperament. He will have nothing to do with the small towns-people ; he says they are ' ignoble.' He can't endure his mother's friends—the old ladies and the ministers and the tea-party people ; they bore him to death. So he comes and lounges here and rails at everything and every one."

This youthful scoffer reappeared a couple of evenings later and confirmed the friendly feeling he had excited on Rowland's part. He was in an easier mood than before, he chattered less extravagantly, and asked Rowland a number of rather primitive questions about the condition of the fine arts in New York and Boston. Cecilia, when he had gone, said that this was the wholesome effect of

Rowland's eulogy of his statuette. Roderick was acutely sensitive, and Rowland's intelligent praise had sobered him; he was ruminating the full-flavoured verdict of culture. Rowland took a great fancy to him, to his personal charm and his probable genius. He had an indefinable attraction—the something tender and divine of unspotted, exuberant, confident youth. The next day was Sunday, and Rowland proposed that they should take a long walk and that Roderick should show him the country. The young man assented gleefully, and in the morning, as Rowland at the garden gate was giving his hostess Godspeed on her way to church, he came striding along the grassy margin of the road and out-whistling the music of the church bells. It was one of those lovely days of the last of August when summer seems to balance in the scale with autumn. "Remember the day, and take care you rob no orchards," said Cecilia, as they separated.

The young men walked away at a steady pace, over hill and dale, through woods and fields, and at last found themselves on a grassy elevation studded with mossy rocks and red cedars. Just beneath them, in a great shining curve, flowed the generous Connecticut. They flung themselves on the grass and tossed stones into the river; they talked like old friends. Rowland lit a cigar and Roderick refused one with a grimace of extravagant disgust. He thought them vile things; he didn't see how decent people could tolerate them. Rowland was amused —he wondered what it was that made this ill-mannered speech seem perfectly inoffensive on Roderick's lips. He belonged to the race of mortals, to be pitied or envied according as we view the matter, who are not held to a strict account for their aggressions. Looking at him as he lay stretched in the shade, Rowland vaguely likened him to some beautiful, supple, restless, bright-eyed animal, whose motions should have no deeper warrant than the tremulous delicacy of its structure and seem graceful even when they were most inconvenient. Rowland watched the shadows on Mount Holyoke, listened to the gurgle of the river, and sniffed the balsam of the pines. A gentle breeze had begun to tickle their summits, and brought the smell of the mown grass across from the elm-dotted river meadows. He sat up beside his companion and looked away at the far-spreading view. It seemed to him beautiful, and suddenly a strange feeling of prospective regret took possession of him. Something seemed to tell him that later, in a foreign land, he should remember it with longing and regret.

"It's a wretched business," he said, "this virtual quarrel of ours with our own country, this everlasting impatience to get out of it. Is one's only safety then in flight? This is an American day, an American landscape, an American atmosphere. It certainly has its merits, and some day when I am shivering with ague in classic Italy I shall accuse myself of having slighted them."

Roderick kindled with a sympathetic glow, and declared that America was good enough for him and that he had always thought it the duty of an honest citizen to stand by his own country and help it on. He had evidently thought nothing whatever about it—he was launching his doctrine on the inspiration of the moment. The doctrine expanded with the occasion, and he declared that he was above all an advocate for American art. He didn't see why we shouldn't produce the greatest works in the world. We were the biggest people, and we ought to have the biggest conceptions. The biggest conceptions of course would bring forth in time the biggest performances. We had only to be true to ourselves, to pitch in and not be afraid, to fling Imitation overboard and fix our eyes upon our National Individuality. "I declare," he cried, "there's a career for a man, and I have twenty minds to embrace it on the spot—to be the typical, original, national American artist! It's inspiring!"

Rowland burst out laughing and told him that he liked his practice better than his theory, and that a saner impulse than this had inspired his little Water-drinker. Roderick took no offence, and three minutes afterwards was talking volubly of some humbler theme—only half heeded by his companion, who had returned to his cogitations. At last Rowland delivered himself of the upshot of these reflections. "How should you like," he suddenly demanded, "to go to Rome?"

Hudson stared, and with a laugh which speedily consigned our National Individuality to perdition, responded that he should like it reasonably well. "And I should like by the same token," he added, "to go to Athens, to Constantinople, to Damascus, to the holy city of Benares, where there is a golden statue of Brahma twenty-feet tall."

"No," said Rowland soberly, "if you were to go to Rome you should settle down and work. Athens might help you, but for the present I shouldn't recommend Benares."

"It will be time to arrange details when I pack my trunk," said Hudson.

"If you mean to turn sculptor the sooner you pack your trunk the better."

"Oh, but I'm a practical man! What is the smallest sum per annum on which one can keep alive the sacred fire?"

"What is the largest sum at your disposal?"

Roderick stroked his light moustache, gave it a twist, and then announced with mock pomposity—"Three hundred dollars!"

"The money question could be arranged," said Rowland. "There are ways of raising money."

"I should like to know a few! I never yet discovered one."

"One of them consists," said Rowland, "in having a friend with a good deal more than he wants and not being too proud to accept a part of it."

Roderick stared a moment and his face flushed. "Do you mean—do you mean?" .... He stammered. He was greatly excited.

Rowland got up, blushing a little, and Roderick sprang to his feet. "In three words, if you are to be a sculptor you ought to go to Rome and study the antique. To go to Rome you need money. I am fond of fine statues, but unfortunately I can't make them myself. I have to order them. I order a dozen from you, to be executed at your convenience. To help you I pay you in advance."

Roderick pushed off his hat and pressed his forehead, still gazing at his companion. "You believe in me!" he cried at last.

"Allow me to explain," said Rowland. "I believe in you if you are prepared to work and to wait and to struggle and to exercise a great many virtues. And then

I am afraid to say it, lest I should disturb you more than
I should help you. You must decide for yourself. I
simply offer you an opportunity."

Hudson stood for some time, profoundly meditative.
"You have not seen my other things," he said suddenly.
"Come and look at them."

"Now?"

"Yes, we will walk home. We will settle the question."

He passed his hand through Rowland's arm and they
retraced their steps. They reached the town and made
their way along a broad country street, dusky with the
shade of magnificent elms. Rowland felt his companion's
arm trembling in his own. They stopped at a large white
house, flanked with melancholy hemlocks, and passed
through a little front garden, paved with moss-coated
bricks and ornamented with parterres bordered with high
box edges. The mansion had an air of antiquated dignity,
but it had seen its best days and evidently sheltered a
shrunken household. Mrs. Hudson, Rowland was sure,
might be seen in the garden of a morning, in a white
apron and a pair of old gloves, engaged in frugal horti-
culture. Roderick's studio was behind, in the basement ;
a large empty room, with the paper peeling off the walls.
This represented, in the fashion of fifty years ago, a series
of small fantastic landscapes of a hideous pattern, and
the young sculptor had presumably torn it away in great
scraps, in moments of æsthetic exasperation. On a board
in a corner was a heap of clay, and on the floor, against
the wall, stood some dozen medallions, busts, and figures, in
various stages of completion. To exhibit them Roderick
had to place them one by one on the end of a long packing-
box, which served as a pedestal. He did so silently,
making no explanations and looking at them himself with
a strange air of quickened curiosity. Most of the things
were portraits, and the three at which he looked longest
were finished busts. One was a colossal head of a negro,
tossed back, defiant, with distended nostrils ; one was the
portrait of a young man whom Rowland immediately perceived by the resemblance to be his lost brother ; the last
represented a gentleman with a pointed nose, a long close-
shaven upper lip and a tuft on the end of his chin. This

was a face peculiarly unadapted to sculpture; but as a
piece of modelling it was the best, and it was admirable.
It reminded Rowland in its homely veracity, its artless
artfulness, of the works of the early Italian Renaissance.
On the pedestal was cut the name—Barnaby Striker, Esq.
Rowland remembered that this was the appellation of the
legal luminary from whom his companion had undertaken
to borrow a reflected ray, and although in the bust there
was nothing grossly satirical, it betrayed comically to one
who could relish the secret that the features of the
original had often been scanned with an irritated eye.
Besides these there were several rough studies of the nude
and two or three figures of a fanciful kind. The most
noticeable (and it had singular beauty) was a small
modelled design for a sepulchral monument; that evidently
of Stephen Hudson. The young soldier lay sleeping
eternally with his hand on his sword—like an old crusader
in a Gothic cathedral.

Rowland made no haste to pronounce; too much depended
on his judgment. "Upon my word," cried Hudson at last,
" they seem to me very good ! "

And in truth as Rowland looked he saw they were good.
They were youthful, awkward, ignorant; the effort often
was more apparent than the success. But the effort was
signally powerful and intelligent; it seemed to Rowland
that it might easily hit the mark. Here and there the
mark had been hit with a masterly ring. Rowland turned
to his companion, who stood with his hands in his pockets
and his hair very much crumpled, looking at him askance.
The light of admiration was in Rowland's eyes, and it
speedily kindled a wonderful illumination on Hudson's
handsome brow. Rowland said at last simply, " You have
only to work ! "

" I think I know what that means," Roderick answered.
He turned away, threw himself on a rickety chair, and
sat for some moments with his elbows on his knees and
his head in his hands. " Work—work ? " he said at last,
looking up; " ah, if I could only begin ! " He glanced
round the room a moment and his eye encountered on the
mantelshelf the vivid physiognomy of Mr. Barnaby Striker.
His smile vanished—he stared at it with an air of concentrated enmity. " I want to begin," he cried, " and I can't

make a better beginning than this! Good-bye, Mr. Barnaby
Striker!"   He strode across the room, seized a hammer
that lay at hand, and before Rowland could interfere, in
the interest of art if not of morals, dealt a merciless blow
upon Mr. Striker's skull. The bust cracked into a dozen
pieces, which toppled with a great crash upon the floor.
Rowland relished neither the destruction of the image nor
his companion's look in working it, but as he was about
to express his displeasure the door opened and gave passage
to a young girl. She came in with a rapid step and startled
face, as if she had been alarmed by the noise. Seeing the
heap of shattered clay and the hammer in Roderick's hand,
she gave a cry of horror. Her voice died away when she
perceived that Rowland was a stranger, but she murmured
reproachfully, "Why, Roderick, what have you done?"

Roderick gave a joyous kick to the shapeless fragments.
"I have driven the money-changers out of the temple!"
he cried.

The traces retained shape enough to be recognised, and
she gave a little moan of pity. She seemed not to understand the young man's allegory, but yet to feel that it
pointed to some great purpose, which must be an evil one
from being expressed in such a lawless fashion, and to
perceive that Rowland was in some way accountable for it.
She looked at him with a sharp frank mistrust and turned
away through the open door. Rowland looked after her
with quickened interest.

III.

EARLY on the morrow he received a visit from his new
friend. Roderick was in a state of extreme exhilaration,
tempered however by a certain amount of righteous wrath.
He had had a domestic struggle, but he had remained
master of the situation. He had shaken the dust of Mr.
Striker's office from his feet.

"I had it out last night with my mother," he said. "I

dreaded the scene, for she takes things terribly hard. She doesn't scold nor storm, and she doesn't argue nor insist. She sits with her eyes full of tears that never fall, and looks at me, when I vex her, as if I were a monster of depravity. And the trouble is that I was born to vex her. She doesn't trust me ; she never has and she never will. I don't know what I have done to set her against me, but ever since I can remember I have been looked at with tears. The trouble is," he went on, giving a twist to his moustache, " I have been too great a mollycoddle. I have been sprawling all my days by the maternal fireside, and my dear mother has grown used to bullying me. I have made myself cheap ! If I am not in my bed by eleven o'clock, the cook is sent out to explore with a lantern. When I think of it I despise my docility. It's rather a hard fate, to live like a saint and to pass for a sinner. I should like for six months to lead Mrs. Hudson the life some fellows lead their mothers ! "

" Allow me to believe," said Rowland, " that you would like nothing of the sort. If you have been a good boy, don't spoil it by pretending you don't like it. You have been very happy in spite of your virtues, and there are worse fates in the world than being loved too well. I have not had the pleasure of seeing your mother, but I will lay you a wager that this is where the shoe pinches. She is passionately fond of you, and her hopes, like all intense hopes, keep trembling into fears." Rowland, as he spoke, had an instinctive vision of how this beautiful youth must be loved by his female relatives.

Roderick frowned, and with an impatient gesture, " I do her justice," he cried—" may she never do me less ! " Then after a moment's hesitation, " I will tell you the perfect truth," he went on ; " I have to fill a double place. I have to be my brother as well as myself. It's a good deal to ask of a man, especially when he has so little talent as I for being what he is not. When we were both young together I was the curled darling. I had the silver mug and the biggest piece of pudding, and I stayed in-doors to be kissed by the ladies while he made mud-pies in the garden. In fact he was worth fifty of me ! When he was brought home from Vicksburg with a piece of shell in his skull, my poor mother began to think she hadn't loved

him enough. I remember, as she hung round my neck
sobbing, before his coffin, she told me that I must be to
her everything that he would have been. I made no end
of vows, but I haven't kept them all. I have been very
different from Stephen. I have been idle, restless, egotistical, discontented. I have done no harm I believe, but
I have done no good. My brother, if he had lived, would
have made fifty thousand dollars, and had the parlour
done up. My mother, brooding night and day on her
bereavement, has come to fix her ideal in little attentions of that sort. Judged by that standard I'm nowhere."

Rowland was at a loss what to believe of this account
of his friend's domestic circumstances; it was plaintive,
yet it seemed to him rather rough. "You must lose no
time in making a masterpiece," he answered; "then with
the proceeds you can do up the whole house."

"So I have told her; but she only half believes in the
thing. She can see no good in my making statues; they
seem to her a snare of the enemy. She would fain see me
all my life tethered to the law, like a browsing goat to a
stake. In that way I am in sight. 'It's a more regular
occupation!'—that's all I can get out of her. A more
regular damnation! Is it a fact that artists in general are
such wicked men? I never had the pleasure of knowing
one, so I couldn't refute her with an example. She had
the advantage of me, because she formerly knew a portrait-
painter at Richmond, who did her miniature in black lace
mittens (you may see it on the parlour table), who used to
drink raw brandy and beat his wife. I promised her that
whatever I might do to my wife I would never beat my
mother, and that as for brandy, raw or diluted, I detested
it. She sat silently crying for an hour, during which I
expended treasures of eloquence. It's a good thing to have
to take stock of one's intentions, and I assure you, as I
pleaded my cause, I was most agreeably impressed with the
elevated character of my own. I kissed her solemnly
at last, and told her that I had said everything and that
she must make the best of it. This morning she has dried
her eyes, but I warrant you it isn't a cheerful house. I
long to be out of it!"

"I am extremely sorry to have made such a rumpus."

said Rowland. "I owe your mother some amends; will it be possible for me to see her?"

"If you will see her, it will smooth matters vastly; though to tell the truth she will need all her courage to face you, for she considers you an agent of the foul fiend. She doesn't see why you should have come here and set me by the ears: you are made to ruin young law-sludents and desolate doting mothers. I leave it to you personally to answer these charges. You see, what she can't forgive—what she will not really ever forgive—is your taking me off to Rome. Rome is an evil word in my mother's vocabulary, to be said in a whisper, as you'd say 'damnation.' Northampton is in the centre of Christendom and Rome far away in outlying dusk, into which it can do no proper moral man any good to penetrate. And there was I but yesterday a regular attendant at that repository of every virtue, Mr. Striker's office!"

"And does Mr. Striker know of your decision?" asked Rowland.

"To a certainty! Mr. Striker, you must know, is not simply a good-natured attorney who lets me dog's-ear his law-books. He's a particular friend and general adviser. He looks after my mother's property and kindly consents to regard me as part of it. Our opinions have always been painfully divergent, but I freely forgive him his zealous attempts to unscrew my head-piece and set it on another way. He never understood me, and it was useless to try to make him. We speak a different language—we are made of a different clay. I had a fit of rage yesterday, when I smashed his bust, at the thought of all the bad blood he had stirred up in me; it did me good, and it's all over now. I don't hate him any more; I am rather sorry for him. See how you have improved me! I must have seemed to him wilfully, wickedly stupid, and I am sure he only tolerated me on account of his great regard for my mother. This morning I grasped the bull by the horns. I took an armful of law-books that have been gathering the dust in my room for the last year and a half, and presented myself at the office. 'Allow me to put these back in their places,' I said. 'I shall never have need for them more—never more, never more, never more!' 'So you have learned everything they contain?' says the great

Striker, leering over his spectacles; 'better late than
never!' 'I have learned nothing that you can teach me,'
I cried. 'But I shall tax your patience no longer. I am
going to be a sculptor. I am going to Rome. I won't bid
you good-bye just yet; I shall see you again. But I bid
good-bye here with enthusiasm to these four detested
walls—to this living tomb! I didn't know till now how
I hated the place! My compliments to Mr. Spooner, and
my thanks for all you have not made of me!'"

"I am glad to know you are to see Mr. Striker again,"
Rowland answered, correcting a primary inclination to
smile. "You certainly owe him a respectful farewell, even
if he has not understood you. I confess you rather puzzle
me. There is another person," he presently added, "whose
opinion as to your new career I should like to know.
What does Miss Garland think?"

Hudson looked at him keenly, with a slight blush.
Then with a conscious smile, "What makes you suppose
she thinks anything?" he asked.

"Because, though I saw her but for a moment yesterday,
she struck me as a very intelligent girl, and I am sure she
has opinions."

The smile on Roderick's mobile face passed rapidly into
a frown. "Oh, she thinks what I think!" he answered.

Before the two young men separated Rowland attempted
to give as harmonious a shape as possible to his companion's
future. "I have launched you, as I may say," he said;
"and I feel as if I ought to see you into port. I am older
than you and know the world better, and it seems well
that we should voyage a while together. It's on my conscience that I ought to take you to Rome, walk you through
the Vatican, and then lock you up with a heap of clay. I
sail on the 5th of September; can you make your preparations to start with me?"

Roderick assented to all this with an air of candid
confidence in his friend's wisdom that expressed more than
formal pledges. "I have no preparations to make," he
said with a smile, raising his arms and letting them fall,
as if to indicate his unencumbered condition. "What I
am to take with me I carry here!" and he tapped his
forehead.

"Happy man!" murmured Rowland with a sigh, thinking of the light stowage in his own organism, in the region indicated by Roderick, and of the heavy one in deposit at his banker's, of bags and boxes.

When his companion had left him he went in search of Cecilia. She was sitting at work at a shady window, and welcomed him to a low chintz-covered chair. He sat some time thoughtfully snipping wools with her scissors ; he expected criticism and he was preparing a rejoinder. At last he told her of Roderick's decision and of his own part in the matter. Cecilia, besides an extreme surprise, exhibited a certain fine displeasure at his not having asked her advice.

"What would you have said if I had ? " he demanded.

"I should have said in the first place, 'Oh for pity's sake don't carry off the person in all Northampton who amuses me most ! ' I should have said in the second place, 'Nonsense ! the boy is doing very well. Let well alone ! ' "

"That in the first five minutes. What would you have said later ? "

"That for a man who is generally averse to meddling, you were suddenly rather officious."

Rowland's countenance fell ; he frowned in silence. Cecilia looked at him askance ; gradually the spark of irritation faded from her eye.

"Excuse my sharpness," she resumed at last. "But I am literally in despair at losing Roderick Hudson. His visits in the evening, for the past year, have kept me alive. They have given a point to a very dull life—a kind of silver-tip to days that seemed made of a baser metal. I don't say he is a phœnix—but I liked to see him. Of course, however, that I shall miss him sadly is not a reason for his not going to seek his fortune. Men must work and women must weep ! "

"Decidedly not ! " said Rowland, with a good deal of emphasis. He had suspected from the first hour of his stay that Cecilia had a private satisfaction, and he discovered that she found it in Hudson's lounging visits and boyish chatter. Now he wondered whether, judiciously viewed, her gain in the matter were not her young friend's loss. It was evident that Cecilia was not judicious, and that her good sense, habitually rigid under the demands of domestic economy, indulged itself with a certain agreeable laxity on this particular point. She liked her young friend just as he was; she humoured him, flattered him, laughed at him, caressed him—did everything but advise him. It was a flirtation without the benefits of a flirtation. She was too old to let him fall in love with her, which might have done him good; and her inclination was to keep him young, so that the nonsense he talked might never transgress a certain line. It was quite conceivable that poor Cecilia should relish a pastime; but if one had philanthropically embraced the idea that something considerable might be made of Roderick, it was impossible not to see that her friendship was not what might be called tonic. So Rowland reflected, in the glow of an almost creative ardour. There was a later time when he would have been grateful if Hudson's susceptibility to the relaxing influence of lovely women might have been limited to such inexpensive tribute as he rendered the excellent Cecilia.

"I only wish to remind you," she went on, "that you are likely to have your hands full."

"I have thought of that and I rather like the idea; liking as I do the man. I told you the other day, you know, that I longed to have something on my hands. When it first occurred to me that I might start our young friend on the path of glory, I felt as if I had an unimpeachable inspiration. Then I remembered there were dangers and difficulties, and asked myself whether I had a right to drag him out of his obscurity. My notion of his really having a great talent answered the question. He is made to do the things that we are the better for having. I can't do such things myself, but when I see a young man of genius standing helpless and hopeless for want of capital, I feel—and it's no affectation of humility, I assure you—as if it would give at least a reflected usefulness to my own life to offer him his opportunity."

"In the name of the general public I suppose I ought to thank you. But I want first of all to profit myself. You guarantee us at any rate, I hope, the master-pieces?"

"A master-piece a year," said Rowland, smiling, "for the next quarter of a century."

"It seems to me that we have a right to ask more—to

demand that you guarantee us not only the development of the artist but the security of the man."

Rowland became grave again. "His security?"

"His moral, his sentimental security. Here you see, it's perfect. We are all under a tacit compact to keep him quiet. Perhaps you believe in the necessary turbulence of genius, and you intend to enjoin upon your *protégé* the importance of cultivating his passions."

"On the contrary, I believe that a man of genius owes as much deference to his passions as any other man, but not a particle more, and I confess I have a strong conviction that the artist is better for leading a quiet life. That is what I shall preach to my *protégé*, as you call him, by example as well as by precept. You evidently believe," he added in a moment, "that he will lead me a dance!"

"No, I prophesy nothing. I only think that circumstances, with our young man, have a great influence; as is proved by the fact that although he has been fuming and fretting here for the last five years, he has nevertheless managed to make the best of it and found it easy on the whole to vegetate. Transplanted to Rome, I fancy he will put forth some wonderful flowers. I should like vastly to see the change. You must write me about it from stage to stage. I hope with all my heart that the fruit will be proportionate to the foliage. Don't think me a bird of ill omen; only remember that you will be held to a strict account."

"A man should make the most of himself and be helped if he needs help," Rowland answered after a long pause. "Of course when a body begins to expand, there comes in the possibility of bursting; but I nevertheless approve of a certain tension of one's being. It's what a man is meant for. And then I believe in the essential salubrity of genius—true genius."

"Very good," said Cecilia, with an air of resignation which made Rowland for the moment seem to himself culpably eager. "We will drink then to-day at dinner to the health of our friend!"

Having it much at heart to convince Mrs. Hudson of the purity of his intentions, Rowland waited upon her that evening. He was ushered into a large parlour, which by the light of a couple of candles he perceived to be very

meagrely furnished and very tenderly and sparingly used.
The windows were open to the air of the summer night,
and a circle of three persons was temporarily awed into
silence by his appearance. One of these was Mrs. Hudson,
who was sitting at one of the windows, empty-handed save
for the pocket-handkerchief in her lap, which was held
with an air of familiarity with its sadder uses. Near her,
on the sofa, half sitting, half lounging, in the attitude of
a visitor outstaying ceremony, with one long leg flung over
the other and a large foot in a clumsy boot swinging to
and fro continually, was a lean, sandy-haired gentleman
whom Rowland recognised as the original of the portrait
of Mr. Barnaby Striker. At the table, near the candles,
busy with a substantial piece of needlework, sat the young
girl of whom he had had a moment's quickened glimpse
in Roderick's studio and whom he had learned to be Miss
Garland, his companion's kinswoman. This young lady's
limpid penetrating gaze was the most effective greeting he
received. Mrs. Hudson rose with a soft, vague sound of
distress and stood looking at him shrinkingly and waver-
ingly, as if she were sorely tempted to retreat through
the open window. Mr. Striker swung his long leg a trifle
defiantly. No one evidently was used to offering hollow
welcomes or telling polite fibs. Rowland introduced
himself; he had come he might say upon business.

"Yes," said Mrs. Hudson tremulously; "I know—my
son has told me. I suppose it is better I should see you.
Perhaps you will take a seat?"

With this invitation Rowland prepared to comply, and
turning, grasped the first chair that offered itself.

"Not that one," said a full grave voice; whereupon he
perceived that a thick skein of sewing-silk had been suspended and entangled over the back, for the purpose of
being wound on reels. He felt the least bit irritated at
the curtness of the warning, coming as it did from a young
woman whose countenance he had mentally pronounced
interesting and with regard to whom he was conscious of
the germ of the inevitable desire to produce a responsive
interest. And then he thought it would break the ice to
say something playfully urbane.

"Oh, you should let me take the chair," he answered,
"and have the pleasure of holding the skein myself!"

For all reply to this sally he received a stare of undisguised amazement from Miss Garland, who then looked across at Mrs. Hudson with a glance which plainly said, "You see he's quite the insinuating foreigner we feared." The elder lady however sat with her eyes fixed on the ground and her two hands tightly clasped. But as regards Mrs. Hudson, Rowland felt much more compassion than resentment; her attitude was not coldness, it was a kind of dread, almost a terror. She was a small eager woman, with a pale troubled face which added to her apparent age. After looking at her for some minutes Rowland saw that she was still young and that she must have been a very girlish bride. She had been a pretty one too, though she probably had looked terribly frightened at the altar. She was very delicately shaped, and Roderick had come honestly by his physical slimness and elegance. She wore no cap, and her flaxen hair, which was of extraordinary fineness, was smoothed and confined with Puritanic precision. She was excessively shy and evidently very humble-minded; it was singular to see a woman to whom the experience of life had conveyed such scanty reassurance. Rowland began immediately to like her, and to feel impatient to persuade her that there was no harm in him. He foresaw that she would be easy to persuade and that a benevolent conversational tone would probably make her pass fluttering from distrust into an oppressive extreme of confidence. But he had an indefinable sense that the person who was testing that strong young eyesight of hers in the dim candle-light was less readily beguiled from her mysterious feminine preconceptions. Miss Garland, according to Cecilia's judgment, as Rowland remembered, had not a countenance to inspire a sculptor; but it seemed to Rowland that her countenance might fairly inspire a man whose relation to the beautiful was amateurish. She was not pretty, as the eye of habit judges prettiness, but when you made the observation you somehow failed to set it down against her, for you had already passed from measuring contours to tracing meanings. In Mary Garland's face there were many possible ones, and they gave you the more to think about that it was not—like Roderick Hudson's, for instance —a quick and mobile face, over which expression flickered like a candle in a wind. They followed each other slowly, distinctly, sincerely, and you might almost have fancied that, as they came and went, they gave her a sort of pain. She was tall and slender, and had an air of maidenly strength and decision. She had a broad forehead and dark eyebrows, a trifle thicker than those of classic beauties; her grey eye was clear but not brilliant, and her features were bravely irregular. Her mouth enabled her smile—which was the principal grace of her physiognomy —to display itself with magnificent amplitude. Rowland, indeed, had not yet seen this smile in operation; but something assured him that her rigid gravity had a radiant counterpart. She wore a scanty white dress, and had a nameless rustic, provincial air; she looked like a distinguished villager. She was evidently a girl of a great personal force, but she lacked pliancy. She was hemming a kitchen towel with the aid of a large steel thimble. She bent her serious eyes at last on the work again and let Rowland explain himself.

"I have become suddenly so very intimate with your son," he said at last, addressing himself to Mrs. Hudson, "that it seems proper I should make your acquaintance."

"Very proper," murmured the poor lady, and after a moment's hesitation was on the point of adding something more; but Mr. Striker here interposed, after a prefatory clearance of the throat:

"I should like to take the liberty of addressing you a simple question! For how long a period of time have you been acquainted with our young friend?" He continued to kick the air, but his head was thrown back and his eyes fixed on the opposite wall, as if to avert themselves from the spectacle of Rowland's inevitable confusion.

"A very short time, I confess. Hardly three days."

"And yet you call yourself intimate, eh? I have been seeing Mr. Roderick daily these three years, and yet it was only this morning that I felt as if I had at last the right to say that I knew him. We had a few moments' conversation in my office which supplied the missing links in the evidence. So that now I do venture to say I'm acquainted with Mr. Roderick! But wait three years, sir, like me!" and Mr. Striker laughed, with a closed mouth and a noiseless shake of all his long person.

Mrs. Hudson smiled confusedly, at hazard; Miss Garland

kept her eyes on her stitches.   But it seemed to Rowland
that the latter coloured a little.   "Oh, in three years, of
course," he said, " we shall know each other better.   Before
many years are over, madam," he pursued, " I expect the
world to know him.   I expect him to be a great man ! "

Mrs. Hudson looked at first as if this could be but an
insidious device for increasing her distress by the assistance of irony.   Then reassured little by little by Rowland's
frank smile, she gave him an appealing glance and a timorous " Really ? "

But before Rowland could respond, Mr. Striker again
intervened.   " Do I fully apprehend your expression ? " he
asked.   " Our young friend is to become _a great man ? _ "

" A great artist, I hope," said Rowland.

" This is a new and interesting view," said Mr. Striker,
with an assumption of judicial calmness.   " We have had
hopes for Mr. Roderick, but I confess that if I have rightly
understood them they stopped short of greatness.   We
shouldn't have taken the responsibility of claiming it for
him.   What do you say, ladies ?   We all feel about him here
—his mother, Miss Garland and myself—as if his merits
were rather in the line of the "—and Mr. Striker waved
his hand with a series of fantastic flourishes in the air
—" of the light ornamental ! "   Mr. Striker bore his re-
calcitrant pupil a grudge ; yet he was evidently trying both
to be fair and to respect the susceptibilities of his companions.   But he was unversed in the mysterious processes
of feminine emotion.   Ten minutes before there had been
a general harmony of sombre views ; but on hearing
Roderick's limitations thus distinctly formulated to a
stranger, the two ladies mutely protested.   Mrs. Hudson
uttered a short faint sigh, and Miss Garland raised her
eyes toward their advocate and visited him with a short
cold glance.

" I am afraid, Mrs. Hudson," Rowland pursued, evading
the discussion of Roderick's possible greatness, " that you
don't at all thank me for stirring up your son's ambition
for objects that lead him so far from home.   I suspect
I have made you my enemy."

Mrs. Hudson covered her mouth with her finger-tips and
looked painfully perplexed between the desire to confess
the truth and the fear of being impolite.   " My cousin is

no one's enemy," Miss Garland hereupon declared gently, but with that same fine deliberateness with which she had made Rowland relax his grasp of the chair.

"Does she leave that to you?" Rowland ventured to ask with a smile.

"We are inspired with none but Christian sentiments," said Mr. Striker; "Miss Garland perhaps most of all. Miss Garland," and Mr. Striker waved his hand again as if to perform an introduction which had been regrettably omitted, "is the daughter of a minister, the grand-daughter of a minister, the sister of a minister." Rowland bowed deferentially, and the young girl went on with her sewing, with nothing apparently either of embarrassment or elation at the promulgation of these facts. Mr. Striker continued —"Mrs. Hudson, I see, is too deeply agitated to converse with you freely. She will allow me to address you a few questions. Would you kindly inform her as exactly as possible just what you propose to do with her son?"

The poor lady fixed her eyes appealingly on Rowland's face and seemed to say that Mr. Striker had spoken her desire, though she herself would have expressed it less defiantly. But Rowland saw in Mr. Striker's many wrinkled light blue eye, shrewd at once and good-natured, that he had no intention of defiance, and that he was simply pompous and conceited and sarcastically compassionate of any view of things in which Roderick Hudson was regarded in a serious light.

"Do, my dear madam?" demanded Rowland. "I don't propose to do anything. He must do for himself. I simply offer him the chance. He is to study, to work— hard I hope."

"Not too hard please," murmured Mrs. Hudson, pleadingly, wheeling about from recent visions of dangerous leisure. "He's not very strong, and I am afraid the climate of Europe is very relaxing."

"Ah, study!" repeated Mr. Striker. "To what line of study is he to direct his attention?" Then suddenly, with an impulse of disinterested curiosity on his own account, "How do you study sculpture, anyhow?"

"By looking at models and imitating them."

"At models, eh? To what kind of models do you refer?"

" To the antique in the first place."

" Ah, the antique," repeated Mr. Striker with a jocose intonation. " Do you hear, madam? Roderick is going off to Europe to learn to imitate the antique."

"I suppose it's all right," said Mrs. Hudson, twisting herself in a sort of delicate anguish.

" An antique as I understand it," the lawyer continued, "is an image of a pagan deity, with considerable dirt sticking to it, and no arms, no nose, and no clothing. A precious model certainly ! "

" That's a very good description of many," said Rowland, with a laugh.

" Mercy ! Truly ? " asked Mrs. Hudson, borrowing courage from his urbanity.

" But a sculptor's studies, you intimate, are not confined to the antique," Mr. Striker resumed. " After he has been looking three or four years at the objects I describe—"

" He studies the living model," said Rowland.

" Does it take three or four years ? " asked Mrs. Hudson imploringly.

" That depends upon the artist's aptitude. After twenty years a real artist is still studying."

" Oh, my poor boy ! " moaned Mrs. Hudson, finding the prospect, under every light, still terrible.

" Now this study of the living model," Mr. Striker pursued. " Give Mrs. Hudson a sketch of that."

" Oh dear, no ! " cried Mrs. Hudson, shrinkingly.

" That too," said Rowland, " is one of the reasons for studying in Rome. It's a handsome race, you know, and you find very well-made people."

"I suppose they're no better made than a good tough Yankee," objected Mr. Striker, transposing his interminable legs. " The same God made us ! "

" Surely," sighed Mrs. Hudson, but with a questioning glance at her visitor which showed that she had already begun to concede much weight to his opinion. Rowland hastened to express his assent to Mr. Striker's proposition.

Miss Garland looked up, and, after a moment's hesitation —" Are the Roman women very beautiful ? " she asked.

Rowland too, in answering, hesitated ; he was looking

straight at the young girl. "On the whole I prefer ours," he said.

She had dropped her work in her lap; her hands were crossed upon it, her head thrown a little back. She had evidently expected a more impersonal answer, and she was dissatisfied. For an instant she seemed inclined to make a rejoinder, but she slowly picked up her work in silence, and drew her stitches again.

Rowland had for the second time the feeling that she judged him to be a person of a disagreeably sophisticated tone. He noticed too that the kitchen towel she was hemming was terribly coarse. And yet his answer had a resonant inward echo, and he repeated to himself, "Yes, on the whole I prefer ours."

"Well, these models," began Mr. Striker. "You put them into an attitude, I suppose?"

"An attitude, exactly."

"And then you sit down and look at them?"

"You must not sit too long. You must go at your clay and try to build up something that looks like them."

"Well, there you are with your model in an attitude on one side, yourself in an attitude too I suppose on the other, and your pile of clay in the middle, building up as you say. So you pass the morning. After that I hope you go out and take a walk and rest from your exertions."

"Unquestionably. But to a sculptor who loves his work there is no time lost. Everything he looks at teaches or suggests something."

"That's a tempting doctrine to young men with a taste for sitting by the hour with the page unturned, watching the flies buzz, or the frost melt on the window-pane. Our young friend in this way must have laid up stores of information which I never suspected!"

"It is very possible," said Rowland with an unresentful smile, "that he will prove some day the completer artist for some of those lazy reveries."

This theory was apparently very grateful to Mrs. Hudson, who had never had the case put for her son with such ingenious hopefulness, and who found herself disrelishing the singular situation of seeming to side against her own flesh and blood with a lawyer whose conversational tone betrayed the habit of cross-questioning.

"My son then," she ventured to ask, "my son has great —what you would call great powers?"

"To my sense very great powers."

Poor Mrs. Hudson actually smiled, broadly, gleefully, and glanced at Miss Garland as if to invite her to do likewise. But the young girl's face remained as serious as the eastern sky when the opposite sunset is too feeble to make it glow. "Do you really know?" she asked, looking at Rowland.

"One can't *know* in such a matter save after proof, and proof takes time. But one can believe."

"And you believe?"

"I believe."

But even then Miss Garland vouchsafed no smile; her face became graver than ever.

"Well, well," said Mrs. Hudson, "we must hope that it is all for the best."

Mr. Striker eyed his old friend for a moment with a look of some displeasure; he saw that this was but a cunning feminine imitation of resignation, and that, through some untraceable process of transition, she was now taking more comfort in the opinions of this sophistical stranger than in his own tough dogmas. He rose to his feet, without pulling down his waistcoat, but with a wrinkled grin at the inconsistency of women. "Well, sir, Mr. Roderick's powers are nothing to me," he said, "no, nor the use he makes of them. Good or bad, he's no son of mine. But in a friendly way I'm glad to hear so fine an account of him. I'm glad, madam, you're so satisfied with the prospect. Affection, sir, you see must have its guarantees!" He paused a moment, stroking his beard, with his head inclined and one eye half-closed, looking at Rowland. The look was grotesque, but it was significant, and it puzzled Rowland more than it amused him. "I suppose you are a very brilliant young man," he went on, "very enlightened, very cultivated, quite up to the mark in the fine arts and all that sort of thing. I'm a plain practical old boy, content to follow an honourable profession in a free country. I didn't go off to the Old World to learn my business; no one took me by the hand; I had to grease my wheels myself, and such as I am I'm a self-made man, every inch of me! Well, if our young friend is booked for fame and

fortune I don't suppose his going to Rome will stop him.
But, mind you, it won't help him such a long way either.
If you have undertaken to put him through, there's a thing
or two you had better remember. The crop we gather
depends upon the seed we sow. He may be the biggest
genius of the age; his potatoes won't come up without his
hoeing them. If he takes things so almighty easy as—
well, as one or two young fellows of genius I've had under
my eye—his produce will never gain the prize. Take the
word for it of a man who has made his way inch by inch
and doesn't believe that we wake up to find our work done
because we have lain all night a-dreaming of it; anything
worth doing is devilish hard to do! If your young gentleman finds things easy and has a good time of it and says
he likes the life, it's a sign that—as I may say—you had
better step round to the office and look at the books.
That's all I desire to remark. No offence intended. I
hope you'll have a first-rate time."

Rowland could honestly reply that this seemed pregnant
sense, and he offered Mr. Striker a friendly hand-shake as
the latter withdrew. But Mr. Striker's rather grim view
of matters cast a momentary shadow on his companions,
and Mrs. Hudson seemed to feel that it necessitated between them some little friendly agreement not to be
overawed.

Rowland sat for some time longer, partly because he
wished to please the two women and partly because he was
strangely pleased himself. There was something touching
in their unworldly fears and diffident hopes, something
almost terrible in the way poor little Mrs. Hudson seemed
to flutter and quiver with intense maternal passion. She
put forth one timid conversational venture after another,
and asked Rowland a number of questions about himself,
his age, his family, his occupations, his tastes, his religious
opinions. Rowland had an odd feeling at last that she
had begun to believe him very exemplary and that she
might make later some perturbing discovery. He tried
therefore to invent something that would prepare her to
find him fallible. But he could think of nothing. It only
seemed to him that Miss Garland secretly mistrusted him
and that he must leave her to render him the service,
after he had gone, of making him the object of a little

conscientious derogation. Mrs. Hudson talked with low-voiced eagerness about her son.

"He's very lovable, sir, I assure you. When you come to know him you will find him very lovable. He's a little spoiled, of course; he has always done with me as he pleased; but he's a good boy, I am sure he's a good boy. And every one thinks him very attractive: I am sure he would be noticed anywhere. Don't you think he's very handsome, sir? He is the very copy of his poor father. I had another—perhaps you have been told. He was killed." And the poor little lady bravely smiled, for fear of doing worse. "He was a very fine boy, but very different from Roderick. Roderick is a little strange; he has never been an easy boy. Sometimes I feel like the goose—wasn't it a goose, dear?" and startled by the audacity of her comparison she appealed to Miss Garland—"the goose or the hen, who hatched a swan's egg. I have never been able to give him what he needs. I have always thought that in more—in more brilliant circumstances he might find his place and be happy. But at the same time I was afraid of the world for him; it was so dangerous and dreadful—so mixed. No doubt I know very little about it. I never suspected, I confess, that it contained persons of such liberality as yours."

Rowland replied that evidently she had done the world but scanty justice.

"No," objected Miss Garland after a pause, "it is like something in a fairy tale."

"What, pray?"

"Your coming here all unknown, so rich and so polite, and carrying off my cousin in a golden cloud."

If this was badinage Miss Garland had the best of it, for Rowland almost fell a-musing silently over the question whether there were a possibility of irony in the young lady's lucid glance. Before he withdrew Mrs. Hudson made him tell her again that Roderick's powers were extraordinary. He had inspired her with a clinging, caressing faith in his wisdom. "He will really do great things?" she asked—"the very greatest?"

"I see no intrinsic reason why he should not."

"Well, we shall think of that as we sit here alone," she rejoined. "Mary and I will sit here and talk about it.

So I give him up," she went on, as he was going. "I am sure you will be the best of friends to him; but if you should ever forget him or grow tired of him—if you should lose your interest in him and he should come to any harm or any trouble, please sir, remember—" and she paused, with a tremulous voice.

"Remember, my dear madam?"

"That he is all I have—that he is everything—and that it would be very terrible."

"In so far as I can help him he shall succeed," was all Rowland could say. He turned to Miss Garland to bid her good-night, and she rose and put out her hand. She was very straightforward, but he could see that if she was too modest to be bold she was much too simple to be shy. "Have you no injunctions to give me?" he asked—to ask her something.

She looked at him a moment and then, although she was not shy, she blushed. "Make him do his best," she said.

Rowland noted the soft intensity with which the words were uttered. "Do you take a great interest in him?" he demanded.

"Certainly."

"Then if he will not do his best for you he will not do it for me." She turned away with another blush and Rowland took his leave.

He walked homeward, thinking of many things. The great Northampton elms inter-arched far above in the darkness, but the moon had risen and through scattered apertures was hanging the dusky vault with silver lamps. There seemed to Rowland something intensely serious in the scene in which he had just taken part. He had laughed and talked and braved it out in self-defence; but when he reflected that he was really meddling with the simple stillness of this little New England home, and that he had ventured to disturb so much living security in the interest of a far-away fantastic hypothesis, he paused, amazed at his temerity. It was true, as Cecilia had said, that for an unofficious man it was a singular position. There stirred in his mind an odd feeling of annoyance with Roderick for having so peremptorily taken possession of his mind. As he looked up and down the long vista, and saw the clear white houses glancing here and there in the broken moonshine, he could almost have believed that the happiest lot for any man was to make the most of life in some such tranquil spot as that. Here were kindness, comfort, safety, the warning voice of duty, the perfect absence of temptation. And as Rowland looked along the arch of silvered shadow and out into the lucid air of the American night, which seemed so doubly vast, somehow, and strange and nocturnal, he felt like declaring that here was beauty too—beauty sufficient for an artist not to starve upon it. As he stood there lost in the darkness, he presently heard a rapid tread on the other side of the road, accompanied by a loud jubilant whistle, and in a moment a figure emerged into an open gap of moonshine. He had no difficulty in recognising Hudson, who was presumably returning from a visit to Cecilia. Roderick stopped suddenly and stared up at the moon, with his face vividly illumined. He broke out into a snatch of song—

> " The splendour falls on castle walls
> And snowy summits old in story ! "

And with a great musical roll of his voice he went swinging off into the darkness again, as if his thoughts had lent him wings. He was dreaming of the inspiration of foreign lands—of castled crags and historic landscapes. What a pity after all, thought Rowland, as he went his own way, that he shouldn't have a taste of it!

IV.

IT had been a very just remark of Cecilia's that Roderick would change with a change in his circumstances. Rowland had telegraphed to New York for another berth on his steamer, and from the hour the answer came Hudson's spirits rose to incalculable heights. He was radiant with good humour, and his charming gaiety seemed the pledge of a brilliant future. He had forgiven his old enemies

and forgotten his old grievances—he seemed every way
reconciled to a world in which he was going to count as an
active force. He was inexhaustibly jocose and suggestive,
and as Cecilia said, he had suddenly become so good that
it was only to be feared he was going to start not for the
Old World, but for the Next! He took long walks with
Rowland, who felt more and more the fascination of his
brilliant disposition. Rowland returned several times to
Mrs. Hudson's, and found the two ladies doing their best
to be happy in their companion's happiness. Mary Garland, he thought, was succeeding better than her demeanour on his first visit had promised. He tried to have some
especial talk with her, but her extreme reserve forced him
to content himself with such response to his rather urgent
overtures as might be extracted from a keenly attentive
smile. It must be confessed however that if the response
was vague, the satisfaction was great, and that Rowland
after his second visit kept seeing a lurking reflection of
this smile in the most unexpected places. It seemed
strange that she should please him so well at so slender
a cost; but please him she did, extraordinarily, and his
pleasure had a quality altogether new to him. It made
him restless and a trifle melancholy; he walked about
absently, wondering and wishing. He wondered among
other things why fate should have condemned him to
make the acquaintance of a girl whom he would make
a sacrifice to know better, just as he was leaving the
country for years. It seemed to him that he was turning
his back on a chance of happiness—happiness of a sort
of which the slenderest germ should be cultivated. He
asked himself whether, feeling as he did, if he had only
himself to please he should give up his journey and—wait.
He had Roderick to please now, for whom disappointment
would be cruel; but he said to himself that certainly had
there been no Roderick in the case the ship should sail
without him. He asked Hudson several questions about
his cousin, but Roderick, confidential on most points,
seemed to have reasons of his own for being reticent on
this one. His measured answers quickened Rowland's
curiosity, for the girl, with her irritating half-suggestions,
had only to be a subject of guarded allusion in others to
become intolerably interesting. He learned from Roderick

that she was the daughter of a country minister, a far-away cousin of his mother, settled in another part of the State ; that she was one of a half-a-dozen daughters, that the family was very poor, and that she had come a couple of months before to pay his mother a long visit. " It is to be a very long one now," he said, " for it is settled that she is to remain while I am away."

The fermentation of contentment in Roderick's soul reached its climax a few days before the young men were to make their farewells. He had been sitting with his friends on Cecilia's verandah, but for half an hour past he had said nothing. Lounging back against a column muffled in creepers, and gazing idly at the stars, he kept carolling softly to himself with that indifference to ceremony for which he always found allowance, though it had nothing conciliatory but what his good looks gave it. At last, springing up—" I want to strike out hard ! " he exclaimed. " I want to do something violent, to let off steam ! "

" I'll tell you what to do, this lovely weather," said Cecilia. " Give a picnic. It can be as violent as you please, and it will have the merit of leading off our over emotion into a safe channel, as well as yours."

Roderick laughed uproariously at Cecilia's very practical remedy for his sentimental need, but a couple of days later nevertheless the picnic was given. It was to be a family party, but Roderick in his magnanimous geniality insisted on inviting Mr. Striker, a decision which Rowland mentally applauded. " And we will have Mrs. Striker too," he said, " if she will come, to keep my mother in countenance ; and at any rate we will have Miss Striker—the divine Petronilla ! " The young lady thus denominated formed with Mrs. Hudson, Miss Garland and Cecilia the feminine half of the company. Mr. Striker presented himself, sacrificing a morning's work, with a magnanimity greater even than Roderick's, and foreign support was further secured in the person of Mr. Whitefoot, the young Orthodox minister. Roderick had chosen the feasting place ; he knew it well and had passed many a summer afternoon there, lying at his length on the grass and gazing at the blue undulations of the horizon. It was a meadow on the edge of a wood, with mossy rocks protruding through the grass and a little lake on the other side. It was a cloudless August day; Rowland always remembered it, and the scene, and everything that was said and done, with extraordinary distinctness. Roderick surpassed himself in friendly jollity, and at one moment, when exhilaration was at the highest, was seen in Mr. Striker's high white hat, drinking champagne from a broken tea-cup to Mr. Striker's health. Miss Striker had her father's pale blue eye; she was dressed as if she had been going to sit for her photograph, and remained for a long time with Roderick on a little promontory overhanging the lake. Mrs. Hudson sat all day with a little meek apprehensive smile. She was afraid of an "accident," though unless Miss Striker (who indeed was a little of a romp) should push Roderick into the lake, it was hard to see what accident could occur. Mrs. Hudson was as neat and crisp and uncrumpled at the end of the festival as at the beginning. Mr. Whitefoot, who but a twelvemonth later became a convert to Episcopacy and was already cultivating a certain conversational sonority, devoted himself to Cecilia. He had a little book in his pocket, out of which he read to her at intervals, lying stretched at her feet; and it was a lasting joke with Cecilia afterwards that she would never tell what Mr. Whitefoot's little book had been. Rowland had placed himself near Miss Garland while the feasting went forward on the grass. She wore a so-called gipsy hat—a little straw hat, tied down over her ears, so as to cast her eyes into shadow, by a ribbon passing outside of it. When the company dispersed after lunch, he proposed to her to take a stroll in the wood. She hesitated a moment and looked towards Mrs. Hudson, as if for permission to leave her. But Mrs. Hudson was listening to Mr. Striker, who sat gossiping to her with relaxed consistency, his waistcoat unbuttoned and his hat on his nose.

"You can give your cousin your society at any time," said Rowland. "But me perhaps you will never see again."

"Why then should we wish to be friends, if nothing is to come of it?" she asked, with homely logic. But by this time she had consented, and they were treading the fallen pine-needles.

"Oh, one must take all one can get," said Rowland. "If we can be friends for half an hour it's so much gained."

"Do you expect never to come back to Northampton again?"

"'Never' is a good deal to say. But I go to Europe for a long stay."

"Do you prefer it so much to your own country?"

"I will not say that. But I have the misfortune to be a rather idle man, and in Europe the burden of idleness is less heavy than here."

She was silent for a few minutes; then at last, "In that then we are better than Europe," she said. To a certain point Rowland agreed with her, but he demurred, to make her say more.

"Wouldn't it be better," she asked, "to work to get reconciled to America than to go to Europe to get reconciled to idleness?"

"Doubtless; but you know work is hard to find."

"I come from a little place where every one has plenty," said Mary Garland. "We all work; every one I know works. And really," she added presently, "I look at you with curiosity; you are the first unoccupied man I ever saw."

"Don't look at me too hard," said Rowland, smiling. "I shall sink into the earth. What is the name of your little place?"

"West Nazareth," said Mary Garland with her usual directness. "It is not so very little, though it's smaller than Northampton."

"I wonder whether I could find any work at West Nazareth," Rowland said.

"You would not like it," Miss Garland declared reflectively. "Though there are far finer woods there than this. We have miles and miles of woods."

"I might chop down trees," said Rowland. "That is if you allow it."

"Allow it? Why, where should we get our fire-wood?" Then noticing that he had spoken jestingly she glanced at him askance, though with no visible diminution of her gravity. "Don't you know how to do anything? Have you no profession?"

Rowland shook his head. "Absolutely none."

"What do you do all day?"

"Nothing worth relating. That's why I am going to

Europe. There at least if I do nothing I shall see a great deal; and if I am not a producer I shall at any rate be an observer."

" Can't we observe everywhere ? "

" Certainly ; and I really think that in that way I make the most of my opportunities. Though I confess," he continued, " that I often remember there are things to be seen here to which I probably have not done justice. I should like, for instance, to see West Nazareth."

She looked round at him, open-eyed ; not apparently that she exactly supposed he was jesting, for the expression of such a desire was not necessarily facetious ; but as if he must have spoken with an ulterior motive. In fact, he had spoken from the simplest of motives. The girl beside him pleased him immensely, and suspecting that her charm was essentially her own and not reflected from social circumstance, he wished to give himself the satisfaction of contrasting her with the meagre influences of her education. Miss Garland's second movement was to take him at his word. " Since you are free to do as you please, why don't you go there ? "

" I am not free to do as I please now. I have offered your cousin to bear him company to Europe, he has accepted with enthusiasm, and I can't back out."

" Are you going to Europe simply for his sake ? "

Rowland hesitated for a moment. "I think I may almost say so."

Mary Garland walked along in silence. "Do you mean to do a great deal for him ? " she asked at last.

" What I can. But my power of helping him is very small beside his power of helping himself."

For a moment she was silent again. " You are very generous," she said, almost solemnly.

" No, I am simply very shrewd. Roderick will repay me. It's a speculation. At first, I think," he added shortly afterwards, " you would not have paid me that little compliment. You didn't believe in me."

She made no attempt to deny it. " I didn't see why you should wish to make Roderick discontented. I thought you were rather frivolous."

" You did me injustice. I don't think I am that."

"It was because you are unlike other men—those at least whom I have seen."

"In what way?"

"Why, as you describe yourself. You have no duties, no profession, no home. You live for your pleasure."

"That's all very true. And yet I maintain I am not frivolous."

"I hope not," said Mary Garland simply. They had reached a point where the wood-path forked and put forth two divergent tracks which lost themselves in a verdurous tangle. The young girl seemed to think that the difficulty of choice between them was a reason for giving them up and turning back. Rowland thought otherwise, and detected agreeable grounds for preference in the left-hand path. As a compromise, they sat down on a fallen log. Looking about him, Rowland espied a curious wild shrub, with a spotted crimson leaf; he went and plucked a spray of it and brought it to his companion. He had never observed it before, but she immediately called it by its name. She expressed surprise at his not knowing it; it was extremely common. He presently brought her a specimen of another delicate plant, with a little blue-streaked flower. "I suppose that's common too," he said, "but I have never seen it—or noticed it at least." She answered that this one was rare, and meditated a moment before she could remember its name. At last she re-called it and expressed surprise at his having found the plant in the woods; she supposed it grew only in the marshes. Rowland complimented her on her fund of useful information.

"It's not especially useful," she answered; "but I like to know the name of plants as I do those of my acquaintances. When we walk in the woods at home—which we do so much—it seems as unnatural not to know what to call the flowers as it would be to see some one in the town with whom we should not be on speaking terms."

"*Apropos* of frivolity," Rowland said, "I am sure you yourself have very little of it, unless at West Nazareth it is considered frivolous to walk in the woods and nod to the nodding flowers. Do kindly tell me a little about yourself." And to compel her to begin, "I know you come of a race of theologians," he went on.

"No," she replied, deliberating; "they are not theologians, though they are ministers. We don't take a very firm stand upon doctrine; we are practical rather. We write sermons and preach them, but we do a great deal of hard work besides."

"And of this hard work what has your share been?"

"The hardest part—doing nothing."

"What do you call nothing?"

"I taught some small children their lessons once; I must make the most of that. But I confess I didn't like it. Otherwise, I have only done little things at home, as they turned up."

"What kind of things?"

"Oh, every kind. If you had seen my home you would understand."

Rowland would have liked to make her specify; but he felt a sort of luxurious pleasure in being discreet. "To be happy, I imagine," he contented himself with saying, "you need to be occupied. You need to have something to expend yourself upon."

"That is not so true as it once was; now that I am older I am sure I am less impatient of leisure. Certainly these two months that I have been with Mrs. Hudson I have had a terrible amount of it. And yet I have liked it! And now that I am probably to be with her all the while that her son is away, I look forward to more with dreadful resignation."

"It is settled then that you are to remain with your cousin?"

"It depends upon their writing from home that I may stay. But that is probable. Only I must not forget," she said, rising, "that the ground for my doing so is that she shall not be left alone."

"I am glad to know that I shall probably often hear about you. I assure you I shall often think about you!" These words of Rowland's were half impulsive, half deliberate. They were the simple truth, and he had asked himself why he should not tell her the truth. And yet they were not all of it; her hearing the rest would depend upon the way she received this. She received it not only, as Rowland foresaw, without a shadow of coquetry, of any apparent thought of listening to it gracefully, but with a slight movement of nervous deprecation which seemed to betray itself in the quickening of her step. Evidently, if Rowland was to take pleasure in hearing about her, it would have to be a highly disinterested pleasure. She answered nothing, and Rowland too, as he walked beside her, was silent; but as he looked along the shadow-woven wood-path, what he was really facing was a level three years of disinterestedness. He ushered them in by talking composed civility until he had brought Miss Garland back to her companions.

He saw her but once again. He was obliged to be in New York a couple of days before sailing, and it was arranged that Roderick should overtake him at the last moment. The evening before he left Northampton he went to say farewell to Mrs. Hudson. The ceremony was brief. Rowland soon perceived that the poor little lady was in the melting mood, and as he dreaded her tears he compressed a multitude of solemn promises into a silent hand-shake and took his leave. Mary Garland she had told him was in the back-garden with Roderick; he might go out to them. He did so, and as he drew near he heard Roderick's high-pitched voice ringing behind the shrubbery. In a moment, emerging, he found the girl leaning against a tree, with her cousin before her talking with great emphasis. He asked pardon for interrupting them and said he wished only to bid her good-bye. She gave him her hand and he held it an instant, saying nothing. "Don't forget," he said to Roderick as he turned away. "And don't, in this company, repent of your bargain."

"I shall not let him," said Mary Garland, with something very like gaiety. "I shall see that he is punctual. He must go! I owe you an apology for having doubted that he ought to go!" And in spite of the dusk, Rowland could see that she had even a sweeter smile than he had supposed.

Roderick was punctual, eagerly punctual, and they went. Rowland for several days was occupied with material cares, and lost sight of his sentimental perplexities. But they only slumbered and they were sharply awakened. The weather was fine, and the two young men always sat together upon deck late into the evening. One night, towards the last, they were at the stern of the great ship, watching her grind the solid blackness of the ocean into phosphorescent foam. ' They talked on these occasions of everything conceivable, and had the air of having no secrets from each other. But it was on Roderick's conscience that this air belied him, and he was too frank by nature, moreover, for permanent reticence on any point.

"I must tell you something," he said at last. "I should like you to know it, and you will be so glad to know it. Besides, it's only a question of time; three months hence probably you would have guessed it. I am engaged to Mary Garland."

Rowland sat staring; though the sea was calm it seemed to him that the ship gave a great dizzying lurch. But in a moment he contrived to answer coherently—"Engaged to Mary Garland! I never supposed—I never imagined—"

"That I was in love with her?" Roderick interrupted. "Neither did I until this last fortnight. But you came and put me into such ridiculous good-humour that I felt an extraordinary desire to tell some woman that I adored her. Mary Garland is a magnificent girl; you know her too little to do her justice. I have been quietly learning to know her these past three months, and have been falling in love with her without suspecting it. It appeared when I spoke to her that she thought me a charming fellow! So the thing was settled. I must of course make some money before we can marry. It's rather awkward, certainly, to engage one's self to a girl whom one is going to leave for years the next day. We shall be condemned for some time to come to do a terrible deal of abstract thinking about each other. But I wanted her blessing and I couldn't help asking for it. Unless a man is unnaturally selfish he needs to work for some one else than himself, and I am sure I shall run a smoother and swifter course for knowing that that capital creature is waiting at Northampton for news of my greatness. If ever I am a dull companion and over-addicted to moping, remember in justice to me that I am in love, and that my sweetheart is five thousand miles away."

Rowland listened to all this with a feeling that fortune had played him an elaborately-devised trick. It had lured him out into mid-ocean and smoothed the sea and stilled the winds and given him a singularly sympathetic comrade, and then it had turned and delivered him a thumping blow in mid-chest. " Yes," he said, after an attempt at the usual formal congratulation, " you certainly ought to do better—with Miss Garland waiting for you at Northampton ! "

Roderick, now that he had broken ground, was eloquent, and rung a hundred changes on the assurance that he was a very happy man. Then at last, suddenly, his climax was a yawn, and he declared that he must go to bed. Rowland let him go alone, and sat there late between sea and sky.

V.

ONE warm still day, late in the Roman autumn, our two young men were sitting beneath one of the high-stemmed pines of the Villa Ludovisi. They had been spending an hour in the mouldy little garden-house where the colossal mask of the famous Juno looks out with blank eyes from that dusky corner which must seem to her the last possible stage of a lapse from Olympus. Then they had wandered out into the gardens, and were lounging away the morning under the spell of their magical picturesqueness. Roderick declared that he would go nowhere else; that after the Juno it was a profanation to look at anything but sky and trees. There was a fresco of Guercino, to which Rowland, though he had seen it on his former visit to Rome, went dutifully to pay his respects. But Roderick, though he had never seen it, declared that it couldn't be worth a fig, and that he didn't care to look at ugly things. He remained stretched on his overcoat, which he had spread on the grass, while Rowland went off envying the intellectual comfort of genius which can arrive at serene conclusions without disagreeable processes. When the latter came back, his friend was sitting with his elbows on his knees and his head in his hands. Rowland, in the geniality of a mood attuned to the mellow charm of a Roman villa, found a good word to say for the Guercino ; but he chiefly talked of the view from the little belvedere on the roof of

the casino and how it looked like the prospect from a castle
turret in a fairy tale.

"Very likely," said Roderick, throwing himself back
with a yawn. "But I must let it pass. I have seen
enough for the present; I have reached the top of the hill.
I have an indigestion of impressions; I must work them
off before I go in for any more. I don't want to look at
any more of other people's works for a month—not even
at Nature's own. I want to look at Roderick Hudson's!
The result of it all is that I am not afraid. I can but try,
as well as the rest of them! The fellow who did that
gazing goddess yonder only made an experiment. The
other day, when I was looking at Michael Angelo's Moses,
I was seized with a kind of defiance—a reaction against
all this mere passive enjoyment of grandeur. It was a
rousing great success, certainly, that sat there before me,
but somehow it was not an inscrutable mystery, and it
seemed to me, not perhaps that I should some day do as
well, but that at least I *might!*"

"As you say, you can but try," said Rowland. "Success
is only passionate effort."

"Well, the passion is blazing; we have been piling on
fuel handsomely. It came over me just now that it is
exactly three months to a day since I left Northampton.
I can't believe it!"

"It certainly seems more."

"It seems like ten years. What an exquisite ass I
was!"

"Do you feel so wise now?"

"Verily! Don't I look so? Surely I haven't the same
face. Haven't I a different eye, a different expression,
a different voice?"

"I can hardly say, because I have watched the transformation. But it's very likely. You are in the literal
sense of the word more civilised. I dare say," added
Rowland, "that Miss Garland would think so."

"That's not what she would call it; she would say I am
corrupted."

Rowland asked few questions about Mary Garland, but
he always listened narrowly to his companion's voluntary
observations. "Are you very sure?" he replied.

"Why, she's a stern moralist, and she would infer from

my appearance that I had become a gilded profligate."
Roderick had in fact a Venetian watch-chain round his
neck and a magnificent Roman intaglio on the third finger
of his left hand.

"Shall you think I take a liberty," asked Rowland, "if
I say you judge her superficially?"

"For heaven's sake," cried Roderick laughing, "don't
tell me she's not a moralist! It was for that I fell in love
with her—and with rigid virtue in her person."

"She is a moralist, but not as you imply a narrow one.
That's more than a difference in degree; it's a difference in
kind. I don't know whether I ever mentioned it, but I
have a great notion of Miss Garland. There is nothing
narrow about her but her experience; everything else is
large. My impression of her is that she is very intelligent,
but that she has never had a chance to prove it. Some
day or other I am sure she will judge fairly and wisely of
everything."

"Stay a bit!" cried Roderick; "you are a better Catholic
than the Pope. I shall be content if she judges fairly of
me—of my merits, that is. The rest she must not judge
at all. She's a grimly devoted little creature; may she
always remain so! Changed as I am, I adore her none
the less. What becomes of all our emotions, our impressions," he went on after a long pause, "all the material
of thought that life pours into us at such a rate during
such a memorable three months as these? There are
twenty moments a week—a day, for that matter, some
days—that seem supreme, twenty impressions that seem
ultimate, that appear to form an intellectual era. But
others come treading on their heels and sweeping them
along, and they all melt like water into water and settle
the question of precedence among themselves. The
curious thing is that the more the mind takes in, the more
it has space for, and that all one's ideas are like the Irish
people at home who live in the different corners of a room
and take boarders."

"I fancy it is our peculiar good luck that we don't see
the limits of our minds," said Rowland. "We are young,
compared with what we may one day be. That belongs
to youth; it is perhaps the best part of it. They say
that old people do find themselves at last face to face

with a solid blank wall and stand thumping against it in
vain. It resounds, it seems to have something beyond it,
but it won't move! That's only a reason for living with
open doors as long as we can! "

"Open doors?" murmured Roderick. "Yes, let us close
no doors that open upon Rome. For this, for the mind, is
eternal warm weather! But though my doors may stand
open to-day," he presently added, "I shall see no visitors.
I want to pause and breathe; I want to dream of a statue.
I have been working hard for three months; I have earned
a right to a reverie."

Rowland, on his side, was not without provision for
reflection, and they lingered on in gentle desultory gossip.
Rowland felt the need for intellectual rest, for a truce to
present care for churches, statues, and pictures on even
better grounds than his companion, inasmuch as he had
really been living Roderick's intellectual life the past three
months as well as his own. As he looked back on these
animated weeks he drew a long breath of satisfaction—
almost of relief. Roderick so far had justified his confidence and flattered his perspicacity; he was giving a
splendid account of himself. He was changed even more
than he himself suspected; he had stepped without
faltering into his birthright, and was spending money,
intellectually, as lavishly as a young heir who has just
won an obstructive lawsuit. Roderick's glance and voice
were the same, doubtless, as when they enlivened the
summer dusk on Cecilia's verandah, but in his person
generally there was an indefinable expression of experience
rapidly and easily assimilated. Rowland had been struck
at the outset with the instinctive quickness of his observation and his free appropriation of whatever might serve
his purpose. He had not been for instance half an hour
on English soil before he perceived that he was dressed
provincially, and he had immediately reformed his toilet
with the most unerring tact. His appetite for novelty was
insatiable, and for everything characteristically foreign,
as it presented itself, he had an extravagant greeting; but
in half an hour the novelty had faded, he had guessed the
secret, he had plucked out the heart of the mystery and
was clamouring for a keener sensation. At the end of a
month he presented a puzzling spectacle to his companion.

He had caught instinctively the key-note of the Old World. He observed and enjoyed, he criticised and rhapsodised, but though all things interested him and many delighted him, none surprised him; he invented short cuts and anticipated the unexpected. Witnessing the rate at which he did intellectual execution on the general spectacle of European life, Rowland at moments felt vaguely uneasy for the future; the boy was living too fast, he would have said, and giving alarming pledges to ennui in his later years. But we must live as our pulses are timed, and Roderick's struck the hour very often. He was by imagination, though he never became in manner, a natural man of the world; he had intuitively, as an artist, what one may call the historic consciousness. He asked Rowland questions which this halting dilettante was quite unable to answer, and of which he was equally unable to conceive where he had picked up the data. Roderick ended by answering them himself, tolerably to his satisfaction, and in a short time he had almost turned the tables, and become in their walks and talks the accredited fountain of criticism. Rowland took a generous pleasure in his companion's confident *coup d'œil*; Roderick was so much younger than he himself had ever been! Surely youth and genius hand in hand were the most beautiful sight in the world. Roderick added to this the charm of his more immediately personal qualities. The vivacity of his perceptions, the audacity of his imagination, the picturesqueness of his phrase when he was pleased—and even more when he was displeased—his abounding good-humour, his candour, his unclouded frankness, his unfailing impulse to share every emotion and impression with his friend; all this made comradeship a high felicity, and interfused with a deeper amenity the wanderings and contemplations that beguiled their pilgrimage to Rome.

They had gone almost immediately to Paris, and had spent their days at the Louvre and their evenings at the theatre. Roderick was divided in mind as to whether Titian or Mademoiselle Delaporte were the greater artist. They had come down through France to Genoa and Milan, had spent a fortnight in Venice and another in Florence, and had now been a month in Rome. Roderick had said that he meant to spend three months in simply looking, absorbing, and reflecting, without putting pencil to paper. He looked indefatigably, and certainly saw great things—things greater doubtless at times than the intention of the artist. And yet he made few false steps, and wasted little time in theories of what he ought to like and to dislike. He judged instinctively and passionately, but never vulgarly. At Venice for a couple of days he had half a fit of melancholy over the pretended discovery that he had missed his way, and that the only proper vestment of plastic conceptions was the colouring of Titian and Paul Veronese. Then one morning the two young men had themselves rowed out to Torcello, and Roderick lay back for a couple of hours watching a brown-breasted gondolier making superb muscular movements, in high relief, against the sky of the Adriatic, and at the end jerked himself up with a violence that nearly swamped the gondola, and declared that the only thing worth living for was to make a colossal bronze and set it aloft in the light of a public square. In Rome his first care was for the Vatican; he went there again and again. But the old imperial and papal city altogether delighted him; only there he really found what he had been looking for from the first—the complete contradiction of Northampton. And indeed Rome is the natural home of those spirits with which we just now claimed fellowship for Roderick—the spirits with a deep relish for the artificial element in life and the infinite superpositions of history. It is the immemorial city of convention; and in that still recent day the most impressive convention in all history was visible to men's eyes in the reverberating streets, erect in a gilded coach drawn by four black horses. Roderick's first fortnight was a high æsthetic revel. He declared that Rome made him feel and understand more things than he could express; he was sure that life must have there for all one's senses an incomparable fineness; that more interesting things must happen to one there than anywhere else. And he gave Rowland to understand that he meant to live freely and largely and be as interested as occasion demanded. Rowland saw no reason to regard this as a menace of grossness, because in the first place there was in all dissipation, refine it as one might, a vulgarity which would disqualify it for Roderick's favour; and because in the second the young sculptor was a man to regard all things in the light of his art, to hand over his passions to his genius to be dealt with, and to find that he could live largely enough without exceeding the circle of pure delights. Rowland took immense satisfaction in his companion's lively desire to transmute all his impressions into production. Production indeed was not always working at a clay model, but the form it sometimes took was none the less a safe one. He wrote frequent long letters to Mary Garland; when Rowland went with him to post them he thought wistfully of the fortune of the large loosely-written missives, which cost Roderick unconscionable sums in postage. He received punctual answers of a more frugal shape, written in a clear and delicate hand, on paper vexatiously thin. If Rowland was present when they came, he turned away and thought of other things —or tried to think. These were the only moments when his sympathy halted, and they were brief. For the rest he let the days go by unprotestingly, and enjoyed Roderick's serene efflorescence as he would have done a beautiful summer sunrise. Rome for the past month had been delicious. The annual descent of the Goths had not yet begun, and sunny leisure seemed to brood over the city.

Roderick had taken out a note-book and was roughly sketching a memento of the great Juno. Suddenly there was a noise on the gravel, and the young men, looking up, saw three persons advancing. One was a woman of middle age, with a rather grand air and a great many furbelows. She looked very hard at our friends as she passed, and glanced back over her shoulder as if to hasten the step of a young girl who slowly followed her. She had such an expansive majesty of mien that Rowland supposed she must have some proprietary right in the villa and was not just then in an hospitable mood. Beside her walked a little elderly man, tightly buttoned in a shabby black coat, but with a flower in his lappet and a pair of soiled light gloves. He was a grotesque-looking personage, and might have passed for a gentleman of the old school reduced by adversity to playing cicerone to foreigners of distinction. He had a little black eye which glittered like a diamond, and rolled about like a ball of quicksilver, and a white moustache, cut short and stiff, like a worn-out brush. He was smiling with extreme urbanity and talking in a low

mellifluous voice to the lady, who evidently was not listening to him. At a considerable distance behind this couple
strolled a young girl, apparently of about twenty. She
was tall and slender and dressed with extreme elegance ;
she led by a cord a large poodle of the most fantastic
aspect. He was combed and decked like a ram for sacrifice ; his trunk and haunches were of the most transparent
pink, his fleecy head and shoulders as white as jeweller's
cotton, his tail and ears ornamented with long blue ribbons.
He stepped along stiffly and solemnly beside his mistress,
with an air of conscious elegance. There was something
at first slightly ridiculous in the sight of a young lady
gravely appended to an animal of these incongruous attributes, and Roderick, with his customary frankness, greeted
the spectacle with a confident smile. The young girl perceived it and turned her face full upon him, with a gaze
intended apparently to enforce greater deference. It was
not deference, however, her countenance provoked, but
startled submissive admiration ; Roderick's smile fell dead
and he sat eagerly staring. A pair of extraordinary dark
blue eyes, a mass of dusky hair over a low forehead, a
blooming oval of perfect purity, a flexible lip just touched
with disdain, the step and carriage of a tired princess—
these were the general features of his vision. The young
lady was walking slowly and letting her long dress rustle
over the gravel ; the young men had time to see her distinctly before she averted her face and went her way. She
left a vague sweet perfume behind her as she passed.

"Immortal powers !" cried Roderick ; "what a vision !
In the name of transcendent perfection who is she ?" He
sprang up and stood looking after her until she rounded a
turn in the avenue. "What a movement, what a manner,
what a poise of the head ! I wonder if she would sit
to me ?"

"You had better go and ask her," said Rowland, laughing. "She is certainly most beautiful."

"Beautiful ? She's beauty itself—she's a revelation.
I don't believe she is living—she's a phantasm, a vapour,
an illusion !"

"The poodle," said Rowland, "is certainly alive."

"No, he too may be a grotesque phantom, like the black
dog in *Faust*."

"I hope at least that the young lady has nothing in common with Mephistopheles. She looked dangerous."

"If beauty is immoral, as people think at Northampton," said Roderick, "she is the incarnation of evil. The mamma and the queer old gentleman moreover are a pledge of her reality. Who are they all?"

"The Prince and Princess Ludovisi and the *principessina*," suggested Rowland.

"There are no such people," said Roderick. "Besides, the little old man is not the papa." Rowland smiled, wondering how he had ascertained these facts, and the young sculptor went on. "The old man is a Roman, a hanger-on of the mamma, a useful personage who now and then gets asked to dinner. The ladies are foreigners from some Northern country; I won't say which."

"Perhaps from the State of Maine," said Rowland.

"No, she is not an American, I will lay a wager on that. She is a daughter of this elder world. We shall see her again, I pray my stars; but if we don't I shall have done something I never expected—I shall have had a glimpse of ideal beauty." He sat down again and went on with his sketch of the Juno, scrawled away for ten minutes, and then handed the result in silence to Rowland. Rowland uttered an exclamation of surprise and applause. The drawing represented the Juno as to the position of the head, the brow and the broad fillet across the hair; but the eyes, the mouth, the physiognomy were a vivid portrait of the young girl with the poodle. "I have been wanting a subject," said Roderick; "there's one made to my hand! And now for work!"

They saw no more of the young girl, though Roderick looked hopefully for some days into the carriages on the Pincian. She had evidently only been passing through Rome; Naples or Florence now happily possessed her, and she was guiding her fleecy companion through the Villa Reale or the Boboli Gardens with the same superb defiance of irony. Roderick went to work and spent a month shut up in his studio; he had an idea and he was not to rest till he had embodied it. He had established himself in the basement of a huge, dusky, dilapidated old house, in that long tortuous and preeminently Roman street which leads from the Corso to the Bridge of

St. Angelo. The black archway which admitted you might
have served as the portal of the Augean stables, but you
emerged presently upon a mouldy little court, of which the
fourth side was formed by a narrow terrace overhanging
the Tiber. Here, along the parapet, were stationed half
a dozen shapeless fragments of sculpture, with a couple of
meagre orange-trees in terra-cotta tubs and an oleander
that never flowered. The unclean historic river swept
beneath; behind were dusky, reeking walls, spotted here
and there with hanging rags and flower-pots in windows;
opposite, at a distance, were the bare brown banks of the
stream, the huge rotunda of St. Angelo, tipped with its
seraphic statue, the dome of St. Peter's and the broad-
topped pines of the Villa Pamfili. The place was crumbling
and shabby and melancholy, but the river was delightful,
the rent was a trifle and everything was picturesque.
Roderick was in the best humour with his quarters from
the first, and was certain that the faculty of production
would be intenser there in an hour than in twenty years
at Northampton. His studio was a large empty room
with a vaulted ceiling, covered with vague dark traces of
an old fresco which Rowland when he spent an hour with
his friend used to stare at vainly for some surviving cohe-
rence of floating draperies and clasping arms. Roderick
had lodged himself economically in the same quarter. He
occupied a fifth floor on the Ripetta, but he was only at
home to sleep, for when he was not at work he was either
lounging in Rowland's more luxurious rooms or strolling
through streets and churches and gardens.

Rowland had found a convenient corner in a stately old
palace close to the Fountain of Trevi, and made himself
a home to which books and pictures and prints and odds
and ends of curious furniture gave an air of leisurely per-
manence. He had the tastes of a collector; he spent half
his afternoons ransacking the dusky magazines of the
curiosity-mongers, and he often made his way in quest
of a prize into the heart of impecunious Roman house-
holds which had been prevailed upon to listen — with
closed doors and an impenetrably wary smile—to proposals for an hereditary " antique." In the evening often,
under the lamp, amid dropped curtains and the scattered
gleam of firelight upon polished carvings and mellow

paintings, the two friends sat with their heads together, criticising intaglios and etchings, water-colour drawings and illuminated missals. Roderick's quick appreciation of every form of artistic beauty reminded his companion of the flexible temperament of those Italian artists of the sixteenth century who were indifferently painters and sculptors, sonneteers and engravers. At times when he saw how the young sculptor's day passed in a single sustained pulsation, while his own was broken into a dozen conscious devices for disposing of the hours, and intermingled with sighs, half suppressed, some of them, for conscience' sake, over what he failed of in action and missed in possession—he felt a pang of something akin to envy. But Rowland had two substantial aids for giving patience the air of contentment; he was an inquisitive reader and a passionate rider. He plunged into bulky German octavos on Italian history, and he spent long afternoons in the saddle, ranging over the grassy desolation of the Campagna. As the season went on and the social groups began to constitute themselves, he found that he knew a great many people, and that he had easy opportunity for knowing others. He enjoyed a quiet corner of a drawing-room beside an agreeable woman, and although the machinery of what calls itself society seemed to him to have many superfluous wheels, he accepted invitations and made visits punctiliously, from the conviction that the only way not to be overcome by the ridiculous side of most of such observances is to take them with exaggerated gravity. He introduced Roderick right and left, and suffered him to make his way himself—an enterprise for which Roderick very soon displayed an all-sufficient capacity. Wherever he went he made, not exactly what is called a favourable impression, but what, from a practical point of view, is better—a puzzling one. He took to evening parties as a duck to water, and before the winter was half over was the most freely and frequently discussed young man in the heterogeneous foreign colony. Rowland's theory of his own duty was to let him run his course and play his cards, only holding himself ready to point out shoals and pitfalls and administer a friendly propulsion through tight places. Roderick's manners on the precincts of the Pincian were quite the same as his

manners on Cecilia's verandah; that is, they were no
manners at all. But it remained as true as before that
it would have been impossible on the whole to violate
ceremony with less of lasting offence. He interrupted,
he contradicted, he spoke to people he had never seen,
and left his social creditors without the smallest conversational interest on their loans; he lounged and yawned,
he talked loud when he should have talked low, and low
when he should have talked loud. Many people in consequence thought him insufferably conceited and declared
that he ought to wait till he had something to show for
his powers before he assumed the airs of a spoiled celebrity.
But to Rowland and to most friendly observers this judgment was quite beside the mark, and the young man's
undiluted naturalness was its own justification. He was
impulsive, spontaneous, sincere; there were so many people
at dinner-tables and in studios who were not that it
seemed worth while to allow this rare specimen all possible
freedom of action. If Roderick took the words out of
your mouth when you were just prepared to deliver them
with the most effective accent, he did it with a perfect
good conscience, and with no pretension of a better right
to being heard, but simply because he was full to overflowing of his own momentary thought and it sprang from
his lips without asking leave. There were persons who
waited on your periods much more deferentially, that were
a hundred times more capable than Roderick of a reflective
impertinence. Roderick received from various sources,
chiefly feminine, enough finely-adjusted advice to have
established him in life as an embodiment of the pro-
prieties, and he received it, as he afterwards listened to
criticisms on his statues, with unfaltering candour and
good-humour. Here and there doubtless as he went he
took in a reef in his sail; but he was too adventurous a
spirit to be successfully tamed, and he remained at most
points the florid, rather strident young Virginian whose
brilliant aridity had been the despair of Mr. Striker. All
this was what friendly commentators (still chiefly feminine)
alluded to when they spoke of his delightful freshness,
and critics of harsher sensibilities (of the other sex) when
they denounced his damned impertinence. His appearance
enforced these impressions—his handsome face, his radiant

unaverted eyes, his childish unmodulated voice. Afterwards, when those who loved him were in tears, there was something in all this unspotted comeliness that seemed to lend a mockery to the causes of their sorrow.

Certainly, among the young men of genius who for so many ages have gone up to Rome to test their powers, none ever made a fairer beginning than Roderick. He rode his two horses at once with extraordinary good fortune; he established the happiest *modus vivendi* betwixt work and play. He wrestled all day with a mountain of clay in his studio, and chattered half the night away in Roman drawing-rooms. It all seemed part of a kind of divine facility. He was passionately interested, he was feeling his powers; now that they had thoroughly kindled in the glowing æsthetic atmosphere of Rome the ardent young fellow should be pardoned for believing that he never was to see the end of them. He enjoyed immeasurably, after the chronic obstruction of home, the downright act of production. He kept models in his studio till they dropped with fatigue; he drew on other days at the Capitol and the Vatican till his own head swam with his eagerness and his limbs stiffened with the cold. He had promptly set up a life-sized figure which he called an "Adam," and was pushing it rapidly towards completion. There were naturally a great many wiseheads who smiled at his precipitancy and cited him as one more example of Yankee crudity—a capital recruit to the great army of those who wish to dance before they can walk. They were right, but Roderick was right too, for the success of his statue was not to have been foreseen; it partook really of the miraculous. He never surpassed it afterwards, and a good judge here and there has been known to pronounce it the finest piece of sculpture of our modern time. To Rowland it seemed to justify superbly the highest hopes of his friend, and he said to himself that if he had staked his reputation on bringing out a young lion he ought now to pass for a famous connoiseur. In his elation he travelled up to Carrara and selected at the quarries the most magnificent block of marble he could find, and when it came down to Rome the two young men had a "celebration." They drove out to Albano, breakfasted boisterously (in their respective measure) at the

inn, and lounged away the day in the sun on the top of
Monte Cavo. Roderick's head was full of ideas for other
works, which he described with infinite spirit and eloquence,
as vividly as if they were ranged on their pedestals before
him. He had an indefatigable fancy; things he saw in
the streets, in the country, things he heard and read,
effects he saw just missed or half expressed in the works
of others, acted upon his mind as a kind of challenge, and
he was terribly uneasy until in some form or other he had
taken up the glove and set his lance in rest.

The Adam was put into marble, and all the world came
to see it. Of the criticisms passed upon it this history
undertakes to offer no record; over many of them the two
young men had a daily laugh for a month, and certain
of the formulas of the connoisseurs, restrictive or indul-
gent, furnished Roderick with a permanent supply of
humorous catchwords. But people enough spoke flattering good sense to make Roderick feel as if he were already
half famous. The statue passed formally into Rowland's
possession; it was paid for as if an illustrious name had
been chiselled on the pedestal. Poor Roderick owed
every franc of the money. It was not for this however, but
because he was so gloriously in the mood, that, denying
himself all breathing time, on the same day he had given
the last touch to the Adam, he began to shape the rough
contour of an Eve. This experiment went forward with
equal rapidity and success. Roderick lost his temper time
and again with his models, who offered but a gross de-
generate image of his splendid ideal; but his ideal, as he
assured Rowland, became gradually such a fixed vivid
presence that he had only to shut his eyes to behold a
creature far more to his purpose than the poor girl who
stood posturing at forty sous an hour. The Eve was
finished in three months, and the feat was extraordinary,
as well as the statue, which represented an admirably
beautiful woman. When the spring began to muffle the
rugged old city with its tremulous festoons it seemed to him
that he had done a handsome winter's work and had fairly
earned a holiday. He took a liberal one, and lounged
away the lovely Roman May, doing nothing. He looked
very contented; with himself perhaps at times a trifle too
obviously. But who could have said without good reason?

He was "flushed with triumph;" this classic phrase portrayed him to Rowland's sense. He would lose himself in long reveries and emerge from them with a quickened smile and heightened colour. Rowland grudged him none of his smiles and took an extreme satisfaction in his two statues. He had these productions transported to his own apartment, and one warm evening in May he gave a little dinner in honour of the artist. It was small, but Rowland had meant it should be very agreeably composed. He thought over his friends and chose four. They were all persons with whom he lived in a certain intimacy.

VI.

ONE of them was an American sculptor of French extraction, or remotely perhaps of Italian, for he rejoiced in the somewhat fervid name of Gloriani. He was a man of forty, he had been living for years in Paris and in Rome, and he now drove a very pretty trade in sculpture of the ornamental and fantastic sort. In his youth he had had money; but he had spent it recklessly, much of it scandalously, and at twenty-six had found himself obliged to make capital of his talent. This was quite inimitable, and fifteen years of indefatigable exercise had brought it to perfection. Rowland admitted its power, though it gave him very little pleasure; what he relished in the man was the extraordinary vivacity and frankness, not to call it the impudence, of his opinions. He had a definite, practical scheme of art, and he knew at least what he meant. In this sense he was solid and complete. There were so many of the æsthetic fraternity who were floundering in unknown seas, without a notion of which way their noses were turned, that Gloriani, conscious and compact, unlimitedly intelligent and consummately clever, dogmatic only as to his own duties and at once gracefully deferential and profoundly indifferent to those of others, had for Rowland a certain intellectual refreshment quite independent of the

character of his works. These were considered by most
people to belong to a very corrupt, and by many to a positively indecent, school. Others thought them tremendously
knowing and paid enormous prices for them ; and indeed
to be able to point to one of Gloriani's figures in a shady
corner of your library was tolerable proof that you were
not a fool. Corrupt things they certainly were ; in the
line of sculpture they were quite the latest fruit of time.
It was the artist's opinion that there is no essential difference between beauty and ugliness ; that they overlap
and intermingle in a quite inextricable manner ; that there
is no saying where one begins and the other ends ; that
hideousness grimaces at you suddenly from out of the very
bosom of loveliness, and beauty blooms before your eyes in
the lap of vileness ; that it is a waste of wit to nurse
metaphysical distinctions and a sadly meagre entertainment
to caress imaginary lines ; that the thing to aim at is the
expressive and the way to reach it is by ingenuity ; that
for this purpose everything may serve, and that a consummate work is a sort of hotch-potch of the pure and the
impure, the graceful and the grotesque. Its prime duty
is to amuse, to puzzle, to fascinate, to savour of a complex
imagination. Gloriani's statues were florid and meretri-
cious ; they looked like magnified goldsmith's work. They
were extremely elegant, but they had no charm for Rowland. He never bought one, but Gloriani was such an
independent fellow, and was withal so deluged with orders,
that this made no difference in their friendship. The artist
might have passed for a Frenchman. He was a great
talker, and a very picturesque one ; he was almost bald ;
he had a small bright eye, a broken nose and a moustache
with waxed ends. When sometimes he received you at
his lodging, he introduced you to a lady with a plain face
whom he called Madame Gloriani—which she was not.

Rowland's second guest was also an artist, but of a very
different type. His friends called him Sam Singleton ; he
was an American, and he had been in Rome a couple of
years. He painted small landscapes, chiefly in water-
colours ; Rowland had seen one of them in a shop window,
had liked it extremely, and, ascertaining his address, had
gone to see him and found him established in a very humble
studio near the Piazza Barberini, where apparently fame

and fortune had not yet found him out. Rowland took a fancy to him and bought several of his pictures; Singleton made few speeches, but he was grateful. Rowland heard afterwards that when he first came to Rome he painted worthless daubs and gave no promise of talent. Improvement had come however hand in hand with patient industry, and his talent, though of a slender and delicate order, was now incontestable. It was as yet but scantily recognised, and he had hard work to live. Rowland hung his little water-colours on the library wall and found that as he lived with them he grew very fond of them. Singleton was a diminutive attenuated personage; he looked like a precocious child. He had a high protuberant forehead, a transparent brown eye, a perpetual smile, an extraordinary expression of modesty and patience. He listened much more willingly than he talked, with a little fixed grateful grin; he blushed when he spoke, and always offered his ideas in a sidelong fashion, as if the presumption were against them. His modesty set them off and they were eminently to the point. He was so perfect an example of the little noiseless laborious artist whom chance, in the person of a moneyed patron, has never taken by the hand, that Rowland would have liked to befriend him by stealth. Singleton had expressed a fervent admiration for Roderick's productions, but he had not yet met the young master. Roderick was lounging against the chimney-piece when he came in, and Rowland presently introduced him. The little water-colourist stood with folded hands, blushing, smiling and looking up at him as if Roderick had been himself a statue on a pedestal. Singleton began to murmur something about his pleasure, his admiration; the desire to say something very appreciative gave him almost a look of distress. Roderick looked down at him, surprised, and suddenly burst into a laugh. Singleton paused a moment and then, with an intenser smile, went on— " Well, sir, your statues are beautiful, all the same ! "

Rowland's two other guests were ladies, and one of them, Miss Blanchard, belonged also to the artistic fraternity. She was an American, she was young, she was pretty, and she had made her way to Rome alone and unaided. She lived alone, or with no other duenna than a bushy-browed old serving-woman, though indeed she had a friendly neighbour in the person of a certain Madame Grandoni, who in various social emergencies lent her a protecting wing and had come with her to Rowland's dinner. Miss Blanchard had a small fortune, but she was not above selling her pictures. These represented generally a bunch of dew-sprinkled roses, with the dew-drops very highly finished, or else a wayside shrine and a peasant woman with her back turned kneeling before it. She did backs very well, but she was a little weak in faces. Flowers however were her speciality, and though her touch was a little old-fashioned and finical, she painted them with remarkable skill. Her pictures were chiefly bought by the English. Rowland had made her acquaintance early in the winter, and as she kept a saddle horse and rode a great deal he had asked permission to be her cavalier. In this way they had become almost intimate. Miss Blanchard's name was Augusta; she was slender, pale and elegant; she had a very pretty head and brilliant auburn hair, which she braided with classic simplicity. She talked in a sweet soft voice, used language at times a trifle superfine, and made literary allusions. These had often a patriotic strain, and Rowland had more than once been treated to quotations from Mrs. Sigourney in the cork-woods of Monte Mario, and from Mr. Willis among the ruins of Veii. Rowland was of a dozen different minds about her, and was half surprised at times to find himself treating it as a matter of serious moment that he should like her or not. He admired her, and indeed there was something admirable in her combination of beauty and talent, of isolation and self-support. He used sometimes to go into the little high-niched ordinary room which served her as a studio, and find her working at a panel six inches square, at an open casement, profiled against the deep blue Roman sky. She received him with a meek-eyed dignity that made her seem like a painted saint on a church-window, receiving the daylight in all her being. The breath of vulgar rumour passed her by with folded wings. And yet Rowland wondered why he did not like her better. If he failed, the reason was not far to seek. There was another woman whom he liked better, an image in his heart which gave itself little airs of exclusiveness.

On that evening to which allusion has been made, when

Rowland was left alone between the starlight and the waves with the sudden knowledge that Mary Garland was to become another man's wife, he had made after a while the simple resolution to forget her. And every day since, like a famous philosopher who wished to abbreviate his mourning for a faithful servant, he had said to himself in substance—" Remember to forget Mary Garland." Sometimes it seemed as if he were succeeding; then, suddenly, when he was least expecting it, he would find her name inaudibly on his lips, and seem to see her eyes meeting his eyes. All this made him uncomfortable, and seemed to portend a possible discord. Discord was not to his taste; he shrank from imperious passions, and the idea of finding himself jealous of an unsuspecting friend was simply disgusting. More than ever, then, the path of good manners was to forget Mary Garland, and he cultivated oblivion, as we may say, in the person of Miss Blanchard. Her fine temper, he said to himself, was a trifle cold and conscious, her purity prudish perhaps, her culture pedantic. But since he was obliged to give up hopes of Mary Garland, Providence owed him a compensation, and he had fits of angry sadness in which it seemed to him that to attest his right to sentimental satisfaction he should indulge in some defiantly incongruous passion. And what was the use after all of bothering about a possible which was only perhaps a dream? Even if Mary Garland had been free, what right had he to assume that he should have pleased her? The actual was good enough. Miss Blanchard had beautiful hair, and if she were a trifle old-maidish, there was nothing like matrimony for curing old-maidishness.

Madame Grandoni, who had formed with the companion of Rowland's rides an alliance which might have been called defensive on the part of the former and attractive on that of Miss Blanchard, was an excessively ugly old lady, highly esteemed in Roman society for her homely benevolence and her shrewd and humorous good sense. She had been the widow of a German archæologist who came to Rome in the early ages, as an attaché of the Prussian legation on the Capitoline. Her good sense had been wanting on but a single occasion, that of her second marriage. This occasion was certainly a momentous one, but these are by common consent not test cases. A

couple of years after her first husband's death she had
accepted the hand and the name of a Neapolitan music-
master, ten years younger than herself and with no fortune but his fiddle-bow. The marriage was most unhappy,
and the Maestro Grandoni was suspected of using the
fiddle-bow as an instrument of conjugal correction. He
had finally run off with a *prima donna assoluta*, who it
was to be hoped had given him a taste of the quality
implied in her title. He was believed to be living still,
but he had shrunk to a small black spot in Madame
Grandoni's life, and for ten years she had not mentioned
his name. She wore a light flaxen wig, which was never
very artfully adjusted; but this mattered little, as she
made no secret of it. She used to say, "I was not always
so ugly as this; as a young girl I had beautiful golden
hair, very much the colour of my wig." She had worn
from time immemorial an old blue satin dress and a white
crape shawl embroidered in colours; her appearance was
ridiculous, but she had an interminable Teutonic pedigree,
and her manners in every presence were easy and jovial,
as became a lady whose ancestor had been cup bearer to
Frederick Barbarossa. Thirty years' observation of Roman
society had sharpened her wits and given her an inexhaustible store of anecdotes; but she had beneath her
crumpled bodice a deep-welling fund of Teutonic sentiment, which she communicated only to the objects of her
particular favour. Rowland had a great regard for her,
and she repaid it by wishing him to get married. She
never saw him without whispering to him that Augusta
Blanchard was just the girl.

It seemed to Rowland a sort of foreshadowing of
matrimony to see Augusta Blanchard standing gracefully on his hearth-rug and blooming behind the central
bouquet at his circular dinner-table. The dinner was
very prosperous, and Roderick amply filled his position
as hero of the feast. He had always an air of joyous
intentness, but on this occasion he manifested a good deal
of harmless pleasure in his glory. He drank freely and
talked bravely; he leaned back in his chair with his hands
in his pockets, and flung open the gates of his eloquence.
Singleton sat gazing and listening open-mouthed, as if
Phœbus Apollo had been talking. Gloriani showed a

twinkle in his eye and an evident disposition to draw Roderick out. Rowland was rather regretful, for he knew that theory was not his friend's strong point and that it was never fair to take his measure from his language.

"As you have begun with Adam and Eve," said Gloriani, "I suppose you are going straight through the Bible." He was one of the persons who thought Roderick delightfully fresh.

"I may make a David," said Roderick, "but I shall not try any more of the Old Testament people. I don't like the Jews; I don't like pendulous noses. David, the boy David, is rather an exception; you can think of him and treat him as a young Greek. Standing forth there on the plain of battle between the contending armies, rushing forward to let fly his stone, he looks like a beautiful runner at the Olympic games. After that I shall skip to the New Testament. I mean to make a Christ."

"You will put nothing of the Olympic games into him, I hope," said Gloriani.

"Oh, I shall make him very different from the Christ of tradition; more—more—" and Roderick paused a moment to think. This was the first that Rowland had heard of his Christ.

"More rationalistic, I suppose," suggested Miss Blanchard.

"More idealistic!" cried Roderick. "The perfection of form, you know, to symbolise the perfection of spirit."

"For a companion-piece," said Miss Blanchard, "you ought to make a Judas."

"Never! I mean never to make anything ugly. The Greeks never made anything ugly, and I am a Hellenist; I am not a Hebraist! I have been thinking lately of making a Cain, but I should never dream of making him ugly. He should be a very handsome fellow, and he should lift up the murderous club with the beautiful movement of the fighters in the Greek friezes who are chopping at their enemies."

"There is no use trying to be a Greek," said Gloriani. "If Phidias were to come back he would recommend you to give it up. I am half Italian and half French, and, as a whole, a Yankee. What sort of a Greek should I make? I think the Judas is a capital idea for a statue.

Much obliged to you, madam, for the suggestion. What an insidious little scoundrel one might make of him, sitting there nursing his money-bag and his treachery! There may be a great deal of expression in a pendulous nose, my dear sir—especially if one has put it there!"

"Very likely," said Roderick. "But it is not the sort of expression I care for. I care only for perfect beauty. There it is, if you want to know it! That is as good a profession of faith as another. In future, so far as my things are not positively beautiful you may set them down as failures. For me, it's either that or nothing. It is against the taste of the day, I know; we have really lost the faculty to understand beauty in the large ideal way. We stand like a race with shrunken muscles, staring helplessly at the weights our forefathers easily lifted. But I don't hesitate to proclaim it—I mean to lift them again! I mean to go in for big things; that is my notion of my art. I mean to do things that will be simple and vast and infinite. You shall see if they won't be infinite! Excuse me if I brag a little; all those Italian fellows in the Renaissance used to brag. There was a sensation once common, I am sure, in the human breast—a kind of religious awe in the presence of a marble image newly created and expressing the human type in superhuman purity. When Phidias and Praxiteles had their statues of goddesses unveiled in the temples of the Ægean, don't you suppose there was a passionate beating of hearts, a thrill of mysterious terror? I mean to bring it back; I mean to thrill the world again! I mean to produce a Juno that will make you tremble, a Venus that will make you grow faint."

"So that when we come and see you," said Madame Grandoni, "we must be sure and bring our smelling-bottles. And pray have a few sofas conveniently placed."

"Phidias and Praxiteles," Miss Blanchard remarked, "had the advantage of believing in their goddesses. I insist on believing, for myself, that the pagan mythology is not a fiction, and that Venus, and Juno, and Apollo, and Mercury used to come down in a cloud into this very city of Rome where we sit talking nineteenth-century English."

"Nineteenth-century nonsense, my dear!" cried Madame Grandoni. "Mr. Hudson may be a new Phidias, but Venus and Juno—that's you and I—arrived to-day in a very dirty cab; and were cheated by the driver too."

"But, my dear fellow," objected Gloriani, "you don't mean to say you are going to make over in cold blood those poor old exploded Apollos and Hebes."

"It won't matter what you call them," said Roderick. "They shall be simply divine forms. They shall be Beauty; they shall be Wisdom; they shall be Power; they shall be Genius; they shall be Daring. That's all the Greek divinities were."

"That's rather abstract, you know," said Miss Blanchard.

"My dear fellow," cried Gloriani, "you are delightfully young!"

"I hope you will not grow any older," said Singleton, with a flush of sympathy across his large white forehead. "You can do it if you try."

"Then there are all the Forces, and Elements, and Mysteries of Nature," Roderick went on. "I mean to do the Morning; I mean to do the Night! I mean to do the Ocean and the Mountains; the Moon and the West Wind. I mean to make a magnificent statue of America!".

"America—the Mountains—the Moon!" said Gloriani. "You will find it rather hard, I'm afraid, to compress such subjects into classic forms."

"Oh, there's a way," cried Roderick, "and I shall think it out. My figures shall make no contortions, but they shall mean a tremendous deal."

"I am sure there are contortions enough in Michael Angelo," said Madame Grandoni; "perhaps you don't approve of him."

"Oh, Michael Angelo was not me!" said Roderick with sublimity. There was a great laugh; but after all Roderick had done some fine things.

Rowland had bidden one of the servants to bring him a small portfolio of prints, and had taken out a photograph of Roderick's little statue of the youth drinking. It pleased him to see his friend sitting there in radiant ardour, defending idealism against so knowing an apostle of corruption as Gloriani, and he wished to help the elder artist to be confuted. He silently handed him the photograph.

" Bless me ! " cried Gloriani, " did he do this ? "

" Ages ago," said Roderick.

Gloriani looked at the photograph a long time, with evident admiration.

" It's deucedly pretty," he said at last. " But, my dear young friend, you can't keep this up."

" I shall do better," said Roderick.

" You will do worse ! You will become weak. You will have to take to violence, to contortions, to romanticism in self-defence. This sort of thing is like a man trying to lift himself up by the seat of his trousers. He may stand on tiptoe, but he can't do more. Here you stand on tiptoe, very gracefully I admit ; but you can't fly ; there's no use trying."

" My ' America ' shall answer you ! " said Roderick, shaking towards him a tall glass of champagne and drinking it down.

Singleton had taken the photograph, and was poring over it with a little murmur of delight.

" Was this done in America ? " he asked.

" In a square white wooden house at Northampton, Massachusetts," Roderick answered.

" Dear old white wooden houses ! " said Miss Blanchard.

" If you could do as well as this there," said Singleton, blushing and smiling, " one might say that really you had only to lose by coming to Rome."

" Our host is to blame for that," said Roderick. " But I am willing to risk the loss."

The photograph had been passed to Madame Grandoni. " It reminds me," she said, " of the things a young man used to do whom I knew years ago, when I first came to Rome. He was a German, a pupil of Overbeck, and a votary of spiritual art. He used to wear a black velvet tunic and a very low shirt-collar ; he had a neck like a sickly crane, and he let his hair grow down to his shoulders. His name was Herr Schaafgans. He never painted anything so profane as a man taking a drink, for none of his people had anything so vulgar as an appetite. They were all angles and edges—they looked like diagrams of human nature. They were figures if you please—but geometrical figures. He would not have agreed with Gloriani any more than you. He used to come and see me very often, and in those days I thought his tunic and his long neck infallible symptoms of genius. His talk was all of gilded aureoles and beatific visions; he lived on weak wine and biscuits and wore a lock of Saint Some-body's hair in a little bag round his neck. If he was not a Beato Angelico it was not his own fault. I hope with all my heart that Mr. Hudson will do the fine things he talks about, but he must bear in mind the history of dear Mr. Schaafgans as a warning against high-flown preten-sions. One fine day this poor young man fell in love with a Roman model, though she had never sat to him I believe, for she was a buxom, bold-faced, high-coloured creature, and he painted none but pale and sickly women. He offered to marry her, and she looked at him from head to foot, gave a shrug and consented. But he was ashamed to set up his ménage in Rome. They went to Naples, and there, a couple of years afterwards, I saw him. The poor fellow was ruined. His wife used to beat him and he had taken to drinking. He wore a ragged black coat and he had a blotchy red face. Madame had turned washer-woman and used to make him go and fetch the dirty linen. His talent had gone heaven knows where! He was getting his living by painting views of Vesuvius in eruption on the little boxes they sell at Sorrento."

"Moral: don't fall in love with a buxom Roman model," said Roderick. "I am much obliged to you for your story, but I don't mean to fall in love with any one."

Gloriani had possessed himself of the photograph again, and was looking at it curiously. "It's a happy bit of youth," he said. "But you can't keep it up—you can't keep it up!"

The two sculptors pursued their discussion after dinner in the drawing-room. Rowland left them to have it out in a corner, where Roderick's Eve stood over them in the shaded lamplight, in vague white beauty, like the guardian angel of the young idealist. Singleton was listening to Madame Grandoni, and Rowland took his place on the sofa near Miss Blanchard. They had a good deal of familiar desultory talk; every now and then Madame Grandoni looked round at them. Miss Blanchard at last asked Rowland certain questions about Roderick—who he was, where he came from, whether it was true, as she had

heard, that Rowland had discovered him and brought him
out at his own expense. Rowland answered her questions;
to the last he gave a vague affirmative. Finally, after a
pause, looking at him, " You are very generous," Miss
Blanchard said. The declaration was made with a certain
richness of tone, but it brought to Rowland's sense neither
delight nor confusion. He had heard the words before;
he suddenly remembered the grave sincerity with which
Mary Garland had uttered them as he strolled with her in
the woods on the day of Roderick's picnic. They had
pleased him then; now he asked Miss Blanchard whether
she would have some tea.

When the two ladies withdrew he went with them to
their hackney-coach. Coming back to the drawing-room,
he paused outside the open door; he was struck by the
group formed by the three men. They were standing
before Roderick's statue of Eve, and the young sculptor
had lifted up the lamp and was showing different parts
of it to his companions. He was talking ardently—the
lamplight covered his head and face. Rowland stood
looking on, for the group struck him with its picturesque
symbolism. Roderick, bearing the lamp and glowing in
its radiant circle, seemed the beautiful image of a genius
which combined sincerity with power. Gloriani, with his
head on one side, pulling his long moustache and looking
keenly from half-closed eyes at the lighted marble, represented art with a worldly motive, skill unleavened by
faith, the mere base maximum of cleverness. Poor little
Singleton, on the other side, with his hands behind him,
his head thrown back and his eyes following devoutly
the course of Roderick's explanations, might pass for an
embodiment of aspiring candour afflicted with feebleness
of wing. In all this, Roderick's was certainly the *beau
rôle*.

Gloriani turned to Rowland as he came up, and pointed
back with his thumb to the statue, with a smile half
sardonic, half good-natured. " A pretty thing—a devilish
pretty thing," he said. " It's as fresh as the foam
in the milk-pail. He can do it once, he can do it
twice, he can do it at a stretch half a dozen times.
But—*but*—"

He was returning to his former refrain, but Rowland

intercepted him. "Oh, he will keep it up," he said, smiling, "I will answer for him!"

Gloriani was not encouraging, but Roderick had listened smiling. He was floating on the tide of his deep self-confidence. Now, suddenly, however, he turned with a flash of irritation in his eye, and demanded in a ringing voice, "In a word then you prophesy that I shall fail?"

Gloriani answered imperturbably, patting him kindly on the shoulder. "My dear fellow, passion burns out, inspiration runs to seed. Some fine day every artist finds himself sitting face to face with his lump of clay, with his empty canvas, with his sheet of blank paper, waiting in vain for the revelation to be made, for the Muse to descend. He must learn to do without the Muse! When the fickle jade forgets the way to your studio, don't waste any time in tearing your hair and meditating on suicide. Come round and see me and I will show you how to console yourself."

"If I break down," said Roderick passionately, "I shall stay down. If the Muse deserts me, she shall at least have her infidelity on her conscience!"

"You have no business," Rowland said to Gloriani, "to talk lightly of the Muse in this company. Mr. Singleton too has received pledges from her which place her constancy beyond suspicion." And he pointed out on the wall, near by, two small landscapes by the modest water-colourist.

The sculptor examined them with deference, and Singleton himself began to laugh nervously; he was trembling with hope that the great Gloriani would be pleased. "Yes, these are fresh too," Gloriani said; "extraordinarily fresh! How old are you?"

"Twenty-six, sir," said Singleton.

"For twenty-six they are famously fresh. They must have taken you a long time; you work slowly."

"Yes, unfortunately I work very slowly. One of them took me six weeks, the other two months."

"Upon my word! The Muse pays you long visits." And Gloriani turned and looked from head to foot at so unlikely an object of her favours. Singleton smiled and began to wipe his forehead very hard. "Oh, you," said the sculptor—"you'll keep it up!"

A week after his dinner party, Rowland went into

Roderick's studio and found him sitting before an unfinished piece of work, with a hanging head and a heavy
eye. He might have fancied that the fatal hour foretold
by Gloriani had struck. Roderick rose with a sombre
yawn and flung down his tools. "It's no use," he said,
"I give it up!"

"What is it?"

"I have struck a shallow! I have been sailing bravely,
but for the last day or two my keel has been grinding the
bottom."

"A difficult place?" Rowland asked, with a sympathetic
inflection, looking vaguely at the roughly modelled figure.

"Oh, it's not the poor old clay!" Roderick answered.
"The difficult place is *here!*" And he struck a blow on
his heart. "I don't know what's the matter with me.
Nothing comes; all of a sudden I hate things. My old
things look ugly; everything looks stupid."

Rowland was perplexed. He was in the situation of a man
who has been riding a blood-horse at a steady elastic galop,
and of a sudden feels him stumble and balk. As yet he
reflected, he had seen nothing but the sunshine of genius;
he had forgotten that it has its storms. Of course it has!
And he felt a flood of comradeship rise in his heart which
would float them both safely through the worst weather.
"Why, you are tired!" he said. "Of course you are
tired. You have a right to be."

"Do you think I have a right to be?" Roderick asked,
looking at him.

"Unquestionably, after all you have done."

"Well, then, right or wrong, I am tired. I certainly
have done a fair winter's work. I want a change."

Rowland declared that it was certainly high time they
should be leaving Rome. They would go north and travel.
They would go to Switzerland, to Germany, to Holland,
to England. Roderick assented, his eye brightened, and
Rowland talked of a dozen things they might do. Roderick
walked up and down; he seemed to have something to say
which he hesitated to bring out. He hesitated so rarely
that Rowland wondered, and at last asked him what was
on his mind. Roderick stopped before him frowning a
little.

"I have such unbounded faith in your good-will," he

said, "that I believe nothing I can say would offend you."

"'Try it!'" said Rowland.

"Well, then, I think my journey will do me more good if I take it alone. I needn't say I prefer your society to that of any man living. For the last six months it has been a fund of comfort. But I have a perpetual feeling that you are expecting something of me, that you are measuring my doings by a terrifically high standard. You are watching me; I don't want to be watched! I want to go my own way; to work when I choose and to loaf when I choose. It is not that I don't know what I owe you: it is not that we are not friends. It is simply that I want a taste of perfect freedom. Therefore I say let us separate."

Rowland shook him by the hand. "Willingly—do as you desire! I shall miss you, and I venture to believe you will pass some lonely hours. But I have only one request to make—that if you get into trouble of any kind whatever, you will immediately let me know."

They began their journey however together, crossing the Alps side by side, muffled in one rug, on the top of the St. Gothard coach. Rowland was going to England to pay some promised visits; his companion had no plan save to ramble through Switzerland and Germany as fancy should guide him. He had money that would outlast the summer; when it was spent he would come back to Rome and make another statue. At a little mountain-village by the way Roderick declared that he would stop; he would scramble about a little in the high places and doze in the shade of the pine-forests. The coach was changing horses; the two young men walked along the village street, picking their way between dung-hills, breathing the light cool air, and listening to the plash of the fountain and the tinkle of cattle-bells. The coach overtook them, and then Rowland, as he prepared to mount, felt an almost overmastering reluctance.

"Say the word," he exclaimed, "and I will stop too!"

Roderick frowned. "Ah, you don't trust me; you don't think I am able to take care of myself! That proves that I was right in feeling as if I were watched!"

"Watched, my dear fellow?" said Rowland, "I hope

you may never have anything worse to complain of than being watched in the spirit in which I watch you. But I will spare you even that. Good-bye!" Standing in his place as the coach rolled away, he looked back at his friend lingering by the roadside. A great snow-mountain, behind Roderick, was beginning to turn pink in the sunset. The slim and straight young figure waved its hat with a sort of mocking solemnity. Rowland settled himself in his place, reflecting after all that this was a salubrious beginning of independence. Roderick was among forests and glaciers, leaning on the pure bosom of nature. And then—and then—was it not in itself a guarantee against folly to be engaged to Mary Garland?

VII.

ROWLAND passed the summer in England, staying with several old friends and two or three new ones. On his arrival he felt it on his conscience to write to Mrs. Hudson and inform her that her son had relieved him of his tutelage. He felt that she thought of him as an incorruptible Mentor, following Roderick like a shadow, and he wished to let her know the truth. But he made the truth very comfortable, and gave a detailed account of the young man's brilliant beginnings. He owed it to himself, he said, to remind her that he had not judged lightly, and that Roderick's present achievements were more profitable than his inglorious drudgery at Messrs. Striker & Spooner's. He was now taking a well-earned holiday and proposing to see a little of the world. He would work none the worse for this; every artist needed to knock about and look at things for himself. They had parted company for a couple of months, for Roderick was now a great man and beyond the need of going about with a keeper. But they were to meet again in Rome in the autumn, and then he should be able to send her more good news. Meanwhile he was very happy in what Roderick had already done—especially happy in the happiness it must have brought his mother. He ventured to ask to be kindly commended to Miss Garland.

His letter was promptly answered—to his surprise in the hand of the latter lady. The same post brought also an epistle from Cecilia. The document was voluminous, and we must content ourselves with giving an extract.

" Your letter was filled with an echo of that brilliant Roman world which made me almost ill with envy. For a week after I got it I thought Northampton really unpardonably tame. But I am drifting back again to my old deeps of resignation, and I rush to the window, when any one passes, with all my old gratitude for small favours. So Roderick Hudson is already a great man, and you turn out to be a great prophet ? My compliments to both of you ; I never saw a trick so prettily played ! And he takes it all very quietly, and doesn't lose his balance nor let it turn his head ? You judged him then in a day better than I had done in six months, for I really did not expect that he would behave so properly. I believed he would do fine things, but I was sure he would intersperse them with a good many follies and that his beautiful statues would spring up out of the midst of a dense plantation of wild oats. But from what you tell me, Mr. Striker may now go hang himself. . . . There is one thing, however, to say as a friend, in the way of warning. That candid soul can keep a secret, and he may have private designs on your peace of mind. What do you think of his being engaged to Mary Garland ? The two ladies had given no hint of it all winter, but a fortnight ago, when those big photographs of his statues arrived, they first pinned them up on the wall, and then trotted out into the town and made a dozen calls, announcing the news. Mrs. Hudson did, at least ; Miss Mary, I suppose, sat at home writing letters. To me, I confess, the thing was a brutal surprise. I had not a suspicion that all the while he was coming so regularly to make himself agreeable on my verandah, he was quietly preferring his cousin to any one else. Not, indeed, that he was ever at particular pains to make himself agreeable ! I suppose he has picked up a few graces in Rome. But he must not pick up too many ; if he is too polite when he comes back, Miss G. will count him as one

of the lost. She will be a very good wife for a man of
genius, and such a one as they are often shrewd enough
to take. She will darn his stockings and keep his accounts,
and sit at home and trim the lamp and keep up the fire,
while he studies the Beautiful in pretty neighbours at
dinner-parties. The two ladies are evidently very happy,
and, to do them justice, very humbly grateful to you.
Mrs. Hudson never speaks of you without tears in her
eyes, and I am sure she regards you as our leading philan-
thropist. Verily, it's a good thing for a woman to be in
love ; Mary Garland has grown almost pretty. 1 met her
the other night at a tea-party ; she had a white rose in
her hair and sang a sentimental ballad in a fine contralto
voice."

Mary Garland's letter was so much shorter that we may
give it entire :—

" My dear Sir,—Mrs. Hudson, as I suppose you know,
has been for some time unable to use her eyes. She
requests me therefore to answer your beautiful letter of
the 22nd of June. She thanks you extremely for writing,
and wishes me to say that she considers herself under great
obligations to you. Your account of her son's progress
and the high esteem in which he is held has made her
very happy, and she earnestly prays that all may go on
well. He sent us a short time ago several large photographs of his two statues, taken from different points of
view. We know little about such things, but they seem
to us wonderfully beautiful. We sent them to Boston to
be handsomely framed, and the man, on returning them,
wrote us that he had exhibited them for a week in his
gallery and that they had attracted great attention. The
frames are magnificent, and the pictures now hang in a row
on the parlour wall. Our only quarrel with them is that
they make the old papering and the engravings look
dreadfully shabby. Mr. Striker stood and looked at them
the other day full five minutes, and said at last that if
Roderick's head had been running on such things it was no
wonder he could not learn to draw up a deed. We lead here
so quiet and monotonous a life that I am afraid I can tell
you nothing that will interest you. Mrs. Hudson requests
me to say that the little that might happen to us—more

or less—is of small importance, as we live in our thoughts, which are fixed on her dear son. She thanks Heaven he has so good a friend. Mrs. Hudson says that this is too short a letter, but I can say nothing more.

"Yours most respectfully,
"MARY GARLAND."

It is a question whether the reader will know why, but this letter gave Rowland extraordinary pleasure. He liked its shortness and meagreness, and there seemed to him an exquisite modesty in its saying nothing from the young girl herself. He delighted in the formal address and conclusion; they pleased him as he had been pleased by an angular gesture in some expressive girlish figure in an early painting. The letter renewed that impression of fine feeling combined with an almost rigid simplicity, which Roderick's betrothed had personally given him. And its homely stiffness seemed a vivid reflection of a life concentrated, as the young girl had borrowed warrant from her companion to say, in a single devoted idea. The monotonous days of the two women seemed to Rowland's fancy to follow each other like the tick-tick of a great timepiece, marking off the hours which separated them from the supreme felicity of clasping the far-away son and lover to lips sealed with the intensity of joy.

He was left to vain conjectures however as to Roderick's own state of mind. He knew he was no letter writer, and that in the young sculptor's own phrase he would at any time rather build a monument than write a note. But when a month had passed without news of him, he began to be half anxious and half angry, and wrote him three lines, in the care of a Continental banker, begging him at least to give some sign of life. A week afterwards came an answer —brief, and dated Baden-Baden. "I know I have been a great brute," Roderick wrote, "not to have sent you a word before; but really I don't know what has got into me. I have lately learned terribly well how to do nothing. I am afraid to think how long it is since I wrote to my mother or to Mary. Heaven help them—poor patient trustful creatures! I don't know how to tell you what I am doing or not doing. It seems all amusing enough while it lasts, but it would make a poor show in a narrative

intended for your formidable eyes. I found Baxter in
Switzerland, or rather he found me, and he grabbed me
by the arm and brought me here. I was walking twenty
miles a day in the Alps, drinking milk in lonely chalets,
sleeping as you sleep, and thinking it was all very good
fun; but Baxter told me it would never do, that the Alps
were 'damned rot,' that Baden-Baden was the place, and
that if I knew what was good for me I would come along
with him. It is a wonderful place certainly, though,
thank the Lord, Baxter departed last week, blaspheming
horribly at *trente et quarante*. But you know all about it,
and what one does—what one is liable to do. I have
succumbed, in a measure, to the liabilities, and I wish I
had some one here to give me a kicking. Not you—you
would kick me with your boots off; you are too devilish
generous. I have fits of horrible homesickness for my
studio, and I shall be devoutly grateful when the summer
is over and I can go back and potter about there. I feel
as if nothing but the chisel would satisfy me; as if I
could rush in a rage at a block of unshaped marble, like
Michael A. There are a lot of Roman people here,
English and American; I live in the midst of them, and
talk nonsense from morning till night. There is also
some one else; and to her I don't talk sense, nor, thank
Heaven, mean what I say. I confess I need a month's
work to recover my self-respect."

These lines brought Rowland a large perturbation; the
more that what they seemed to point to surprised him.
During the nine months of their companionship Roderick
had shown so little taste for disorderly doings that Rowland
had come to think of these things as a cancelled danger,
and it greatly perplexed him to learn that his friend had
apparently proved so pliant to opportunity. But Roderick's
allusions were ambiguous, and it was possible they might
simply mean that he was out of patience with a frivolous
way of life, and fretting wholesomely over his absent work.
It was a very good thing certainly that idleness should
prove on experiment to sit heavily on his conscience.
Nevertheless the letter needed to Rowland's mind a key:
the key arrived a week later. "In common charity,"
Roderick wrote, "lend me a hundred pounds! I have
gambled away my last franc—I have made a villanous

heap of debts. Send me the money first; lecture me afterwards!" Rowland sent the money by return of post; then he proceeded, not to lecture, but to think. He hung his head—he was acutely disappointed. He had no right to be, he assured himself; but so it was. Roderick was young, impulsive, unpractised in stoicism; it was a hundred to one that he was to pay the usual vulgar tribute to folly. But his friend had regarded it as securely gained to his own belief in virtue that he was not as other foolish youths are, and that he would have been capable of looking at folly in the face and passing on his way. Rowland for a while felt a sore sense of wrath. What right had a man who was engaged to that delightful girl in Northampton to behave as if his consciousness were a common blank, to be overlaid with coarse sensations? Yes, distinctly, he was disappointed. He had accompanied his missive with an urgent recommendation to leave Baden-Baden immediately, and an offer to meet Roderick at any point he would name. The answer came promptly; it ran as follows: "Send me another fifty pounds! I have been back to the tables. I will leave as soon as the money comes, and meet you at Geneva. There I will tell you everything."

There is an ancient terrace at Geneva, planted with trees and studded with benches, overlooked by stately houses and overlooking the distant Alps. A great many generations have made it a lounging-place, a great many friends and lovers strolled there, a great many confidential talks and momentous interviews gone forward. Here, one morning, sitting on one of the battered green benches, Roderick, as he had promised, told his friend everything. He had arrived late the night before; he looked tired, and yet flushed and excited. He made no professions of penitence, but he practised an unmitigated frankness, and his remorse might be taken for granted. He implied in every phrase that he had done with licentious experiments and that he was counting the hours till he should get back to work. We shall not rehearse his confession in detail; its main outline will be sufficient. He had fallen in with some very idle people, and had discovered the charms of emulation. What could he do? He never read books, and he had no studio; in one way or another he had to pass the time. He passed it in dangling about several very pretty women, and reflecting that it was always something gained for a sculptor to sit under a tree looking at his leisure into a charming face, and saying things that made it smile and play its muscles and part its lips and show its teeth. Attached to these ladies were certain gentlemen who walked about in clouds of fragrance, rose at mid-day, and supped at mid-night. Roderick had found himself in the mood for thinking them very amusing fellows. He was surprised at his own taste, but he let it take its course. It led him to the discovery that to live with ladies who expect you to present them with expensive bouquets, to ride with them in the Black Forest on well-looking horses, to arrange parties for the opera on nights when Patti sang and the prices were consequent, to propose light suppers at the Kursaal or drives by moonlight to the Castle, to be always arrayed and anointed, trinketted and gloved—that to move in such society, we say, though it might be a privilege, was a privilege with a penalty attached. But the tables made such things easy; half the Baden world lived by the tables. Roderick tried them and found them at first a wonderful help. The help however was only momentary, for he soon perceived that to seem to have money, and to have it in fact, exposed a good-looking young man to peculiar liabilities. At this point of his friend's narrative Rowland was reminded of Madame de Cruchecassée in Thackeray's novel, and though he had listened in tranquil silence to the rest of it, he found it hard not to say that all this had been under the circumstances a very bad business. Roderick admitted it with bitterness, and then told how much—measured simply financially—it had cost him. His luck had changed; the tables had ceased to back him, and he had found himself up to his knees in debt. Every penny had gone of the solid sum which had seemed a large equivalent of those shining statues in Rome. He had been an ass, but it was not irreparable; he could make another statue in a couple of months.

Rowland frowned. "For heaven's sake," he said, "don't play such dangerous games with your facility. If you have got facility, revere it, respect it, adore it, hoard it—don't speculate on it." And he wondered what his companion, up to his knees in debt, would have done if there had been no good-natured Rowland Mallet to lend a helping hand. But he did not express his curiosity audibly, and the contingency seemed not to have presented itself to Roderick's imagination. The young sculptor reverted to his late adventures again in the evening, and this time talked of them more objectively, as the phrase is ; more as if they had been the adventures of another person. He related half a dozen droll things that had happened to him, and, as if his responsibility had been disengaged by all this free discussion, he laughed extravagantly at the memory of them. Rowland sat perfectly grave, on principle. Then Roderick began to talk of half a dozen statues that he had in his head, and set forth his ideas with his usual vividness. Suddenly, as it was relevant, he declared that his Baden doings had not been altogether fruitless, for the lady who had reminded Rowland of Madame de Cruchecassée was tremendously statuesque. Rowland at last said that such experiments might pass if one felt one was really the wiser for them. " By the wiser," he added, " I mean the stronger in purpose, in will."

" Oh don't talk about will ! " Roderick answered, throwing back his head and looking at the stars. This conversation also took place in the open air, on the little island in the shooting Rhone, where Jean-Jacques has a monument. " The will, I believe, is the mystery of mysteries. Who can answer for his will ? who can say beforehand that it's strong ? There are all kinds of indefinable currents moving to and fro between one's will and one's inclinations. People talk as if the two things were essentially distinct ; on different sides of one's organism, like the heart and the liver. Mine I know are much nearer together. It all depends upon circumstances. I believe there is a certain group of circumstances possible for every man, in which his will is destined to snap like a dry twig."

" My dear boy," said Rowland, " don't talk about the will being ' destined.' The will is destiny itself. That's the way to look at it."

" Look at it, my dear Rowland," Roderick answered, " as you find most comfortable. One conviction I have gathered from my summer's experience," he went on— " it's as well to look it frankly in the face—is that I possess an almost unlimited susceptibility to the influence of a beautiful woman."

Rowland stared, then strolled away, softly whistling to himself. He was unwilling to admit even to himself that this speech had really the ominous meaning it seemed to have. In a few days the two young men made their way back to Italy, and lingered a while in Florence before going on to Rome. In Florence Roderick seemed to have won back his old innocence and his preference for the pleasures of study. Rowland began to think of the Baden episode as a bad dream, or at the worst as a mere sporadic escapade, without roots in his companion's character. They passed a fortnight looking at pictures and exploring for out of the way fragments of fresco and carving, and Roderick recovered all his earlier energy of appreciation and criticism. In Rome he went eagerly to work again, and finished in a month two or three small things he had left standing on his departure. He talked the most joyous nonsense about finding himself back in his old quarters. On the first Sunday afternoon following their return, on their going together to Saint Peter's, he delivered himself of a lyrical greeting to the great church and to the city in general, in a tone of voice so irrepressibly elevated that it rang through the nave in an almost scandalous fashion and arrested a procession of canons who were marching across to the choir. He began to model a new statue—a female figure of which he had said nothing to Rowland. It represented a woman leaning lazily back in her chair, with her head drooping as if she were listening, a vague smile on her lips and a pair of remarkably beautiful arms folded in her lap. With rather less softness of contour it would have resembled the noble statue of Agrippina in the Capitol. Rowland looked at it and was not sure he liked it. "Who is it? what does it mean?" he asked.

"Anything you please!" said Roderick, with a certain petulance. "I call it 'A Lady Listening.'"

Rowland then remembered that one of the Baden listeners had been "statuesque," and asked no more questions. This after all was a way of profiting by experience. A few days later he took his first ride of the season on the Campagna, and as on his homeward way he was passing across the long shadow of a ruined tower, he perceived a small figure

at a short distance, bent over a sketch-book. As he drew
near he recognised his friend Singleton. The honest little
painter's face was scorched to flame-colour by the light of
southern suns, and borrowed an even deeper crimson from
his gleeful greeting of his most appreciative patron. He
was making a careful and charming little sketch. On
Rowland's asking him how he had spent his summer he
gave an account of his wanderings which made our poor
friend sigh with a sense of more contrasts than one. He
had not been out of Italy, but he had been delving deep
into the picturesque heart of the lovely land and gathering
a wonderful store of subjects. He had rambled about
among the unvisited villages of the Apennines, pencil in
hand and knapsack on back, sleeping on straw and eating
black bread and beans, but feasting on local colour, rioting
on chiaroscuro, and laying up a treasure of reminiscences.
He took a devout satisfaction in his hard-earned knowledge
and his happy frugality. Rowland went the next day by
appointment to look at his sketches, and spent a whole
morning turning them over. Singleton talked more than
he had ever done before, explained them all, and told some
comical anecdote about the production of each.

"Dear me, how I have chattered!" he said, at last. "I
am afraid you would rather have looked at the things in
peace and quiet. I didn't know I could talk so much. But
somehow I feel very happy; I feel as if I had improved."

"That you have," said Rowland. "I doubt whether
an artist ever got more out of three months. You must
feel much more sure of yourself."

Singleton looked for a long time with great intentness
at a knot in the floor. "Yes," he said at last in a fluttered
tone, "I feel much more sure of myself. I have got more
facility!" And he lowered his voice as if he were com-
municating a secret which it took some courage to impart.
"I hardly like to say it, for fear I should after all be mistaken. But since it strikes you, perhaps it's true. It's a
great happiness; I would not exchange it for a great deal
of money."

"Yes, I suppose it's a great happiness," said Rowland.
"I shall really think of you as living here in a state of
scandalous bliss. I don't believe it's good for an artist to
be in such brutally high spirits."

Singleton stared for a moment, as if he thought Rowland was in earnest; then suddenly fathoming the kindly jest, he walked about the room agitating his head and laughing intensely to himself. "And Mr. Hudson?" he said, as Rowland was going; "I hope he is well and happy."

"He is very well," said Rowland. "He is back at work again."

"Ah, there's a man," cried Singleton, "who has taken his start once for all and doesn't need to stop and ask himself in fear and trembling every month or two whether he is going on. When he stops, it's to rest! And where did he spend his summer?"

"The greater part of it at Baden-Baden."

"Ah, that's in the Black Forest," cried Singleton, with profound simplicity. "They say you can make capital studies of trees there."

"No doubt," said Rowland, with a smile, laying an almost paternal hand on the little artist's stooping shoulder. "Unhappily, trees are not Roderick's line. Nevertheless he tells me that at Baden he made some studies. Come when you can, by the way," he added after a moment, "to his studio, and tell me what you think of something he has lately begun." Singleton declared that he would come delightedly, and Rowland left him at his work.

He met a number of his last winter's friends and found that Madame Grandoni, Miss Blanchard and Gloriani had again taken up the golden thread of Roman life. The ladies gave an excellent account of themselves. Madame Grandoni had been taking sea-baths at Rimini, and Miss Blanchard painting wild flowers in the Tyrol. Her complexion was somewhat browned, which was very becoming, and her flowers were uncommonly pretty. Gloriani had been in Paris and had come away in high good-humour, finding no one there in the artist-world cleverer than himself. He came in a few days to Roderick's studio, one afternoon when Rowland was present. He examined the new statue with great deference, said it was very promising, and abstained considerably from irritating prophecies. But Rowland fancied he observed certain signs of inward jubilation on the clever sculptor's part, and walked away with him to learn his private opinion.

"Certainly; I liked it as well as I said," Gloriani

declared, in answer to Rowland's anxious query; "or rather I liked it a great deal better. I didn't say how much, for fear of making your friend angry. But one can leave him alone now, for he's coming round. I told you he couldn't keep up the transcendental style, and he has already broken down. Don't you see it yourself, man?"

"I don't particularly like this new statue," said Rowland.

"That's because you are a purist. It's deuced clever, it's deuced knowing, it's deuced pretty, but it isn't the topping high art of three months ago. He has taken his turn sooner than I supposed. What has happened to him? Has he been disappointed in love? But that's none of my business. I congratulate him on having become a practical man."

Roderick, however, was less to be congratulated than Gloriani had taken it into his head to believe. He was discontented with his work, he applied himself to it by fits and starts, he declared that he didn't know what was coming over him; he was turning into a man of moods. "Is this of necessity what a fellow must come to,"—he asked of Rowland, with a sort of peremptory flash in his eye, which seemed to imply that his companion had undertaken to insure him against perplexities and was not fulfilling his contract—"this damnable uncertainty when one goes to bed at night· as to whether one is going to wake up in an ecstasy or in a tantrum? Have we only a season, over before we know it, in which we can call our faculties our own? Six months ago I could stand up to my work like a man, day after day, and never dream of asking myself how I felt. But now, some mornings, it's the very devil to get going. My statue looks so bad when I come into the studio that I have twenty minds to smash it on the spot, and I lose three or four hours in sitting there moping and getting used to it."

Rowland said that he supposed that this sort of thing was the lot of every artist, and that the only remedy was plenty of courage and faith. And he reminded him of Gloriani's having forewarned him against these sterile moods the year before.

"Gloriani's an ass!" said Roderick, almost fiercely. He

hired a horse and began to ride with Rowland on the
Campagna. This delightful amusement restored him in
a measure to cheerfulness, but it seemed to Rowland on
the whole not to stimulate his industry. Their rides were
always very long, and Roderick insisted on making them
longer by dismounting in picturesque spots and stretching himself in the sun among a heap of over-tangled
stones. He let the scorching Roman luminary beat down
upon him with a bravery which Rowland found it hard to
emulate. But in this situation Roderick talked so much
amusing nonsense that for the sake of his company Rowland consented to be uncomfortable, and often forgot that,
though in these diversions the days passed quickly, they
brought forth neither high art nor low. And yet it was
perhaps by their help after all that Roderick secured several
mornings of ardent work on his new figure and brought it
to rapid completion. One afternoon when it was finished
Rowland went to look at it and Roderick asked him for
his opinion.

"What do you think yourself?" Rowland demanded—
not from pusillanimity but from real uncertainty.

"I think it is curiously bad," Roderick answered. "It
was bad from the first; it has fundamental vices. I have
shuffled them out of sight in a sort of way, but I have not
corrected them. I can't—I can't—I can't!" he cried
passionately. "They stare me in the face—they are all
I see!"

Rowland offered several criticisms of detail and suggested
certain practicable changes. But Roderick differed with
him on each of these points; the thing had faults enough,
but they were not those faults. Rowland unruffled, concluded by saying that whatever its faults might be, he had
an idea people in general would like it.

"I wish to heaven some person in particular would buy
it, and take it off my hands and out of my sight!"
Roderick cried. "What am I to do now?" he went on.
"I haven't an idea. I think of subjects, but they remain
mere lifeless names. They are mere words—they are not
images. What am I to do?"

Rowland was a trifle annoyed. "Be a man," he was on
the point of saying, "and don't, for heaven's sake, talk in
that confoundedly querulous voice!" But before he had

uttered the words there rang through the studio a loud peremptory ring at the outer door.

Roderick broke into a laugh. "Talk of the devil and you see his horns! If that's not a customer it ought to be."

VIII.

THE door of the studio was promptly flung open, and a lady advanced to the threshold—an imposing voluminous person who quite filled up the doorway. Rowland immediately felt that he had seen her before, but he recognised her only when she moved forward and disclosed an attendant in the person of a little bright-eyed elderly gentleman with a bristling white moustache. Then he remembered that just a year before he and his companion had seen in the Ludovisi gardens a wonderfully beautiful girl strolling in the train of this conspicuous couple. He looked for her now, and in a moment she appeared, following her companions with the same maidenly majesty as before, and leading her great snow-white poodle, who was decorated as before with motley ribbons. The elder lady offered the two young men a sufficiently gracious salute ; the little old gentleman bowed and smiled with extreme alertness. The young girl, without casting a glance either at Roderick or at Rowland, looked about for a chair, and, on perceiving one, sank into it listlessly, pulled her poodle towards her and began to re-arrange his top-knot. Rowland saw that, even with her eyes dropped, her beauty was still dazzling.

"I trust we are at liberty to enter," said the elder lady with urbanity. "We were told that Mr. Hudson had no fixed day, and that we might come at any time. Let us not disturb you."

Roderick, as one of the newer lights of the Roman art-world, had not hitherto been subject to incursions from inquisitive tourists, and, having no regular reception day, was not versed in the usual arts of hospitality. He said

nothing, and Rowland, looking at him, saw that he was
gazing amazedly at the young girl, and was apparently
unconscious of everything else. "By Jove!" he cried
precipitately, "it's that goddess of the Villa Ludovisi!"
Rowland, in some confusion, did the honours as he could,
but the little old gentleman begged him with the most
obsequious of smiles to give himself no trouble. "I have
been in many a studio!" he said, with his finger in the
air, and a strong Italian accent.

"We are going about everywhere," said his companion.
"I am passionately fond of art!"

Rowland smiled sympathetically and let them turn to
Roderick's statue. He glanced again at the young sculptor,
to invite him to bestir himself, but Roderick was still
staring wide-eyed at the beautiful young mistress of the
poodle, who by this time had looked up and was gazing
straight at him. There was nothing bold in her look; it
expressed a kind of languid imperturbable indifference.
Her beauty was extraordinary; it grew and grew as the
young man observed her. In such a face the maidenly
custom of averted eyes and ready blushes would have
seemed an anomaly; nature had produced it for man's
delight and meant that it should surrender itself freely
and coldly to admiration. It was not immediately apparent however that the young lady found an answering
entertainment in the physiognomy of her host; she turned
her head after a moment and looked idly round the
room, and at last let her eyes rest on the statue of the
woman seated. It being left to Rowland to stimulate
conversation, he began by complimenting her on the
beauty of her dog.

"Yes, he is very handsome," she murmured. "He is
a Florentine. The dogs in Florence are handsomer than
the people," and on Rowland's caressing him—"His name
is Stenterello," she added. "Stenterello, give your hand to
the gentleman." This order was given in Italian. "Say
buon giorno a Lei."

Stenterello thrust out his paw and gave four short shrill
barks; upon which the elder lady turned round and raised
her forefinger.

"My dear, my dear, remember where you are! Excuse
my foolish child," she added, turning to Roderick with

an agreeable smile. "She can think of nothing but her poodle."

"I am teaching him to talk for me," the young girl went on, without heeding her mother; "to say little things in society. It will save me a great deal of trouble. Stenterello, love, give a pretty smile and say *tanti complimenti!*" The poodle wagged his white pate—it looked like one of those little pads in swan's-down, for applying powder to the face—and repeated the barking process.

"He is a wonderful beast," said Rowland.

"He is not a beast," said the young girl. "A beast is something black and dirty—something you can't touch."

"He is a very valuable dog," the elder lady explained. "He was presented to my daughter by a Florentine nobleman."

"It is not for that I care about him. It is for himself. He is better than the Duke!"

"My precious love!" exclaimed the mother in deprecating accents, but with a significant glance at Rowland which seemed to bespeak his attention to the glory of possessing a daughter who could deal in that light fashion with the aristocracy.

Rowland remembered that when their unknown visitors had passed before them, a year previous, in the Villa Ludovisi, Roderick and he had exchanged conjectures as to their nationality and social quality. Roderick had declared that they were old-world people; but Rowland now needed no telling to feel that he might claim the elder lady as a fellow-countrywoman. She was a person of what is called a great deal of presence, with the faded traces, artfully revived here and there, of once brilliant beauty. Her daughter had come lawfully by her loveliness, but Rowland mentally made the distinction that the mother was silly, and the daughter was not. The mother had a fatuous countenance—a countenance, Rowland suspected, capable of expressing an inordinate degree of fatuity. The young girl, in spite of her childish satisfaction in her poodle, was not a person of a weak understanding. Rowland received an impression that for reasons of her own she was playing a part. What was the part and what were her reasons? She was interesting; Rowland wondered what were her domestic secrets. If her mother were a

daughter of the great Republic it was to be supposed that
the young girl was a flower of the American soil; but her
beauty had a large firmness that is uncommon in the somewhat relaxed robustness of our western maidenhood. She
spoke with a vague foreign accent, as if she had spent her
life in strange countries. The little Italian apparently
divined Rowland's mute imaginings, for he presently
stepped forward, with a bow like a master of ceremonies.
" I have not done my duty," he said " in not announcing
these ladies. Mrs. Light, Miss Light ! "

Rowland was not materially the wiser for this information,
but Roderick was aroused by it to the exercise of some
slight civility. He altered the light, pulled forward two
or three figures and made an apology for not having more
to show. "I don't pretend to have anything of an exhibition—I am only a novice."

" Indeed ?—a novice ! For a novice this is very well,"
Mrs. Light declared. " Cavaliere, we have seen nothing
better than this."

The Cavaliere smiled rapturously. " It is stupendous ! "
he murmured. " And we have been to all the studios."

" Not to all—Heaven forbid ! " cried Mrs. Light. " But
to a number that I have had pointed out by artistic friends.
I delight in studios—I should have been so happy myself
to be a little quiet artist ! And if you are a novice, Mr.
Hudson," she went on, " you have already great admirers.
Half a dozen people have told us that yours were quite
among the things to see." This gracious speech went
unanswered; Roderick had already wandered across to
the other side of the studio and was revolving about
Miss Light. " Ah, he's gone to look at my beautiful
daughter; he is not the first that has had his head
turned," Mrs. Light resumed, lowering her voice to a
confidential undertone; a favour which, considering the
shortness of their acquaintance, Rowland was bound to
appreciate. " The artists are all crazy about her. When
she goes into a studio she is fatal to the pictures. And
when she goes into the ball-room what do the other women
say ? Eh, Cavaliere ? "

" She is very beautiful," Rowland said, simply.

Mrs. Light, who through her long gold-cased glasses was
looking a little at everything and at nothing as if she saw

it, interrupted her random murmurs and exclamations and surveyed Rowland from head to foot. She looked at him all over; apparently he had not been mentioned to her as a feature of Roderick's establishment. It was the gaze, Rowland felt, which the vigilant and ambitious mother of a beautiful daughter has always at her command for well-appointed young men. Her inspection in this case seemed satisfactory. "Are you also an artist?" she inquired with an almost affectionate inflection. It was clear that what she meant was something of this kind: "Be so good as to assure me without delay that you are really the amiable young man of fortune that you appear."

But Rowland answered simply the formal question—not the latent one. "Dear me, no; I am only a friend of Mr. Hudson."

Mrs. Light, with a sigh, returned to the statues, and after mistaking the Adam for a gladiator and the Eve for a gipsy, declared that she could not judge of such things unless she saw them in the marble. Rowland hesitated a moment and then, speaking in the interest of Roderick's renown, said that he was the happy possessor of several of his friend's works and that she was welcome to come and see them at his rooms. She bade the Cavaliere make a note of his address. "Ah, you are a patron of the arts," she said. "That's what I should like to be if I had a little money. I revel in beauty in every form. But all these people ask such monstrous prices. One must be a millionaire to think of such things, eh? Twenty years ago my husband had my portrait painted, here in Rome, by Papucci, who was the great man in those days. I was in a ball-dress, with all my jewels, and my shoulders and arms—which were not a *petite affaire*. The man got six hundred francs and thought he was very well treated. Those were the days when a family could live like princes in Italy for five thousand scudi a year. The Cavaliere once upon a time was a great dandy—don't blush, Cavaliere; any one can see that, just as any one can see what I was! Get him to tell you what he made a figure upon. The railroads have brought in the vulgarians. That's what I call it now—the invasion of the vulgarians! What are poor *we* to do?"

Rowland had begun to murmur some remedial proposition

when he was interrupted by the voice of Miss Light calling
across the room, " Mamma ! "

" My own love ? "

" This gentleman wishes to model my bust. Please
speak to him."

The Cavaliere gave a little chuckle. " Already ? " he
cried.

Rowland looked round, equally surprised at the promp-
titude of the proposal. Roderick stood planted before the
young girl with his arms folded, looking at her as he would
have done at the Medicean Venus. He never paid compliments, and Rowland, though he had not heard him speak,
could imagine the startling distinctness with which he
made his request.

" He saw me a year ago," the young girl went on, " and
he has been thinking of me ever since." Her tone in
speaking was peculiar ; it had a kind of studied inexpressiveness which was yet not the vulgar device of a drawl.

" I *must* make your daughter's bust—that's all madam ! "
cried Roderick with warmth.

" I would rather you should make the poodle's," said
the young girl. " Is it very tiresome ? I have spent half
my life sitting for my photograph, in every conceivable
attitude and with every conceivable coiffure. I think I
have posed enough."

" My dear child," said Mrs. Light, " it may be one's
duty to pose ! But as to my daughter's sitting to you,
sir—to a young artist whom we don't know—it is a matter
that one must look at a little. It is not a favour that's
to be had for the mere asking."

" If I don't make her from life," said Roderick with
energy, " I will make her from memory, and if the thing's
to be done you had better have it done as well as
possible."

" Mamma hesitates," said Miss Light, " because she
doesn't know whether you mean she shall pay you for the
bust. I can assure you that she will not pay you a
sou."

" My daughter, you forget yourself," said Mrs. Light,
with an attempt at a high tone. " Of course," she added
in a moment, with a change of note, " the bust would be
my own property."

" Of course ! " cried Roderick, impatiently.

" Dearest mother," interposed the young girl, " how can you carry a marble bust about the world with you ? Is it not enough to drag the poor original ? "

" My dear, you are nonsensical ! " cried Mrs. Light, almost angrily.

" You can always sell it," said the young girl, with the same artful artlessness.

Mrs. Light turned to Rowland, who pitied her, flushed and irritated. " She is very wicked to-day ! "

The Cavaliere grinned in silence and walked away on tiptoe, with his hat to his lips, as if to leave the field clear for action. Rowland on the contrary wished to mediate. " You had better not refuse," he said to Miss Light, " until you have seen Mr. Hudson's things in the marble. Your mother is to come and look at some that I possess."

" Thank you ; I have no doubt you will see us. I dare say Mr. Hudson is very clever ; but I don't care for modern sculpture. I can't look at it ! "

" You shall care for my bust, I promise you ! " cried Roderick, with a laugh.

" To satisfy Miss Light," said the Cavaliere, " one of the old Greeks ought to come to life."

" It would be worth his while," said Roderick, paying, to Rowland's knowledge, his first compliment.

" I might sit to Phidias, if he would promise to be very amusing and make me laugh. What do you say, Stenterello ? would *you* sit to Phidias ? "

" We must talk of this some other time," said Mrs. Light. " We are in Rome for the winter. Many thanks. Cavaliere, call the carriage." The Cavaliere led the way out, backing like a silver-stick, and Miss Light following her mother, nodded without looking at them, to each of the young men.

" Immortal powers, what a head ! " cried Roderick, when they were gone. " There's my fortune ! "

" She is certainly very beautiful," said Rowland. " But I am sorry you have undertaken her bust."

" And why, pray ? "

" I suspect it will bring trouble with it."

" What kind of trouble ? "

" I hardly know. They are queer people. The mamma,

I suspect, is a bit of an advenuress. Heaven knows what
the daughter is."

"She's a goddess!" cried Roderick.

"Just so. She is all the more dangerous."

"Dangerous? What will she do to me? She doesn't
bite, I imagine."

"It remains to be seen. There are two kinds of women
—you ought to know by this time—the safe and the
unsafe. Miss Light, if I am not mistaken, is one of the
unsafe. A word to the wise!"

"Much obliged!" said Roderick, and he began to whistle
a triumphant air, in honour apparently of the advent of
his beautiful model.

In calling this young lady and her mamma queer people
Rowland but roughly expressed his sentiment. They were
so marked a variation from the monotonous troop of his
compatriots that he felt much curiosity as to the sources
of the change, especially since he doubted greatly whether
on the whole it elevated the type. For a week he saw the
two ladies driving daily in a well-appointed landau, with
the Cavaliere and the poodle in the front seat. From Mrs.
Light he received a gracious salute, tempered by her native
majesty; but the young girl, looking straight before her,
seemed profoundly indifferent to observers. Her extraordinary beauty however had already made observers
numerous, and given the habitués of the Pincian plenty
to talk about. The echoes of their commentary reached
Rowland's ears; but he had little taste for unsifted rumour,
and he desired a veracious informant. He found one in
the person of Madame Grandoni, for whom Mrs. Light and
her beautiful daughter were a pair of old friends.

"I have known the mamma for twenty years," said this
judicious critic, "and if you ask any of the people who
have been living here as long as I, you will find they
remember her well. I have held the beautiful Christina
on my knee when she was a little wizened baby with a
very red face and no promise of beauty but those magnificent eyes. Ten years ago Mrs. Light disappeared, and
has not since been seen in Rome, except for a few days
last winter, when she passed through on her way to Naples.
Then it was you met the trio in the Ludovisi gardens.
When I first knew her she was the unmarried but very

marriageable daughter of an old American painter of very
bad landscapes, which people used to buy from charity and
use for fire-boards. His name was Savage; it used to
make every one laugh, he was such a mild, melancholy,
pitiful old gentleman. He had married a horrible wife, an
Englishwoman who had been on the stage. It was said
she used to beat poor Savage with his mahl-stick, and,
when the domestic finances were low, to lock him up in
his studio and tell him he shouldn't come out until he
had painted half a dozen of his daubs. She had a good
deal of showy beauty. She would go forth with the
key in her pocket, and, her beauty helping, she would
make certain people take the pictures. It helped her
at last to make an English lord run away with her.
At the time I speak of she had quite disappeared. Mrs.
Light was then a very handsome girl, though by no means
so handsome as her daughter has now become. Mr. Light
was an American consul, newly appointed at one of the
Adriatic ports. He was a mild, fair-whiskered young man,
with some little property, and my impression is that he
had got into bad company at home, and that his family
procured him his place to keep him out of harm's way.
He came up to Rome on a holiday, fell in love with Miss
Savage and married her on the spot. He had not been
married three years when he was drowned in the Adriatic,
no one ever knew how. The young widow came back to
Rome, to her father, and here shortly afterwards, in the
shadow of Saint Peter's, her little girl was born. It might
have been supposed that Mrs. Light would marry again,
and I know she had opportunities. But she overreached
herself. She would take nothing less than a title and a
fortune, and they were not forthcoming. She was admired
and very fond of admiration; very vain, very worldly, very
silly. She remained a pretty widow with a surprising
variety of bonnets and a dozen men always in her train.
Giacosa dates from this period. He calls himself a Roman,
but I have an impression he came up from Ancona with
her. He was *l'ami de la maison*. He used to hold her
bouquets, clean her gloves and satin shoes, run her errands,
get her opera-boxes, fight her battles with the shopkeepers.
For this he needed courage, for she was smothered in debt.
She at last left Rome to escape her creditors. Many of

them must remember her still, but she seems now to have
money to satisfy them. She left her poor old father here
alone—helpless, infirm, and unable to work. A subscription
was shortly afterwards taken up among the foreigners, and
he was sent back to America, where, as I finally heard, he
died in some sort of asylum. From time to time, for several
years, I heard vaguely of Mrs. Light as a wandering beauty
at French and German watering-places. Once came a rumour
that she was going to make a grand marriage in England :
then we heard that the gentleman had thought better of
it and left her to keep afloat as she could. She was a
terribly scatter-brained creature. She pretends to be a
great lady, but I consider that old Filomena, my washer-
woman, is in essentials a greater one. But certainly after
all she has been fortunate. She embarked at last on a
lawsuit about some property, with her husband's family,
and went to America to attend to it. She came back
triumphant, with a long purse. She reappeared in Italy
and established herself for a while in Venice. Then she
came to Florence, where she spent a couple of years and
where I saw her. Last year she passed down to Naples,
which I should have said was just the place for her, and
this winter she had laid siege to Rome. She seems very
prosperous. She has taken a floor in the Palazzo F——,
she keeps her carriage, and Christina and she, between
them, must have a pretty milliner's bill. Giacosa has
turned up again, looking as if he had been kept in ice at
Ancona for her return."

"What sort of education," Rowland asked, "do you
imagine the mother's adventures to have been for the
daughter ?"

"A strange school ! But Mrs. Light told me in Florence
that she had given her child the education of a princess.
In other words I suppose she speaks three or four languages
and has read several hundred French novels. Christina I
suspect is very clever. When I saw her I was amazed at
her beauty, and certainly if there is any truth in faces she
ought to have the soul of an angel. Perhaps she has. I don't
judge her ; she's an extraordinary young person. She has
been told twenty times a day by her mother, since she was
five years old, that she is a beauty of beauties, that her
face is her fortune, and that if she plays her cards she

may marry a duke. If she has not been fatally corrupted
she is a very superior girl. My own impression is that
she is a mixture of good and bad, of ambition and indifference. Mrs. Light having failed to make her own
fortune in matrimony has transferred her hopes to her
daughter and nursed them till they have become a mono-
mania. She has a hobby, which she rides in secret; but
some day she will let you see it. I am sure that if you go
in some evening unannounced, you will find her scanning
the tea-leaves in her cup or telling her daughter's fortune
with a greasy pack of cards, kept sacredly for the purpose.
She promises her a prince—a reigning prince. But if
Mrs. Light is a fool she is a practical one, and lest con-
siderations of state should deny her prince the luxury of
a love-match she keeps on hand a few common mortals.
At the worst she would take a duke, an English lord, or
even a young American with a proper number of millions.
The poor woman must be rather uncomfortable. She is
always building castles and knocking them down again
—always casting her nets and pulling them in. If her
daughter were less of a beauty her restless ambition would
be simply grotesque; but there is something in the girl,
as one looks at her, that seems to make it very possible
she is marked out for one of those wonderful romantic
fortunes that history now and then relates. 'Who, after all,
was the Empress of the French?' Mrs. Light is for ever
saying. 'And beside Christina the Empress is a dowdy!'"

"And what does Christina say?"

"She makes no scruple, as you know, of saying that her
mother is an idiot! What she thinks Heaven knows. I
suspect that practically she does not commit herself. She
is excessively proud and thinks herself good enough to
occupy the highest station in the world; but she knows
that her mother talks nonsense and that even a beautiful
girl may look awkward in making unsuccessful advances.
So she remains superbly indifferent and lets her mother
take the risks. If the Prince is secured, so much the
better; if he is not she need never confess to herself that
even a prince has slighted her."

"Your report is as solid," Rowland said to Madame
Grandoni, thanking her, "as if it had been drawn up for
the Academy of Sciences;" and he congratulated himself

on having listened to it when a couple of days later Mrs.
Light and her daughter, attended by the Cavaliere and the
poodle, came to his rooms to look at Roderick's statues.
It was more comfortable to know just with whom he was
dealing.

Mrs. Light was prodigiously gracious, and showered
down compliments not only on the statues but on all his
possessions. "Upon my word," she said, "you rich young
men know how to make yourselves comfortable. If one
of us poor women had half as many easy-chairs and knick-
knacks we should be famously abused. It's really selfish
to be living all alone in such a place as this. Cavaliere,
how should you like this suite of rooms and a fortune to
fill them with pictures and statues? Christina love, look at
that mosaic table. Mr. Mallet, I could almost beg it from
you! Yes, that Eve is certainly very fine. We needn't be
ashamed of such a great-grandmother as that. If she was
really such a beautiful woman, it accounts for the good looks
of some of us. Where is Mr. What's-his-name, the young
sculptor? Why isn't he here to be complimented?"

Christina had remained but for a moment in the chair
which Rowland placed for her, had given but a cursory
glance at the statues, and then, leaving her seat, had
begun to wander round the room—looking at herself in
the mirror, touching the ornaments and curiosities, glancing
at the books and prints. Rowland's sitting-room was encumbered with bric-à-brac ånd she found plenty of
occupation. Rowland presently joined her and pointed
out some of the objects he most valued.

"It's an odd jumble," she said frankly. "Some things
are very pretty—some are very ugly. But I like ugly
things when they have a certain look. Prettiness is
terribly vulgar nowadays, and it is not every one that knows
just the sort of ugliness that has *chic*. But chic is getting
dreadfully common too. There's a hint of it even in
Madame Baldi's bonnets. I like looking at people's
things," she added in a moment, turning to Rowland and
resting her eyes on him. "It helps you to find out their
characters."

"Am I to suppose," asked Rowland smiling, "that you
have arrived at any conclusions as to mine?"

"I am rather *intriguée*; you have too many things; one

seems to contradict another. You are very artistic and yet you are very prosaic; you have what is called a 'catholic' taste, and yet you are full of obstinate little prejudices and preferences which, if I knew you, I should find very tiresome. I don't think I like you."

"You make a great mistake," laughed Rowland; "I assure you I am very amiable."

"Yes, I am probably wrong, and if I knew you, I should find out I was wrong, and that would irritate me and make me dislike you more. So you see we are necessarily enemies."

"No, I don't dislike you!"

"Worse and worse; for you certainly will not like me."

"You are very discouraging."

"I am fond of facing the truth, though some day you will deny even that. Where is that queer friend of yours?"

"You mean Roderick Hudson? He is represented by these beautiful works."

Miss Light looked for some moments at Roderick's statues. "Yes," she said, "they are not so silly as most of the things we have seen. They have no chic, and yet they are beautiful."

"You describe them perfectly," said Rowland. "They are beautiful, and yet they have no chic. That's it!"

"If he will promise to put no chic into my bust, I have a mind to let him make it. A request made in those terms deserves to be granted."

"In what terms?"

"Didn't you hear him? 'Mademoiselle, you almost satisfy my conception of the beautiful. I must model your bust.' That *almost* should be rewarded! He is like me, he likes to face the truth. I think we should get on together."

The Cavaliere approached Rowland to express the pleasure he had derived from his beautiful "collection." His smile was exquisitely bland, his accent appealing, flattering, insinuating. But he gave Rowland an odd sense of looking at a little waxen image adjusted to perform certain gestures and emit certain sounds. It had once contained a soul, but the soul had leaked away. Nevertheless, Rowland reflected, there are more graceless things than mere manner and

posture, in an old-fashioned Italian. And the Cavaliere too
had soul enough left to desire to speak a few words on his
own account, and call Rowland's attention to the fact that
he was not after all a hired cicerone, but an ancient Roman
gentleman. Rowland felt sorry for him; he hardly knew
why. He assured him in a friendly fashion that he must
come again; that his house was always at his service. The
Cavaliere bowed down to the ground. "You do me too
much honour," he murmured. "If you will allow me—it
is not impossible! "

Mrs. Light meanwhile had prepared to depart. "If you
are not afraid to come and see two quiet little women,
we shall be most happy ! " she said. "We have no statues
nor pictures — we have nothing but each other. Eh,
darling ? "

"I beg your pardon," said Christina.

"Oh, and the Cavaliere," added her mother.

"The poodle please ! " cried the young girl.

Rowland glanced at the Cavaliere; he was smiling more
blandly than ever.

A few days later Rowland presented himself, as civility
demanded, at Mrs. Light's door. He found her living in
one of the stately houses of the Via dell' Angelo Custode,
and rather to his surprise was told she was at home. He
passed through half a dozen rooms and was ushered into an
immense saloon, at one end of which sat the mistress of
the establishment with a piece of embroidery. She received him very graciously, and then pointing mysteriously
to a large screen which was unfolded across the embrasure
of one of the deep windows, "I am keeping guard ! "
she said. Rowland looked interrogative; whereupon she
beckoned him forward and motioned him to look behind
the screen. He obeyed, and for some moments stood
gazing. Roderick, with his back turned, stood before an
extemporised pedestal, ardently shaping a formless mass
of clay. Before him sat Christina Light, in a white dress,
with her shoulders bare, her magnificent hair twisted into
a classic coil, her head admirably poised. Meeting Rowland's gaze she smiled a little, only in the depths of her
blue-grey eyes, without moving. She looked divinely
beautiful.

IX.

The brilliant Roman winter came round again, and Rowland enjoyed it in a certain way more deeply than before. He grew passionately, unreasoningly fond of all Roman sights and sensations, and to breathe the Roman atmosphere seemed a needful condition of being. He could not have defined and explained the nature of his great relish, nor have made up the sum of it by adding together his calculable pleasures. It was a large, vague, idle, half profitless emotion, of which perhaps the most pertinent thing that may be said is that it brought with it a sort of relaxed acceptance of the present, the actual, the sensuous—of life on the terms of the moment. It was perhaps for this very reason that in spite of the charm which Rome flings over one's mood there ran through Rowland's meditations an undertone of melancholy natural enough in a mind which finds its horizon sensibly limited —even by a magic circle. Whether it be that one tacitly concedes to the Roman Church the monolopy of a guarantee of immortality, so that if one is indisposed to bargain with her for the precious gift one must do without it altogether ; or whether in an atmosphere so heavily weighted with echoes and memories one grows to believe that there is nothing in one's consciousness that is not foredoomed to moulder and crumble and become dust for the feet and possible malaria for the lungs, of future generations—the fact at least remains that one parts half willingly with one's hopes in Rome and misses them only under some very exceptional stress of circumstance. For this reason it may perhaps be said that there is no other place in which one's daily temper has such a mellow serenity, and none at the same time in which acute attacks of depression are more intolerable. Rowland found, in fact, a perfect response to his prevision that to live in Rome was an education to the senses and the imagination ; but he sometimes wondered whether this were not a questionable gain in case of one's not being prepared to subside into soft dilettantism. His customary tolerance of circumstances

seemed sometimes to pivot about by a mysterious inward
impulse and look his conscience in the face. "But afterwards . . . . ?" it seemed to ask, with a long reverbera-
tion; and he could give no answer but a shy affirmation
that there was no such thing as to-morrow and that to-day
was uncommonly fine. He often felt heavy-hearted; he
was sombre without knowing why; there were no visible
clouds in his heaven, but there were cloud-shadows on his
mood. Shadows projected they often were, without his
knowing it, by an undue apprehension that things after
all might not go so ideally well with Roderick. When he
caught himself fidgeting it vexed him, and he rebuked
himself for taking things unmanfully hard. If Roderick
chose to follow a crooked path, it was no fault of his;
he had given him, he would continue to give him, all that
he had offered him—friendship, sympathy, advice. He
had not undertaken to make him over!

If Rowland felt his roots striking and spreading in the
Roman soil, Roderick also surrendered himself with renewed liberality to the local influence. More than once
he declared to his companion that he meant to live and
die within the shadow of St. Peter's, and that he cared
little if he should never again draw breath in American
air. "For a man of my temperament Rome is the only
possible place," he said; "it's better to recognise the fact
early than late. So I shall never go home unless I am
absolutely forced."

"What is your idea of 'force'?" asked Rowland,
smiling. "It seems to me you have an excellent reason
for going home some day or other."

"Ah, you mean my engagement?" Roderick answered
with unaverted eyes. "Yes, there is a little understanding
of that sort at Northampton!" And he gave a little
vaguely appreciative sigh. "To reconcile Northampton
and Rome is rather a problem. Mary had better come
out here. Even at the worst I have no intention of
giving up Rome for six or eight years, and a union
deferred for that length of time would be rather absurd."

"Miss Garland could hardly leave your mother,"
Rowland observed.

"Oh, of course my mother should come! I think I will
suggest it in my next letter. It will take her a year or

two to make up her mind to it, but if she consents it will brighten her up. It's too small and dry a life over there, even for a timid old lady. It is hard to imagine," he added, "any change in Mary being a change for the better; but I should like her to take a look at the world and have her ideas enlarged a little. One is never so good, I suppose, but that one can improve."

"If you wish your mother and Miss Garland to come," Rowland suggested, "you had better go home and bring them."

"Oh, I can't think of leaving Europe for many a day. At present it would quite break the charm. I am just beginning to profit, to get used to things and take them naturally. I am sure the sight of Northampton Main Street would permanently upset me."

It was reassuring to hear that Roderick in his own view was but "just beginning" to spread his wings, and Rowland, if he had had any forebodings, might have suffered them to be modified by this declaration. This was the first time since their meeting at Geneva that Roderick had mentioned his cousin's name, but the ice being broken he indulged for some time afterwards in frequent allusions to his betrothed, which always had an accent of scrupulous, of almost studied, consideration. An uninitiated observer, hearing him, would have imagined her to be a person of a certain age—possibly an affectionate maiden aunt—who had once done him a kindness which he highly appreciated; perhaps presented him with a cheque for a thousand dollars. Rowland noted the difference between his present frankness and his reticence during the first six months of his engagement, and sometimes wondered whether it were not rather an anomaly that he should expatiate more largely as the happy event receded. He had wondered over the whole matter first and last in a great many different ways—he had looked at it in all possible lights. There was something uncommonly hard to explain in the fact of his having fallen in love with his cousin. She was not, as Rowland conceived her, the sort of girl he would have been likely to fancy, and the operation of sentiment, in all cases so mysterious, was particularly so in this one. Just why it was that Roderick should not in consistency have been captivated, his companion would have

been at a loss to say; but I think the conviction had its
roots in an unformulated comparison between himself and
the accepted suitor. Roderick and he were as different as
two men could be, and yet Roderick had taken it into his
head to fall in love with a woman for whom he himself
had been keeping in reserve for years a deeply characteristic passion. That if Rowland Mallet happened to be
very much struck with the merits of Roderick's mistress,
the irregularity here was hardly Roderick's, was a view of
the case to which our virtuous hero did scanty justice.
There were women, he said to himself, whom it was every
one's business to fall in love with a little—women beautiful,
brilliant, artful, easily fascinating. Miss Light, for instance, was one of these; every man who spoke to her
did so, if not in the language, at least with something of
the agitation, the divine tremor, of a lover. There were
other women—they might have great beauty, they might
have small; perhaps they were generally to be classified as
plain—whose triumphs in this line were rare, but immutably
permanent. Such a one, conspicuously, was Mary Garland.
Upon the doctrine of probabilities it was unlikely that she
should have had an equal charm for each of them, and was
it not possible therefore that the charm for Roderick had
been simply the charm imagined, unquestionably accepted,
the general charm of youth, sympathy, kindness—of the
present feminine, in short—enhanced indeed by the advantage of an expressive countenance? The charm in
this case for Rowland was—*the* charm!—the mysterious,
individual, essential woman. There was an element in
the charm, as his companion saw it, which Rowland was
obliged to recognise, but which he forbore to linger upon;
the rather important attraction, namely, of reciprocity.
As to the girl being in love with Roderick and com-
mending herself by this accident, this was a point with
which his imagination ventured to take no liberties;
partly because it would have been indelicate, and partly
because it would have been vain. He contented himself
with feeling that she was still as vivid an image in his
own memory as she had been five days after he left her,
and with drifting nearer and nearer to the conviction that
at just that crisis any other girl would have answered
Roderick's sentimental needs as well. Any other woman,

indeed, would do so still! Roderick had confessed as much to him at Geneva in saying that he had been taking at Baden the measure of his susceptibility.

His extraordinary success in modelling the bust of the beautiful Miss Light was pertinent evidence of this amiable quality. She sat to him repeatedly for a fortnight, and the work was rapidly finished. On one of the last days Roderick asked Rowland to come and give his opinion as to what was still wanting; for the sittings had continued to take place in Mrs. Light's apartment, the studio being pronounced too damp for the fair model. When Rowland presented himself, Christina, still in her white dress, with her shoulders bare, was standing before a mirror readjusting her hair, the arrangement of which on this occasion had apparently not met the young sculptor's approval. He stood beside her, directing the operation with a peremptoriness of tone which seemed to Rowland to denote a considerable advance in intimacy. As Rowland entered, Christina was losing patience, "Do it yourself then!" she cried, and with a rapid movement unloosed the great coil of her tresses and let them fall over her shoulders.

They were magnificent, and with her perfect face dividing their rippling flow she looked like some immaculate saint of legend being led to martyrdom. Rowland's eyes presumably betrayed his admiration, but her own manifested no consciousness of it. If Christina was a coquette, as the remarkable timeliness of this incident might have suggested, she was not a superficial one.

"Hudson's a sculptor," said Rowland, with warmth. "But if I were only a painter!"

"Thank Heaven you are not!" said Christina. "I am having quite enough of this minute inspection of my charms."

"My dear young man, hands off!" cried Mrs. Light, coming forward and seizing her daughter's hair. "Christina, love, I am surprised."

"Is it indelicate?" Christina asked. "I beg Mr. Mallet's pardon." Mrs. Light gathered up the dusky locks and let them fall through her fingers, glancing at her visitor with a significant smile. Rowland had never been in the East, but if he had attempted to make a sketch of an old slave-merchant calling attention to the "points" of a

Circassian beauty, he would have depicted such a smile
as Mrs. Light's. "Mamma is not really shocked," added
Christina in a moment, as if she had guessed her mother's
by-play. "She is only afraid that Mr. Hudson might
have injured my hair, and that *per consequenza*, I should
sell for less."

"You unnatural child!" cried mamma. "You deserve
that I should make a fright of you!" And with half a
dozen skilful passes she twisted the tresses into a single
picturesque braid, placed high on the head, as a kind of
coronal.

"What does your mother do when she wants to do you
justice?" Rowland asked, observing the admirable line
of the young girl's neck.

"I do her justice when I say she says very improper
things. What is one to do with such a thorn in the
flesh?" Mrs. Light demanded.

"Think of it at your leisure, Mr. Mallet," said Christina,
"and when you have discovered something let us hear.
But I must tell you that I shall not willingly believe in
any remedy of yours, for you have something in the
expression of your face that particularly provokes me to
make the remarks that my mother so sincerely deplores.
I noticed it the first time I saw you. I think it's because
your face is so broad. For some reason or other broad
faces exasperate me; they fill me with a kind of *rabbia*.
Last summer at Carlsbad there was an Austrian count,
with enormous estates and some great office at court. He
was very attentive—seriously so; he was really very far
gone. *Cela ne tenait qu'à moi!* But I couldn't; he was
impossible! He must have measured from ear to ear at
least a yard and a half. And he was blond too, which
made it worse—as blond as Stenterello; pure fleece! So
I said to him frankly, 'Many thanks, Herr Graf; your
uniform is magnificent but your face is too fat.'"

"I am afraid that mine also," said Rowland with a
smile, "seems just now to have assumed an unpardonable
latitude."

"Oh, I take it you know very well that we are looking
for a husband and that none but tremendous swells need
apply. Surely before these gentlemen, mamma, I may
speak freely; they are disinterested. Mr. Mallet won't

do, because, though he is rich, he is not rich enough. Mamma made that discovery the day after we went to see you, moved to it by the promising look of your furniture. I hope she was right, eh? Unless you have millions, you know, you have no chance."

"I feel like a beggar," said Rowland.

"Oh, some better girl than I will decide some day, after mature reflection, that on the whole you have enough. Mr. Hudson, of course, is nowhere; he has nothing but his genius and his *beaux yeux*."

Roderick had stood looking at Christina intently while she delivered herself, softly and slowly, of this surprising nonsense. When she had finished, she turned and looked at him; their eyes met and he blushed a little. "Let me model you, and he who can may marry you!" he said, abruptly.

Mrs. Light, while her daughter talked, had been adding a few touches to her coiffure. "She is not so silly as you might suppose," she said to Rowland with dignity. "If you will give me your arm we will go and look at the bust."

"Does that represent a silly girl?" Christina demanded when they stood before it.

Rowland transferred his glance several times from the portrait to the original. "It represents a young lady whom I should not pretend to judge off-hand."

"She may be a fool, but you are not sure. Many thanks! You have seen me half a dozen times. You are either very slow or I am very deep."

"I am certainly slow," said Rowland. "I don't expect to make up my mind about you within six months."

"I give you six months if you will promise then a perfectly frank opinion. Mind, I shall not forget; I shall insist upon it."

"Well, though I am slow I am tolerably brave," said Rowland. "We shall see."

Christina looked at the bust with a sigh. "I am afraid after all," she said, "that there's very little wisdom in it save what the artist has put there. Mr. Hudson looked particularly wise while he was working; he scowled and growled, but he never opened his mouth. It is very kind of him not to have represented me yawning."

"If I had felt obliged to talk a lot of rubbish to you," said Roderick roundly, "the thing would not have been a tenth so good."

"Is it good after all ? Mr. Mallet is a famous connoisseur ; has he not come here to pronounce ?"

The bust was in fact a very happy performance— Roderick had risen to the level of his subject. It was thoroughly a portrait, and not a vague fantasy executed on a graceful theme, as the busts of pretty women in modern sculpture are apt to be. The resemblance was deep and vivid ; there was extreme fidelity of detail, and yet a noble simplicity. One could say of the head that, without idealisation, it was a representation of ideal beauty. Rowland however, as we know, was not fond of exploding into superlatives, and after examining the piece he contented himself with suggesting two or three alterations of detail.

"Ah, how can you be so cruel ?" demanded Mrs. Light, with soft reproachfulness. "It is surely a wonderful thing !"

"Rowland knows it's a wonderful thing," said Roderick smiling. "I can tell that by his face. The other day I finished something he thought bad, and he looked very differently from this."

"How did Mr. Mallet look ?" asked Christina.

"My dear Rowland, " said Roderick, "I am speaking of my seated woman. You looked as if you had on a pair of tight boots."

"Ah, my child, you'll not understand that !" cried Mrs. Light. "You never yet had a pair that were small enough."

"It's a pity, Mr. Hudson," said Christina gravely, "that you could not have introduced my feet into the bust. But we can hang a pair of slippers round the neck !"

"I nevertheless like your statues, Roderick," Rowland rejoined, "better than your jokes. This is admirable. Miss Light, you may be proud !"

"Than you, Mr. Mallet, for the permission," rejoined the young girl.

"I am dying to see it in the marble, with a red velvet screen behind it," said Mrs. Light.

"Placed there under the Sassoferrato !" Christina went

on. "I hope you keep well in mind, Mr. Hudson, that you have not a grain of property in your work, and that if mamma chooses she may have it photographed and the copies sold in the Piazza di Spagna at five francs apiece, without your having a sou of the profits."

"Amen!" said Roderick. "It was so nominated in the bond. My profits are here!" and he tapped his forehead.

"It would be prettier if you said *here!*" And Christina touched her heart.

"My precious child, how you do run on!" murmured Mrs. Light.

"It is Mr. Mallet," the young girl answered. "I can't talk a word of sense so long as he is in the room. I don't say that to make you go," she added; "I say it simply to justify myself."

"The noble art of self-defence!" said Rowland.

Roderick declared that he must get at work and requested Christina to take her usual position, and Mrs. Light proposed to her visitor that they should adjourn to her boudoir. This was a small room, hardly more spacious than an alcove, opening out of the drawing-room and having no other issue. Here, as they entered, on a divan near the door, Rowland perceived the Cavaliere Giacosa, with his arms folded, his head dropped upon his breast and his eyes closed.

"Sleeping at his post!" said Rowland, smiling.

"That's a punishable offence," rejoined Mrs. Light sharply. She was on the point of calling him in the same tone, when he suddenly opened his eyes, stared a moment, and then rose with a smile and a bow.

"Excuse me, dear lady," he said, "I was overcome by the—the great heat."

"Nonsense, Cavaliere!" cried the lady, "you know we are perishing here with the cold! You had better go and cool yourself in one of the other rooms."

"I obey, dear lady," said the Cavaliere; and with another salutation to Rowland he departed, walking very discreetly on his toes. Rowland outstayed him but a short time, for he was not fond of Mrs. Light, and he found nothing very inspiring in her frank intimation that if he chose he might become a favourite. He was disgusted with himself for pleasing her; he confounded his fatal urbanity. In the

courtyard of the palace he overtook the Cavaliere, who had
stopped at the porter's lodge to say a word to his little
girl. She was a young lady of very tender years and she
wore a very dirty pinafore. He had taken her up in his
arms and was singing an infantine rhyme to her, and she
was staring at him with big soft Roman eyes. On seeing
Rowland he put her down with a kiss, and stepped forward
with a conscious grin, an unresentful admission that he
was sensitive both to chubbiness and to ridicule. Rowland
began to pity him again ; he had taken his dismissal from
the drawing-room so meekly.

"You don't keep your promise to come and see me,"
said the young man, "Don't forget it. I want you to
tell me about Rome thirty years ago."

"Thirty years ago ? Ah, dear sir, Rome is Rome
still ; a place where strange things happen ! But happy
things too, since I have your renewed permission to call.
You do me too much honour. Is it in the morning or in
the evening that I should least intrude ? "

"Take your own time, Cavaliere ; only come some time.
I depend upon you," said Rowland.

The Cavaliere thanked him with a humble obeisance.
To old Giacosa too, he felt that he was, in Roman phrase,
sympathetic ; but the idea of pleasing this extremely reduced gentleman was not disagreeable to him.

Miss Light's bust stood for a while on exhibition in
Roderick's studio, and half the foreign colony came to see
it. With the completion of his work, however, Roderick's
visits at the Palazzo F—— by no means came to an end.
He spent half his time in Mrs. Light's drawing-room, and
began to be talked about as "attentive" to Christina.
The success of the bust restored his equanimity, and in the
garrulity of his good-humour he suffered Rowland to see
that she was just now the object uppermost in his thoughts.
Rowland, when they talked of her, was rather listener
than speaker ; partly because Roderick's own tone was so
resonant and exultant, and partly because, when his companion laughed at him for having called her unsafe, he
was too perplexed to defend himself. The impression
remained that she was unsafe ; that she was a complex,
wilful, passionate, creature who might easily engulph a too
confiding spirit in the eddies of her capricious temper.

And yet he strongly felt her charm ; the eddies had a strange fascination ! Roderick, in the glow of that renewed admiration provoked by the fixed attention of portrayal, was never weary of descanting on the extraordinary perfection of her beauty.

"I had no idea of it," he said, "till I began to look at her with an eye to reproducing line for line and curve for curve. Her face is the most exquisite piece of modelling that ever came from creative hands. Not a line without meaning, not a hair's breadth that is not admirably finished. And then her mouth ! It is as if a pair of lips had been shaped to utter pure truth without doing it dishonour !" Later, after he had been working for a week, he declared that if the girl had been inordinately plain she would still be the most fascinating of women. "I have quite forgotten her beauty," he said, "or rather I have ceased to perceive it as something distinct and defined, something independent to the rest of her. She is all one, and all consummately interesting !

"What does she do—what does she say, that is so remarkable ?" Rowland had asked.

"Say ? Sometimes nothing—sometimes everything. She is never the same. Sometimes she walks in and takes her place without a word, without a smile, gravely, stiffly, as if it were an awful bore. She hardly looks at me, and she walks away without even glancing at my work. On other days she laughs and chatters and asks endless questions and pours out the most irresistible nonsense. She is a creature of moods ; you can't count upon her ; she keeps observation on the stretch. And then, bless you, she has seen so much of the world ! Her talk is full of the strangest allusions ! "

"It is altogether a very singular type of young lady," said Rowland, after the visit which I have related at length. "It may be a charm, but it is certainly not the orthodox charm of marriageable maidenhood, the charm of shrinking innocence and soft docility. Our American girls are accused of being more knowing than any others, and this wonderful damsel is nominally an American. But it has taken twenty years of Europe to make her what she is ! The first time we saw her, I remember you called her a product of the old world, and certainly you were not far wrong."

"Ah, she has an atmosphere," said Roderick, in a tone of high appreciation.

"Young unmarried women should be careful not to have too much!"

"Ah, you don't forgive her for hitting you so hard! A man ought to be flattered at such a girl as that taking so much notice of him."

"A man is never flattered at a woman's not liking him," said Rowland.

"Are you sure she doesn't like you? That's to the credit of your humility. A fellow of more vanity might, on the evidence, persuade himself that he was in favour."

"He would have also," said Rowland laughing, "to be a fellow of remarkable ingenuity!" He asked himself privately how the deuce Roderick reconciled it to his conscience to think so much more of the girl he was not engaged to than of the other. But it amounted almost to arrogance in poor Rowland, you may say, to pretend to know how often Roderick thought of Mary Garland. He wondered gloomily at any rate whether for men of his companion's large easy power there was not a larger moral law than for narrow mediocrities like himself, who, yielding Nature a meagre interest on her investment (such as it was), had no reason to expect from her this affectionate laxity as to their accounts. Was it not a part of the eternal fitness of things that Roderick, while rhapsodising about Christina Light, should have it at his command to look at you with eyes of the most guileless and unclouded blue, and to shake off your musty imputations by a toss of his picturesque brown locks? Or had he, in fact, no conscience to speak of? Happy fellow either way!

Our friend Gloriani came, among others, to congratulate Roderick on his model and what he had made of her. "Devilish pretty, through and through!" he said as he looked at the bust. "Capital handling of the neck and throat; lovely work on the nose. You are a detestably lucky fellow, my boy! But you ought not to have squandered such material on a simple bust; you should have made a great imaginative figure. If I could only have got hold of her I would have put her into a statue in

spite of herself.   What a pity she is not a ragged Traste-
verine whom we might have for a franc an hour !   I have
been carrying about in my head for years a delicious design
for a fantastic figure, but it has always stayed there for
want of a tolerable model.   I have seen intimations of the
type, but this consummate creature is the perfection of it.
As soon as I saw her I said to myself, ' By Jove, there's
my statue in the flesh ! ' "

"What is your subject ?" asked Roderick.

"Don't take it ill," said Gloriani.   "You know I am
the very deuce for observation.   She would make a magnificent Herodias ! "

If Roderick had taken it ill (which was unlikely, for
we know he thought Gloriani an ass and expected little of
his wisdom), he might have been soothed by the candid
incense of Sam Singleton, who came and sat for an hour
in a sort of mental prostration before both bust and artist.
But Roderick's attitude in regard to his patient little
devotee was one of undisguised, though friendly amusement ; and, indeed, from a strictly plastic point of view the
poor fellow's diminutive stature and grotesque physiognomy
were a bribe to levity.   "Ah, don't envy our friend,"
Rowland said to Singleton afterwards, on his expressing
with a little groan of depreciation of his own paltry performances his sense of the brilliancy of Roderick's talent.
"You sail nearer the shore, but you sail in smoother
waters.   Be contented with what you are and paint me
another picture."

"Oh, I don't envy Hudson anything he possesses,"
Singleton said, "because to take anything away would
spoil his beautiful completeness.   ' Complete,' that's what
he is ; while we little clevernesses are like half ripened
plums, only good eating on the side that has had a glimpse
of the sun.   Nature has made him so, and fortune confesses
to it !   He is the handsomest fellow in Rome, he has the
most genius, and as a matter of course the most beautiful
girl in the world comes and offers to be his model.   If that
is not completeness where shall we find it ? "

X.

ONE morning, going into Roderick's studio, Rowland
found the young sculptor entertaining Miss Blanchard—
if this is not too flattering a description of his gracefully
passive tolerance of her presence. He had never liked
her and never climbed into her sky studio to observe her
wonderful manipulation of petals. He had once quoted
Tennyson against her—

> "And is there any moral shut
>   Within the bosom of the rose?"

" In all Miss Blanchard's roses you may be sure there is
a moral," he had said. " You can see it sticking out its
head, and if you go to smell the flower it scratches your
nose." But on this occasion she had come with a propitia-
tory gift—introducing her friend Mr. Leavenworth. Mr.
Leavenworth was a tall, expansive, bland gentleman, with
a carefully brushed whisker and a spacious, fair, well-
favoured face, which seemed somehow to have more room
in it than was occupied by a smile of superior benevolence,
so that (with his smooth white forehead) it bore a certain
resemblance to a large parlour with a very florid carpet,
but no pictures on the walls. He held his head high,
talked impressively, and told Roderick within five minutes
that he was a widower, travelling to distract his mind, and
that he had lately retired from the proprietorship of large
mines of borax in Pennsylvania. Roderick supposed at
first that under the influence of his bereavement he had
come to order a tombstone; but observing the extreme
blandness of his address to Miss Blanchard he credited
him with a judicious prevision that by the time the tombstone should be completed, a monument of his inconsolability
might have become an anachronism. Mr. Leavenworth,
however, was disposed to order something.

" You will find me eager to patronise our indigenous
talent," he said. " You may be sure that I have employed
a native architect for the large residential structure that

I am erecting on the banks of the Ohio. I have sustained a considerable loss; but are we not told that art is a consolation? That's why I have come to you, sir. In a tasteful home, surrounded by the memorials of my wanderings, I hope to recover my moral tone. I ordered in Paris the complete appurtenances of a dining-room. Do you think you could do something for my library? It is to be filled with well-selected authors, and I think a pure white image in this style"—pointing to one of Roderick's statues—"standing out against the morocco and gilt, would have a noble effect. The subject I have already fixed upon. I desire an allegorical representation of Culture. Do you think now," asked Mr. Leavenworth, encouragingly, "you could rise to the conception?"

"A most interesting subject for a truly serious mind," remarked Miss Blanchard.

Roderick looked at her a moment, and then—"The simplest thing I could do," he said, "would be to make a full-length portrait of Miss Blanchard. I could give her a scroll in her hand. and that would do for the allegory."

Miss Blanchard coloured; the compliment might be ironical; and there was ever afterwards a reflection of her uncertainty in her opinion of Roderick's genius. Mr. Leavenworth responded that with all deference to Miss Blanchard's beauty he desired something colder, more monumental, more impersonal. "If I were to be the happy possessor of a likeness of Miss Blanchard," he added, "I should prefer to have it in no factitious disguise!"

Roderick consented to entertain the proposal, and while they were discussing it, Rowland had a little talk with the judicious Augusta. "Who is your friend?" he asked.

"A very worthy man. The architect of his own fortune —which is magnificent. One of nature's gentlemen!"

This was a trifle sententious, and Rowland turned to the bust of Miss Light. Like every one else in Rome by this time, Miss Blanchard had an opinion on the young girl's beauty, and in her own fashion she expressed it in a quotable phrase. "She looks half like a Madonna and half like a *ballerina!*"

Mr. Leavenworth and Roderick came to an understanding,

and the young sculptor good-naturedly promised to do his
best to rise to his patron's conception. "His conception
be hanged!" Roderick exclaimed after he had departed.
"His conception is sitting on an india-rubber cushion,
with a pen in her ear and the lists of the stock exchange
in her hand. I shall have to invent something myself.
For the money I ought to be able to!"

Mrs. Light meanwhile had fairly established herself in
Roman society. "Heaven knows how!" Madame Grandoni
said to Rowland, who had mentioned to her several evidences
of the lady's prosperity. "In such a case there is nothing
like audacity. A month ago she knew no one but her
washerwoman, and now I am told that the cards of Roman
princesses are to be seen on her table. She is evidently
determined to play a great part, and she has the wit to
perceive that, to make remunerative acquaintances, you
must seem yourself to be worth knowing. You must
have striking rooms and a bewildering variety of dresses,
you must give dinners and dances and concerts. She is
spending a lot of money, and you'll see that in two or
three weeks she will take upon herself to open the season
by giving a magnificent ball. Of course it is Christina's
beauty that floats her. People go to see her because they
are curious."

"And they go again because they are charmed," said
Rowland. "Miss Christina is a very remarkable young
woman."

"Oh, I know it well; I had occasion to say so to
myself the other day. She came to see me of her own
free will, and for an hour she was deeply interesting.
I think she is an actress, but she believes in her part
while she is playing it. She took it into her head the
other day to believe that she was very unhappy, and she
sat there, where you are sitting, and told me a tale of her
miseries which brought tears into my eyes. She cried pro-
fusely, and as naturally as possible. She said she was
weary of life and that she knew no one but me she could
speak frankly to. She must speak, or she should go mad.
She sobbed as if her heart would break. I assure you it's
well for you susceptible young men that you don't see her
when she sobs. She said in so many words that her mother
was an immoral woman. Heaven knows what she meant!

She meant I suppose that she makes debts that she knows
she can't pay. She said the life they led was horrible;
that it was monstrous a poor girl should be dragged about
the world to be sold to the highest bidder. She was meant
for better things; she could be perfectly happy in poverty.
It was not money she wanted. I might not believe her,
but she really cared for serious things. Sometimes she
thought of taking poison!"

"What did you say to that?"

"I recommended her to come and see me instead. I
would help her about as much, and I was on the whole less
unpleasant. Of course I could help her only by letting
her talk herself out, and kissing her, and patting her
beautiful hands, and telling her to be patient and she
would be happy yet. About once in two months I expect
her to reappear on the same errand, and meanwhile to quite
forget my existence. I believe I melted to the point of
telling her that I would find some good, kind, quiet
husband for her; but she declared, almost with fury,
that she was sick of the very name of husbands, which
she begged I would never mention again. And in fact it
was a rash offer; for I am sure that there is not a man
of the kind that might really make a woman happy but
would be afraid to marry mademoiselle. Looked at in
that way she is certainly very much to be pitied, and
indeed, altogether, though I don't think she either means
all she says, or, by a great deal, says all that she means,
I feel very sorry for her."

Rowland met the two ladies about this time at several
entertainments, and looked at Christina with a kind of
imaginative *attendrissement*. He suspected more than once
that there had been a passionate scene between them about
coming out, and he wondered what arguments Mrs. Light
had found effective. But Christina's face told no tales,
and she moved about, beautiful and silent, looking absently
over people's heads, barely heeding the men who pressed
about her, and suggesting somehow that the soul of a
world-wearied mortal had found its way into the blooming
body of a goddess. "Where in the world has Miss Light
been before she is twenty," observers asked, "to have left
all her illusions behind?" And the general verdict was
that though she was incomparably beautiful she was

intolerably proud. Young ladies to whom the former distinction was not conceded were free to reflect that she was
"not at all liked."

It would have been difficult to guess, however, how they
reconciled this conviction with a variety of contradictory
evidence, and in especial with the spectacle of Roderick's in-
veterate devotion. All Rome might behold that he at least
"liked" Christina Light. Wherever she appeared he was
either awaiting her or immediately followed her. He was
perpetually at her side, trying apparently to preserve some
broken thread of talk, the fate of which was, to judge by
her face, profoundly immaterial to the young lady. People
in general smiled at the radiant good faith of the handsome young sculptor and asked each other whether he
really supposed that beauties of that quality were meant
to give themselves to juvenile artists. But although
Christina's deportment, as I have said, was one of superb
inexpressiveness, Rowland had derived from Roderick no
suspicion that he suffered from snubbing, and he was
therefore surprised at an incident that occurred one evening
at a large musical party. Roderick as usual was in the
field, and on the ladies taking the chairs which had been
arranged for them he immediately placed himself beside
Christina. As most of the gentlemen were standing, his
position made him as conspicuous as Hamlet at Ophelia's
feet. Rowland was leaning somewhat apart, against the
chimney-piece. There was a long solemn pause before the
music began, and in the midst of it Christina rose, left her
place, came the whole length of the immense room, with
every one looking at her, and stopped before him. She
was neither pale nor flushed; she had a soft smile.

"Will you do me a favour?" she asked.

"A thousand!"

"Not now, but at your earliest convenience. Please
remind Mr. Hudson that he is not in a New England
village—that it is not the custom in Rome to address one's
conversation exclusively, night after night, to the same
poor girl, and that——"

The music broke out with a great blare and covered her
voice. She made a gesture of impatience, and Rowland
offered her his arm and led her back to her seat.

The next day he repeated her words to Roderick, who

burst into joyous laughter. "She has a delightful un-
expectedness!" he cried. "She must do everything that
comes into her head!"

"Had she never asked you before not to talk to her so
much?"

"On the contrary, she has often said to me, 'Mind you
now, I forbid you to leave me. Here comes that tiresome
So-and-so.' She cares as little about the custom as I do.
What could be a better proof than her walking up to you
with five hundred people looking at her? Is that the
custom for young girls in Rome?"

"Why then should she take such a step?"

"Because as she sat there it came into her head. That's
reason enough for her! I have imagined she wishes me
well, as they say here—though she has never distinguished
me in such a way as that!"

Madame Grandoni had foretold the truth; Mrs. Light
a couple of weeks later convoked all Roman society to a
brilliant ball. Rowland went late, and found the staircase
so encumbered with flower-pots and servants that he was
a long time making his way into the presence of the
hostess. At last he approached her as she stood making
curtsies at the door with her daughter by her side. Some
of Mrs. Light's curtsies were very low, for she had the
happiness of receiving a number of the social potentates
of the Roman world. She was rosy with triumph, to say
nothing of a less metaphysical cause, and was evidently
vastly contented with herself, with her company, and with
the general attitude of destiny. Her daughter was less
overtly jubilant, and distributed her greetings with impartial frigidity. She had never been so beautiful.
Dressed simply in vaporous white, relieved with half a
dozen white roses, the perfection of her features and of her
person, and the mysterious depth of her expression, seemed
to glow with the white light of a splendid pearl. She
recognised no one individually, and made her salutation
slowly, gravely, with her eyes on the ground. Rowland
fancied that, as he stood before her, her obeisance was
slightly exaggerated, as with an intention of irony; but
he smiled philosophically to himself, and reflected as
he passed on that if she disliked him he had nothing to
reproach himself with. He walked about, had a few

words with Miss Blanchard, who with a fillet of cameos in her hair was leaning on the arm of Mr. Leavenworth, and at last came upon the Cavaliere Giacosa, modestly stationed in a corner. The little gentleman's coat lappet was decorated with an enormous bouquet, and his neck encased in a voluminous white handkerchief of the fashion of thirty years ago. His arms were folded, and he was surveying the scene with contracted eyelids, through which you saw the glitter of his intensely dark vivacious pupil. He immediately embarked on an elaborate apology for not having yet manifested as he felt it his sense of the honour Rowland had done him.

" I am always on service with these ladies, you see," he explained, "and that is a duty to which one would not willingly be faithless for an instant."

"Evidently," said Rowland, "you are a very devoted friend. Mrs. Light, in her situation, is very happy in having you."

" We are old friends," said the Cavaliere, gravely. " Old friends. I knew the signora many years ago, when she was the prettiest woman in Rome—or rather in Ancona, which is even better. The beautiful Christina now is perhaps the most beautiful young girl in Europe ! "

" Very likely," said Rowland.

" Very well, sir, I taught her to read ; I guided her little hands to touch the piano." And at these faded memories the Cavaliere's eyes glittered more brightly. Rowland half expected him to proceed with a little flash of long-repressed passion, " And now—and now sir, they treat me as you observed the other day ! " But the Cavaliere only looked out at him keenly from among his wrinkles, and seemed to say with all the vividness of the Italian glance, " Oh, I say nothing more. I am not so shallow as to complain ! "

Evidently the Cavaliere was not shallow, and Rowland repeated respectfully, " You are a devoted friend."

"That's very true. I am a devoted friend. A man may do himself justice after twenty years ! "

Rowland after a pause made some remark about the beauty of the ball. It was very brilliant.

"Stupendous ! ' said the Cavaliere solemnly. " It is a great day. We have four Roman princes, to say nothing

of others." And he counted them over on his fingers and
held up his hand triumphantly. "And there she stands,
the girl to whom I—I, Giuseppe Giacosa—taught her
alphabet and her piano scales; there she stands in her
incomparable beauty, and Roman princes come and bow
to her! Here, in his quiet corner, her old master permits
himself to be proud."

"It is very friendly of him," said Rowland smiling.

The Cavaliere contracted his lids a little more and gave
another keen glance. "It is very natural, signore. The
Christina is a good girl; she remembers my little services.
But here comes," he added in a moment, "the young Prince
of the Fine Arts. I am sure he has bowed lowest of all."

Rowland looked round and saw Roderick moving slowly
across the room and casting about him his usual luminous,
unshrinking looks. He presently joined them, nodded
familiarly to the Cavaliere, and immediately demanded of
Rowland, "Have you seen her?"

"I have seen Miss Light," said Rowland. "She's
magnificent."

"I'm intoxicated with her beauty!" cried Roderick; so
loud that several persons turned round.

Rowland saw that he was flushed, and laid his hand on
his arm. Roderick was trembling. "If you will go away,"
Rowland said instantly, "I will go with you."

"Go away?" cried Roderick, almost angrily. "I intend
to dance with her!"

The Cavaliere had been watching him attentively; he
gently laid his hand on his other arm. "Softly, softly,
dear young man," he said. "Let me speak to you as
a friend."

"Oh, speak even as an enemy and I shall not mind it,"
Roderick answered frowning.

"Be very reasonable then and go away."

"Why the devil should ı go away?"

"Because you are in love," said the Cavaliere.

"I might as well be in love here as in the streets."

"Carry your love as far as possible from Christina. She
will not listen to you—she can't."

"She 'can't'?" demanded Roderick. "She is not a
person of whom you may say that. She can if she will;
the does as she chooses."

"Up to a certain point. It would take too long to explain; I only beg you to believe that if you continue to love Miss Light you will be very unhappy. Have you a princely title? have you a princely fortune? Otherwise you can never have her."

And the Cavaliere folded his arms again, like a man who has done his duty. Roderick wiped his forehead and looked askance at Rowland; he seemed to be guessing his thoughts and they made him blush a little. But he smiled blandly, and addressing the Cavaliere, "I am much obliged to you for the information," he said. "Now that I have obtained it, let me tell you that I am no more in love with Miss Light than you are. My friend here knows that. I admire her—yes, immensely. But that's no one's business but my own, and though I have as you say neither a princely title nor a princely fortune, I mean to suffer neither those advantages nor those who possess them to diminish my right."

"If you are not in love, my dear young man," said ·the Cavaliere with his hand on his heart and an apologetic smile, "so much the better! But let me entreat you as an affectionate friend to keep a watch on your emotions. You are young, you are handsome, you have a brilliant genius and a generous heart, but—I may say it almost with authority—Christina is not for you!"

Whether Roderick were in love or not, he was nettled by what apparently seemed to him an obtrusive negation of an inspiring possibility. "You speak as if she had made her choice!" he cried. "Without pretending to confidential information on the subject, I am sure she has not."

"No, but she must make it soon," said the Cavaliere. And raising his forefinger, he laid it against his under lip. "She must choose a name and a fortune—and she will!"

"She will do exactly as her inclination prompts! She will marry the man who pleases her, if he hasn't a dollar! I know her better than you."

The Cavaliere turned a little paler than usual and smiled more urbanely. "No, no, my dear young man, you do not know her better than I. You have not watched her day by day for twenty years. I too have admired her. She is a good girl; she has never said an unkind word to me; the blessed Virgin be thanked! But she must have a brilliant destiny; it has been marked out for her and she will submit. You had better believe me; it may save you much suffering."

"We shall see!" said Roderick, with an excited laugh.

"Certainly we shall see. But I retire from the discussion," the Cavaliere added. "I have no wish to provoke you to attempt to prove to me that I am wrong. You are already excited."

"No more than is natural to a man who in an hour or so is to dance a cotillon with a divinity."

"A cotillon? has she promised?"

Roderick patted the air with a grand confidence. "You'll see!" His gesture might almost have been taken to mean that the state of his relations with the "divinity" was such that they quite dispensed with vain preliminaries.

The Cavaliere gave an exaggerated shrug. "You will make a great many mourners!"

"He has made a mourner already!" Rowland murmured to himself. This was evidently not the first time that reference had been made between Roderick and the Cavaliere to the young man's possible passion, and Roderick had failed to consider it the simplest and most natural course to say in three words to the vigilant little gentleman that there was no cause for alarm—his affections were preoccupied. Rowland hoped silently with some dryness that his motives for reticence were of a finer kind than they seemed to be. He turned away; it was irritating to look at Roderick's radiant unscrupulous eagerness. The tide was setting towards the supper-room and he drifted with it to the door. The crowd at this point was dense, and he was obliged to wait for some minutes before he could advance. At last he felt his neighbours dividing behind him, and turning he saw Christina pressing her way forward alone. She was looking at no one, and save for the fact of her being alone you would not have supposed she was in her mother's house. As she recognised Rowland she beckoned to him, took his arm, and motioned him to lead her into the supper-room. She said nothing until he had forced a passage and they stood somewhat isolated.

"Take me into the most out-of-the-way corner you can

find," she then said, "and then go and get me a piece of bread."

"Nothing more? There seems to be everything conceivable."

"A simple roll. Nothing more on your peril. Only bring something for yourself."

It seemed to Rowland that the embrasure of a window (embrasures in Roman palaces are deep) was a retreat sufficiently obscure for Christina to execute whatever design she might have contrived against his equanimity. A roll, after he had found her a seat, was easily procured. As he presented it, he remarked that, frankly speaking, he was at a loss to understand why she should have selected for the honour of a *tête-à-tête* an individual for whom she had so little taste.

"Ah yes, I dislike you!" said Christina. "To tell the truth I had forgotten it. There are so many people here whom I dislike more that when I espied you just now you seemed like an intimate friend. But I have not come into this corner to talk nonsense," she went on. "You must not think I always do, eh ?"

"I have never heard you do anything else," said Rowland, deliberately, having decided that he owed her no compliments.

"Very good. I like your frankness. It's quite true. You see I am a strange girl. To begin with I am frightfully egotistical. Don't flatter yourself you have said anything very clever if you ever take it into your head to tell me so. I know it much better than you. So it is, I can't help it. I am tired to death of myself; I would give all I possess to get out of myself; but somehow at the end I find myself so vastly more interesting than nine-tenths of the people I meet. If a person wished to do me a favour I would say to him, 'I beg you with tears in my eyes to interest me. Be strong, be positive, be imperious, if you will; only be *something*—something that in looking at I can forget my detestable self!' Perhaps that is nonsense too. If it is, I can't help it. I can only apologise for the nonsense that I know to be such, and that I talk—oh, for more reasons than I can tell you! I wonder whether if I were to try you would understand me."

"I am afraid I should never understand," said Rowland, "why a person should willingly talk nonsense."

"That proves how little you know about women. But I like your frankness. When I told you the other day that you displeased me I had an idea you were more formal —how do you say it ?—more *guindé*. I am very capricious. To-night I like you better."

"Oh, I am not *guindé*," said Rowland gravely.

"I beg your pardon then for thinking so. Now I have an idea that you would make a useful friend—an intimate friend—a friend to whom one could tell everything. For such a friend what wouldn't I give !"

Rowland looked at her in some perplexity. Was this touching sincerity or unfathomable coquetry ? Her beautiful eyes looked divinely candid ; but then if candour was beautiful, beauty was apt to be subtle. "I hesitate to recommend myself out and out for the office," he said, "but I believe that if you were to depend upon me for anything that a friend may do I should not be found wanting."

"Very good. One of the first things one asks of a friend is to judge one not by isolated acts, but by one's whole conduct. I care for your opinion—I don't know why."

"Nor do I, I confess !" said Rowland, with a laugh.

"What do you think of this affair?" she continued, without heeding his laugh.

"Of your ball ? Why, it's a very grand affair."

"It's horrible—that's what it is! It's a mere rabble! There are people here whom I never saw before, people who were never asked. Mamma went about inviting every one, asking other people to invite any one they knew, doing anything to have a crowd. I hope she is satisfied ! It is not my doing. I feel weary, I feel angry, I feel like crying. I have twenty minds to escape into my room and lock the door, and let mamma go on with it as she can. By the way," she added in a moment, without a visible reason for the transition, "can you tell me something to read ?"

Rowland stared at the disconnectedness of the question.

"Can you recommend me some books?" she repeated. "I know you are a great reader. I have no one else to ask. We can buy no books. We can make debts for jewellery and bonnets and ten-button gloves, but we can't spend a sou for ideas. And yet, though you may not believe it, I like ideas quite as well."

"I shall be most happy to lend you some books," Rowland said. "I will pick some out to-morrow and send them to you."

"No novels, please! I am tired of novels. I can imagine better stories for myself than any I read. Some good poetry, if there is such a thing nowadays, and some memoirs and histories and books of facts."

"You shall be served. Your taste agrees with my own."

She was silent a moment, looking at him. Then suddenly —"Tell me something about Mr. Hudson," she exclaimed. "You are great friends!"

"Oh, yes," said Rowland; "we are great friends."

"Tell me about him. Come, begin!"

"Where shall I begin? You know him for yourself."

"No, I don't know him; I don't find him so easy to know. Since he has finished my bust and begun to come here disinterestedly, he has become a great talker. He says very fine things; but does he mean all he says?"

"Few of us do that."

"You do, I imagine. You ought to know, for he tells me you discovered him." Rowland was silent, and Christina continued, "Do you consider him very clever?"

"Unquestionably."

"His talent is really something out of the common way?"

"So it seems to me."

"In short, he is a man of genius?"

"Yes, call it genius."

"And you found him vegetating in a little village, and took him by the hand and set him on his feet in Rome?"

"Is that the popular legend?" asked Rowland.

"Oh, you needn't be modest. There was no great merit in it; there would have been none at least on my part in the same circumstances. Real geniuses are not so common, and if I had discovered one in the wilderness, I should have brought him out in the market-place to see how he would behave. It would be excessively amusing. You must find it so to watch Mr. Hudson, eh? Tell me this: do you think he is going to be a great man—become famous, have his life written and all that?"

"I don't prophesy, but I have good hopes."

Christina was silent. She stretched out her bare arm and looked at it a moment absently, turning it so as to see —or almost to see—the dimple in her elbow. This was apparently a frequent gesture with her; Rowland had already observed it. It was as coolly and naturally done as if she had been alone before her toilet-table. "So he is a man of genius," she suddenly resumed. "Don't you think I ought to be extremely flattered to have a man of genius perpetually hanging about? He is the first I ever saw, but I should have known he was not a common mortal. There is something strange about him. To begin with, he has no manners. You may say that it's not for me to blame him, for I have none myself. That's very true, but the difference is that I can have them when I wish to (and very charming ones too; I will show you some day); whereas Mr. Hudson will never have them. And yet somehow one sees he is a gentleman. He seems to have something urging, driving, pushing him, making him restless and defiant. You see it in his eyes. They are the finest, by the way, I ever saw. When a person has such eyes as that, you can forgive him his bad manners. I suppose that is what they call the sacred fire."

Rowland made no answer except to ask her in a moment if she would have another roll. She merely shook her head and went on—

"Tell me how you found him. Where was he—how was he?"

"He was in a place called Northampton. Did you ever hear of it? He was studying law—but not learning it."

"It appears it was something horrible, eh?"

"Something horrible?"

"This little village. No society, no pleasures, no beauty, no life."

"You have received a false impression. Northampton is not so gay as Rome, but Roderick had some charming friends."

" Tell me about them. Who were they ? "

" Well, there was my cousin, through whom I made his acquaintance—a delightful woman."

" Young—pretty ? "

" Yes, a good deal of both. And very clever."

" Did he make love to her ? "

" Not in the least."

" Well, who else ? "

" He lived with his mother. She is the best of women."

" Ah, yes, I know all that one's mother is. But she does not count as society. And who else ? "

Rowland hesitated. He wondered whether Christina's insistence were the result of a general interest in Roderick's antecedents or of a particular suspicion. He looked at her; she was looking at him a little askance, waiting for his answer. As Roderick had said nothing about his engagement to the Cavaliere, it was probable that with this beautiful girl he had not been more explicit. And yet the thing was announced, it was public; that other girl was happy in it, proud of it. Rowland felt a kind of dumb anger rising in his heart. He deliberated a moment intently.

" What are you frowning at ? " Christina asked.

" There was another person," he answered, " the most important of all—the young girl to whom he is engaged."

Christina stared a moment, raising her eyebrows. " Ah, Mr. Hudson is engaged ? " she said, very simply. " Is she pretty ? "

" She is not called a beauty." Rowland meant to practise great brevity, but in a moment he added, " I have seen beauties however who pleased me less."

" Ah, she pleases *you* too ? Why don't they marry ? "

" Roderick is waiting till he can afford to marry."

Christina slowly put out her arm again and looked at the dimple in her elbow. " Ah, he's engaged ? " she repeated in the same tone. " He never told me."

Rowland perceived at this moment that the people about them were beginning to return to the dancing-room, and immediately afterwards he saw Roderick making his way towards themselves. Roderick presented himself before Miss Light.

" I don't claim that you have promised me the cotillon,"
he said, " but I consider that you have given me hopes
which warrant the confidence that you will dance with
me."

Christina looked at him a moment. " Certainly I have
made no promises," she said. " It seemed to me that as
the daughter of the house, I should keep myself free, and
let it depend on circumstances."

" I beseech you to dance with me ! " said Roderick, with
vehemence.

Christina rose and began to laugh. " You say that very
well, but the Italians do it better."

This assertion seemed likely to be put to the proof.
Mrs. Light hastily approached, leading, rather than led
by, a tall slim young man, of an unmistakably Southern
physiognomy. " My precious love," she cried, " what a
place to hide in ! We have been looking for you for
twenty minutes; I have chosen a cavalier for you—and
chosen well ! "

The young man disengaged himself, made a ceremonious
bow, joined his two hands and murmured with an ecstatic
smile, " May I venture to hope, dear signorina, for the
honour of your hand ? "

" Of course you may ! " said Mrs. Light. " The honour
is for us ! "

Christina hesitated but for a moment, then swept the
young man a curtsey as profound as his own salutation.
" You are very kind, but you are too late. I have just
accepted ! "

" Ah, my own darling ! " murmured—almost moaned—
Mrs. Light.

Christina and Roderick exchanged a single glance—
a glance brilliant on each side. She passed her hand
into his arm; he tossed his clustering locks and led her
away.

A short time afterwards Rowland saw the young man
she had rejected leaning against a doorway. He was ugly,
but what is called distinguished-looking. He had a heavy
black eye, a sallow complexion, a long thin neck; his hair
was cropped *en brosse*. He looked very young, yet extremely bored. He was staring at the ceiling and stroking
an imperceptible moustache. Rowland espied the Cavaliere

Giacosa hard by, and having joined him asked him the young man's name.

"Oh," said the Cavaliere, "he is a *pezzo grosso!* A Neapolitan. Prince Casamassima."

XI.

ONE day on entering Roderick's lodging (not the modest rooms on the Ripetta which he had first occupied, but a much more sumptuous apartment on the Corso), Rowland found a letter on the table addressed to himself. It was from Roderick, and consisted of but three lines. "I am gone to Frascati—for meditation. If I am not at home on Friday you had better join me." On Friday he was still absent, and Rowland went out to Frascati. Here he found his friend living at the inn and spending his days according to his own account lying under the trees of the Villa Mondragone and reading Ariosto. He was in a sombre mood; "meditation" seemed not to have been fruitful. Nothing especially pertinent to our narrative had passed between the two young men since Mrs. Light's ball save a few words bearing on an incident of that entertainment. Rowland informed Roderick the next day that he had told Miss Light of his engagement. "I don't know whether you will thank me," he had said, "but it is my duty to let you know it. Miss Light perhaps has already done so."

Roderick looked at him a moment intently, with his colour slowly rising. "Why should I not thank you?" he asked. "I am not ashamed of my engagement."

"As you had not spoken of it yourself I thought you might have a reason for not having it known."

"A man doesn't gossip about such a matter with strangers," Roderick rejoined, with the ring of irritation in his voice.

"With strangers—no!" said Rowland smiling.

Roderick continued his work; but after a moment,

turning round with a frown—" If you supposed I had a reason for being silent, pray why should you have spoken ? "

"I did not speak idly, my dear Roderick. I weighed the matter before I spoke, and promised myself to let you know immediately afterwards. It seemed to me that Miss Light had better know that your affections are pledged."

"The Cavaliere then has put it into your head that I am making love to her ? "

"No ; in that case I should not have spoken to her first."

"Do you mean, then, that she is making love to me ? "

"This is what I mean," said Rowland after a pause. "That girl finds you interesting and she is pleased, even though she may feign indifference, at your finding her so. I said to myself that it might save her some sentimental disappointment to know without delay that you are not at liberty to become indefinitely interested in other women."

"You seem to have taken the measure of my liberty with extraordinary minuteness !" cried Roderick.

"You must do me justice. I am the cause of your separation from Miss Garland, the cause of your being exposed to temptations which she hardly even suspects. How could I ever meet her again," Rowland demanded with much warmth of tone, "if at the end of it all she should be unhappy ? "

"I had no idea that she had made such an impression on you ! You are too zealous. I take it she didn't charge you to look after her interests."

"If anything happens to you I am accountable. You must understand that."

"That's a view of the situation I can't accept; in your own interest no less than in mine ! It can only make us both very uncomfortable. I know all I owe you ; I feel it ; you know that ! But I am not a small boy nor an amiable simpleton any longer, and whatever I do I do with my eyes open. When I do well the 'merit's my own ; if I do ill the fault's my own ! The idea that I make you nervous is ridiculous. Dedicate your nerves to some better cause and believe that if Miss Garland and I have a quarrel we shall settle it between ourselves."

Rowland had found himself wondering shortly before
whether possibly his brilliant young friend were without
a conscience ; now it dimly occurred to him that he was
without a heart. Rowland as we have already intimated
was a man with a moral passion, and no small part of it
had gone forth into this adventure. There had been from
the first no protestations of friendship on either side, but
Rowland had implicitly offered everything that belongs to
friendship, and Roderick had apparently as deliberately
accepted it. Rowland indeed had taken an exquisite
satisfaction in his companion's easy inexpressive assent to
his interest in him. " Here is an uncommonly fine thing,"
he said to himself ; " a nature unconsciously grateful, a
man in whom friendship does the thing that love alone
generally has the credit of—knocks the bottom out of
pride ! " His reflective judgment of Roderick, as time
went on, had indulged in a great many irrepressible
vagaries ; but his affection, his sense of something in his
companion's whole personality that appealed to his
tenderness and charmed his imagination, had never for
an instant faltered. He listened to Roderick's last
words, and then smiled as he rarely smiled—with
bitterness.

" I don't at all like your telling me I am too zealous,"
he said. " If I had not been zealous I should never have
cared a fig for you ! "

Roderick flushed deeply and thrust his modelling tool
up to the handle into the clay. " Say it outright ! You
have been a great fool to believe in me."

" I don't desire to say it, and you don't honestly believe
I do ! " said Rowland. " It seems to me I am really very
good-natured even to reply to such nonsense."

Roderick sat down, crossed his arms and fixed his eyes
on the floor. Rowland looked at him for some moments ;
it seemed to him that he had never so clearly perceived
his strangely commingled character—his strength and his
weakness, his picturesque personal attractiveness and his
urgent egotism, his exalted ardour and his puerile petulance. It would have made him almost sick however to
think that on the whole Roderick was not a generous
fellow, and he was so far from having ceased to believe in
him that he felt just now more than ever that all this was

but the painful complexity of genius. Rowland, who had not a grain of genius either to make one say he was an interested reasoner or to enable one to feel that he could afford a dangerous theory or two, adhered to his conviction of the essential salubrity of genius. Suddenly he felt an irresistible pity for his companion; it seemed to him that his beautiful faculty of production was a double-edged instrument, susceptible of being dealt in back-handed blows at its possessor. Genius was priceless, inspired, divine; but it was also at its hours capricious, sinister, cruel; and men of genius accordingly were alternately very enviable and very helpless. It was not the first time he had had a sense of Roderick's standing passive in the clutch of his temperament. It had shaken him as yet but with a half good-humoured wantonness; but henceforth possibly it meant to handle him more roughly. These were not times therefore for a friend to have a short patience.

"When you err you say the fault's your own," he said at last. "It is because your faults are your own that I heed them."

Rowland's voice, when he spoke with feeling, had an extraordinary amenity. Roderick sat staring a moment longer at the floor, then he sprang up and laid his hand affectionately on his friend's shoulder. "You are the best man in the world," he said, "and I am a vile brute. Only," he added in a moment, "*you don't understand me!*" And he looked at him with eyes of such pure expressiveness that one might have said (and Rowland did almost say so himself) that it was the fault of one's own grossness if one failed to read to the bottom of that beautiful soul.

Rowland smiled sadly. "What is it now? Explain."

"Oh, I can't explain!" cried Roderick impatiently, returning to his work. "I have only one way of expressing my deepest feelings—it's this." And he swung his tool. He stood looking at the half wrought clay for a moment and then flung the instrument down. "And even this half the time plays me false!"

Rowland felt that his irritation had not subsided, and he himself had no taste for saying disagreeable things. Nevertheless he saw no sufficient reason to forbear uttering the words he had had on his conscience from

the beginning. "We must do what we can and be thankful," he said. "And let me assure you of this—that it
won't help you to become entangled with Miss Light."

Roderick pressed his hand to his forehead with vehemence
and then shook it in the air despairingly; a gesture that
had become frequent with him since he came to Italy. "No,
no, it's no use; you don't understand me! But I don't
blame you. You can't!"

"You think it *will* help you then?" said Rowland
wondering.

"I think that when you expect a man to produce beautiful and wonderful works of art you ought to allow him a
certain freedom of action, you ought to give him a long
rope, you ought to let him follow his fancy and look for
his material wherever he thinks he may find it! A mother
can't nurse her child unless she follows a certain diet; an
artist can't bring his visions to maturity unless he has
a certain experience. You demand of us to be imaginative,
and you deny us the things that feed the imagination. In
labour we must be as passionate as the inspired sibyl; in life
we must be mere machines. It won't do! When you have
got an artist to deal with, you must take him as he is,
good and bad together. I don't say they are pleasant
fellows to know, or easy fellows to live with; I don't say
they satisfy themselves any better than other people. I only
say that if you want them to produce you must let them
conceive. If you want a bird to sing, you must not cover
up its cage. Shoot them, the poor devils, drown them,
exterminate them, if you will, in the interest of public
morality; it may be morality would gain—I dare say it
would! But if you suffer them to live, let them live on
their own terms and according to their own inexorable
needs!"

Rowland burst out laughing. "I have no wish whatever
either to shoot you or to drown you!" he said. "Why
defend yourself with such very big guns against a warning
offered you altogether in the interest of your freest development? Do you really mean that you have an inexorable
need of embarking on a flirtation with Miss Light?—a
flirtation as to the felicity of which there may be differences of opinion, but which cannot at best, under the
circumstances, be called innocent. Your last summer's

adventures were more so! As for the terms on which you are to live, I had an idea you had arranged them otherwise!"

"I have arranged nothing—thank God! I don't pretend to arrange. I am young and ardent and inquisitive, and I am preoccupied with that girl. That's enough. I shall go as far as the fancy leads me. I am not afraid. Your genuine artist may be sometimes half a madman, but he's not acoward!"

"I see; it's a speculation. But suppose that in your speculation you should come to grief artistically as well as sentimentally?"

"Come what come will! If I'm to fizzle out, the sooner I know it the better. Sometimes I half suspect it. But let me at least go out and reconnoitre for the enemy, and not sit here waiting for him, cudgelling my brains for ideas that won't come!"

Do what he would, Rowland could not think of Roderick's theory of unlimited experimentation, especially as applied in the case under discussion, as anything but a pernicious illusion. But he saw it was vain to discuss the matter, for inclination was powerfully on Roderick's side. He laid his hand on the young man's shoulder, looked at him a moment with troubled eyes, then shook his head mournfully and turned away.

"I can't work any more," said Roderick. "You have upset me! I'll go and stroll on the Pincian." And he tossed aside his working-jacket and prepared himself for the street. As he was arranging his cravat before the glass, something occurred to him which made him thoughtful. He stopped a few moments afterwards as they were going out, with his hand on the door-knob. "You did from your own point of view an indiscreet thing," he said, "to tell Miss Light of my engagement."

Rowland looked at him with a glance which was partly an interrogation, but partly also an admission.

"If she's the coquette you say," Roderick added, "you have given her a reason the more!"

"And that's the girl you propose to devote yourself to?" cried Rowland.

"Oh, I don't say it, mind! I only say that she's the most interesting creature in the world! The next time you

mean to render me a service pray give me notice beforehand ! "

It was perfectly characteristic of Roderick that a fortnight later he should have let his friend know that he
depended upon him for society at Frascati as freely as if
no irritating topic had ever been discussed between them.
Rowland thought him generous, and he had at any rate
a liberal faculty of forgetting that he had given you any
reason to be displeased with him. It was equally characteristic of Rowland that he complied with his friend's
summons without a moment's hesitation. His cousin
Cecilia had once told him that he was the dupe of his
perverse benevolence. She put the case with too little
favour, or too much, as the reader chooses ; it is certain
at least that he had a constitutional tendency to magnanimous interpretations. Nothing happened however to
suggest to him that he was deluded in thinking that
Roderick's secondary impulses were wiser than his primary
ones, and that the rounded total of his nature had a harmony perfectly attuned to the most amiable of its brilliant
parts. Roderick's humour, for the time, was pitched in
a minor key ; he was lazy, listless, and melancholy, but
he had never been so softly submissive. Winter had
begun by the calendar, but the weather was divinely
mild, and the two young men took long slow strolls on
the hills and lounged away the mornings in the villas. The
villas at Frascati are delicious places and replete with
romantic suggestiveness. Roderick as he had said was
meditating, and if a masterpiece was to come of his meditations Rowland was perfectly willing to bear him company
and coax it along. But Roderick let him know from the
first that he was in a miserably sterile mood, and, cudgel
his brains as he would, could think of nothing that would
serve for the statue he was to make for Mr. Leavenworth.

" It is worse out here than in Rome," he said, " for here
I am face to face with the dead blank of my mind ! There
I couldn't think of anything either, but there I found
things to make me forget that I needed to think ! " This
was as frank an allusion to Christina Light as could have
been expected under the circumstances ; it seemed indeed
to Rowland surprisingly frank—a pregnant example of his
companion's strangely irresponsible way of looking at

harmful facts. Roderick was silent sometimes for hours,
with a puzzled look on his face and a constant fold between
his even eyebrows; at other times he talked unceasingly,
with a sort of impartial contemplative drawl. Rowland was
half a dozen times on the point of asking him what was
the matter with him; he was afraid he was going to be
ill. Roderick had taken a great fancy to the Villa Mondragone and used to declaim fantastic compliments to it as
they strolled in the winter sunshine on the great terrace
which looks towards Tivoli and the iridescent Sabine mountains. He carried his volume of Ariosto in his pocket, and
took it out every now and then to spout half a dozen stanzas
to his companion. He was as a general thing very little of
a reader; but at intervals he would take a fancy to one of
the classics and peruse it for a month in disjointed scraps.
He had picked up Italian without study, and had a wonderfully proper accent, though in reading aloud he ruined the
sense of half the lines he rolled off so sonorously. Rowland,
who pronounced badly but understood everything, once said
to him that Ariosto was not the poet for a man of his craft;
a sculptor should make a companion of Dante. So he lent
him the *Inferno*, which he had brought with him, and
advised him to look into it. Roderick took it with some
eagerness; perhaps it would brighten his wits. He returned it the next day with disgust; he had found it
intolerably depressing.

"A sculptor should model as Dante writes—you are
right there,' he said. "But when his genius is in eclipse
Dante is a dreadfully smoky lamp. By what perversity of
fate," he went on, "has it come about that I am a sculptor
at all? A sculptor is such a confoundedly special genius;
there are so few subjects he can treat, so few things in
life that bear upon his work, so few moods in which he
himself is inclined to it." (It may be noted that Rowland
had heard him a dozen times affirm the flat reverse of all
this.) "If I had only been a painter—a little, quiet, docile,
matter-of-fact painter like our friend Singleton—I should
only have to open my Ariosto here to find a subject, to
find colour and attitudes, stuffs and composition; I should
only have to look up from the page at that mouldy old
fountain against the blue sky, at that cypress alley wandering away like a procession of priests in couples, at the

crags and hollows of the Sabine hills, to find my picture begun ! Best of all would it be to be Ariosto himself or one of his brotherhood. Then everything in nature would give you a hint, and every form of beauty be part of your stock. You wouldn't have to look at things only to say— with tears of rage half the time—' Oh, yes, it's wonderfully pretty, but what the devil can I do with it ? ' But a sculptor now ! That's a pretty trade for a fellow who has got his living to make, and yet is so damnably constituted that he can't work to order, and considers that, æsthetically, clock ornaments don't pay ! You can't model the serge-coated cypresses, nor those mouldering old Tritons, and all the sunny sadness of that dried-up fountain ; you can't put the light into marble—the lovely caressing consenting Italian light that you get so much of for nothing ! Say that a dozen times in his life a man has a completely plastic vision—a vision in which the imagination recognises a subject and the subject reacts on the imagination. It is a remunerative rate of work, and the intervals are comfortable ! "

One morning as the two young men were lounging on the sun-warmed grass at the foot of one of the slanting pines of the Villa Mondragone, Roderick delivered himself of a tissue of lugubrious speculations as to the possible mischances of one's genius. " What if the watch should run down," he asked, "and you should lose the key ? What if you should wake up some morning and find it stopped—inexorably, appallingly stopped ? Such things have been, and the poor devils to whom they happened have had to grin and bear it. The whole matter of genius is a mystery. It bloweth where it listeth and we know nothing of its mechanism. If it gets out of order we can't mend it ; if it breaks down altogether we can t set it going again. We must let it choose its own pace and hold our breath lest it should lose its balance. It's dealt out in different doses, in big cups and little, and when you have consumed your portion it's as *naïf* to ask for more as it was for Oliver Twist to ask for more porridge. Lucky for you if you have got one of the big cups ; we drink them down in the dark, and we can't tell their size until we tip them up and hear the last gurgle. Those of some men last for life ; those of others for a couple of

years. Come, what are you grinning at ? " he went on.
" Nothing is more common than for an artist who has set
out on his journey on a high-stepping horse to find himself
all of a sudden dismounted and invited to go his way on
foot. You can number them by the thousand—the people
of two or three successes ; the poor fellows whose candle
burnt out in a night. Some of them groped their way
along without it, some of them gave themselves up for
blind and sat down by the wayside to beg. Who shall
say that I am not one of these ? Who shall assure me
that my credit is for an unlimited sum ? Nothing proves
it and I never claimed it ; or if I did, I did so in the mere
boyish joy of shaking off the dust of Northampton ! If
you believed so, my dear fellow, you did so at your own
risk ! What am I, what are the best of us, but an experiment ? Do I succeed—do I fail ? It doesn't depend on
me ! I am prepared for failure. It won't be a disappointment, simply because I sha'n't survive it. The end of my
work shall be the end of my life. When I have played
my last card, I shall cease to care for the game. I am not
making vulgar threats of suicide ; for destiny, I trust,
won't add insult to injury by putting me to that abomin-
able trouble. But I have a conviction that if the hour
strikes *here*," and he tapped his forehead, " I shall dis-
appear, dissolve, be carried off in a cloud ! For the past
ten days I have had the vision of some such fate perpetually swimming before my eyes. My mind is like a dead
calm in the tropics, and my imagination as motionless as
the phantom ship in the ' Ancient Mariner ' ! "

Rowland listened to this fine monologue, as he often had
occasion to listen to Roderick's flights of eloquence, with
a number of mental restrictions. Both in gravity and in
gaiety he said more than he meant, and you did him
simple justice if you privately concluded that neither the
glow of purpose nor the chill of despair was of so intense
a character as his copiousness of illustration implied. The
moods of an artist, his exultations and depressions, Rowland had often said to himself, were like the pen-flourishes
a writing master makes in the air when he begins to set
his copy. He may bespatter you with ink, he may hit you
in the eye, but he writes a magnificent hand. It was
nevertheless true that at present poor Roderick gave

unprecedented tokens of moral stagnation, and as for
genius being held by the precarious tenure he had sketched,
Rowland was at a loss to see where he could borrow the
authority to contradict him. He sighed to himself and
wished that his companion had a trifle more of little Sam
Singleton's vulgar steadiness. But then, was Sam Singleton a man of genius? He answered that such reflections
seemed to him unprofitable, not to say morbid; that the
proof of the pudding was in the eating; that he did not
know about bringing a dead genius back to life again, but
that he was satisfied that vigorous effort was a cure for a
great many ills that seemed far gone. "Don't bother about
your mood," he said, "and don't believe there is any calm
so dead that your own lungs can't ruffle it with a breeze.
If you have work to do, don't wait to feel like it; set to
work and you *will* feel like it."

"Set to work and produce abortions!" cried Roderick
with ire. "Preach that to others. Production with me
must be either pleasure or nothing. As I said just now,
I must either stay in the saddle or not go at all. I won't
do second-rate work; I can't if I would. I have no
cleverness apart from inspiration. I am not a Gloriani!
You are right," he added after a while; "this is unprofitable talk, and it makes my head ache. I shall take a nap
and see if I can dream of a bright idea or two."

XII.

HE turned his face upward to the parasol of the great
pine, closed his eyes, and in a short time forgot his sombre
fancies. January though it was, the mild stillness seemed
to vibrate with faint midsummer sounds. Rowland sat
listening to them and wishing that for the sake of their
common comfort Roderick's temper had been graced with
a certain absent ductility. He was brilliant, but was he,
like many brilliant things, brittle? Suddenly, to his
musing sense, the soft atmospheric hum was overscored

with distincter sounds. He heard voices beyond a mass of shrubbery, at the turn of a neighbouring path. In a moment one of them began to seem familiar, and an instant later a large white poodle emerged into view. He was slowly followed by his mistress. Miss Light paused a moment on seeing Rowland and his companion; but though the former perceived that he was recognised she gave no greeting. Presently she walked directly towards him. He rose and was on the point of waking Roderick, but she laid her finger on her lips and motioned him to forbear. She stood a moment looking at Roderick's handsome slumber.

"What delicious oblivion!" she said. "Happy man! Stenterello"—and she pointed to his face—"wake him up!"

The poodle extended a long pink tongue and began to lick Roderick's cheek.

"Why," asked Rowland, "if he is happy?"

"Oh, I want companions in misery! Besides, I want to show off my dog." Roderick roused himself, sat up and stared. By this time Mrs. Light had approached, walking with a gentleman on each side of her. One of these was the Cavaliere Giacosa; the other was Prince Casamassima. "I should have liked to lie down on the grass and go to sleep," Christina added. "But it would have been unheard of."

"Oh, not quite," said the Prince, in English, in a tone of great precision. "There was already a Sleeping Beauty in the Wood!"

"Charming!" cried Mrs. Light. "Do you hear that, my dear?"

"When the Prince says a brilliant thing it would be a pity to lose it," said the young girl. "Your servant, sir!" And she smiled at him with a grace that might have reassured him if he had thought her compliment ambiguous.

Roderick meanwhile had risen to his feet, and Mrs. Light began to exclaim on the oddity of their meeting, and to explain that the day was so lovely that she had been charmed with the idea of spending it in the country. And who would ever have thought of finding Mr. Mallet and Mr. Hudson sleeping under a tree?

"Oh, I beg your pardon; I was not sleeping," said
Rowland.

"Don't you know that Mr. Mallet is Mr. Hudson's
sheep-dog?" asked Christina. "He was mounting guard
to keep away the wolves."

"To indifferent purpose, madam!" said Rowland,
indicating the young girl.

"Is that the way you spend your time?" Christina
demanded of Roderick. "I never yet happened to learn
what men were doing when they supposed women were not
watching them but it was something vastly below their
reputation."

"When, pray," said Roderick, smoothing his ruffled locks,
"are women not watching them?"

"We shall give you something better to do at any rate.
How long have you been here? It's an age since I have
seen you. We consider you an old inhabitant, and expect
you to play host and entertain us."

Roderick said that he could offer them nothing
but to show them the great terrace and its view; and
ten minutes later the little group was assembled there.
Mrs. Light was extravagant in her satisfaction; Christina
looked away at the Sabine mountains in silence. The
Prince stood by, frowning at the raptures of the elder
lady.

"This is nothing," he said at last. "My word of honour.
Have you seen the terrace at San Gaetano?"

"Ah, that terrace," murmured Mrs. Light, amorously.
"I suppose it is magnificent!"

"It is four hundred feet long, and paved with marble.
And the view is a thousand times more beautiful than this.
You see far away the blue, blue sea, and the little smoke of
Vesuvio!"

"Christina love," cried Mrs. Light forthwith, "the
Prince has a terrace four hundred feet long, all paved
with marble!"

The Cavaliere gave a little cough and began to wipe his
eye-glass.

"Stupendous!" said Christina. "To go from one end
to the other the Prince must have out his golden carriage."
This was apparently an allusion to one of the other items
of the young man's grandeur.

"You always laugh at me," said the Prince. "I know no more what to say!"

She looked at him with a sad smile and shook her head. "No, no, dear Prince, I don't laugh at you. Heaven forbid! You are much too serious an affair. I assure you I feel your importance. What did you inform us was the value of the hereditary diamonds of the Princess Casamassima?"

"Ah, you are laughing at me yet!" said the poor young man, standing rigid and pale.

"It does not matter," Christina went on. "We have a note of it; mamma writes all those things down in a little book!"

"If you are laughed at, dear Prince, at least it's in company," said Mrs. Light caressingly; and she took his arm, as if to combat his possible displacement under the shock of her daughter's sarcasm. But the Prince looked heavy-eyed at Rowland and Roderick, to whom the young girl was turning, as if he had much rather his lot were cast with theirs.

"Is the villa inhabited?" Christina asked, pointing to the vast melancholy structure which rises above the terrace.

"Not privately," said Roderick. "It is occupied by a Jesuits' college for little boys."

"Can women go in?"

"I am afraid not." And Roderick began to laugh. "Fancy the poor little devils looking up from their Latin declensions and seeing Miss Light shining down on them!"

"I should like to see the poor little devils, with their rosy cheeks, and their long black gowns, and when they were pretty I shouldn't scruple to kiss them. But if I can't have that amusement I must have some other. We must not stand planted on this enchanting terrace as if we were stakes driven into the earth. We must dance, we must feast, we must do something picturesque. Mamma has arranged I believe that we are to go back to Frascati to lunch at the inn. I decree that we lunch here and send the Cavaliere to the inn to get the provisions! He can take the carriage, which is waiting below."

Miss Light carried out this programme with unfaltering

ardour. The Cavaliere was summoned, and he stood to
receive her commands hat in hand, with his eyes cast down,
as if she had been a princess addressing her major-domo.
She however laid her hand with friendly grace upon his
button-hole and called him a dear good old Cavaliere for
being always so obliging. Her spirits had risen with the
occasion and she talked irresistible nonsense. " Bring the
best they have," she said, " no matter if it ruins us ! And
if the best is very bad it will be all the more amusing. I
shall enjoy seeing Mr. Mallet try to swallow it for propriety's sake ! Mr. Hudson will say out like a man that
it's horrible stuff and that he'll be choked first ! Be sure
you bring a dish of maccaroni ; the Prince must have the
diet of the Neapolitan nobility. But I leave all that to
you, my poor dear Cavaliere ; you know what's good !
Only be sure above all you bring a guitar. Mr. Mallet
will play us a tune, I will dance with Mr. Hudson, and
mamma will pair off with the Prince, of whom she is so
fond ! "

And as she concluded her recommendations, she patted
her discreet old servitor tenderly on the shoulder. He
looked askance at Rowland ; his little black eye glittered ;
it seemed to say, " Didn't I tell you she was a good
girl ? "

The Cavaliere returned with zealous speed, accompanied
by one of the servants of the inn, laden with a basket
containing the materials of a rustic luncheon. The porter
of the villa was easily induced to furnish a table and half
a dozen chairs, and the repast when set forth was pronounced a perfect success ; not so good as to fail of the
proper picturesqueness, nor yet so bad as to defeat the
proper function of repasts. Christina continued to display
the most charming animation, and compelled Rowland to
reflect privately that, think what one might of her, the
harmonious gaiety of a beautiful girl was the most delightful sight in nature. Her good-humour was contagious.
Roderick, who an hour before had been descanting on madness and suicide, commingled his laughter with her lightest
sallies ; Prince Casamassima stroked his young moustache
and found a fine cool smile for everything ; his neighbour
Mrs. Light, who had Rowland on the other side, made
the friendliest confidences to each of the young men, and

the Cavaliere contributed to the general hilarity by the solemnity of his attention to his plate. As for Rowland, the spirit of kindly mirth prompted him to propose the health of this useful old gentleman. A moment later he wished he had held his tongue, for although the toast was drunk with demonstrative good-will, the Cavaliere received it with various small signs of eager self-effacement which suggested to Rowland that his diminished gentility but half relished honours which had a flavour of patronage. To perform punctiliously his mysterious duties towards the two ladies, and to elude or to baffle observation on his own merits—this seemed the Cavaliere's modest programme. Rowland perceived that Mrs. Light, who was not always remarkable for tact, seemed to have divined his humour on this point. She touched her lips with her glass, but she said nothing gracious, and she immediately gave another direction to the conversation. The old man had brought no guitar, so that when the feast was over there was nothing to hold the little group together. Christina wandered away with Roderick to another part of the terrace; the Prince, whose smile had vanished, sat gnawing the head of his cane, near Mrs. Light, and Rowland strolled apart with the Cavaliere, to whom he wished to address a friendly word in compensation for the discomfort he had inflicted on his modesty. The Cavaliere was a mine of information upon all Roman places and people; he told Rowland a number of curious anecdotes about the old Villa Mondragone. "If history could always be taught in this fashion!" thought Rowland. "It's the ideal—strolling up and down on the very spot commemorated, hearing out-of-the-way anecdotes from deeply indigenous lips." At last, as they passed, Rowland observed the mournful physiognomy of Prince Casamassima, and glancing towards the other end of the terrace saw that Roderick and Christina had disappeared from view. The young man was sitting upright in an attitude, apparently habitual, of ceremonious rigidity; but his lower jaw had fallen and was propped up with his cane, and his dull dark eye was fixed upon the angle of the villa which had just eclipsed Miss Light and her companion. His features were grotesque and his expression was vacuous; but there was a lurking delicacy in his face which seemed to tell you that nature had been making

Casamassimas for a great many centuries, and, though she adapted her mould to circumstances, had learned to mix her material to an extraordinary fineness and to perform the whole operation with extreme smoothness. The Prince was stupid, Rowland suspected, but he imagined he was amiable, and he saw that at any rate he had the great quality of regarding himself in a thoroughly serious light. Rowland touched his companion's arm and pointed to the melancholy nobleman.

"Why in the world does he not go after her and insist on being noticed?" he asked.

"Oh, he's very proud!" said the Cavaliere.

"That's all very well, but a gentleman who cultivates a passion for that young lady must be prepared to make sacrifices."

"He thinks he has already made a great many. He comes of a very great family—a race of princes who for six hundred years have married none but the daughters of princes. But he is seriously in love and he would marry her to-morrow."

"And she will not have him?"

"Ah, she is very proud too!" The Cavaliere was silent a moment, as if he were measuring the propriety of frankness. He seemed to have formed a high opinion of Rowland's discretion, for he presently continued—"It would be a great match, for she brings him neither a name nor a fortune—nothing but her beauty. But the signorina will receive no favours; I know her well! She would rather have her beauty blasted than seem to care about the marriage, and if she ever accepts the Prince it will be only after he has implored her on his knees!"

"But she does care about it," said Rowland, "and to bring him to his knees she is working upon his jealousy by pretending to be interested in my friend Hudson. If you said more, you would say that, eh?"

The Cavaliere's shrewdness exchanged a glance with Rowland's. "By no means. Christina is a singular girl; she has many romantic ideas. She would be quite capable of interesting herself seriously in a remarkable young man like your friend, and doing her utmost to discourage a splendid suitor like the Prince. She would act sincerely and she would go very far. But it would be unfortunate

for the remarkable young man," he added, after a pause,
"for at the last she would go back!"

"A singular girl indeed!"

"She would accept the more brilliant *parti*. I can
answer for it."

"And what would be her motive?"

"She would be forced. There would be circumstances
. . . . I can't tell you more."

"But this implies that the rejected suitor would come
back to her. He might grow tired of waiting."

"Oh, this one is good! Look at him now." Rowland
looked, and saw that the Prince had left his place by Mrs.
Light and was marching restlessly to and fro between the
villa and the parapet of the terrace. Every now and then
he looked at his watch. "In this country, you know," said
the Cavaliere, "a young lady never goes walking alone with
a handsome young man. It seems to him very strange."

"It must seem to him monstrous, and if he overlooks
it he must be very much in love."

"Oh, he will overlook it. He is far gone."

"Who is this exemplary lover then; what is he?"

"A Neapolitan; one of the oldest houses in Italy. He
is a prince in your English sense of the word, for he has
a princely fortune. He is very young; he is only just of
age; he saw the signorina last winter in Naples. He fell
in love with her from the first, but his family interfered,
and an old uncle, an ecclesiastic, Monsignor B——, hurried
up to Naples, seized him and locked him up. Meantime
he has passed his majority and he can dispose of himself.
His relations are moving heaven and earth to prevent his
marrying Miss Light, and they have sent us word that he
forfeits his property if he takes his wife out of a certain
line. I have investigated the question, and I find this is
but a fiction to frighten us. He is perfectly free; but the
estates are such that it is no wonder they wish to keep
them in their own hands. For Italy, it is an extraordinary
case of unincumbered property. The Prince has been an
orphan from his third year; he has therefore had a long
minority and made no inroads upon his fortune. Besides,
he is very prudent and orderly; I am only afraid that
some day he will pull the purse-strings too tight. All
these years his affairs have been in the hands of Monsignor

B——, who has managed them to perfection—paid off mortgages, planted forests, opened up mines. It is now a magnificent fortune ; such a fortune as with his name would justify the young man in pretending to any alliance whatsoever. And he lays it all at the feet of that young girl who is wandering in yonder *boschetto* with a penniless artist."

"He is certainly a phœnix of princes ! The signora must be in a state of bliss."

The Cavaliere looked imperturbably grave. "The signora has a high esteem for his character."

"His character, by the way," rejoined Rowland, with a smile ; "what sort of a character is it ? "

"Eh, Prince Casamassima is a veritable prince ! He is a very good young man. He is not brilliant nor witty, but he will not let himself be made a fool of. He is a faithful son of the Church—though he does propose to marry a Protestant. He will handle that point after marriage. He's as you see him there : a young man without many ideas, but with a very firm grasp of a single one—the conviction that Prince Casamassima is a very great person, that he greatly honours any young lady by asking for her hand, and that things are going very strangely when the young lady turns her back upon him. The poor young man is terribly puzzled. But I whisper to him every day, ' Pazienza, Signor Principe ! ' "

"So you firmly believe," said Rowland, in conclusion, "that Miss Light will accept him just in time not to lose him ? "

"I count upon it. She would make too perfect a princess to miss her destiny."

"And you hold that nevertheless in the meanwhile in listening to, say, my friend Hudson, she will have been acting in good faith ? "

The Cavaliere lifted his shoulders a trifle, and gave an inscrutable smile. "Eh, dear signore, the Christina is very romantic ! "

"So much so, you intimate, that she will eventually pivot round in consequence not of a change of sentiment, but of a mysterious outward pressure ? "

"If everything else fails, there is that resource. But it is mysterious, as you say, and you needn't try to guess it. You will never know."

"The poor signorina then will suffer ! "

" Not too much, I hope."

" And the remarkable young man ? You maintain that there is nothing but disappointment in store for the infatuated youth who loses his heart to her."

The Cavaliere hesitated. " He had better," he said in a moment, " go and pursue his studies in Florence. There are very fine antiques in the Uffizi ! "

Rowland presently joined Mrs. Light, to whom her restless *protégé* had not yet returned. " That's right," she said ; " sit down here ; I have something serious to say to you. I am going to talk to you as a friend. I want your assistance. In fact, you *must* help me ; it's your duty. Look at that unhappy young man."

" Yes," said Rowland, " he seems unhappy."

" He is just come of age, he bears one of the greatest names in Italy, and owns one of the greatest properties, and he is pining away with love for my daughter."

" So the Cavaliere tells me."

" The Cavaliere shouldn't gossip," said Mrs. Light dryly. " Such information should come from me. The Prince is pining, as I say ; he's consumed, he's devoured. It's a real Italian passion ; I know what that means ! " And the lady gave a speaking glance, which seemed to coquet for a moment with retrospect. " Meanwhile, if you please, my daughter is hiding in the woods with your dear friend Mr. Hudson. I could cry with rage ! "

" If things are as bad as that," said Rowland, " it seems to me that you should find nothing easier than to despatch the Cavalier to bring the guilty couple back."

" Never in the world ! My hands are tied. Do you know what Christina would do ? She would tell the Cavaliere to go about his business—Heaven forgive her !—and send me word that if she had a mind to she would walk in the woods till midnight. Fancy the Cavaliere coming back and delivering such a message as that before the Prince ! Think of a girl wantonly making light of such a chance as hers ! He would marry her to-morrow at six o'clock in the morning."

" It is certainly very sad," said Rowland.

" That costs you little to say ! If you had left your precious young meddler to vegetate in his native village you would have saved me a world of bother ! "

"Ah, you marched into the jaws of danger," said Rowland. "You came and knocked at poor Hudson's door."

"In an evil hour! I wish to Heaven you would talk with him."

"I have done my best."

"I wish then you would take him away. You have plenty of money. Do me a favour. Take him to travel. Go to the East—go to Timbuctoo. Then, when Christina is Princess Casamassima," Mrs. Light added in a moment, "he may come back if he chooses!"

"Does she really care for him?" Rowland asked, abruptly.

"She thinks she does, possibly. She is a living riddle. She must needs follow out every idea that comes into her head. Fortunately most of them don't last long; but this one may last long enough to give the Prince a fit of disgust. If that were to happen, I don't know what I should do! I should be the most miserable of women. It would be too cruel, after all I have suffered to make her what she is, to see the labour of years blighted by a caprice. For I can assure you, sir," Mrs. Light went on, "that if my daughter is the greatest beauty in the world some of the credit is mine."

Rowland promptly remarked that this was obvious. He saw that the lady's irritated nerves demanded comfort from flattering reminiscence, and he assumed designedly the attitude of a zealous auditor. She began to tell the story of her efforts, her hopes, her dreams, her presentiments, her disappointments, in this exalted cause of catching a great husband for her daughter. It was a wonderful rigmarole of strange confidences, and while it went on the Prince continued to pass to and fro, stiffly and solemnly, like a pendulum marking the time allowed for the young lady to come to her senses. Mrs. Light evidently, at an early period had gathered her maternal hopes into a sacred parcel, to which she said her prayers and burnt incense—which she treated generally as a sort of fetish. These things had been her religion; she had none other, and she performed her devotions bravely and cheerily, in the light of day. The poor old fetish had been so caressed and manipulated, so thrust in and out of its niche, so passed from hand to hand, so dressed and undressed, so mumbled and fumbled over, that it had lost by this time much of its early freshness, and seemed a rather battered and disfeatured divinity. But it was still brought forth in moments of trouble, to have its tinselled petticoat twisted about and be set up on its altar. Rowland observed that Mrs. Light had a real maternal conscience; she considered that she had been performing a pious duty in bringing up Christina to set her cap for a prince; and when the future looked dark she found consolation in thinking that destiny could never have the heart to deal a blow at so deserving a person. This conscience upside down presented to Rowland's fancy a sort of physical image; he was on the point half a dozen times of laughing out.

"I don't know whether you believe in presentiments," said Mrs. Light, "and I don't care! I have had one for the last fifteen years. People have laughed at it, but they have not laughed me out of it. It has been everything to me; I couldn't have lived without it. One must believe in something! It came to me in a flash, when Christina was five years old. I remember the day and the place, as if it were yesterday. She was a very ugly baby; for the first two years I could hardly bear to look at her, and I used to spoil my own looks with crying about her. She had an Italian nurse who was very fond of her, and insisted that she would grow up pretty. I couldn't believe her, I used to contradict her, and we were for ever squabbling. I was just a little silly in those days—surely I may say it now—and I was very fond of being amused. If my daughter was ugly, it was not that she resembled her mamma; I had no lack of amusement. People accused me, I believe, of neglecting my little girl; if I ever did I have made up for it since. One day I went to drive on the Pincio—I was in very low spirits. A certain person —I needn't name him—had trifled with my generous confidence. While I was there he passed me in a carriage, driving with a horrible woman who had made trouble between us. I got out of my carriage to walk about, and at last sat down on a bench. I can show you the spot at this hour. While I sat there a child came wandering along the path—a little girl of four or five, very

fantastically dressed, in all the colours of the rainbow.
She stopped in front of me and stared at me, and I
stared at her queer little dress, which was a cheap imitation of the costume of one of these *contadine*. At last I
looked up at her face and said to myself, 'Bless me, what
a beautiful child! what a splendid pair of eyes, what a
magnificent head of hair! If my poor little Christina
were only like that!' The child turned away slowly,
but looking back with its eyes fixed on me. All of a
sudden I gave a cry, pounced on it, pressed it in my
arms, covered it with kisses. It *was* Christina, my
own precious child, so disguised by the ridiculous dress
which the nurse had amused herself in making for her,
that her own mother had not recognised her! She knew
me, but she said afterwards that she had not spoken to me
because I looked so angry. Of course, my face was sad!
I rushed with my child to the carriage, drove home post-
haste, pulled off her rags, and, as I may say, wrapped her
up in cotton. I had been blind, I had been insane; she
was a creature in ten millions, she was to be a beauty of
beauties, a priceless treasure! Every day, after that, the
certainty grew. From that time I lived only for my
daughter. I watched her, I fondled her from morning
till night, I worshipped her. I went to see doctors about
her, I took every sort of advice. I was determined she
should be perfection. The things that have been done for
that girl, sir—you wouldn't believe them; they would
make you smile! Nothing was spared; if I had been
told that she must have a bath every morning of molten
pearls I would have found means to give it to her. She
never raised a finger for herself, she breathed nothing but
perfumes, she walked upon velvet. She never was out of
my sight, and from that day to this I have never said a
sharp word to her. By the time she was ten years old
she was beautiful as an angel, and so noticed, wherever we
went, that I had to make her wear a veil like a woman of
twenty. Her hair reached down to her feet; her hands
were the hands of an empress. Then I saw that she was
as clever as she was beautiful, and that she had only to
play her cards. She had masters, professors, every educa-
tional advantage. They told me she was a little prodigy.
She speaks French, Italian, German, better than most

natives. She has a wonderful genius for music, and might make her fortune as a pianist if it were not made for her otherwise! I travelled all over Europe, every one told me she was a marvel. The director of the opera in Paris saw her dance at a child's party at Spa, and offered me an enormous sum if I would give her up to him and let him have her educated for the ballet. I said, 'No, I thank you, sir; she is meant to be something finer than a *princesse de théâtre*.' I had a passionate belief that she might marry absolutely whom she chose, that she might be a princess out and out. I have never given it up, and I can assure you that it has sustained me in many embarrassments. Financial, some of them; I don't mind confessing it! I have raised money on that girl's face! I have taken her to the Jews and bidden her put up her veil, and asked if the mother of that young lady was not safe! She, of course, was too young to understand me. And yet, as a child, you would have said she knew what was in store for her; before she could read she had the manners, the tastes, the instincts of a little aristocrat. She would have nothing to do with shabby things or shabby people; if she stained one of her frocks she was seized with a kind of frenzy—she would tear it to pieces. At Nice, at Baden, at Brighton, wherever we stayed, she used to be sent for by all the great people to play with their children. She has played at kissing-games with people who now stand on the steps of thrones! I have gone so far as to think at times that those childish kisses were a sign—a symbol—a pledge! You may laugh at me if you like, but haven't such things happened again and again without half so good a cause, and doesn't history notoriously repeat itself? There was a little Spanish girl at a second-rate English boarding-school thirty years ago! . . . . The Empress certainly is a pretty woman; but what is my Christina, pray? I have dreamt of it sometimes, every night for a month. I won't tell you I have been to consult those old women who advertise in the newspapers; you'll call me an old imbecile. Imbecile, if you please! I have refused magnificent offers because I believed that somehow or other—if wars and revolutions were needed to bring it about—we should have nothing less than *that*. There might be another *coup d'état* somewhere, and another brilliant young sovereign looking out for a wife! At last, however," Mrs. Light proceeded with incomparable gravity, "since the overturning of the poor king of Naples and that charming queen, and the expulsion of all those dear little old-fashioned Italian grand-dukes, and the dreadful radical talk that is going on all over the world, it has come to seem to me that with Christina in such a position I should be really very nervous. Even in such a position she would hold her head very high, and if anything should happen to her she would make no concessions to the popular fury. The best thing, if one would be prudent, seems to be a nobleman of the highest possible rank short of belonging to a reigning stock. There you see one striding up and down looking at his watch and counting the minutes till my daughter reappears!"

Rowland listened to all this with a large compassion for the heroine of the tale. What an education, what a history, what a school of character and of morals! He looked at the Prince and wondered whether he too had heard Mrs. Light's story. If he had he was a brave man. "I certainly hope you will nail him," he said to Mrs. Light. "You have played a dangerous game with your daughter; it would be a pity not to win! But there is hope for you yet; here she comes at last!

Christina reappeared as he spoke these words, strolling beside her companion with the same indifferent tread with which she had departed. Roderick imagined that there was a faint pink flush in her cheek which she had not carried away with her, and there was certainly a light in Roderick's eyes which he had not seen there for a week.

"Bless my soul, how they are all looking at us!" she cried as they advanced. "One would think we were prisoners of the Inquisition!" And she paused and glanced from the Prince to her mother, and from Rowland to the Cavaliere, and then threw back her head and burst into far-ringing laughter. "What is it pray? Have I been very improper? Am I ruined for ever? Dear Prince, you are looking at me as if I had committed the unpardonable sin!"

"I myself," said the Prince, "would never have ventured to ask you to walk with me alone in the country for an hour!"

"The more fool you, dear Prince, as the vulgar say! Our walk has been charming. I hope you, on your side, have enjoyed each other's society."

"My dear daughter," said Mrs. Light, taking the arm of her predestined son-in-law, "I shall have something serious to say to you when we reach home. We will go back to the carriage."

"Something serious! Decidedly, it *is* the Inquisition. Mr. Hudson, stand firm, and let us agree to make no confessions without conferring previously with each other! They may put us on the rack first. Mr. Mallet I see also," Christina added, "has something serious to say to me!"

Rowland had been looking at her with the shadow of his lately-stirred pity in his eyes. "Possibly," he said. "But it must be for some other time."

"I am at your service. I see our good humour is gone. And I only wanted to be amiable! It is very discouraging. Cavaliere, you alone look as if you had a little of the milk of human kindness left; from your dear old stupid face, at least, there is no telling what you think. Give me your arm and take me away!"

The party took its course back to the carriage, which was waiting in the grounds of the villa, and Rowland and Roderick bade their friends farewell. Christina threw herself back in her seat and closed her eyes; a manœuvre for which Rowland imagined the Prince was grateful, as it enabled him to look at her without seeming to depart from his attitude of distinguished disapproval.

Rowland found himself aroused from sleep early the next morning, to see Roderick standing before him, dressed for departure, with his bag in his hand. "I am off," he said. "I am back to work. I have an idea. I must strike while the iron is hot! Farewell!" And he departed by the first train. Rowland went alone by the next.

XIII.

ROWLAND went very often to the Coliseum; he was never tired of inspecting this monument. One morning about a month after his return from Frascati, as he was strolling across the vast arena, he observed a young woman seated on one of the fragments of stone which are ranged along the line of the ancient parapet. It seemed to him that he had seen her before, but he was unable to localise her face. Passing her again he perceived that one of the little red-legged French soldiers who were at that time on guard there had approached her and was gallantly making himself agreeable. She smiled brilliantly, and Rowland recognised the smile (it had always pleased him) of a certain comely Assunta who sometimes opened the door for Mrs. Light's visitors. He wondered what she was doing alone in the Coliseum, and conjectured that Assunta had admirers as well as her young mistress, but that being without the same domiciliary conveniences she was using this massive heritage of her Latin ancestors as a boudoir. In other words, she had an appointment with her lover, who would do well from present appearances to be punctual. It was a long time since Rowland had ascended to the ruinous upper tiers of the great circus, and as the day was radiant and the distant views promised to be particularly clear he determined to give himself this pleasure. The custodian unlocked the great wooden wicket, and he climbed through the winding shafts where the eager Roman crowds had billowed and trampled, not pausing till he reached the highest accessible point of the ruin. The views were as fine as he had supposed; the lights on the Sabine mountains had never been more lovely. He gazed to his satisfaction and retraced his steps. In a moment he paused again on an abutment somewhat lower, from which the glance dropped dizzily into the interior. There are accidents of ruggedness in the upper portions of the Coliseum which offer a very fair imitation of the mighty excrescences in the face of an Alpine cliff. In those days a multitude of delicate flowers and sprays of wild herbage had found a friendly soil in the hoary crevices, and they bloomed and nodded amid the antique masonry as naturally as if it were the boulders of a mountain. Rowland was turning away when he heard a sound of voices rising up from below. He had but to step slightly forward to find himself overlooking two persons who had seated themselves on a narrow ledge in a sunny corner. They had apparently an eye to extreme privacy, but they had not observed that their position was commanded by the abutment on which Rowland stood. One of these airy adventurers was a lady, thickly veiled, so that even if he had not been placed directly above her Rowland could not have seen her face. The other was a young man whose face was also invisible, but who presently gave a toss of his clustering locks which was equivalent to a master's signature. A moment's reflection satisfied him of the identity of the lady. He had been unjust to poor Assunta, sitting patient in the gloomy arena ; she had not come on her own errand. Rowland's discoveries made him hesitate. Should he retire as noiselessly as possible, or should he call out a friendly good morning ? While he was debating the question he found himself hearing his friend's words. They were of such a nature as to make him unwilling to retreat, and yet to make it awkward to be discovered in a position where it would be apparent that he had been an auditor.

"If what you say is true," said Christina, with her usual soft deliberateness—it made her words rise with peculiar distinctness to Rowland's ear—"you are simply weak. I am sorry ! I hoped—I really believed—you were not."

"No, I am not weak," answered Roderick with vehemence ; "I maintain that I am not weak ! I am incomplete perhaps ; but I can't help that. Weakness is a man's own fault ! "

"Incomplete then !" said Christina with a laugh. "It's the same thing, so long as it keeps you from splendid achievement. Is it written then that I shall really never know what I have so often dreamed of ? "

"What have you dreamed of ? "

"A man whom I can perfectly respect," cried the young girl with a sudden flame. "A man whom I can unrestrictedly admire ! I meet one, as I have met more

than one before, whom I fondly believe to be cast in a
larger mould than most of the vulgar human breed—to be
large in character, great in talent, strong in will ! In such
a man as that, I say, one's weary imagination at last may
rest ; or it may wander if it will, yet never need to wander
far from the deeps where one's heart is anchored. When I
first knew you I gave no sign, but you had struck me. I
observed you as women observe, and I fancied you had the
sacred fire."

"Before Heaven I believe I have ! " cried Roderick.

"Ah, but so little ! It flickers and trembles and
sputters ; it goes out, you tell me, for whole weeks together. From your own account it's highly probable that
you are a failure."

"I say those things sometimes myself, but when I hear
you say them they make me feel as if I could do all sorts
of great things."

"Ah, the man who is strong with what I call strength,"
Christina replied, "would neither rise nor fall by anything
I could say ! I am a poor weak woman ; I have no strength
myself, and I can give no strength. I am a miserable
medley of vanity and folly. I am silly, I am ignorant,
I am affected, I am false. . I am the fruit of a horrible
education sown on a worthless soil. I am all that, and yet
I believe I have one merit ! I should know a great
character when I saw it, and I should delight in it with a
generosity which would do something towards the remission
of my sins. For a man who should really give me a certain
feeling—I have never had it, but I should know it when it
came—I would send Prince Casamassima and his millions
to perdition. I don't know what you think of me for
saying all this ; I suppose we have not climbed up here
under the skies to play propriety. Why have you been at
such pains to assure me after all that you are a little man
and not a great one, a weak one and not a strong ? I
innocently imagined that your eyes declared you were
strong. But your voice condemns you ; I always wondered
at it ; it's not the voice of a conqueror ! "

"Give me something to conquer," cried Roderick, "and
when I say that I thank you from my soul, my voice,
whatever you think of it, shall speak the truth ! "

Christina for a moment said nothing. Rowland was too

interested to think of moving. "You pretend to such devotion," she went on, "and yet I am sure you have never really chosen between me and that person in America."

"Do me the favour not to speak of her," said Roderick imploringly.

"Why not? I say no ill of her, and I think all kinds of good. I am certain she is a far better girl than I, and far more likely to make you happy."

"This is happiness, this present palpable moment," said Roderick; "though you *have* such a genius for saying the things that torture me!"

"It's greater happiness than you deserve then! You have never chosen, I say; you have been afraid to choose. You have never really looked in the face the fact that you are false, that you have broken your faith. You have never looked at it and seen that it was hideous, and yet said, 'No matter, I will brave the penalty, I will bear the shame!' You have closed your eyes; you have tried to stifle remembrance, to persuade yourself that you were not behaving so badly as you seemed to be, that there would be some way after all of doing what you liked and yet escaping trouble. You have faltered and drifted, you have gone on from accident to accident, and I am sure that at this present moment you can't tell what it is you really desire!"

Roderick was sitting with his knees drawn up and bent, and his hands clasped round his legs. He bent his head and rested his forehead on his knees.

Christina went on with a sort of infernal calmness. "I believe that really you don't greatly care for your friend in America any more than you do for me! You are one of the men who care only for themselves and for what they can make of themselves. That's very well when they can make something great, and I could interest myself in a man of extraordinary power who should wish to turn all his passions to account. But if the power should turn out to be after all rather ordinary? Fancy feeling one's self ground in the mill of a third-rate talent! If you have doubts about yourself I can't reassure you; I have too many doubts myself about everything in this weary world. You have gone up like a rocket in your profession they

tell me ; are you going to come down like the stick ? I
don't pretend to know ; I repeat frankly what I have
said before—that all modern sculpture seems to me vulgar,
and that the only things I care for are some of the most
battered of the antiques of the Vatican. No, no, I can't
reassure you ; and when you tell me—with a confidence
in my discretion of which certainly I am duly sensible—
that at times you feel terribly small, why, I can only
answer, ' Ah then, my poor friend, I am afraid you are
small ! ' The language I should like to hear, from
a certain person, would be the language of absolute
decision."

Roderick raised his head, but he said nothing ; he
seemed to be exchanging a long glance with his companion.
The result of it was to make him fling himself back with
an inarticulate murmur. Rowland, admonished by the
silence, was on the point of turning away, but he was
arrested by a gesture of the young girl. She pointed
for a moment into the blue air. Roderick followed the
direction of her gesture.

" Is that little flower we see outlined against that dark
niche," she asked, "as intensely blue as it looks through
my veil ? " She spoke apparently with the amiable
design of directing the conversation into a less painful
channel.

Rowland, from where he stood, could see the flower she
meant—a delicate plant of radiant hue, which sprouted
from the top of an immense fragment of wall some twenty
feet from Christina's place.

Roderick turned his head and looked at it without
answering. At last glancing round, " Put up your veil ! "
he said. Christina complied. " Does it look as blue now ? "
he asked.

" Ah, what a lovely colour ! " she murmured, leaning
her head on one side.

" Should you like to have it ? "

She stared a moment and then broke into a loud laugh.

" Should you like to have it ? " he repeated in a ringing
voice.

" Don't look as if you would eat me up," she answered.
" It's harmless if I say yes ! "

Roderick rose to his feet and stood looking at the little

flower. It was separated from the ledge on which he stood by a rugged surface of vertical wall, which dropped straight into the dusky vaults behind the arena. Suddenly he took off his hat and flung it behind him. Christina then sprang to her feet.

"I will bring it to you," he said.

She seized his arm. "Are you crazy? Do you mean to kill yourself?"

"I shall not kill myself. Sit down!"

"Excuse me. Not till you do!" and she grasped his arm with both hands.

Roderick shook her off and pointed with a violent gesture to her former place. "Go there!" he cried fiercely.

"You can never, never!" she murmured beseechingly, clasping her hands. "I implore you!"

Roderick turned and looked at her, and then in a voice which Rowland had never heard him use, a voice almost thunderous, a voice which awakened the echoes of the mighty ruin, he repeated, "Sit down!" She hesitated a moment, and then she dropped on the ground and buried her face in her hands.

Rowland had seen all this, and he saw what followed. He saw Roderick clasp in his left arm the jagged corner of the vertical partition on which he proposed to try his experiment, then stretch out his leg and feel for a resting-place for his foot. Rowland had measured with a glance the possibility of his holding on and pronounced it uncommonly small. The wall was garnished with a series of narrow projections, the remains apparently of a brick cornice supporting the arch of a vault which had long since collapsed. It was by lodging his toes on these loose brackets and grasping with his hands at certain mouldering protuberances on a level with his head that Roderick intended to proceed. The relics of the cornice were utterly worthless as a support. Rowland had observed this, and yet for a moment he had hesitated. If the thing were possible he felt a sudden admiring glee at the thought of Roderick's doing it. It would be finely done, it would be gallant, it would have a sort of masculine eloquence as an answer to Christina's sinister *persiflage*. But it was not possible! Rowland left his place with a bound and scrambled down some neighbouring steps, and

the next moment a stronger pair of hands than Christina's
were laid upon Roderick's shoulder.

He turned, staring, pale and angry. Christina rose,
pale and staring too, but beautiful in her wonder and
alarm. "My dear Roderick," said Rowland, "I am only
preventing you from doing a very foolish thing. That's
an exploit for spiders, not for young sculptors of
promise."

Roderick wiped his forehead, looked back at the wall, and
then closed his eyes, as if with a spasm of retarded dizzi-
ness. "I won't resist you," he said. "But I have made
you obey," he added, turning to Christina. "Am I weak
now?"

She had recovered her composure; she looked straight
past him and addressed Rowland. "Be so good as to
show me the way out of this horrible place!"

He helped her back into the corridor; Roderick followed
after a short interval. Of course, as they were descending
the steps, came questions for Rowland to answer, and more
or less surprise. Where had he come from? how happened
he to have appeared at just that moment? Rowland
answered that he had been rambling overhead and that,
looking out of an aperture, he had seen a gentleman preparing to undertake a preposterous gymnastic feat and a lady
swooning away in consequence. Interference seemed justi-
fiable and he had made it as prompt as possible. Roderick
was far from hanging his head like a man who has been
caught in the perpetration of an extravagant folly; but
if he held it more erect than usual Rowland believed that
this was much less because he had made a show of personal
daring than because he had triumphantly proved to Christina
that like a certain person she had dreamed of he too could
speak the language of decision. Christina descended to
the arena in silence, apparently occupied with her own
thoughts. She betrayed no sense of the privacy of her
interview with Roderick needing an explanation; she
seemed to imply that Rowland had seen stranger things
in New York. The only evidence of her recent agitation
was that on being joined by her maid she declared that
she was unable to walk home—she must have a carriage.
A fiacre was found resting in the shadow of the Arch of
Constantine, and Rowland suspected that after she had got

into it she disburdened herself under her veil of a few
natural tears.

Rowland had played eavesdropper to so good a purpose
that he might justly have omitted the ceremony of de-
nouncing himself to Roderick. He preferred however to
let him know that he had overheard a portion of his talk
with Christina.

"Of course it seems to you," Roderick said, "a proof
that I am thoroughly infatuated."

"Miss Light seemed to me to know very well how far
she could go," Rowland answered. "She was twisting you
round her finger. I don't think she exactly meant to defy
you; but your preposterous attempt to pluck the flower
was a proof that she could go all lengths in the way of
making a fool of you."

"Yes," said Roderick, meditatively; "she is making
a fool of me."

"And what do you expect to come of it?"

"Nothing good!" And Roderick put his hands into his
pockets and looked as if he had announced the most
colourless fact in the world.

"And in the light of your late interview, what do you
make of your young lady?"

"If I could tell you that, it would be plain sailing. But
she will not tell me again I am weak!"

"Are you very sure you are not weak?"

"I may be, but she shall never dare—she shall never
care—to say it!"

Rowland said no more until they reached the Corso,
when he asked his companion whether he were going to
his studio.

Roderick started out of a reverie and passed his hands
over his eyes. "Oh no, I can't settle down to work after
such a scene as that. I was not afraid of breaking my
neck then, but I feel in a devil of a tremor now. I will go
—I will go and sit in the sun on the Pincio!"

"Promise me this first," said Rowland very solemnly—
"that the next time you meet Miss Light it shall be on
the earth and not in the air!"

Since his return from Frascati Roderick had been working doggedly at the statue ordered by Mr. Leavenworth.
To Rowland's eye he had made a very fair beginning, but

he had himself insisted from the first that he liked neither his subject nor his patron, and that it was impossible to feel any warmth of interest in a work which was to be incorporated into the ponderous personality of Mr. Leavenworth. It was all against the grain; he wrought without love. Nevertheless after a fashion he wrought, and the figure grew beneath his hands. Miss Blanchard's friend was ordering works of art on every side, and his purveyors were in many cases persons whom Roderick declared it was an infamy to be associated with. There had been famous tailors, he said, who declined to make you a coat unless you should get the hat you were to wear with it from an artist of their own choosing. It seemed to him that he had an equal right to exact that his statue should not form part of the same system of ornament as the " Pearl of Perugia," a picture by an American *confrère* who had in Mr. Leavenworth's opinion a prodigious eye for colour. As a liberal customer, Mr. Leavenworth used to drop into Roderick's studio to see how things were getting on, and give a friendly hint or exert an enlightened control. He would seat himself squarely, plant his gold-topped cane between his legs, which he held very much apart, rest his large white hands on the head, and enunciate the principles of spiritual art—a species of fluid wisdom which appeared to rise in bucketfuls, as he turned the crank, from the well-like depths of his moral consciousness. His benignant and imperturbable pomposity gave Roderick the sense of suffocating beneath an immense feather-bed, and the worst of the matter was that the good gentleman's placid vanity had an integument impenetrable to sarcastic shafts. Roderick admitted that in thinking over the tribulations of struggling genius the danger of dying of too much attention had never occurred to him.

The deterring effect of the episode of the Coliseum was apparently of long continuance; if Roderick's nerves had been shaken his hand needed time to recover its steadiness. He cultivated composure upon principles of his own; by frequenting entertainments from which he returned at four o'clock in the morning and lapsing into habits which might fairly be called irregular. He had hitherto made few friends among the artistic fraternity; chiefly because he had taken no trouble about it, and there was in his demeanour an elastic independence of the favour of his fellow-mortals which made social advances on his own part peculiarly necessary. Rowland had told him more than once that he ought to fraternise a trifle more with the other artists, and he had always answered that he had not the smallest objection to fraternising: let them come! But they came on rare occasions, and Roderick was not punctilious about returning their visits. He declared there was not one of them the fruits of whose genius gave him the least desire to delve in the parent soil. For Gloriani he professed an ineffable contempt, and having been once to look at his wares never crossed his threshold again. The only one of the fraternity for whom by his own admission he cared a straw was little Singleton; but he took an exclusively facetious view of this humble genius whenever he encountered him, and quite forgot his existence in the intervals. He had never been to see him, but Singleton edged his way from time to time timidly into Roderick's studio and agreed with characteristic modesty that brilliant fellows like Hudson might consent to receive homage but could hardly be expected to render it. Roderick never acknowledged 'applause, and apparently failed to observe whether poor Singleton spoke in admiration or in blame. Roderick's taste as to companions was singularly capricious. There were very good fellows that were disposed to cultivate him who bored him to death; and there were others in whom even Rowland's good-nature was unable to discover a pretext for tolerance in whom he appeared to find the highest social qualities. He gave the most fantastic reasons for his likes and dislikes. He would declare he could not speak a civil word to a man who brushed his hair in a certain fashion, and he would explain his unaccountable fancy for an individual of imperceptible merit by telling you that he had an ancestor who in the thirteenth century had walled up his wife alive. "I like to talk to a man whose ancestor has walled up his wife alive," he would say. "You may not see the fun of it, and think poor P—— is a very dull fellow. It's very possible; I don't ask you to admire him. But for reasons of my own I like to see him about. The old fellow left her for three days with her face uncovered and placed a looking-glass opposite to her, so that she could see, as he said, if her gown was a fit!"

His relish for an odd flavour in his friends had led him
to make the acquaintance of a number of people outside
of Rowland's well-ordered circle, and he made no secret
of their being very queer fish. He formed an intimacy,
among others, with a crazy fellow who had come to Rome
as an emissary of one of the Central American republics,
to drive some ecclesiastical bargain with the papal govern-
ment. The Pope had given him the cold shoulder, but
since he had not prospered as a diplomatist he had sought
compensation as a man of the world, and his great flam-
boyant curricle and negro lackeys were for several weeks
one of the striking ornaments of the Pincian. He spoke
a queer jargon of Italian, Spanish, French, and English,
humorously relieved with scraps of ecclesiastical Latin,
and to those who inquired of Roderick what he found to
interest him in this pretentious jackanapes, the latter
would reply, looking at his interlocutor with his lucid
blue eyes, that it was worth any sacrifice to hear him
talk nonsense ! The two had gone together one night to
a ball given by a lady of some renown in the Spanish
colony, and very late, on his way home, Roderick came up
to Rowland's rooms, in the windows of which he had seen
a light. Rowland was going to bed, but Roderick flung
himself into an arm-chair and chattered for an hour. The
friends of the Costa Rican envoy were as amusing as himself, and in very much the same line. The mistress of the
house had worn a yellow satin dress and gold heels on her
slippers, and at the close of the entertainment had sent
for a pair of castanets, tucked up her petticoats and danced
a fandango, while the gentlemen sat cross-legged on the
floor. "It was awfully low," Roderick said ; "all of a
sudden I perceived it and bolted. Nothing of that kind
ever amuses me to the end ; before it's half over it bores
me to death ; it makes me sick. Hang it, why can't a
poor fellow enjoy things in peace ? My illusions are all
broken-winded ; they won't carry me twenty paces ! I
can't laugh and forget ; my laugh dies away before it
begins. Your friend Stendhal writes on his book-covers
(I never got further) that he has seen too early in life
la beauté parfaite. I don't know how early he saw it ; I
saw it before I was born—in another state of being ! I
can't describe it positively ; I can only say I don't find it

anywhere now. Not at the bottom of champagne glasses ; not, strange as it may seem, in that extra half-yard or so of shoulder that some women have their ball-dresses cut to expose. I don't find it at noisy supper-tables where half a dozen ugly men with pomatumed heads are rapidly growing uglier still with heat and wine ; nor when I come away and walk through these squalid black streets and go out into the Forum and see a few old battered stone posts standing there like gnawed bones stuck into the earth. Everything is mean and dusky and shabby, and the men and women who make up this so-called brilliant society are the meanest and shabbiest of all. They have no real spontaneity ; they are nothing but parrots and popinjays. They have no more dignity than so many grasshoppers. Nothing is good but one ! " And he jumped up and stood looking at one of his statues, which shone vaguely across the room in the dim lamplight.

" Yes, do tell us," said Rowland, " what to hold on by ! "

" Those things of mine were tolerably good," he answered. " But my idea was better—and that's what I mean ! "

Rowland said nothing. He was willing to wait for Roderick to complete the circle of his metamorphoses, but he had no desire to officiate as chorus to the play.

" You think I have the ' cheek ' of the devil himself," the latter said at last, " coming up to moralise at this hour of the night ! You think I want to throw dust into your eyes, to put you off the scent. That's your eminently rational view of the case."

" Excuse me from taking any view at all," said Rowland.

" You have given me up, then ? "

" No, I have merely suspended judgment. I am waiting."

Roderick looked at him a moment. " What are you waiting for ? "

Rowland made an angry gesture. " Oh, miserable boy ! When you have hit your mark and made people care for you, you shouldn't twist your weapon about at that rate in their vitals. Allow me to say I am sleepy. Good night ! "

XIV.

SOME days afterwards it happened that Rowland, on a long afternoon ramble, took his way through one of the quiet corners of the Trastevere. He was particularly fond of this part of Rome, though he could hardly have expressed the charm he found in it. As you pass away from the dusky swarming purlieus of the Ghetto, you emerge into a region of empty, soundless, grass-grown lanes and alleys, where the shabby houses seem mouldering away in disuse and yet your footstep brings figures of startling Roman type to the doorways. There are few monuments here, but no part of Rome seemed more historic, in the sense of being weighted with a ponderous past, blighted with the melancholy of things that had had their day. When the yellow afternoon sunshine slept on the sallow battered walls and lengthened the shadows in the grassy courtyards of small closed churches the place acquired a strange fascination. The church of St. Cecilia has one of these sunny waste-looking courts ; the edifice seems abandoned to silence and the charity of chance devotion. Rowland never passed it without going in, and he was generally the only visitor. He entered it now, but he found that two persons had preceded him. Both were women. One was at her prayers at one of the side-altars ; the other was seated against a column at the upper end of the nave. Rowland walked to the altar and paid in a momentary glance at the clever statue of the saint in death in the niche beneath it the usual tribute to the charm of polished ingenuity. As he turned away he looked at the person seated and recognised Christina Light. Seeing that she perceived him he advanced to speak to her.

She was sitting in a listless attitude, with her hands in her lap ; she seemed to be tired. She was dressed very simply, as if for walking and escaping observation. When he had greeted her he glanced back at her companion and recognised the faithful Assunta.

Christina smiled. " Are you looking for Mr. Hudson ? He is not here I am happy to say."

"If he were here one might understand," said Rowland. "This is a strange place to find you alone."

"Not at all! People call me a strange girl, and I might as well have the comfort of it. I came to take a walk; that by the way is part of my strangeness. I can't loll all the morning on a sofa and sit perched all the afternoon in a carriage. I get horribly restless; I must move; I must do something and see something. Mamma suggests a cup of tea. Meanwhile I put on an old dress and half a dozen veils, I take Assunta under my arm and we start on a pedestrian tour. It's a bore that I can't take the poodle, but he attracts attention. We trudge about everywhere; there is nothing I like so much. I hope you will congratulate me on the simplicity of my tastes."

"I congratulate you on your wisdom. To live in Rome and not to walk about would, I think, be poor pleasure. But you are terribly far from home, and I am afraid you are tired."

"A little—enough to sit here a while."

"Might I offer you my company while you rest?"

"If you will promise to amuse me. I am in dismal spirits."

Saying he would do what he could, Rowland brought a chair and placed it near her. He was not in love with her; he disapproved of her; he distrusted her; and yet he felt it a kind of privilege to watch her and he found a peculiar excitement in talking to her. The background of her nature, as he would have called it, was large and mysterious, and it emitted strange fantastic gleams and flashes. Watching for these rather quickened one's pulses. Moreover it was not a disadvantage to talk to a girl who made one keep guard on one's composure; it diminished one's usual liability to utter something less than revised wisdom.

Assunta had risen from her prayers, and as he took his place was coming back to her mistress. But Christina motioned her away. "No, no; while you are about it say a few dozen more!" she said. "Pray for *me*," she added in English. "Pray that I say nothing silly. She has been at it half an hour; I envy her volubility!"

"One often envies good Catholics," said Rowland.

"Oh, speak to me of that; I have been through that

too! There was a time when I wanted immensely to be a
nun; it was not a laughing matter. It was when I was
about sixteen years old. I read the *Imitation* and the *Life
of St. Catherine*. I fully believed in the miracles of the
saints, and I was dying to have one of my own—little of
a saint as I was! The least little accident that could have
been twisted into a miracle would have carried me straight
into the cloister. I had the real religious passion. It
passed away, and as I sat here just now I was wondering
what has become of it!"

Rowland had already been sensible of something in this
young lady's tone which he would have called a want of
veracity, and this epitome of her religious experience failed
to strike him as absolutely historical. But the trait was
not disagreeable, for she herself was evidently the foremost
dupe of her inventions. She had a fictitious history in
which she believed much more fondly than in her real
one, and an infinite capacity for extemporised reminiscence
adapted to the mood of the hour. She liked to idealise
herself, to take interesting and picturesque attitudes to
her own imagination; and the vivacity and spontaneity
of her character gave her really a starting-point in experience, so that the many-coloured flowers of fiction which
blossomed in her talk were not so much perversions as
sympathetic exaggerations of fact. And Rowland felt that
whatever she said of herself might have been, under the
imagined circumstances; energy was there, audacity, the
restless questioning temperament. "I am afraid I am
sadly prosaic," he said, "for in these many months now that
I have been in Rome I have never ceased for a moment
to look at Catholicism simply from the outside. I don't
see an opening as big as your finger-nail where I could creep
into it!"

"What do you believe?" asked Christina, looking at
him. "Are you religious?"

"I am very old fashioned. I believe in God."

Christina let her beautiful eyes wander a while and then
gave a little sigh. "You are much to be envied!"

"You, I imagine, in that line have nothing to envy me."

"Yes, I have. Rest!"

"You are too young to say that."

"I am not young; I have never been young! My

mother took care of that. I was a little wrinkled old woman at ten."

"I am afraid," said Rowland, in a moment, "that you are fond of painting yourself in dark colours."

She looked at him a while in silence. "Do you wish to win my eternal gratitude? Prove to me that I am better than I suppose."

"I should have first to know what you really suppose."

She shook her head. "It wouldn't do! You would be horrified to learn even the things I imagine about myself, and shocked at the knowledge of evil displayed in my very mistakes."

"Well, then," said Rowland, "I will ask no questions. But, at a venture, I promise you to catch you some day in the act of doing something very good."

"Are you too trying to flatter me? I thought you and I had fallen from the first into rather a truth-speaking vein."

"Oh, I have not given it up!" said Rowland; and he determined, since he had the credit of homely directness, to push his advantage farther. The opportunity seemed excellent. But while he was hesitating how to begin, the young girl said, bending forward and clasping her hands in her lap, "Please tell me about your religion."

"Tell you about it? I can't!" said Rowland, with a good deal of emphasis.

She flushed a little. "Is it such a mighty mystery it cannot be put into words nor communicated to my base ears?"

"It is simply a sentiment that makes part of my life, and I can't detach myself from it sufficiently to talk about it."

"Religion, it seems to me, should be eloquent and aggressive. It should wish to make converts, to persuade and illumine, to take possession!"

"One's religion takes the colour of one's general disposition. I am not aggressive, and certainly I am not eloquent."

"Well, I am sure I shouldn't greatly care for anything you might say," Christina rejoined. "It would be sure to be half-hearted. You are not in the least contented."

"How do you know that?"

"Oh, I am an observer!"

"No one is absolutely contented, I suppose—but I assure you I complain of nothing."

"So much the worse for your honesty ! To begin with, you are in love."

"You would not have me complain of that ! "

"And it doesn't go well. There are grievous obstacles. So much I know ! You needn't protest ; I ask no questions. You will tell no one—me least of all. Why does one never see you ? "

"Why, if I came to see you," said Rowland, deliberating, "it wouldn't be, it couldn't be, for a trivial reason—because I had not been in a month, because I was passing, because I admire you. It would be because I should have something very particular to say. I have not come because I have been slow in making up my mind to say it."

"You are simply cruel. Something particular, in this ocean of inanities ? In common charity, speak ! "

"I doubt whether you will like it."

"Oh, I hope to Heaven it's not some tribute to my charms ! "

"It may be called a tribute to your reasonableness. That is one of your charms you know. You perhaps remember that I gave you a hint of it the other day at Frascati."

"Has it been hanging fire all this time ? Explode ! I promise not to stop my ears."

"It relates to my friend Hudson." And Rowland paused. She was looking at him expectantly ; her face gave no sign. " I am rather disturbed in mind about him. He seems to me at times to be in a discouraging way." He paused again, but Christina said nothing. "The case is simply this," he went on. " It was by my advice he gave up his work at home and went in for an artist's life. I made him burn his ships. I brought him to Rome, I launched him in the world, and I have undertaken to answer to—to his mother for his doing well. It is not such smooth sailing as it might be, and I am inclined to put up prayers for fair winds. If he is to succeed, he must work—very quietly and very hard. It is not news to you I imagine that Hudson is a great admirer of yours."

Christina remained silent ; she turned away her eyes with an air, not of confusion, but of deep deliberation.

Surprising frankness had as a general thing struck Rowland as the key-note of her character, but she had more than once given him a suggestion of an unfathomable power of calculation, and her silence now had something which it is hardly extravagant to call portentous. He had of course asked himself how far it was questionable taste to inform an unprotected girl, for the needs of a cause, that another man admired her; the thing superficially had an uncomfortable analogy with treating the young lady as a catspaw. But he decided that even rigid discretion is not bound to take such a person at more than her own valuation, and Christina presently reassured him as to the limits of her susceptibility. "Mr. Hudson is in love with me!" she said.

Rowland flinched a trifle. Then—"Am I," he asked, "from this point of view of mine, to be glad or sorry?"

"I don't understand you."

"Why, is Hudson to be happy or unhappy?"

She hesitated a moment. "You wish him to be great in his profession? And for that you consider that he must be happy in his life?"

"Decidedly. I don't say it's a general rule, but I think it's a rule for him."

"So that if he were very happy he would become very great?"

"He would at least do himself justice."

"And by that you mean a great deal?"

"A great deal."

Christina sank back in her chair and rested her eyes on the cracked and polished slabs of the pavement. At last, looking up, "You have not forgotten, I suppose, that you told me he was engaged to be married?"

"By no means."

"He is still engaged then?"

"To the best of my belief."

"And yet you desire that, as you say, he should be made happy by something I can do for him?"

"What I desire is this. That your great influence with him should be exerted for his good, that it should help him and not retard him. Understand me. You probably know that your admirers have rather a restless time of it. I can answer for two of them. You don't know your own mind very well, I imagine, and as you like being admired, the poor devil on whom you have cast your spell has to pay all the expenses! Since we are really being frank, I wonder whether I might not say the great word."

"You needn't; I know it. I am a horrible coquette."

"No, not a horrible one, since I am making an appeal to your generosity. I am pretty sure you can't imagine yourself marrying my friend."

"There's nothing I can't imagine! That is my difficulty!"

Rowland's brow contracted impatiently. "I can't imagine it then!"

Christina flushed faintly; then very gently—"I am not so bad as you think," she said.

"It is not a question of badness; it is a question of whether circumstances don't make the thing an extreme improbability."

"Worse and worse. I can be bullied, then, or bribed?"

"You are not so candid as you pretend to be. My feeling is this. Hudson, as I understand him, does not need, as an artist, the stimulus of strong emotion, of passion. He is better without it; he is emotional and passionate enough when he is left to himself. The sooner passion is at rest therefore the sooner he will settle down to work, and the fewer emotions he has that are mere emotions and nothing more, the better for him. If you cared for him enough to marry him, I should have nothing to say; I should never venture to interfere. But I strongly suspect you don't, and therefore I suggest most respectfully that you leave him alone."

"If I leave him alone he will go on like a new clock, eh?"

"He will do better. He will have no excuses or pretexts."

"Oh, he makes me a pretext, does he? I am much obliged!" cried Christina, with a laugh. "What is he doing now?"

"I can hardly say. He's like a very old clock indeed. He's moody, desultory, idle, irregular, fantastic."

"Heavens, what a list! And it's all poor me?"

"No, not all. But you are a part of it, and I turn to

you because you are a more tangible, sensible, responsible cause than the other things."

Christina raised her hand to her eyes, and bent her head thoughtfully. Rowland was puzzled to measure the effect of his venture; she rather surprised him by her gentleness. At last, without moving, "If I were to marry him," she asked, "what would have become of his *fiancée* ?"

"I am bound to suppose that she would have become extremely unhappy."

Christina said nothing more, and Rowland, to let her make her reflections, left his place and strolled away. Poor Assunta, sitting patiently on a stone bench and unprovided on this occasion with military consolation, gave him a bright frank smile which might have been construed as an expression of regret for herself and of sympathy for her mistress. Rowland presently seated himself again near Christina.

"What do you think of your friend's infidelity to that young girl in the little village ?" she asked suddenly, looking at him.

"I don't like it."

"Was he very much in love with her ?"

"He asked her to marry him. You may judge."

"Is she rich ?"

"No, she is poor."

"Is she very much in love with him ?"

"I know her too little to say."

She paused again, and then resumed—"You have settled in your mind then that I will never seriously listen to him ?"

"I shall think it unlikely until the contrary is proved."

"How shall it be proved ? How do you know what passes between us ?"

"I can judge, of course, but from appearances ; but, like you, I am no observer. Hudson has not at all the air of a happy lover ! "

"If he is depressed there is a reason. He has a bad conscience. One must hope so at least. On the other hand simply as a friend," she continued, gently, "you think I can do him no good ?"

The humility of her tone combined with her beauty as she made this remark was inexpressibly touching, and

Rowland had an uncomfortable sense of being put at a disadvantage. "There are doubtless many good things you might do if you had proper opportunity," he said. "But you seem to be sailing with a current which leaves you little leisure for quiet benevolence. You live in the whirl and hurry of a world into which a poor artist can hardly find it to his advantage to follow you."

"In plain English I am odiously frivolous. You put it very generously."

"I won't hesitate to say all my thought," said Rowland. "For better or worse you seem to me to belong both by character and by circumstance to what is called the world, the great world. You are made to ornament it magnificently. You are not made to be an artist's wife."

"I see. But even from your point of view that would depend upon the artist. Extraordinary talent might make him a member of the great world."

Rowland smiled. "That is very true."

"If, as it is," Christina continued in a moment, "you take a low view of me—no, you needn't protest—I wonder what you would think if you knew certain things."

"What things do you mean ? "

"Well, for example how I was brought up. I have had a horrible education. There must be some good in me, since I have perceived it, since I have turned and judged my circumstances."

"My dear Miss Light ! " Rowland murmured remonstrantly.

She gave a little quick laugh. "You don't want to hear ! you don't want to have to think about that ! "

"Have I a right to ? You needn't justify yourself."

She turned upon him a moment the quickened light of her beautiful eyes, then fell to musing again. "Is there not some novel or some play," she asked at last, "in which a beautiful wicked woman who has ensnared a young man sees his father come to her and beg her to let him go ? "

"Very likely," said Rowland. "I hope she consents."

"I forget. But tell me," she continued, "shall you consider—admitting your proposition—that in ceasing to be nice to Mr. Hudson, so that he may go about his business, I do something magnanimous, heroic, sublime—something with a fine name like that ? "

Rowland, elated with the prospect of gaining his point, was about to reply that she would deserve the finest name in the world; but he instantly suspected that this tone would not please her, and besides it would not express his meaning.

"You do something I shall greatly respect," he contented himself with saying.

She made no answer, and in a moment she beckoned to her maid. "What have I to do to-day?" she asked.

Assunta meditated. "Eh, it's a very busy day! Fortunately I have a better memory than the signorina," she said, turning to Rowland. She began to count on her fingers, "We have to go to the Piè di Marmo to see about those laces that were sent to be washed. You said also that you wished to say three sharp words to the Buonvicini about your pink dress. You want some moss-rosebuds for to-night, and you won't get them for nothing! You dine at the Austrian Embassy, and that Frenchman is to powder your hair. You're to come home in time to receive, for the signora gives a dance. And so away, away till morning!"

"Ah, yes, the moss-roses!" Christina murmured appreciatively. "I must have a quantity—at least a hundred. Nothing but buds, eh? You must sew them in a kind of immense apron, down the front of my dress. Packed tight together, eh? It will be delightfully barbarous. And then twenty more or so for my hair. They go very well with powder; don't you think so?" And she turned to Rowland. "I am going en Pompadour."

"Going where?"

"To the Spanish Embassy, or whatever it is."

"All down the front, signorina? Dio buono! You must give me time!" Assunta cried.

"Yes, we will go!" And she left her place. She walked slowly to the door of the church, looking at the pavement, and Rowland could not guess whether she was thinking of her apron of moss-rosebuds or of her opportunity for moral sublimity. Before reaching the door she turned away and stood gazing at an old picture, indistinguishable with blackness, over an altar. At last they passed out into the court. Glancing at her in the open air, Rowland was startled; he thought he saw the traces of hastily suppressed tears. They had lost time, she said, and they must hurry; she sent Assunta to look for a coach. She remained silent a while, scratching the ground with the point of her parasol, and then at last looking up she thanked Rowland for his confidence in her "reasonableness." "It's really very comfortable to be expected to do something good, after all the horrid things one has been used to doing—instructed, commanded, forced to do! I will think over what you have said to me." In that deserted quarter coaches are rare, and there was some delay in Assunta's procuring one. Christina talked of the church, of the picturesque old court, of that strange decaying corner of Rome. Rowland was perplexed; he was ill at ease. At last the cab arrived, but she waited a moment longer. "So, decidedly," she suddenly asked, "I can only harm him?"

"You make me feel very brutal," said Rowland.

"And he is such a fine fellow that it would be really a great pity, eh?"

"I shall praise him no more," Rowland said.

She turned away quickly, but she lingered still. "Do you remember promising me, soon after we first met, that at the end of six months you would tell me definitely what you thought of me?"

"It was a foolish promise."

"You gave it. Bear it in mind. I will think of what you have said to me. Farewell." The two women stepped into the carriage and it rolled away. Rowland stood for some minutes looking after it, and then went his way with a sigh. If this expressed general mistrust, he ought three days afterwards to have been reassured. He received by the post a note containing these words:—

"I have done it. Begin and respect me!
                                        "C. L."

To be perfectly satisfactory, indeed, the note required a commentary. Calling that evening upon Roderick, he found one in the information offered him at the door by the old serving-woman—the startling information that the signorino had gone to Naples.

XV.

ABOUT a month later Rowland addressed to his cousin Cecilia a letter, of which the following is a portion :—

. . . "So much for myself; yet I tell you but a tithe of my own story unless I let you know how matters stand with poor Hudson, for he gives me more to think about just now than anything else in the world. I need a good deal of courage to begin this chapter. You warned me, you know, and I made rather light of your warning. I have had all kinds of hopes and fears, but hitherto, in writing to you, I have resolutely put the hopes foremost. Now, however, my pride has forsaken me, and I should like hugely to give expression to a little comfortable despair. I should like to say, ' My dear wise cousin, you were right and I was wrong ; you were a shrewd observer, and I was a meddlesome donkey ! ' When I think of a certain talk we had about the ' salubrity of genius,' I feel my ears tingle. If this is salubrity, give me raging disease ! I am pestered to death ; I go about with a chronic heartache ; there are moments when I could shed salt tears. There's a pretty portrait of the most placid of men . I wish I could make you understand ; or rather I wish you could make me ! I don't understand a jot ; it's a hideous, mocking mystery ; I give it up ! I don't in the least give it up, you know ; I am incapable of giving it up. I sit holding my head by the hour, racking my brain, wondering what to invent. You told me at Northampton that I took the thing too easily ; you would tell me now perhaps that I take it too hard. I do, altogether ; but it can't be helped. Without flattering myself I may say I am sympathetic. Many another man, before this, would have cast his perplexities to the winds, and declared that Master Hudson must lie on his bed as he had made it. Some men perhaps would even say that I am making a mighty ado about nothing, that I have only to give him rope and he will tire himself out. But he tugs at his rope altogether too hard for *me* to hold it comfortably ! I certainly never pretended the thing was anything

but an experiment; I promised nothing, I answered for
nothing; I only said that the case was hopeful, and it
would be a shame not to give him a chance. I have done
my best, and if the machine is running down I have a
right to stand aside and let it rattle. Amen, amen! No,
I can write that, but I can't feel it. I can't be just; I
can only be generous. I am fond of the poor devil, and
I can't give him up. As for understanding him, that's
another matter; nowadays I don't believe even you would.
One's wits are sadly pestered over here, I assure you, and
I am in the way of seeing more than one peculiar specimen
of human nature. Roderick and Miss Light, between
them! . . . . . Haven't I already told you about
Miss Light? Last winter everything was perfection.
Roderick struck out bravely, did really great things, and
proved himself as I supposed thoroughly solid. He was
strong, he was first rate; I felt perfectly secure, and paid
myself all kinds of compliments. We had passed at a
bound into the open sea and left danger behind. But in
the summer I began to be uneasy, though I succeeded in
not being alarmed. When he came back to Rome, however,
I saw that the tide had turned, and that we were close
upon the rocks. It is in fact another case of Ulysses and
the Sirens; only Roderick refuses to be tied to the mast.
He is the most extraordinary being, the strangest mixture
of qualities. I don't understand so much force going with
so much weakness—such a brilliant gift being subject to
such lapses. The poor fellow is incomplete, and it is really
not his own fault; Nature has given him his faculty out
of hand and bidden him be hanged with it! I never knew
a man harder to advise or assist, if he is not in the mood
for listening. I suppose there is some key or other to his
character, but I try in vain to find it; and yet I can't
believe that Providence is so cruel as to have turned the
lock and thrown the key away. He perplexes me to death,
and though he tires out my patience he still fascinates me.
Sometimes I think he has not a grain of conscience, and
sometimes I think that in a way he has an excess. He
takes things at once too easily and too hard; he is both
too lax and too tense, too reckless and too ambitious, too
cold and too passionate. He has developed faster even
than you prophesied, and for good and evil alike he takes

up a formidable space. There's too much of him for me, at any rate. Yes, he *is* hard; there is no mistake about that. He's inflexible, he's brittle; and though he has plenty of spirit, plenty of soul, he hasn't what I call a heart. He has something that Miss Garland took for one, and I am pretty sure she's a judge. But she judged on scanty evidence. He has something that Christina Light, here, makes believe at times that she takes for one, but she is no judge at all! I think it is established that in the long run egotism makes a failure in conduct: is it also true that it makes a failure in the arts? . . . . Roderick's standard is immensely high; I must do him that justice. He will do nothing beneath it, and while he is waiting for inspiration, his imagination, his nerves, his senses must have something to amuse them. This is a highly philosophic way of saying that he has taken to riotous living and has just been spending a month at Naples—a city where 'pleasure' is actively cultivated—in very bad company. Are they all like that, all the men of genius? There are a great many artists here who hammer away at their trade with exemplary industry; in fact I am surprised at their success in reducing the matter to a virtuous habit; but I really don't think that one of them has his exquisite quality of talent. It is in the matter of quantity that he has broken down. Nothing comes out of the bottle; he turns it upside down; it's no use! Sometimes he declares it's empty—that he has done all he was made to do. This I consider great nonsense; but I would nevertheless take him on his own terms if it were only I that was concerned. But I keep thinking of those two praying, trusting neighbours of yours, and I feel uncommonly like a swindler. If his working mood came on but once in five years I would willingly wait for it and keep him on his legs somehow in the intervals; but that would be a sorry account to present to *them!* Five years of this sort of thing moreover would effectually settle the question. I wish he were less of a genius and more of a charlatan! He's too confoundedly all of one piece; he won't throw overboard a grain of the cargo to save the rest. Fancy him thus with all his brilliant personal charm, his handsome head, his careless step, his look as of a nervous nineteenth-century Apollo, and you will

understand that there is mighty little comfort in seeing
him go to the bad. He was tolerably foolish last summer
at Baden-Baden, but he got on his feet and for a while he
was steady. Then he began to waver again and at last
toppled over. Now, literally, he's lying prone! He came
into my room last night miserably tipsy. I assure you it
didn't amuse me. . . . About Miss Light it's a long story.
She is one of the great beauties of all time, and worth
coming barefoot to Rome like the pilgrims of old to see.
Her complexion, her glance, her step, her dusky tresses, may
have been seen before in a goddess, but never in a woman.
And you may take this for truth, because I am not in love
with her. On the contrary! Her education has been
simply infernal. She is corrupt, perverse, as proud as a
potentate, and a coquette of the first magnitude; but she
is generous and intelligent, and if you set rightly to work
you may enlist her imagination in a good cause as well as
in a bad one. The other day I tried to bring it over to
my side. I happened to have some talk with her to which
it was possible to give a serious turn, and I boldly broke
ground and begged her to suffer my poor friend to go in
peace. After leading me rather a dance—in conversation
—she consented, and the next day, with a single word, she
packed him off to Naples to drown his sorrow in debauchery.
I have come to the conclusion that she is more dangerous
in her virtuous moods than in her vicious ones, and that
she probably has a way of turning her back which is the
most provoking thing in the world. She is an actress, she
couldn't forego doing the thing dramatically, and it was the
dramatic touch that made it fatal. I wished her of course
to let him down easily; but she desired to have the curtain
drop on an attitude, and her attitudes have the property
of depriving inflammable young artists of their reason. . . .
Roderick made an admirable bust of her at the beginning
of the winter, and a dozen women came rushing to him to
be done, *mutatis mutandis*, in the same style. They were
all great ladies and ready to take him by the hand, but he
told them all their faces didn't interest him and sent them
away vowing his destruction."

At this stage of his long burst of confidence Rowland
had paused and put by his letter. He kept it three days
and then read it over. He was disposed at first to destroy

it, but he decided finally to keep it, in the hope that it might strike a spark of useful suggestion from the flint of Cecilia's good sense. We know he had a talent for taking advice. And then it might be, he reflected, that his cousin's answer would throw some light on Mary Garland's present vision of things. In his altered mood he added these few lines—

"I unburdened myself the other day of this monstrous load of perplexity ; I think it did me good, and I will let it stand. I was in a melancholy muddle, and I was trying to wriggle out of it. You know I like discussion in a quiet way, and there is no one with whom I can have it as quietly as with you, most sagacious of cousins ! There is an excellent old lady with whom I often chat and who talks very much to the point. But Madame Grandoni has disliked Roderick from the first, and if I were to take her advice I would wash my hands of him. You would laugh at me for my long face, but you would do that in any circumstances. I am half ashamed of my letter, for I have a faith in my friend that is deeper than my doubts. He was here last evening, talking about the Naples Museum, the Aristides, the bronzes, the Pompeian frescoes, with such a beautiful intelligence that doubt of the ultimate future seemed blasphemy. I walked back to his lodging with him, and he was as mild as midsummer moonlight. He has that ineffable something that charms and convinces ; my last word about him shall not be a harsh one."

Shortly after sending his letter, going one day into his friend's studio, he found Roderick suffering the honourable torture of a visit from Mr. Leavenworth. Roderick submitted with extreme ill grace to being bored, and he was now evidently in a state of high exasperation. He had lately begun a representation of a *lazzarone* lounging in the sun ; an image of serene, irresponsible, sensuous life. The real lazzarone, he had admitted, was a vile fellow ; but the ideal lazzarone—and his own had been subtly idealised—was the flower of a perfect civilisation.

Mr. Leavenworth had apparently just transferred his unhurrying gaze to the figure.

"Something in the style of the Dying Gladiator ?" he sympathetically observed.

"Oh no," said Roderick seriously, "he is not dying, he is only drunk!"

"Ah, but intoxication, you know," Mr. Leavenworth rejoined, "is not a proper subject for sculpture. Sculpture should not deal with transitory attitudes."

"Lying dead drunk is not a transitory attitude! Nothing is more permanent, more sculpturesque, more monumental!"

"An entertaining paradox," said Mr. Leavenworth, "if we had time to exercise our wits upon it. I remember at Florence an intoxicated figure by Michael Angelo which seemed to me a deplorable aberration of a great mind. I myself touch liquor in no shape whatever. I have travelled through Europe on cold water. The most varied and attractive lists of wines are offered me, but I brush them aside. No cork has ever been drawn at my command!"

"The movement of drawing a cork calls into play a very pretty set of muscles," said Roderick. "I think I will make a figure in that position."

"A Bacchus realistically treated! My dear young friend, never trifle with your lofty mission. Spotless marble should represent virtue, not vice!" And Mr. Leavenworth placidly waved his hand, as if to exercise the spirit of levity, while his glance journeyed with leisurely benignity to another object—a marble replica of the bust of Christina. "An ideal head I presume," he went on; "a fanciful representation of one of the pagan goddesses—a ·Diana, a Flora, a naiad or dryad? I often regret that our American artists should not boldly cast off that extinct nomenclature."

"She is neither a naiad nor a dryad," said Roderick, "and her name is as good as yours or mine."

"You call her—?" Mr. Leavenworth blandly inquired.

"Christina Light," Rowland interposed in charity.

"Ah, our great American beauty! Not a pagan goddess —an American, Christian lady! Yes, I have had the pleasure of conversing with Miss Light. Her conversational powers are not remarkable, but her beauty is of a high order. I observed her the other evening at a large party, where some of the proudest members of the European aristocracy were present—duchesses, princesses, countesses, and others distinguished by similar titles. But for beauty grace and elegance my fair countrywoman left them all nowhere. What woman can compare with a truly refined American lady? The duchesses the other night had no attractions for my eyes; they looked coarse and sensual! It seemed to me that the tyranny of class distinctions must indeed be terrible when such countenances could inspire admiration. You see more beautiful girls in an hour on Broadway than in the whole tour of Europe. Miss Light now, on Broadway, would excite no particular remark."

"Oh, damn Broadway!" Roderick murmured.

Mr. Leavenworth stared, as if this were unpatriotic; then he resumed, almost severely—"I suppose you have heard the news about our fair countrywoman."

"What news?" Roderick had stood with his back turned, fiercely poking at his *lazzarone;* but at Mr. Leavenworth's last words he faced quickly about.

"It's the news of the hour, I believe. Miss Light is admired by the highest people here. They tacitly recognise her superiority. She has had offers of marriage from various great lords. I was extremely happy to learn this circumstance, and to know that they all had been left sighing. She has not been dazzled by their titles and their gilded coronets. She has judged them simply as men, and found them wanting. One of them however, a young Neapolitan prince I believe, has after a long probation succeeded in making himself acceptable. Miss Light has at last said yes, and the engagement has just been announced. I am not generally a reporter of the gossip of the passing hour, but the fact was alluded to an hour ago by a lady with whom I was conversing, and here in Europe these conventional futilities usurp the lion's share of one's attention. I therefore retained the circumstance in my mind. Yes, I regret that Miss Light should marry one of these used-up foreigners. Americans should stand by each other. If she wanted a brilliant match we could have organised it for her. If she wanted a fine fellow—a fine sharp enterprising modern man—I would have undertaken to find him for her without going out of my native city—Columbus, Ohio. And if she wanted a big fortune, I would have found her twenty that she would have had hard work to spend;

money down—not tied up in fever-stricken lands and worm-
eaten villas! What is the name of the young man? Prince
Castaway, or some such thing!"

It was well for Mr. Leavenworth that he was fond of
listening to his own correct periods; for the current
of his eloquence floated him past the short sharp startled
cry with which Roderick greeted his anecdote. The young
man stood looking at him with parted lips and an excited
eye.

"The position of woman," Mr. Leavenworth thoughtfully resumed, "is certainly a very degraded one in these
countries. I doubt whether a European princess can command the respect which in our country is exhibited towards
the obscurest females. The civilisation of a country
should be measured by the deference shown to the weaker
sex. Judged by that standard, where are they over here?"

Though Mr. Leavenworth had not observed Roderick's
emotion it was not lost upon Rowland, who was making
sundry uncomfortable reflections upon it. He saw that
it had instantly become one with the acute irritation
produced by the poor gentleman's oppressive personality,
and that an explosion of some sort was imminent. Mr.
Leavenworth, with calm unconsciousness, proceeded to fire
the mine.

"And now for our Culture!" he said in the same sonorous tones, demanding with a gesture the unveiling of the
figure, which stood somewhat apart, muffled in a great sheet.

Roderick stood looking at him for a moment with concentrated rancour, and then strode to the statue and twitched
off the cover. Mr. Leavenworth settled himself into his
chair with an air of flattered proprietorship and scanned
the unfinished image. "I can conscientiously express
myself as gratified with the general conception," he said.
"The figure has considerable majesty and the countenance
wears a fine open expression. The forehead, however,
strikes me as not sufficiently intellectual. In the statue
of Culture, you know, that should be the great point. The
eye should instinctively seek the forehead. Couldn't you
elevate it a little?"

Roderick, for all answer, tossed the sheet back over the
statue. "Oblige me, sir," he said, "oblige me! Never
mention that thing again."

"Never mention it ? Why, my dear sir——"

"Never mention it. It's an abomination ! "

"An abomination ! My Culture ! "

"Yours, indeed ! " cried Roderick. "It's none of mine.
I disown it."

"Disown it, if you please," said Mr. Leavenworth,
sternly, " but finish it first ! "

"I would rather smash it ! " cried Roderick.

"This is folly, sir. You must keep your engagements."

"I made no engagement. A sculptor isn't a tailor. Did
you ever hear of inspiration ? Mine is dead ! And it's
no laughing matter. You yourself killed it."

"I—I—killed your inspiration ? " cried Mr. Leavenworth,
with the accent of righteous wrath. "You are a very
ungrateful young man ! If ever I have been encouraging
to any one, I have been so to you ! "

"I appreciate your good intentions and I don't wish to
be uncivil. But your encouragement is—superfluous. I
can't work for you ! "

"I call this ill-humour, my good sir ! " said Mr. Leavenworth, as if he had found the damning word.

"Oh, I'm in an infernal humour ! " Roderick answered.

"Pray, sir, is it my inopportune allusion to Miss Light's
marriage ? "

"It's your inopportune everything ! I don't say that
to offend you ; I beg your pardon if it does. I say it by
way of making our rupture complete, irretrievable ! "

Rowland had stood by in silence, but he now interfered.
"Listen to me," he said, laying his hand on Roderick's
arm. "You are standing on the edge of a gulf. If you
suffer this accident to put you out, you take your plunge.
It's no matter that you don't like your work ; you will do
the wisest thing you ever did if you make the effort of
will necessary for finishing it. Destroy the statue then,
if you like, but make the effort. I speak the truth ! "

Roderick looked at him with eyes that still inexorableness
made almost tender. "You, too ? " he simply said.

Rowland felt that he might as well attempt to squeeze
water from a polished crystal as hope to move him. He
turned away and walked into the adjoining room with
a sense of sickening helplessness. In a few moments he
came back and found that Mr. Leavenworth had departed

—presumably in a manner sufficiently majestic. Roderick was sitting with his elbows on his knees and his head in his hands.

Rowland made one more attempt. "You won't mind me, eh?"

"Be so good as not to mind *me!*"

"There's one more point—that you shouldn't go to Mrs. Light's for a month."

"I shall go there this evening."

"That too is an utter folly."

"There are such things as necessary follies."

"You are not reflecting; you are speaking in passion."

"Why then do you make me speak?"

Rowland meditated a moment. "Is it also necessary that you should lose the best friend you have?"

Roderick looked up. "That's for you to settle!"

His best friend clapped on his hat and strode away; in a moment the door closed behind him.

XVI.

ROWLAND walked hard for a couple of hours. He passed up the Corso, out of the Porta del Popolo and into the Villa Borghese, of which he made a complete circuit. The keenness of his irritation subsided, but it left him with an intolerable weight on his heart. When dusk had fallen he found himself near the lodging of his friend Madame Grandoni. He frequently paid her a visit during the hour which preceded dinner, and he now ascended her unillumined staircase and rang at her relaxed bell-rope with an especial desire for diversion. He was told that for the moment she was occupied, but that if he would come in and wait she would presently be with him. He had not sat musing in the firelight for ten minutes when he heard the jingle of the door-bell and then a rustling and murmuring in the hall. The door of the little parlour opened, but before the visitor appeared he had recognised her voice. Christina

Light swept forward, preceded by her poodle and almost filling the narrow room with the train of her dress. She was coloured here and there by the flickering firelight.

"They told me you were here," she said simply, as she took a seat.

"And yet you came in? It is very brave," said Rowland.

"You are the brave one when one thinks of it! Where is the padrona?"

"Occupied for the moment. But she is coming."

"How soon?"

"I have already waited ten minutes; I expect her from moment to moment."

"Meanwhile, we are alone?" And she glanced into the dusky corners of the room.

"Unless Stenterello counts," said Rowland.

"Oh, he knows my secrets—unfortunate brute!" She sat silent awhile, looking into the firelight. Then at last, glancing at Rowland, "Come! say something pleasant!" she exclaimed.

"I have been very happy to hear of your engagement."

"No, I don't mean that. I have heard that so often, only since breakfast, that it has lost all sense. I mean some of those unexpected charming things that you said to me a month ago at St. Cecilia's."

"I offended you then," said Rowland. "I was afraid I had."

"Ah, it occurred to you? Why haven't I seen you since?"

"Really I don't know." And he began to hesitate for an explanation. "I have called—but you have never been at home."

"You were careful to choose the wrong times. You have a way with a poor girl! You sit down and inform her that she is a person with whom a respectable young man can't associate without contamination; your friend is a very nice fellow, you are very careful of his morals, you wish him to know none but nice people, and you beg me therefore to desist. You request me to take these suggestions to heart and to act upon them as promptly as possible. They are not particularly flattering to my vanity.

Vanity however is a sin, and I listen submissively, with an immense desire to be just. If I have many faults I know it in a general way and I try on the whole to do my best. '*Voyons*,' I say to myself, 'it isn't particularly charming to hear oneself made out such a low person, but it is worth thinking over; there is probably a good deal of truth in it, and at any rate we must be as good a girl as we can.' That's the great point! And then here's a magnificent chance for humility. If there's doubt in the matter, let the doubt count against oneself. That is what Saint Catherine did, and Saint Theresa, and all the others, and they are said to have had in consequence the most ineffable joys. Let us go in for a little ineffable joy! I tried it; I swallowed my rising sobs, I made you my curtsey, I determined I would not be spiteful, nor passionate, nor vengeful, nor anything that is supposed to be particularly feminine. I was a better girl than you made out—better at least than you thought; but I would let the difference go, and do magnificently right lest I should not do right enough. I thought of it a great deal for six hours, when I know I didn't seem to be thinking, and then at last I did it! *Santo Dio!*"

"My dear Miss Light, my dear Miss Light!" said Rowland pleadingly.

"Since then," the young girl went on, "I have been waiting for the ineffable joys. They haven't yet turned up!"

"Pray listen to me!" Rowland urged.

"Nothing, nothing, nothing has come of it. I have passed the dreariest month of my life!"

"You are a very terrible young woman!" cried Rowland.

"What do you mean by that?"

"A good many things. We will talk them over. But, first, forgive me if I have offended you!"

She looked at him a moment, hesitating, and then thrust her hands into her muff. "That means nothing. Forgiveness is between equals, and you don't regard me as your equal."

"Really I don't understand!"

Christina rose and moved for a moment about the room. Then turning suddenly, "You don't believe in me!" she cried, "not a grain! I don't know what I would not give to *force* you to believe in me!"

Rowland sprang up, protesting, but before he had time to go far, one of the scanty *portières* was raised, and Madame Grandoni came in, pulling her wig straight. "But you shall believe in me yet," murmured Christina as she passed towards her hostess.

Madame Grandoni turned tenderly to Christina. "I must give you a very solemn kiss, my dear; you are the heroine of the hour. You have really accepted him, eh?"

"So they say!"

"But you ought to know best."

"I don't know—I don't care!" She stood with her hand in Madame Grandoni's, but looking askance at Rowland.

"That's a pretty state of mind," said the old lady, "for a young person who is going to become a princess."

Christina shrugged her shoulders. "Every one expects me to go into ecstasies over that! Could anything be more vulgar? They may chuckle by themselves! Will you let me stay to dinner?"

"If you can dine on a *risotto*. But I imagine you are expected at home."

"You are right. Prince Casamassima dines there *en famille*. But I am not in his family yet!"

"Do you know you are very wicked? I have half a mind not to keep you."

Christina dropped her eyes reflectively. "I beg you will let me stay," she said. "If you wish to cure me of my wickedness you must be very patient and kind with me. It will be worth the trouble. You must show confidence in me." And she gave another glance at Rowland. Then suddenly, in a different tone, "I don't know what I am saying!" she cried. "I am weary, I am more lonely than ever, I wish I were dead!" The tears rose to her eyes, she struggled with them an instant and buried her face in her muff; but at last she burst into uncontrollable sobs and flung her arms upon Madame Grandoni's neck. This shrewd woman gave Rowland a significant nod and a little shrug, over the young girl's beautiful bowed head, and then led Christina tenderly away into the adjoining room. Rowland, left alone, stood there for an instant, intolerably puzzled, face to face with Miss Light's poodle, who had set up a sharp unearthly cry of sympathy with his mistress.

Rowland vented his confusion in dealing a rap with his
stick at the animal's unmelodious muzzle, and then rapidly
left the house.   He saw Mrs. Light's carriage waiting at
the door, and heard afterwards that Christina went home
to dinner.

A couple of days later he went for a fortnight to
Florence. He had twenty minds to leave Italy altogether;
and at Florence he could at least more freely decide upon
his future movements. He felt deeply, incurably disgusted.
Reflective benevolence stood prudently aside, and for the
time touched the source of his irritation with no softening
side-lights.

It was the middle of March, and by the middle of
March in Florence the spring is already warm and deep.
He had an infinite relish for the place and the season, but
as he strolled by the Arno and paused here and there in
the great galleries they failed to soothe his irritation. He
was sore at heart, and as the days went by the soreness
deepened rather than healed. He felt as if he had a
complaint against fortune; good-natured as he was, his
good-nature this time quite declined to let it pass. He
had tried to be wise, he had tried to be kind, he had engaged in an estimable enterprise; but his wisdom, his
kindness, his energy, had been thrown back in his face.
He was disappointed, and his disappointment had an angry
spark in it. The sense of wasted time, of wasted hope and
faith. kept him constant company. There were times
when the beautiful things about him only exasperated his
discontent. He went to the Pitti Palace, and Raphael's
Madonna of the Chair seemed in its soft serenity to mock
him with the suggestion of unattainable repose. He
lingered on the bridges at sunset and knew that the light
was enchanting and the mountains were divine, but there
seemed to be something horribly invidious and unwelcome
in the fact. He felt, in a word, like a man who has been
cruelly defrauded and who wishes to have his revenge.
Life owed him, he thought, a compensation, and he should
be restless and resentful until he found it. He knew—or
he seemed to know—where he should find it; but he hardly
told himself, and thought of the thing under mental protest, as a man in want of money may think of certain funds
that he holds in trust. In his melancholy meditations the

idea of something better than all this, something that might softly, richly interpose, something that might reconcile him to the future, something that might make one's tenure of life strong and zealous instead of mechanical and uncertain—the idea of concrete compensation in a word—shaped itself sooner or later into the image of Mary Garland.

Very odd, you may say, that at this time of day Rowland should still be brooding over a girl of no brilliancy, of whom he had had but the lightest of glimpses two years before; very odd that so deep an impression should have been made by so lightly pressed an instrument. We must admit the oddity, and remark simply in explanation that his sentiment apparently belonged to that species of emotion of which by the testimony of the poets the very name and essence are oddity. One night he slept but half an hour; he found his thoughts taking a turn which excited him portentously. He walked up and down his room half the night. It looked out on the Arno; the noise of the river came in at the open window; he felt like dressing and going down into the streets. Towards morning he flung himself into a chair; though he was wide awake he was less excited. It seemed to him that he saw his idea from the outside, that he judged it and condemned it; yet it stood there before him, very distinct, and in a certain way imperious. During the day he tried to banish it and forget it; but it fascinated, haunted, at moments frightened him. He tried to amuse himself, paid visits, resorted to several violent devices for diverting his thoughts. If on the morrow he had committed a crime, the persons whom he had seen that day would have testified that he had talked strangely and had not seemed like himself. He felt certainly very unlike himself; long afterwards, in retrospect, he used to reflect that during those days he had for a while been literally *beside* himself. His idea persisted; it clung to him like a sturdy beggar. The sense of the matter, roughly expressed, was this. If Roderick were really going, as he himself had phrased it, to "fizzle out," one might help him on the way—one might smooth the *descensus Averni.* For forty-eight hours there swam before Rowland's eyes a vision of Roderick, graceful and beautiful as he passed, plunging like a diver into a misty gulf. The gulf was destruction, annihilation, death; but if death were decreed, why should not the agony be brief? Beyond this vision there faintly glimmered another, as in the children's game of the magic lantern a picture is superposed on the white wall before the last one has quite faded. It represented Mary Garland standing there with eyes in which the horror seemed slowly, slowly to expire, and hanging motionless hands which at last made no resistance when his own offered to take them. When of old a man was burnt at the stake it was cruel to have to be present; but if one were present it was a charity to lend a hand to pile up the fuel and make the flames do their work quickly and the smoke muffle up the victim. With all deference to your charity, this was perhaps an obligation you would especially feel if you had a reversionary interest in something the victim was to leave behind him.

One morning in the midst of all this Rowland walked heedlessly out of one of the city gates and found himself on the road to Fiesole. It was a completely lovely day; the March sun felt like May, as the English poet of Florence says; the thick-blossomed shrubs and vines that hung over the walls of villa and *podere* flung their odorous promise into the warm still air. Rowland followed the winding climbing lanes; lingered as he got higher beneath the rusty cypresses, beside the low parapets, where you look down on the charming city and sweep the vale of the Arno; reached the little square before the cathedral, and rested awhile in the massive, dusky church; then climbed higher, to the Franciscan convent which is poised on the very apex of the great hill. He rang at the little gateway; a shabby, senile, red-faced brother admitted him with almost maudlin friendliness. There was a dreary chill in the chapel and the corridors, and he passed rapidly through them into the delightfully steep and tangled old garden which runs wild over the forehead of the mountain. He had been in it before, and he was very fond of it. The garden hangs in the air, and you ramble from terrace to terrace and wonder how it keeps from slipping down in full consummation of its dishonour and decay into the nakedly romantic gorge beneath. It was just noon when Rowland went in, and after roaming about awhile he flung himself in the sun on a mossy stone bench and pulled his hat over his eyes. The short shadows of the brown-coated cypresses above him had grown very long, and yet he had not passed back through the convent. One of the monks, in his faded snuff-coloured robe, came wandering out into the garden, reading his greasy little breviary. Suddenly he came towards the bench on which Rowland had stretched himself, and paused a moment attentively. Rowland was lingering there still; he was sitting with his head in his hands and his elbows on his knees. He seemed not to have heard the sandaled tread of the good brother, but as the monk remained watching him he at last looked up. It was not the ignoble old man who had admitted him, but a pale gaunt personage, of a graver and more ascetic, and yet of a benignant aspect. Rowland's face bore the traces of extreme trouble. The *frate* kept his finger in his little book and folded his arms picturesquely across his breast. It can hardly be determined whether his attitude, as he bent his sympathetic Italian eye upon Rowland, was a happy incident or the result of an exquisite spiritual discernment. To Rowland, at any rate, under the emotion of that moment, it seemed blessedly opportune. He rose and approached the monk, laying his hand on his arm.

" My brother," he said, " did you ever see the Devil ? "

The *frate* gazed gravely and crossed himself. " Heaven forbid ! "

" He was here," Rowland went on, " here in this lovely garden, as he was once in Paradise, half an hour ago. But have no fear ; I drove him out." And Rowland stooped and picked up his hat, which had rolled away into a bed of cyclamen in vague symbolism of an actual physical tussle.

" You have been tempted, my brother ? " asked the friar tenderly.

" Hideously ! "

" And you have resisted—and conquered ! "

" I believe I have conquered."

" The blessed Saint Francis be praised ! It is well done. If you like we will offer a mass for you."

" I am not a Catholic," said Rowland.

The *frate* smiled with dignity. " That is a reason the more."

" But it's for you then to choose. Shake hands with me,"

Rowland added; "that will do as well; and suffer me as I go out to stop a moment in your chapel."

They shook hands and separated. The *frate* crossed himself, opened his book, and wandered away in relief against the western sky. Rowland passed back into the convent and paused long enough in the chapel to look for the alms-box. He had had what is vulgarly called a great scare; he believed very poignantly for the time in the Devil, and he felt an irresistible need to subscribe to any institution which engaged to keep him at a distance.

The next day he returned to Rome, and the day after that he went in search of Roderick. He found him on the Pincian, with his back turned to the crowd, looking at the sunset. "I went to Florence," Rowland said, "and I thought of going farther; but I came back on purpose to give you another piece of advice. Decidedly, you won't leave Rome?"

"Never!" said Roderick.

"The only chance that I see then of a revival of your sense of responsibility to—to those various sacred things you have forgotten—is in sending for your mother to join you here."

Roderick stared. "For my mother?"

"For your mother—and for Miss Garland."

Roderick still stared; and then, slowly and faintly, his face flushed. "For Mary Garland—for my mother?" he repeated. "Send for them?"

"Tell me this; I have often wondered, but till now I have forborne to ask. You are still engaged to your cousin?"

Roderick frowned darkly, but assented.

"Wouldn't it give you pleasure then to see her?"

Roderick turned away and for some moments answered nothing. "Pleasure!" he said at last huskily. "Pain will do as well!"

"I regard you as a sick man," Rowland continued. "In such a case Miss Garland would say that her place is at your side."

Roderick looked at him some time askance, mistrustfully. "Is this a deep-laid snare?" he asked slowly.

Rowland had come back with all his patience rekindled, but these words gave it an almost fatal chill. "Heaven forgive you!" he cried bitterly. "My idea has been simply this—try in decency to understand it. I have tried to befriend you, to help you, to inspire you with confidence, and I have failed. I took you from the hands of your mother and that girl, and it seems to me my duty to restore you to their hands. That's all I have to say."

He was going, but Roderick forcibly detained him. It would have been but a rough way of expressing it to say that one could never know how Roderick would take a thing. It had happened more than once that when hit hard deservedly he had received the blow with touching gentleness. On the other hand he had often resented the softest taps. The secondary effect of Rowland's present admonition seemed reassuring. "I beg you to wait," he said, "to forgive that shabby speech and to let me reflect." And he walked up and down awhile reflecting. At last he stopped, with a look in his face that Rowland had not seen all the winter. It was strikingly beautiful.

"How strange it is," he said, "that the simplest devices are the last that occur to one!" And he broke into a light laugh. "To see Mary Garland is just what I want. And my mother—my mother can't hurt me now!"

"You will write then?"

"I will telegraph. They must come at whatever cost. Striker can arrange it all for them."

In a couple of days he told Rowland that he had received a telegraphic answer to his message, informing him that the two ladies were to sail immediately for Leghorn in one of the small steamers which ply between that port and New York. They would arrive therefore in less than a month. Rowland passed this month of expectation in no very serene frame of mind. His suggestion had had its source in the deepest places of his agitated conscience; but there was something intolerable in the thought of the suffering to which the event would probably subject those undefended women. They had scraped together their scanty funds, and embarked at twenty-four hours' notice upon the dreadful sea to journey tremulously to shores darkened by the shadow of deeper alarms. He could only promise himself to be their devoted friend and servant. Preoccupied as he was he was able to observe that expectation, with Roderick, took a form which seemed singular even among his characteristic singularities. If redemption—Roderick seemed to reason—was to arrive with his mother and his affianced bride, these last moments of error should be doubly erratic. He did nothing; but inaction, with him, took on an unwonted air of gentle gaiety, He laughed and whistled and went often to Mrs. Light's; though Rowland failed to guess in what fashion present circumstances had modified his relations with Christina. The month ebbed away and Rowland daily expected to hear from Roderick that he had gone to Leghorn to meet the ship. He heard nothing, and late one evening, not having seen his friend in three or four days, he stopped at Roderick's lodging to assure himself that he had gone at last. A cab was standing in the street, but as it was a couple of doors off he hardly heeded it. The hall at the foot of the staircase was dark, like most Roman halls, and he paused in the open doorway on hearing the advancing footstep of a person with whom he wished to avoid coming into collision. While he did so he heard another footstep behind him, and turning round found that Roderick himself had just overtaken him. At the same moment a woman's figure advanced from within, into the light of the street-lamp, and a face, half startled, glanced at him out of the darkness. He gave a cry—it was the face of Mary Garland. Her glance flew past him to Roderick, and in a second a startled exclamation broke from her own lips. It made Rowland turn again. Roderick stood there, pale, apparently trying to speak, but saying nothing. His lips were parted, and he was wavering slightly with a strange movement—the movement of a man who has drunk too much. Then Rowland's eyes met Miss Garland's again, and her own, which had rested a moment on Roderick's, were formidable.

XVII.

How it occurred that Roderick had failed to be at Leghorn at the moment of his mother's arrival was never clearly ascertained ; for he undertook to give no elaborate explanation of his fault. He never indulged in professions (touching personal conduct) as to the future, or in remorse as to the past, and as he would have asked no praise if he had travelled night and day to embrace Mrs. Hudson as she set foot on shore, he made (in Rowland's presence at least) no apology for having left her to come in search of him. It was to be said that thanks to an unprecedentedly fine season the voyage of the two ladies had been surprisingly rapid, and that according to common probabilities if Roderick had left Rome on the morrow (as he declared that he had intended) he would still have had a day or two of waiting at Leghorn. Rowland's silent inference was that Christina Light had beguiled him into letting the time slip, and it was accompanied with a silent inquiry whether she had done so unconsciously or maliciously. He had told her presumably that his mother and his cousin were about to arrive ; and it was pertinent to remember hereupon that she was a young lady of mysterious impulses. Rowland heard in due time the story of the adventures of the two ladies from Northampton. Mary Garland's wish, at Leghorn, on finding they were left to their own devices, had been to telegraph to Roderick and await an answer ; for she knew that their arrival was a trifle premature. But Mrs. Hudson's maternal heart had taken the alarm. Roderick's sending for them was, to her imagination, a confession of illness, and his not being at Leghorn, a proof of it ; an hour's delay was therefore cruel both to herself and to him. She insisted on immediate departure ; and, unskilled as they were in the mysteries of foreign (or even of domestic) travel, they had hurried in trembling eagerness to Rome. They had arrived late in the evening, and knowing nothing of inns had got into a cab and proceeded to Roderick's lodging. At the door poor Mrs. Hudson's trepidation had overcome her and she had sat quaking and crying in the vehicle. Mary had bravely gone in, groped her way up the dusky staircase, reached Roderick's door and, with the assistance of such acquaintance with the Italian tongue as she had culled from a phrase-book during the calm hours of the voyage, had learned from the old woman who had her cousin's household economy in charge, that he was in the best of health and spirits and had gone forth a few hours before with his hat on his ear *per divertirsi.*

These things Rowland learned during a visit he paid the two ladies the evening after their arrival. Mrs. Hudson spoke of them at great length, and with an air of clinging confidence in Rowland which told him that he was now enshrined in her innermost favour. But her fright was over, though she was still catching her breath a little, like a person dragged ashore out of waters uncomfortably deep. She was excessively bewildered and confused, and seemed more than ever to demand a tender handling from her friends. Before her companion Rowland was distinctly conscious that he trembled. He wondered extremely what was going on in this young lady's mind; what was her silent commentary on the incidents of the night before. He wondered all the more because he immediately perceived that she was now an altered woman and that the difference was not an injury. She was older, easier, more free, she had more of the manner of society. She had more beauty as well, inasmuch as her beauty before had been the quality of her expression, and the sources from which this beauty was fed had in these two years evidently not wasted themselves. Rowland felt almost instantly—he could hardly have said why; it was in her voice, in her tone, in the air—that a total change had passed over her attitude towards himself. She trusted him now absolutely; whether or no she liked him, she believed in his solidity. He felt that during the coming weeks he should need to be solid. Mrs. Hudson was at one of the smaller hotels, and her sitting-room was frugally lighted by a couple of candles. Rowland made the most of this dim illumination to try to detect the afterglow of that frightened flash from Mary's eyes the night before. It had been but a flash, for what provoked it had instantly vanished. Rowland, on this occasion, seeing Roderick instantly perceive what had

happened, had given him a silent blessing. If Roderick
had been drinking, its gravity sobered him on the spot; in
a single moment he collected his wits. The next moment,
with a ringing jovial cry, he was folding the young girl in
his arms, and the next he was beside his mother's carriage,
half smothered in her sobs and caresses. Rowland had
recommended an hotel close at hand and had then discreetly
retired. Roderick was at this time doing his part superbly,
and Mary Garland's brow was serene. It was serene now,
twenty-four hours later; but nevertheless her alarm had
lasted an appreciable moment. What had become of it?
It had dropped down deep into her memory, and it was
lying there for the present in the shade. But from one
day to another, Rowland said to himself, it would hold up
its head—it would begin to watch and listen—it would
stand there confronting him. Meanwhile he made the
most of the hours—he passed them in the consciousness of
being near her. The two ladies had spent the day within
doors, resting from the fatigues of travel. The younger
traveller, Rowland suspected, was not so fatigued as she
suffered it to be assumed. She had remained with Mrs.
Hudson to attend to her personal wants, which the latter
seemed to think now that she was in a foreign land with a
southern climate and a Catholic religion would forthwith
become very complex and formidable, though as yet they
had simply resolved themselves into a desire for a great
deal of tea, and for a certain extremely familiar old black
and white shawl across her feet as she lay on the sofa.
But the sense of novelty was evidently strong upon Mary,
and the light of expectation was in her eye. She was restless and excited; she moved about the room and went
often to the window; she was observing keenly; she
watched the Italian servants as they came and went; she
had already had a long colloquy with the French chamber-
maid, who had expounded her views on the Roman question;
she noted the small differences in the furniture, in the
cookery, in the sounds that came in from the street. Rowland was sure that she observed to good purpose, that she
only needed opportunity, and that she would gather impressions as thickly clustered as the purple bunches of a vintage.
He wished immensely he might have a hand in it; he
wished he might show her Rome. That of course would

be Roderick's office. But he promised himself at least to take advantage of off-hours.

"It behoves you to appreciate your good fortune," he said to her. "To be young and elastic, and yet old enough and wise enough to discriminate and reflect, and to come to Italy for the first time—that is one of the greatest pleasures that life has to offer us. It is but right to remind you of it, so that you may make the most of your chances and may not accuse yourself later of having wasted the precious season."

Mary looked at him, smiling intently, and went to the window again. "I expect to enjoy it," she said. "Don't be afraid; I am not wasteful."

"I am afraid we are not qualified, you know," said Mrs. Hudson. "We are told that you must know so much, that you must have read so many books. Our taste has not been cultivated. When I was a young lady at school I remember I had a medal with a pink ribbon for 'proficiency in ancient history'—the seven kings, or is it the seven hills? and Quintus Curtius and Julius Cæsar, and—and that period, you know. I believe I have my medal somewhere in a drawer now, but I have forgotten all about the kings. But after Roderick came to Italy we tried to learn something about it. Last winter Mary used to read *Corinne* to me in the evenings, and in the mornings she used to read another book to herself. What was it, Mary, that book that was so long, you know—in fifteen volumes?"

"It was Sismondi's *Italian Republics*," said Mary simply.

Rowland could not help laughing; whereupon Mary blushed. "Did you finish it?" he asked.

"Yes, and began another—a shorter one—Roscoe's *Leo the Tenth*."

"Did you find them interesting?"

"Oh yes."

"Do you like history?"

"Some of it."

"That's a woman's answer! And do you like art?"

She paused a moment. "I have never seen it!"

"You have great advantages now, my dear, with Roderick and Mr. Mallet," said Mrs. Hudson. "I am sure no young lady ever had such advantages. You come straight to the highest authorities. Roderick, I suppose, will show you the practice of art, and Mr. Mallet, perhaps, if he will be so good, will show you the theory. As an artist's wife you ought to know something about it."

"One learns a good deal about it here by simply living," said Rowland; "by going and coming about one's daily avocations."

"Dear, dear, how wonderful that we should be here in the midst of it!" murmured Mrs. Hudson. "To think of art being out there in the streets! We didn't see much of it last evening as we drove from the station. But the streets were so dark, and we were so frightened! But we are very easy now; are we not, Mary?"

"I am very happy," said Mary gravely, wandering back to the window again.

Roderick came in at this moment and kissed his mother, and then went over and joined his betrothed. Rowland sat with Mrs. Hudson, who evidently had a word which she deemed of some value for his private ear. She followed Roderick with intensely earnest eyes.

"I wish to tell you, sir," she said, "now very grateful —how very thankful—what a happy mother I am! I feel as if I owed it all to you. To find my poor boy so handsome, so prosperous, so elegant, so famous—and ever to have doubted of you! What must you think of me? You are our guardian angel, sir. I often say so to Mary."

Rowland wore in response to this speech a rather inscrutable countenance. He could only murmur that he was glad she found Roderick looking well. He had of course promptly asked himself whether it would be the best policy just to give her a word of warning—turn the handle of the door through which, later, disappointment might enter. But he had determined to say nothing, and simply to wait for Roderick to find effective inspiration in those confidently expectant eyes. It was to be supposed that he was seeking for it now; he remained some time at the window with his cousin. But at last he turned away and came over to the fireside with a contraction of the eyebrows which seemed to intimate that the young girl's influence was for the moment at least not soothing. She presently followed him, and for an instant Rowland observed her watching him as if she thought him strange. "Strange enough," thought Rowland, "he may seem to her if he will!" Roderick directed his glance to his friend with a certain peremptory air which—roughly interpreted—was equivalent to a request to share the intellectual expense of entertaining the ladies. "Heaven help us!" Rowland cried within himself; "is he already tired of them?"

"To-morrow of course we must begin to put you through the mill," Roderick said to his mother. "And be it hereby known to Mallet that we count upon him to turn the wheel."

"I will do as you please, my son," said Mrs. Hudson. "So long as I have you with me I don't care where I go. We must not take up too much of Mr. Mallet's time."

"His time is inexhaustible; he has nothing under the sun to do. Have you, Rowland? If you had seen the big hole I have been making in it! Where will you go first? You have your choice—from the Scala Santa to the Cloaca Maxima."

"Let us take things in order," said Rowland. "We will go first to Saint Peter's. Miss Garland, I hope you are impatient to see Saint Peter's."

"I should like to go first to Roderick's studio," said Miss Garland.

"It's a very nasty place," said Roderick. "But do what you like."

"Yes we must see your beautiful things before we can look contentedly at anything else," said Mrs. Hudson.

"I have no beautiful things," said Roderick. "You may see what there is! What makes you look so odd?"

This inquiry was abruptly addressed to his mother, who in response glanced appealingly at Mary, and raised a startled hand to her smooth hair.

"No, it's your face," said Roderick. "What has happened to it these two years? It has changed its expression."

"Your mother has prayed a great deal," said Mary, simply.

"I didn't suppos of course it was from doing anything bad! It makes you a very good face—very interesting, very solemn. It has very fine lines in it; something might be done with it." And Rowland held one of the candles near the poor lady's head.

She was covered with confusion. "My son, my son," she said with dignity, "I don't understand you."

In a flash all his old alacrity had come to him. "I suppose a man may admire his own mother!" he cried. "If you please, madam, you will sit to me for that head. I see it, I see it! I will make something that a queen can't get done for her."

Rowland respectfully urged her to assent; he saw Roderick was in the vein and would probably do something eminently original. She gave her promise at last after many soft inarticulate protests and a frightened petition that she might be allowed to keep her knitting.

Rowland returned the next day, with plenty of zeal for the part Roderick had assigned to him. It had been arranged that they should go to Saint Peter's. Roderick was in high good-humour, and in the carriage was watching his mother with a fine mixture of filial and professional interest. Mrs. Hudson looked up mistrustfully at the tall shabby houses, and grasped the side of the barouche in her hand, as if she were in a sail-boat in dangerous waters. Rowland sat opposite to Miss Garland. She was totally oblivious of her companions; from the moment the carriage left the hotel she sat gazing wide-eyed and absorbed at the objects about them. If Rowland had felt disposed he might have made a joke of her intense seriousness. From time to time he told her the name of a place or a building, and she nodded without looking at him. When they emerged into the great square between Bernini's colonnades she laid her hand on Mrs. Hudson's arm and sank back in the carriage, staring up at the vast yellow façade of the church. Inside the church Roderick gave his arm to his mother, and Rowland constituted himself the especial guide of the younger lady. He walked with her slowly everywhere and made the entire circuit, telling her all he knew of the history of the building. This was a great deal, but she listened attentively, keeping her eyes fixed on the dome. To Rowland himself it had never seemed so radiantly sublime as at these moments; he felt almost as if he had designed it

himself and had a right to be proud of it. He left Mary
Garland a while on the steps of the choir, where she had
seated herself to rest, and went to join their companions.
Mrs. Hudson was watching a great circle of tattered
contadini, who were kneeling before the image of Saint
Peter. The fashion of their tatters fascinated her; she
stood gazing at them in a sort of terrified pity, and could
not be induced to look at anything else. Rowland went
back to Mary and sat down beside her.

"Well, what do you think of Europe?" he asked
smiling.

"I think it's dreadful!" she said abruptly.

"Dreadful?"

"I feel so strangely—I could almost cry."

"How is it that you feel?"

"So sorry for the poor past, that seems to have died
here in my heart in an hour!"

"But, surely, you are pleased—you are interested."

"I am overwhelmed. Here in a single hour everything
is changed. It is as if a wall in my mind had been
knocked down at a stroke. Before me lies an immense
new world, and it makes the old one, the poor little
narrow familiar one I have always known, seem pitiful."

"But you didn't come to Rome to keep your eyes
fastened on that narrow little world. Forget it, turn
your back on it and enjoy all this."

"I want to enjoy it; but as I sat here just now, looking
up at that golden mist in the dome, I seemed to see in it
the vague shapes of certain people and things at home.
To enjoy, as you say, as these things demand of one to
enjoy them, is to break with one's past. And breaking
is a pain!"

"Don't mind the pain, and it will cease to trouble you.
Enjoy, enjoy; it is your duty. Yours especially!"

"Why mine especially?"

"Because I am very sure that you have a mind formed
to do justice to everything interesting and beautiful. You
are extremely intelligent."

"You don't know," said the girl simply.

"In that matter one *feels*. I really think that I know
better than you. I don't want to seem patronising, but I
suspect that you are a capital subject for development.

Give yourself the best company, trust yourself, let yourself go!"

She looked away from him for some moments, down the gorgeous vista of the great church. "But what you say," she said at last, "means *change !*"

"Change for the better!" cried Rowland.

"How can one tell? As one stands one knows the worst. It seems to me very frightful to develop," she added, with her complete smile.

"One is in for it in one way or another, and one might as well do it with a good grace as with a bad! Since one can't escape life it is better to take it by the hand."

"Is this what you call life?" she asked.

"What do you mean by 'this'?"

"Saint Peter's—all this splendour, all Rome—pictures, ruins, statues, beggars, monks."

"It is not all of it, but it is a large part of it. All these things are impregnated with life; they are the results of an old and complex civilisation."

"An old and complex civilisation: I am afraid I don't like that."

"Don't conclude on that point just yet. Wait till you have tested it. While you wait you will see an immense number of very beautiful things—things that you are made to understand. They won't leave you as they found you; then you can judge. Don't tell me I know nothing about your understanding. I have a right to count upon it."

Mary gazed awhile aloft into the dome. "I am not sure I understand that," she said, nodding upward.

"I hope at least that at a cursory glance it pleases you," said Rowland. "You needn't be afraid to tell the truth. What strikes some people is' that it is so remarkably small."

"Oh, it's large enough; it's very wonderful. There are things in Rome then," she added in a moment, turning and looking at him, "that are very, *very* beautiful?"

"Lots of them."

"Some of the most beautiful things in the world?"

"Unquestionably."

"What are they? which things have most beauty?"

"That is according to taste. I should say the antique sculpture.'"

"How long will it take to see it all; to know at least something about it?"

"You can see it all, as far as mere seeing goes, in a fortnight. But to know it is a thing for one's leisure. The more time you spend in the midst of it, the more you care for it." After a moment's hesitation he went on, "Why should you grudge time? It's all in your way, since you are to be an artist's wife."

"I have thought of that," she said. "It may be that I shall always live here, among the most beautiful things in the world!"

"Very possibly! I should like to see you ten years hence."

"I dare say I shall seem greatly altered. But I am sure of one thing."

"Of what?"

"That for the most part I shall be quite the same. I ask nothing better than to believe the fine things you say about my understanding, but even if they are true it won't matter. I shall be what I was made, what I am now—a young woman from the country! The fruit of a civilisation not old and complex, but new and simple."

"I am delighted to hear it; that's an excellent basis."

"Perhaps if you show me anything more you will grow rather tired of my basis. Therefore I warn you."

"I am not frightened. I should like extremely to make a request of you. Be what you are, be what you choose; but do, sometimes, as I tell you."

If Rowland was not frightened, neither perhaps was his companion; but she seemed at least slightly disturbed. She proposed that they should join the others.

Mrs. Hudson spoke under her breath; she could not be accused of the want of reverence sometimes attributed to Protestants in the great Catholic temples. "Mary dear," she whispered, "suppose we had to kiss that dreadful brass toe. If I could only have kept our door-knocker at Northampton as bright at that! I think it's so heathenish; but Roderick says he thinks it's sublime."

Roderick had evidently grown a trifle perverse. "It's sublimer than anything that *your* religion asks you to do!" he exclaimed.

"Surely our religion sometimes gives us very difficult duties," said Mary.

"The duty of sitting in a whitewashed meeting-house and listening to a nasal Puritan! I admit that's difficult. But it's not sublime. I am speaking of ceremonies, of forms. It is in my line, you know, to make much of forms. I think this is a very beautiful one. Couldn't you do it?" he demanded, looking at his cousin.

She looked back at him intently and then shook her head. "I think not!"

"Why not?"

"I don't know; I couldn't!"

During this little discussion our four friends were standing near the venerable image of Saint Peter, and a squalid, savage looking peasant, a tattered ruffian of the most orthodox Italian aspect, had been performing his devotions before it. He turned away crossing himself, and Mrs. Hudson gave a little shudder of horror.

"After that," she murmured, "I suppose he thinks he is as good as any one! And here is another. Oh, what a beautiful person!"

A young lady had approached the sacred effigy, after having wandered away from a group of companions. She kissed the brazen toe, touched it with her forehead, and turned round facing our friends. Rowland then recognised Christina Light. He was stupefied at this indication that she had suddenly embraced the Catholic faith, for it was but a few weeks before that she had treated him to a passionate profession of indifference. Had she entered the church to put herself *en règle* with what was expected of a Princess Casamassima? While Rowland was mentally asking these questions she was approaching him and his friends on her way to the great altar. At first she did not perceive them.

Mary Garland had been gazing at her. "You told me," she said gently to Rowland, "that Rome contained some of the most beautiful things in the world. This surely is one of them!"

At this moment Christina's eye met Rowland's and before giving him any sign of recognition she glanced rapidly at his companions. She saw Roderick, but she gave him no bow; she looked at Mrs. Hudson, she looked

at Mary Garland. At Mary Garland she looked fixedly,
piercingly, from head to foot, the slow pace at which she
advanced making it possible. Then suddenly, as if she
had perceived Roderick for the first time, she gave him a
charming nod, a radiant smile. In a moment he was at
her side. She stopped, and he stood talking to her; she
continued to look at Mary.

"Why, Roderick knows her!" cried Mrs. Hudson in an
awe-struck whisper. "I supposed she was some great
princess."

"She is—almost!" said Rowland. "She is the most
beautiful girl in Europe, and Roderick has made her
bust."

"Her bust? Dear, dear!" murmured Mrs. Hudson,
vaguely shocked. "What a strange bonnet!"

"She has very strange eyes," said Mary, turning
away.

The two ladies, with Rowland, began to descend towards
the door of the church. On their way they passed Mrs.
Light, the Cavaliere and the poodle, and Rowland informed
his companions of the relation in which these personages
stood to Roderick's young lady.

"Think of it, Mary!" said Mrs. Hudson. What splendid
people he must know! No wonder he found Northampton
dull!"

"I like the sad little old gentleman," said Mary.

"Why do you call him sad?" Rowland asked, struck
with the observation.

"He seems so!" she answered simply.

As they were reaching the door they were overtaken by
Roderick, whose interview with Miss Light had perceptibly
brightened his eye. "So you are acquainted with princesses?" said his mother softly as they passed into the
portico.

"Miss Light is not a princess!" said Roderick curtly.

"But Mr. Mallet says so," urged Mrs. Hudson, rather
disappointed.

"I meant that she was going to be," said Rowland.

"It's by no means certain that she is even going to
be!" Roderick answered.

"Ah," said Rowland, "I give it up!"

XVIII.

RODERICK almost immediately demanded that his mother should sit to him at his studio for her portrait, and Rowland ventured to add another word of urgency. If Roderick's idea had really taken hold of him it was an immense pity his inspiration should be wasted ; inspiration in these days had become too precious a commodity. It was arranged therefore that for the present, during the mornings, Mrs. Hudson should place herself at her son's service. This involved but little sacrifice, for the good lady's appetite for antiquities was diminutive and bird-like, the usual round of galleries and churches fatigued her, and she was glad to purchase immunity from sight-seeing by a regular afternoon drive. It became natural in this way that Mary Garland having her mornings free, Rowland should propose to be her cicerone. He could not find it in his heart to accuse Roderick of neglect of a girl who was united to him by a double bond, for it was natural that the inspirations of a man of genius should be both capricious and imperious ; but of course he wondered how Mary felt, as the young man's promised wife, on being so summarily handed over to another man to be entertained. However she felt, he was certain he should learn very little about it. There had been between them none but indirect allusions to her intended marriage ; and Rowland had no desire to discuss it more largely, for he had no quarrel with matters as they stood. They wore the same delightful aspect through the lovely month of May, and the ineffable charm of Rome at that period seemed but the radiant sympathy of nature with his happy opportunity. The weather was divine ; each particular morning, as he walked from his lodging to Mrs. Hudson's modest inn, seemed to have a blessing upon it. The elder lady had usually gone off to the studio, and he found Mary sitting alone at the open window, turning the leaves of some book of artistic or antiquarian reference that he had given her. She always had a smile, she was always eager, alert, responsive. She might be grave by nature, she might be sad by circumstance, she might have secret doubts and pangs, but she was essentially young and strong and fresh and able to enjoy. Her enjoyment was not especially demonstrative, but it was curiously diligent. Rowland felt that it was not amusement and sensation that she coveted, but knowledge—facts that she might noiselessly lay away piece by piece in the fragrant darkness of her serious mind, so that under this head at least she should not be a perfectly portionless bride. She never merely pretended to understand; she let things go in her modest fashion at the moment; but she watched them on their way over the crest of the hill, and when her attention seemed not likely to be missed it went hurrying after them and ran breathless at their side and begged them for the secret. Rowland took a high satisfaction in observing that she never mistook the second-best for the best, and that when she was in the presence of a masterpiece she recognised the importance of the occasion. She said many things which he thought very profound—that is if they really had the fine intention he suspected. This point he usually tried to ascertain; but he was obliged to proceed cautiously, for in her mistrustful shyness it seemed to her that cross-examination must necessarily be ironical. She wished to know just where she was going—what she would gain or lose. This was partly on account of the purity and rigidity of a mind that had not lived with its door ajar upon the high-road of thought, for passing ideas to drop in and out at their pleasure, but had made much of a few long visits from guests cherished and honoured—guests whose presence was a solemnity. But it was even more because Mary was conscious of a sort of growing self-respect, a sense of devoting her life not to her own ends, but to those of another whose life would be large and brilliant. She had been brought up to think a great deal of "nature" and nature's innocent laws; but now Rowland had talked to her ingeniously of culture; her fresh imagination had responded, and she was pursuing this mysterious object into retreats where the need for some intellectual effort gave her an air of charming tension. She wished to be very sure, to take only the best, knowing it to be the best. There was something exquisite in her pious desire to improve herself, and Rowland encouraged it none the less that its fruits were not for him. In spite

of her lurking rigidity and angularity it was very evident
that she had a native sense of beauty which only asked to
become pliable, and in which already at moments she lost
herself delightedly. For all that she was not demonstrative,
that her manner was simple and her small-talk of no very
ample flow; for all that, as she has said, she was a young
woman from the country, and the country was West Nazareth, and West Nazareth was in its way a stubborn little
fact, she was feeling the direct influence of the great
amenities of the world, and they were shaping her with
a divinely intelligent touch. "Oh, exquisite virtue of
circumstance!" cried Rowland to himself, "that takes
us by the hand and leads us forth out of corners where
perforce our attitudes are a trifle contracted, and beguiles
us into testing unappreciated faculties!" When he said
to Mary Garland that he wished he might see her ten
years hence, he was paying mentally an equal compliment
to circumstance and to the girl herself. Capacity was
there, it could be freely trusted; observation would have
but to sow its generous seed. "A superior woman"—the
idea had harsh associations, but he watched it imaging
itself in the vagueness of the future with a kind of
hopeless confidence.

They went a great deal to Saint Peter's, and Mary confessed very speedily that to climb the long low yellow
steps, beneath the huge florid façade, and then, pushing the
ponderous leathern apron of the door, find oneself a mere
sentient point in that brilliant immensity, was a sensation of which the keenness never failed to renew itself.
In those days the hospitality of the Vatican had not been
curtailed, and it was an easy and delightful matter to pass
from the gorgeous church to the solemn company of the
antique marbles. Here Rowland had with his companion
a great deal of talk, and found himself expounding æsthe-
tics à perte de vue. He discovered that she made notes
of her likes and dislikes in a new-looking little memoran-
dum book, and he wondered to what extent she reported
his own discourse. These were charming hours. The
galleries had been so cold all winter that Rowland had
been an exile from them; but now that the sun was already
scorching in the great square between the colonnades, where
the twin fountains flashed almost fiercely, the marble

coolness of the long image-bordered vistas made them a delightful refuge. The great herd of tourists had almost departed, and our two friends often found themselves for half an hour at a time in sole and tranquil possession of the beautiful Braccio Nuovo. Here and there was an open window, where they lingered and leaned, looking out into the warm dead air, over the towers of the city, at the soft-hued historic hills, at the stately shabby gardens of the palace, or at some sunny empty grass-grown court lost in the heart of the labyrinthine pile. They went sometimes into the chambers painted by Raphael, and of course paid their respects to the Sistine Chapel; but Mary's evident preference was to linger among the statues. Once, when they were standing before that noblest of sculptured portraits, the so-called Demosthenes, in the Braccio Nuovo, she made the only spontaneous allusion to her plighted faith that had yet fallen from her lips. "I am so glad," she said, "that Roderick is a sculptor and not a painter."

The allusion resided almost exclusively in the extreme earnestness with which the words were uttered. Rowland asked her the reason of her gladness.

"It's not that painting is not fine," she said, "but that sculpture is finer. It is more manly!"

Rowland tried at times to make her talk about herself, but in this she had little skill. She seemed to him so much older, so much more pliant to social uses than when he had seen her at home, that he wished to make her tell him what she had been doing all those two years. He began by telling her that she was very different. "It appears, then," she said, "that after all one can grow in America!"

"Unquestionably, if one has a motive. Your growth then was unconscious? You did not watch yourself and water your roots?"

She paid no heed to his question. "I am willing to grant," she said, "that Europe is more delightful than I supposed; and I don't admit that I had thought meanly of its charms. But you must admit that America is better than you had supposed."

"I have not a fault to find with the country which produced you!"

"And yet you want me to change—to assimilate Europe I suppose you would call it."

"I have felt that desire only on general principles. Shall I tell you what I feel now? America has made you thus far; let America finish you! I should like to ship you back without delay and see what becomes of you. That sounds uncivil, and I admit there is a cold intellectual curiosity in it."

She shook her head. "The charm is broken; the thread is snapped! I prefer to remain here."

Invariably, when he was inclined to make of something they were talking of a direct application to herself, she wholly failed to assist him; she made no response. Once, with a spark of ardent irritation, he told her she was very "secretive." At this she coloured a little, and he said that in default of any larger confidence it would at least be a satisfaction to make her confess to that charge. But even this satisfaction she denied him, and his only revenge was in making, two or three times afterwards, a softly ironical allusion to what he called by way of jocosity her slyness. He told her that she was what is termed in French a *sournoise*. "Very good," she answered, almost indifferently, "and now please tell me again—I have forgotten it—what you said an 'architrave' was."

It was on the occasion of her asking him a question of this kind that he charged her—still by way of jocosity, but in a tone in which, if she had been curious in the matter, she might have detected a spark of restless ardour —with having an insatiable avidity for facts. "You are always snatching at information," he said; "you will never consent to have any disinterested conversation."

She frowned a little, as she always did when he arrested their talk upon something personal. But this time she assented, and said that she knew she was eager for facts. "One must make hay while the sun shines," she added. "I must lay up a store of learning against dark days. After all, I can't believe that I shall be always in Rome."

He knew he had divined her real motive; but he felt that if he might have said to her—what it seemed impossible to say—that fortune possibly had a bitter disappointment in store for her, she would have been capable of answering immediately after the first sense of pain, "Say then that I am laying up resources for solitude!"

But all the accusations were not his own. He had been waiting once while they talked—they were differing and arguing a little—to see whether she would take her forefinger out of her *Murray*, into which she had inserted it to keep her place. It would have been hard to say why this point interested him, for he had not the slightest real apprehension that she was dry or pedantic. The simple human truth was that the poor fellow was jealous of science. In preaching science to her he had over-estimated his powers of self-effacement. Suddenly, sinking science for the moment, she looked at him very frankly and began to frown. At the same time she let the *Murray* slide down to the ground, and he was so charmed with this circumstance that he made no movement to pick it up.

"You are uncommonly inconsistent, Mr. Mallet," she said.

"Oh, nothing is more common than inconsistency."

"Not of your elaborate kind. That first day that we were in Saint Peter's you said things that inspired me. You bade me plunge into all this. I was all ready; I only wanted a little push; you gave me a great one; here I am up to my neck! And now, instead of helping me to swim, you stand on the shore—the shore of superior information—and fling pebbles at me!"

"Pebbles, my dear young lady? They are life-preservers! I must have played my part very ill."

"Your part? What is your part supposed to have been?"

He hesitated a moment. "That of usefulness pure and simple."

"I don't understand you!" she said; and picking up her *Murray* she fairly buried her nose in it.

That evening he said something to her which she perhaps understood as little. "Do you remember my begging you the other day to do occasionally as I told you? It seemed to me you tacitly consented."

"Very tacitly!"

"I have never yet really presumed on your consent. But now I should like you to do this: whenever you catch me in the act of what you call flinging pebbles, ask me the meaning of some architectural term. I shall know what you mean—a word to the wise!"

One morning they spent among the ruins of the Palatine, that sunny desolation of crumbling overtangled fragments, half excavated and half identified, known as the Palace of the Cæsars. Nothing in Rome is more interesting than this confused and crumbling garden, where you stumble at every step on the disinterred bones of the past; where damp frescoed corridors, relics possibly of Nero's Golden House, serve as gigantic bowers, and where in the spring-time you may sit on a Latin inscription in the shade of a flowering almond-tree and admire the composition of the Campagna. The day left a deep impression on Rowland's mind, partly owing to its intrinsic sweetness, and partly because his companion on this occasion let her *Murray* lie unopened for an hour, and asked several questions which had no connection with the Consuls and the Cæsars. She had begun by saying that it was coming over her after all that Rome was a ponderously sad place. The sirocco was gently blowing, the air was heavy, she was tired, she looked a little pale.

"Everything," she said, "seems to say that all things are vanity. If one is doing something I suppose one feels a certain strength within one to say otherwise. But if one is idle, surely it is depressing to live year after year among the ashes of things that once were mighty. If I were to remain here, I should either become permanently 'low,' as they say, or I would take refuge in some practical occupation."

"What occupation?"

"I would open a school for those beautiful little beggars; though I am sadly afraid I should never bring myself to scold them."

"I have no practical occupation," said Rowland, "and yet I have kept up a certain spirit."

"I don't call you unoccupied."

"It is very good of you. Do you remember our talking about that at Northampton?"

"During that walk in the woods? Perfectly. Has your coming abroad succeeded for yourself as well as you hoped?"

"I think I may say that it has turned out as well as I expected."

"Are you happy?"

"Don't I look so?"

"So it seems to me. But"—and she hesitated a moment—"I imagine you look happy whether you are so or not."

"I am like that ancient comic mask that we saw just now in yonder excavated fresco; I am made to grin."

"Shall you come back here next winter?"

"Very probably."

"Are you settled here for ever?"

"'For ever' is a long time. I live only from year to year."

"Shall you never marry?"

Rowland gave a laugh. "'For ever'—'never!' You handle large ideas. I have not taken a vow of celibacy."

"Shouldn't you like to marry?"

"I should like it immensely."

To this she made no rejoinder; but presently she asked, "Why don't you write a book?"

Rowland laughed—this time more freely. "A book! What book should I write?"

"A history; something about art or antiquities."

"I have neither the learning nor the talent."

She made no attempt to contradict him; she simply said she had supposed otherwise. "You ought at any rate," she continued in a moment, "to do something for yourself."

"For myself? I should have supposed that if ever a man seemed to live for himself—"

"I don't know how it seems," she interrupted—"to careless observers. But we know—we know that you have lived—a great deal for us."

Her voice trembled slightly, and she brought out the last words with a little jerk.

"She has had that speech on her conscience," thought Rowland; "she has been thinking she owed it to me, and it seemed to her that now was her time to make it and have done with it."

She went on in a way which confirmed these reflections, speaking with due solemnity. "You ought to be made to know very well what we all feel. Mrs. Hudson tells me that she has told you what she feels. Of course Roderick has expressed himself. I have been wanting to thank you too; I do, from my heart."

Rowland made no answer; his face at this moment resembled the tragic mask much more than the comic. But Mary was not looking at him; she had taken up her eternal *Murray*.

In the afternoon she usually drove with Mrs. Hudson, but Rowland frequently saw her again in the evening. He was apt to spend half an hour in the little sitting-room at the hôtel-pension on the slope of the Pincian, and Roderick, who dined regularly with his mother, was present on these occasions. Rowland saw him little at other times, and for three weeks no observations passed between them on the subject of Mrs. Hudson's advent. To Rowland's vision, as the weeks elapsed, the benefits to proceed from the presence of the two ladies remained shrouded in mystery. Roderick was peculiarly inscrutable. He was preoccupied with his work on his mother's portrait, which was taking a very happy turn; and often when he sat silent with his hands in his pockets, his legs outstretched, his head thrown back and his eyes on vacancy, it was to be supposed that his fancy was hovering about the half-shaped image in his studio, exquisite even in its immaturity. He said little, but his silence did not of necessity imply disaffection, for he evidently found it a deep personal luxury to lounge away the hours in an atmosphere so charged with feminine tenderness. He was not alert, he suggested nothing in the way of excursions (Rowland was the prime mover in such as were attempted), but he conformed passively at least to the tranquil temper of the two women and made no harsh comments nor sombre allusions. Rowland wondered whether he had after all done his friend injustice in denying him the sentiment of duty. He refused invitations, to Rowland's knowledge, in order to dine at the sordid little table-d'hôte; wherever his spirit might be he was present in the flesh with religious constancy. Mrs. Hudson's felicity betrayed itself in a remarkable tendency to finish her sentences and wear her best black silk gown. Her tremors had trembled away; she was like a child who discovers that the shaggy monster

it has so long been afraid to touch is an inanimate terror
compounded of straw and saw-dust, and that it is even a
safe audacity to tickle its nose. As to whether the love-
knot of which Mary Garland had the keeping still held
firm, who should pronounce? The young girl, as we know,
did not wear it on her sleeve. She always sat at the
table, near the candles, with a piece of needlework. This
was the attitude in which Rowland had first seen her, and
he thought, now that he had seen her in several others,
that it was not the least becoming.

XIX.

THERE occurred at last a couple of days during which
Rowland was unable to go to the hotel. Late in the
evening of the second Roderick came into his room. In
a few moments he announced that he had finished the bust
of his mother.

"And it's magnificent: " he declared. "It's one of
the best things I have done."

"I am delighted to hear it," said Rowland. "Never
again talk to me about your inspiration being dead."

"Why not? This may be its last kick! I feel very
tired. But it's a masterpiece, though I do say it. They
tell us we owe so much to our parents. Well, I have paid
the filial debt handsomely!" He walked up and down
the room a few moments, with the purpose of his visit
evidently still hanging fire. "There's one thing more I
want to say," he presently resumed. "I feel as if I ought
to tell you!" He stopped before Rowland with his head
high and his brilliant glance unclouded. "Your invention
is a failure!"

"My invention?" Rowland repeated.

"Bringing out my mother and Mary."

"A failure?"

"It's no use! They don't help me."

Rowland had fancied that Roderick had no more

surprises for him; but he was now staring at him wide-eyed.

"They bore me!" Roderick went on.

"Oh, oh!" cried Rowland.

"Listen, listen!" said Roderick with perfect gentleness. "I am not complaining of them; I am simply stating a fact. I am very sorry for them; I am greatly disappointed."

"Have you given them a fair trial?"

"Shouldn't you say so? It seems to me I have behaved beautifully."

"You have done very well; I have been building great hopes on it."

"I have done too well then. After the first forty-eight hours my own hopes collapsed. But I determined to fight it out; to stand within the temple; to let the spirit of the Lord descend! Do you want to know the result? Another week of it and I shall begin to hate them. I shall want to poison them.'

"Miserable boy!" cried Rowland. "They are the most perfect of women!"

"Very likely! But they mean no more to me than a Bible text means to an atheist!"

"I can say this," said Rowland in a moment. "I don't pretend to understand the state of your relations with Miss Garland."

Roderick shrugged his shoulders and let his hands drop at his sides. "She adores me! That's the state of my relations." And he smiled strangely.

"Have you broken off your engagement?"

"Broken it off? You can't break a ray of moonshine."

"Have you absolutely no affection for her?"

Roderick placed his hand on his heart and held it there a moment. "Dead—dead—dead!" he said at last.

"I wonder," Rowland observed presently, "if you really know what a charming girl she is. She's an awfully charming girl."

"Evidently—or I should not have cared for her!"

"Don't you care for her now then?"

"Oh, don't force a fellow to say rude things!"

"Well, I canhonly say that you don't know what you are giving up."

Roderick gave a quickened glance. "Do *you* know so well?"

"You must admit that you have allowed me time to find out!"

Roderick smiled, I may almost say sympathetically. "Well, you haven't wasted it!"

Rowland's thoughts were crowding upon him fast. If Roderick was resolute, why should he be gainsaid? If Mary was to be sacrificed, why in *that* way try to save her? There was another way; it only needed a little presumption to make it possible. Rowland tried to summon presumption to his aid; but whether it should come or not it was to find conscience there before it. Conscience had only three words, but they were cogent. "For *her* sake —for *her* sake," it dumbly murmured, and Rowland resumed his argument. "I don't know what I wouldn't do," he said, "rather than that Miss Garland should be ill-used."

"There is one thing to be said," Roderick answered reflectively. "She is very strong."

"Well then, if she's strong, believe that with a longer chance, a better chance, she will still regain your affection."

"Do you know what you ask?" cried Roderick. "Make love to a girl I hate?"

"You *hate*?"

"As her lover I should hate her! Do you really urge my marrying a woman who would bore me to death? I shouldn't be long in letting her know it, and then pray where would she be?" Roderick asked impatiently.

Rowland walked the length of the room a couple of times and then stopped suddenly. "Go your way then! Say all this to *her*, not to me!"

"To her? I am afraid of her; I want you to help me."

"My dear Roderick," said Rowland with an eloquent smile, "I can't help you any more!"

Roderick frowned, hesitated a moment, and then took his hat. "Oh well," he said, "I am not so afraid of her as all that!" And he turned as if to depart.

"Stop!" cried Rowland, as he laid his hand on the door.

Roderick paused and stood waiting with his irritated brow.

"Come back; sit down there and listen to me. Of anything you say in your present state of mind you will live most bitterly to repent. You don't know what you really think; you don't know what you really feel. You don't know your own mind; you don't do justice to Miss Garland. All this is impossible here, under these circumstances. You are blind, you are deaf, you are under a spell. To break it you must leave Rome."

"Leave Rome! Rome was never so dear to me."

"That's not of the smallest consequence. Leave it instantly."

"And where shall I go?"

"Go to some place where you may be alone with your mother and your cousin."

"Alone? You will not come?"

"Oh, if you wish it I will come."

Roderick, inclining his head a little, looked at his friend askance. "I don't understand you," he said; "I wish you liked Mary either a little less or a little more."

Rowland felt himself colouring, but he paid no heed to this speech. "You ask me to help you," he went on. "On these present terms I can do nothing. But if you will be perfectly quiet with regard to Miss Garland for a couple of months, and meanwhile leave Rome, leave Italy, I will do what I can to 'help you,' as you say, in the event of your still wishing to be liberated."

"I must do without your help then! Your terms are impossible. I will leave Rome at the time I have always intended—at the end of June. My rooms and my mother's are taken till then; all my arrangements are made accordingly. Then I will go—not before."

"You are not frank," said Rowland. "Your real reason for staying has nothing to do with your rooms."

Roderick's face betrayed neither embarrassment nor resentment. "If I am not frank, it's for the first time in my life. Since you know so much about my real reason, let me hear it! No, stop!" he suddenly added, "I won't trouble you. You are right, I have a motive. On the twenty-fourth of June, Christina Light is to be married.

I take an immense interest in al that concerns her, and
I wish to be present at her marriage."

" But you said the other day at Saint Peter's that it
was by no means certain it would take place."

" Apparently I was wrong ; I am told that the invitations
are going out."

Rowland felt that it would be vain to remonstrate, and
that the only thing for him was to make the best bargain
possible. " If I offer no farther opposition to your waiting
for Christina's marriage," he said, " will you promise, meanwhile and afterwards, for a certain period, to defer to my
judgment—to say or do nothing that may give the alarm
to Miss Garland ? "

" For a certain period ? What period ? " Roderick
demanded.

" Ah, don't screw me down so ! Don't you understand
that I have taken you away from her, that I suffer in
every nerve in consequence, and that I must do what I
can to give you back ? "

" Do what you can then," said Roderick, putting out his
hand. " Do what you can ! " His tone and his hand-shake
seemed to constitute a promise, and upon this they parted.

Roderick's bust of his mother, whether or no it were a
discharge of what he called the filial debt, was at least an
admirable production. Rowland at the time it was finished
met Gloriani one evening, and this unscrupulous genius
immediately began to ask questions about it. " I am told
our high-flying friend has come down," he said. " He has
been doing a queer little old woman."

" A queer little old woman ! " Rowland exclaimed. " My
dear sir, she is Hudson's mother."

" All the more reason for her being queer ! It is a bust
for terra-cotta, eh ? "

" By no means ; it is for marble."

" That's a pity. It was described to me as a charming
piece of quaintness : a little demure, thin-lipped old lady,
with her head on one side and the prettiest wrinkles in
the world—a sort of fairy godmother."

" Go and see it, and judge for yourself," said Rowland.

" No, I see I shall be disappointed. It's quite the other
thing, the sort of thing they put into the campo-santos. I
wish that crazy boy would listen to me for ten minutes ! "

But a day or two later Rowland met him again in the street, and, as they were near, proposed they should adjourn to Roderick's studio. He consented, and on entering they found the young master. Roderick's demeanour to Gloriani was never conciliatory, and on this occasion blank indifference was apparently all he had to offer. But Gloriani, like a genuine connoisseur, cared nothing for his manners; he cared only for his skill. In the bust of Mrs. Hudson there was something almost touching; it was an exquisite example of a ruling sense of beauty. The poor lady's small neat timorous face had certainly no great character, but Roderick had produced its sweetness, its mildness, its minuteness, its still maternal passion, with the most unerring art. The thing was perfectly unflattered and yet admirably tender; it was the poetry of fidelity. Gloriani stood looking at it a long time intently. Roderick wandered away into the neighbouring room.

"I give it up!" said the sculptor at last. "I don't understand it."

"But you like it?" said Rowland.

"Like it? It's a pearl of pearls. Tell me this," he added; "is he very fond of his mother—is he a very good son?" And he gave Rowland a sharp look.

"Why, she adores him," said Rowland, smiling.

"That's not an answer! But it's none of my business. Only if I, in his place, being suspected of having—what shall I call it?—a cold heart, managed to do that piece of work, oh, oh! I should be called a pretty lot of names. Charlatan, *poseur, arrangeur!* But he can do as he chooses! My dear young man, I know you don't like me," he went on as Roderick came back. "It's a pity; you are strong enough not to care about me at all. You are very strong."

"Not at all," said Roderick curtly. "I am very weak!"

"I told you last year that you wouldn't keep it up. I was a great ass. You will!"

"I beg your pardon—I won't!" retorted Roderick.

"Though I'm a great ass all the same, eh? Well, call me what you will, so long as you turn out this sort of thing! I don't suppose it makes any particular difference, but I should like to say now that I believe in you."

Roderick stood looking at him for a moment with a strange hardness in his face. It flushed slowly, and two glittering angry tears filled his eyes. It was the first time Rowland had ever seen them there; he saw them but once again. Poor Gloriani, he was sure, had never in his life spoken with less of the mocking spirit; but to Roderick there was evidently a touch of sarcasm in his profession of faith. He turned away, muttering a passionate imprecation. Gloriani was accustomed to deal with complex problems, but this time he was hopelessly puzzled. "What's the matter with him?" he asked simply.

Rowland gave a sad smile and touched his forehead. "Genius, I suppose."

Gloriani sent another parting, lingering look at the bust of Mrs. Hudson. "Well, it's deuced perfect, it's deuced simple; I *do* believe in him!" he said. "But I am glad I am not a genius. It makes," he added with a laugh, as he looked for Roderick to wave him good-bye and saw his back still turned, "it makes a more sociable studio!"

Rowland had purchased as he supposed temporary tranquillity for Mary Garland; but his own humour in these days was not especially peaceful. He was attempting in a certain sense to lead the ideal life, and he found it at the least not easy. The days passed, but brought with them no official invitation to Christina Light's wedding. He occasionally met her, and he occasionally met Prince Casamassima; but the two were always separate; they were apparently taking their happiness in the inexpressive and isolated manner proper to people of social eminence. Rowland continued to see Madame Grandoni, for whom he felt a confirmed esteem. He had always talked to her with frankness, but now he made her a confidant of all his hidden dejection. Roderick and Roderick's concerns had been a common theme with him, and it was in the natural course to talk of Mrs. Hudson's arrival and Mary Garland's fine smile. Madame Grandoni was an intelligent listener, and she lost no time in putting his case for him in a nutshell. "At one moment you tell me the girl is plain," she said; "the next you tell me she is pretty. I will invite them, and I shall see for myself. But one thing is very clear; you are in love with her!"

Rowland for all answer glanced round to see that no one heard her.

"More than that," she added, "you have been in love with her these two years. There was that certain something about you ! . . . . I knew you were of what we Germans call a subjective turn of mind ; but you had a touch of it more than was natural. Why didn't you tell me at once ? You would have saved me a great deal of trouble. And poor Augusta Blanchard too !" And herewith Madame Grandoni communicated a pertinent fact : Augusta Blanchard and Mr. Leavenworth were going to make a match. The young lady had been staying for a month at Albano, and as Mr. Leavenworth had been dancing attendance the event was a matter of course. Rowland, who had been lately reproaching himself with a failure of attention to Miss Blanchard's doings, made some such observation.

"But you did not find it so !" cried his hostess. "It was a matter of course, perhaps, that Mr. Leavenworth, who seems to be going about Europe with the sole view of picking up furniture for his 'home,' as he calls it, should think Miss Blanchard a very handsome *morceau ;* but it was not a matter of course—or it needn't have been—that she should be willing to become a sort of superior table-ornament. She would have accepted you if you had tried."

"You are supposing the insupposable," said Rowland. "She never gave me a particle of encouragement."

"What would you have had her do ? The poor girl did her best, and I am sure that when she accepted Mr. Leavenworth she thought of you."

"She thought of the pleasure her marriage would give me."

"Ay, pleasure indeed ! She is a thoroughly good girl, but she has her little grain of feminine spite, as well as the rest. Well, he is richer than you, and she will have what she wants ; but before I forgive you I must wait and see this new arrival—what do you call her?—Miss Garland. If I like her I will forgive you ; if I don't I shall always bear you a grudge."

Rowland answered that he was sorry to forfeit any advantage she might offer him, but that his exculpatory passion for Miss Garland was a figment of her fancy. Miss Garland was engaged to another man—he himself had no claims.

"Well, then," said Madame Grandoni, "if I like her we will have it that you ought to be in love with her. If you fail in this it will be a double misdemeanour. The man she has accepted doesn't care a straw for her. Leave me alone and I will tell her what I think of the man she hasn't!"

As to Christina Light's marriage Madame Grandoni could say nothing positive. The young girl of late had made her several flying visits, in the intervals of the usual pre-matrimonial shopping and dress-fitting; she had spoken of the event with a toss of her head, as a matter which with a wise old friend who viewed things in their essence she need not pretend to treat as a solemnity. It was for Prince Casamassima to do that. "It is what they call a marriage of reason," she once said. "That means you know a marriage of madness!"

"What have you said in the way of advice?" Rowland said.

"Very little, but that little has been a good word for the Prince. I know nothing of the mysteries of the young lady's heart. It may be a gold-mine, but at any rate it's at the bottom of a very long shaft. But the marriage in itself is an excellent marriage. It's not only brilliant, but it's safe. I think Christina is quite capable of making it a means of misery; but there is no position that would be sacred to her. Casamassima is an irreproachable young man; there is nothing against him but that he is a prince. It is not often, I fancy, that a prince has been put through his paces at this rate. No one knows the wedding-day; the cards of invitation have been printed half a dozen times over with a different date; each time Christina has destroyed them. There are people in Rome who are furious at the delay; they want to get away; they are in a dreadful fright about the fever, but they are dying to see the wedding, and if the day were fixed, they would make their arrangements to wait for it. I think it very possible that after having kept them for a month and been the cause of a dozen cases of malaria, Christina will be married at sunrise by an old friar, with simply the legal witnesses."

" It is true, then, that she has become a Catholic ? "

" So she tells me. One day she got up in the depths of despair ; at her wits' end, I suppose, in other words, for a new sensation. Suddenly it occurred to her that the Catholic Church might after all hold the key—might give her what she wanted ; she sent for a priest ; he happened to be a clever man and he contrived to interest her. She put on a black dress and a black veil, and, looking handsomer than ever, she rustled into the Catholic church. The Prince, who is very devout and who had her heresy sorely on his conscience, was thrown into an ecstasy. May she never have a caprice that pleases him less ! "

Rowland had already asked Madame Grandoni what to her perception was the present state of matters between Christina and Roderick ; and he now repeated his question with some earnestness of apprehension. " The girl is so deucedly dramatic," he said, " that I don't know what *coup de théâtre* she may have in store for us. Such a stroke was her turning Catholic ; such a stroke would be her some day making her curtsey to a disappointed world as Princess Casamassima, married *en famille*. She might do—she may do—something that would make even more starers ! I am prepared for anything."

" You mean that she might run away with your sculptor, eh ? "

" I am prepared for anything ! "

" Do you mean that he's ready ? "

" Do you mean that *she* is ? "

" They're a precious pair ! This is what I think. You by no means exhaust the subject when you say that Christina is dramatic. It's my belief that in the course of her life she will do a certain number of things from disinterested passion. She's immeasurably proud, and if that is often a fault in a good woman, it may be a merit in a naughty one. She needs to think well of herself ; she knows a fine character easily when she meets one ; she hates to suffer by comparison, even though the comparison be made by herself alone ; and when the estimate she may have made of herself grows vague she needs to do something to give it a definite impressive form. What she will do in such a case will be better or worse, according to her opportunity ; but I imagine it will generally be something that will drive her mother to despair; something of the sort usually termed 'unworldly.'"

Rowland, as he was taking his leave, after some farther exchange of opinions, rendered Christina the tribute of a deeply meditative sigh. "She has bothered me half to death," he said, "but somehow I can't manage as I ought to hate her. I admire her half the time and a good part of the rest I pity her."

"I think as a general thing I pity her!" said Madame Grandoni.

This enlightened woman came the next day to call upon the two ladies from Northampton. She carried their shy affections by storm, and made them promise to drink tea with her on the evening of the morrow. Her visit was an epoch in the life of poor Mrs. Hudson, who did nothing but make sudden desultory allusions to her for the next thirty-six hours. "To think of her being a foreigner!" she would exclaim, after much intent reflection, over her knitting; "she speaks so beautifully!" Then in a little while, "She wasn't so much dressed as you might have expected. Did you notice how easy it was in the waist? I wonder if that's the fashion?" Or, "She's very old to wear a hat; I should never dare to wear a hat!" Or, "Did you notice her hands?—very pretty hands for such a stout person. A great many rings, but nothing very handsome. I suppose they are hereditary." Or, "She's certainly not handsome, but she looks wonderfully clever. I wonder why she doesn't have something done to her teeth." Rowland also received a summons to Madame Grandoni's tea-drinking, and went betimes, as he had been requested. He was eagerly desirous to lend his mute applause to Mary Garland's *début* in the Roman social world. The two ladies had arrived with Roderick, silent and careless, in attendance. Miss Blanchard was also present, escorted by Mr. Leavenworth, and the party was completed by a couple of dozen artists of both sexes and various nationalities. It was a friendly and easy assembly, like all Madame Grandoni's parties, and in the course of the evening there was some excellent music. People played and sang for Madame Grandoni on easy terms who elsewhere were not to be heard for the asking. She was herself a superior musician, and singers found it a privilege to perform to her accompaniment. Rowland talked to various persons, but for the first time in his life his attention visibly wandered; he could not keep his eyes off Mary Garland. Madame Grandoni had said that he sometimes spoke of her as pretty and sometimes as plain; to-night if he had had occasion to describe her appearance he would have called her beautiful. She was dressed more than he had ever seen her; it was becoming, and gave her a deeper colour and a brighter presence. Two or three persons were apparently witty people, for she sat listening to them with her brilliant natural smile. Rowland, from an opposite corner, reflected that he had never varied in his appreciation of Miss Blanchard's classic contour, but that somehow to-night it impressed him hardly more than an effigy stamped upon a coin of low value. Roderick could not be accused of rancour, for he had approached Mr. Leavenworth with unstudied familiarity, and, lounging against the wall with hands in pockets, was discoursing to him with candid serenity. Now that he had done him an impertinence he evidently found him less intolerable. Mr. Leavenworth stood stirring his tea and silently opening and shutting his mouth, without looking at the young sculptor, like a large drowsy dog snapping at flies. Rowland had found it disagreeable to be told Miss Blanchard would have married him for the asking, and he would have felt some embarrassment in going to speak to her if his modesty had not found incredulity so easy. The facile side of a union with Miss Blanchard had never been present to his mind; it had struck him as a thing, in all ways, to be compassed with a great effort. He had half-an-hour's talk with her; a farewell talk as it seemed to him—a farewell not to a real illusion, but to the idea that for him in that matter there could ever be an acceptable *pis-aller*. He congratulated Miss Blanchard upon her engagement, and she received his good wishes with a touch of primness. But she was always a trifle prim, even when she was quoting Mrs. Browning and George Sand, and this harmless defect did not prevent her responding on this occasion that Mr. Leavenworth had a " glorious heart." Rowland wished to manifest an extreme regard, but towards the end of the talk his zeal relaxed and he fell a-thinking that a certain natural ease in a woman was

the most delightful thing in the world. There was Christina
Light, who had too much, and here was Miss Blanchard,
who had too little, and there was Mary Garland, who had
just the right amount.

He went to Madame Grandoni in an adjoining room,
where she was pouring out tea.

" I will make you an excellent cup," she said, " because
I have forgiven you."

He looked at her, answering nothing ; but he swallowed
his tea with great gusto and a slight deepening of his
colour ; by all of which one would have known that he
was gratified. In a moment he intimated that, in so far
as he had sinned, he had forgiven himself.

" She is a delightful creature," said Madame Grandoni.
" She has all sorts of qualities. I have taken a great
fancy to her ; she must let me make a friend of her."

" She is very plain," said Rowland slowly, " very simple,
very ignorant."

" Which, being interpreted, means, ' She is very handsome, very subtle, and has read hundreds of volumes on
winter evenings in the country.' "

" You are a veritable sorceress," cried Rowland ; " you
frighten me away ! " As he was turning to leave her,
there rose above the hum of voices in the drawing-room
the sharp grotesque note of a barking dog. Their eyes
met in a glance of intelligence.

" There is the sorceress ! " said Madame Grandoni.
" The sorceress and her necromantic poodle ! " And she
hastened back to the post of hospitality.

Rowland followed her and found Christina Light standing in the middle of the drawing-room and looking about
in perplexity. Her poodle, sitting on his haunches and
gazing at the company, had apparently been expressing a
sympathetic displeasure at the absence of a welcome. But
in a moment Madame Grandoni had come to the young
girl's relief and Christina had tenderly kissed her hostess.

" I had no idea," said Christina, surveying the assembly,
" that you had such a lot of grand people, or I would not
have come in. The servant said nothing ; he took me for
an *invitée*. I came to spend a neighbourly half-hour ; you
know I haven't many left ! It was too dismally dreary
at home. I hoped I should find you alone, and I brought

Stenterello to play with the cat. I don't know that if
I had known about all this I should have dared to come
in; but since I have stumbled into the midst of it I beg
you to let me stay. I am not dressed, but am I very
hideous? I will sit in a corner and no one will notice me.
My dear sweet lady, do let me stay! Pray, why didn't
you ask me? I never have been to a little party like this.
They must be very charming. No dancing—tea and
conversation? No tea, thank you; but if you could spare
a biscuit for Stenterello; a sweet biscuit please. Really,
why didn't you ask me? Do you have these things often?
Madame Grandoni, it's very unkind!" And the young
girl, who had delivered herself of the foregoing succession
of sentences in her usual low, cool, penetrating voice,
uttered these last words with a certain tremor of feeling.
"I see," she went on, "I do very well for balls and great
banquets, but when people wish to have a cosy, friendly,
comfortable evening, they leave me out with the big
flower-pots and the gilt candlesticks."

"I am sure you are welcome to stay, my dear," said
Madame Grandoni, "and at the risk of displeasing you I
must confess that if I didn't invite you it was because you
are too grand. Your dress will do very well, with its
fifty flounces, and there is no need of your going into a
corner. Indeed, since you are here, I propose to have the
glory of it. You must remain where my people can see
you."

"They are evidently determined to do that by the way
they stare. Do they think I intend to dance a *tarantella*?
Who are they all; do I know them?" And lingering in
the middle of the room, with her arm passed into Madame
Grandoni's, she let her eyes wander slowly from group to
group. They were of course observing her. Standing in
the little circle of lamplight, with the hood of an Eastern
burnous shot with silver threads falling back from her
beautiful head, one hand gathering together its voluminous
shimmering folds and the other playing with the silken
top-knot on the uplifted head of her poodle, she was a
figure of radiant picturesqueness. She seemed to be a sort
of extemporised *tableau vivant*. Rowland's position made
it decoming for him to speak to her without delay. As
she looked at him he saw that, judging by the light of her

beautiful eyes, she was in a humour of which she had not
yet treated him to a specimen. In a simpler person he
would have called it exquisite kindness ; but in this young
lady's deportment the flower was one thing and the perfume
another. "Tell me about these people," she said to him.
"I had no idea there were so many people in Rome I have
not seen. What are they all talking about ? It's all very
clever, I suppose, and quite beyond me. There is Miss
Blanchard sitting as usual in profile against a dark object.
She is like a head on a postage stamp. And there is that
nice little old lady in black, Mrs. Hudson. What a dear
little woman for a mother ! *Comme elle est proprette !* And
the other, the *fiancée*, of course she's here. Ah, I see ! "
She paused ; she was looking intently at Mary Garland.
Rowland measured the intentness of her glance and
suddenly acquired a conviction. "I should like so much
to know her ! " she said turning to Madame Grandoni.
"She has a charming face ; I am sure she is a kind of
saint. I wish very much you would introduce me. No,
on second thoughts I would rather you didn't. I will
speak to her bravely myself, as a friend of her—what do
you call it in English ?—her *promesso*." Madame Grandoni
and Rowland exchanged glances of baffled conjecture, and
Christina flung off her burnous, crumpled it together, and
with uplifted finger, tossing it into a corner, gave it in
charge to her poodle. He stationed himself upon it on his
haunches with upright vigilance. Christina crossed the
room with the step and smile of a ministering angel, and
introduced herself to the young lady from Northampton.
She had once told Rowland that she would show him some
day how gracious her manners could be ; she was now redeeming her promise. Rowland, watching her, saw Mary
Garland rise slowly in response to her greeting and look
at her with serious deep-gazing eyes. The almost dramatic
opposition of these two keenly interesting girls touched
Rowland with a nameless apprehension, and after a
moment he preferred to turn away. In doing so he noticed
Roderick. The young sculptor was standing planted on
the train of a lady's dress, gazing across at Christina's
movements with undisguised earnestness. There were
several more pieces of music ; Rowland sat in a corner
and listened to them. When they were over several

people began to take their leave, Mrs. Hudson among the number. Rowland saw her come up to Madame Grandoni, clinging shyly to Mary Garland's arm. Mary had a brilliant eye and a deep colour in her cheek. The two ladies looked about for Roderick, but Roderick had his back turned. He had approached Christina, who, with an absent air, was sitting alone, where she had taken her place near her innocent rival, looking at the guests pass out of the room. Christina's eye, like Mary's, was bright, but her cheek was pale. Hearing Roderick's voice, she looked up at him sharply; then silently, with a single quick gesture, she motioned him away. He obeyed her and came and joined his mother in bidding good night to Madame Grandoni. Christina in a moment met Rowland's glance and immediately beckoned him to come to her. He was familiar with her spontaneity of movement and was not particularly surprised. She made a place for him on the sofa beside her; he wondered what was coming now. He was not sure it was not a mere fancy, but it seemed to him that he had never seen her look just as she was looking then. It was a humble, touching, appealing glance, which threw into wonderful relief the nobleness of her beauty. "How many more metamorphoses," he asked himself, "am I to be treated to before we have done?"

"I want to tell you," said Christina, "I have taken an immense fancy to Miss Garland. Aren't you glad?"

"Delighted!" exclaimed poor Rowland.

"Ah, you don't believe it," she said with soft dignity.

"Is it so hard to believe?"

"Not that people in general should admire her, but that I should. But I want to tell you; I want to tell some one, and I can't tell Miss Garland herself. She thinks me already a horrid false creature, and if I were to express to her frankly what I think of her I should simply disgust her. She would be quite right; she has repose, and from that point of view I and my doings must seem monstrous. Unfortunately I haven't repose. I am trembling now; if I could ask you to feel my arm, you would see! But I want to tell you that I admire Miss Garland more than any of the people who call themselves her friends—except of course you. Oh, I know that! To begin with she is extremely handsome and she doesn't know it."

"She is not generally thought handsome," said Rowland.

"Evidently! That's the vulgarity of the human mind. Her head has great character, great natural style. If a woman is not to be a brilliant beauty in the regular way, she will choose if she's wise to look like that. She will not be thought pretty by people in general, and desecrated, as she passes, by the stare of every vile wretch who chooses to thrust his nose under her bonnet; but a certain number of intelligent people will find it one of the delightful things of life to look at her. That lot is as good as another! Then she has a beautiful character!"

"You found that out soon!" said Rowland, smiling.

"How long did it take *you?* I found it out before I ever spoke to her. I met her the other day in Saint Peter's; I knew it then. I knew it—do you want to know how long I have known it?"

"Really," said Rowland, "I didn't mean to cross-examine you."

"Do you remember mamma's ball in December? We had some talk and you then mentioned her—not by name. You said but three words, but I saw you admired her, and I knew that if you admired her she must have a beautiful character. That's what you require!"

"Upon my word," cried Rowland, "you make three words go very far!"

"Oh, Mr. Hudson has also spoken of her."

"Ah, that's better!" said Rowland.

"I don't know; he doesn't like her."

"Did he tell you so?" The question left Rowland's lips before he could stay it, which he would have done on a moment's reflection.

Christina looked at him intently. "No!" she said at last. "That would have been dishonourable, wouldn't it? But I know it from my knowledge of him. He doesn't like perfection; he is not bent upon being *safe*, in his likings; he is willing to risk something! Poor fellow, he risks too much!"

Rowland was silent; he did not care for the thrust; but he was profoundly mystified. Christina beckoned to her poodle, and the dog marched stiffly across to her. She gave a loving twist to his rose-coloured top-knot and bade him go and fetch her burnous. He obeyed, gathered it up in his teeth, and returned with great solemnity, dragging it along the floor.

"I do her justice. I do her full justice," she went on with soft earnestness. "I like to say that, I like to be able to say it. She is full of intelligence and courage and devotion. She doesn't do me a grain of justice; but that is no harm. There is something so fine in the aversions of a good woman!"

"If you would give Miss Garland a chance," said Rowland, "I am sure she would be glad to be your friend."

"What do you mean by a chance? She has only to take it. I told her I liked her immensely, and she frowned as if I had said something disgusting. She looks very handsome when she frowns." Christina rose with those words and began to gather her mantle about her. "I don't often like women," she went on. "In fact I generally detest them. But I should like to know that one well. I should like to have a friendship with her; I have never had one; they must be very delightful. But I sha'n't have one now—not if she can help it! Ask her what she thinks of me; see what she will say. I don't want to know; keep it to yourself. It's too sad. So we go through life. It's fatality—that's what they call it, isn't it? We please the people we don't care for, we displease those we do! But I appreciate her, I do her justice; that's the most important thing. It's because I have imagination. She has none. Never mind; it's her only fault. I do her justice; I understand very well." She kept softly murmuring and looking about for Madame Grandoni. She saw the good lady near the door, and put out her hand to Rowland for good night. She held his hand an instant, fixing him with her eyes, the living splendour of which at this moment was something transcendent. "Yes, I do her justice," she repeated. "And you do her more; you would lay down your life for her." With this she turned away, and before he could answer she left him. She went to Madame Grandoni, grasped her two hands and held out her forehead to be kissed. The next moment she was gone.

"That was a happy accident!" said Madame Grandoni. "She never looked so beautiful, and she made my little party brilliant."

"Beautiful verily!" Rowland answered. "But it was no accident."

"What was it, then?"

"It was a plan. She wished to see Mary Garland. She knew she was to be here."

"How so?"

"By Roderick evidently."

"And why did she wish to see Mary Garland?"

"Heaven knows! I give it up!"

"Ah, the wicked girl!" murmured Madame Grandoni.

"No," said Rowland; "don't say that now. She's too beautiful."

"Oh, you men—the best of you!"

"Well, then," cried Rowland, "she's too good!"

XX.

THE opportunity presenting itself the next day, he failed not, as you may imagine, to ask Mary Garland what she thought of Christina. It was a Saturday afternoon, the time at which the beautiful marbles of the Villa Borghese are thrown open to the public. Mary had told him that Roderick had promised to take her to see them with his mother, and he joined the party in the splendid Casino. The warm weather had left so few strangers in Rome that they had the place almost to themselves. Mrs. Hudson had confessed to an invincible fear of treading, even with the help of her son's arm, the polished marble floors, and was sitting patiently on a stool, with folded hands, looking shyly here and there at the undraped paganism around her. Roderick had sauntered off alone, with an irritated brow which seemed to betray the conflict between the instinct of observation and the perplexities of circumstance. His cousin was wandering in another direction, and though she was consulting her catalogue Rowland fancied it was from habit; she too was preoccupied. He joined her, and she presently sat down on a divan rather wearily and closed her *Murray*. Then he asked her abruptly how Christina had pleased her.

She started the least bit at the question, and he felt that she had been thinking of Christina.

" I don't like her ! " she said dryly.

" What do you think of her ? "

" I think she's false." This was said without petulance or bitterness, but with a very positive air.

" But she wished to please you ; she tried," Rowland rejoined in a moment.

" I think not. She wished to please herself ! "

Rowland felt himself at liberty to say no more. No allusion to Christina had passed between them since the day they met her at Saint Peter's, but he knew that she knew by that infallible sixth sense of a woman who loves that this strange and beautiful girl had the power to injure her. To what extent she had the will Mary was uncertain ; but last night's interview apparently had not reassured her. It was under these circumstances equally unbecoming for Rowland either to depreciate or to defend Christina, and he had to content himself with simply having verified the girl's own assurance that she had made a bad impression. He tried to talk of indifferent matters—about the statues and the frescoes ; but to-day plainly æsthetic curiosity, on his companion's part, had folded its wings. Curiosity of another sort had taken its place. Mary was longing, he was sure, to question him about Christina ; but she found a dozen reasons for hesitating. Her questions would imply that Roderick had not treated her with confidence ; for information on this point should properly have come from himself. They would imply that she was jealous, and to betray her jealousy was intolerable to her pride. For some minutes, as she sat scratching the brilliant pavement with the point of her umbrella, it was to be supposed that her pride and her anxiety held an earnest debate. At last anxiety won.

" *A propos* of Miss Light," she asked, " do you know her well ? "

" I can hardly say that. But I have seen her repeatedly."

" Do you like her ? "

" Yes and no. I think I am sorry for her."

Mary had spoken with her eyes on the pavement. At this she looked up. "Sorry for her? Why?"

"Well—she is unhappy."

"What are her miseries?"

"Well—she has a horrible mother and she has had a most injurious education."

For a moment Mary was silent. Then, "Isn't she very beautiful?" she asked.

"Don't you think so?"

"That's measured by what men think! She is extremely clever too."

"Oh, yes—speaking as men think!"

"She has beautiful dresses."

"Any number of them."

"And beautiful manners."

"Yes—sometimes."

"And plenty of money."

"Money enough apparently."

"And she receives great admiration."

"Very true."

"And she is to marry a prince."

"So they say."

Mary rose and turned to rejoin her companions, commenting these admissions with a pregnant silence. "Poor Miss Light!" she said at last simply. And in this it seemed to Rowland there was a touch of serious mockery.

Very late on the following evening his servant brought him the card of a visitor. He was surprised at a visit at such an hour, but it may be said that when he read the inscription—Cavaliere Giuseppe Giacosa—his surprise abated. He had had an unformulated conviction that there was to be a sequel to the apparition at Madame Grandoni's; the Cavaliere had come to usher it in.

He had come evidently on a portentous errand. He was as pale as ashes and prodigiously serious; his little cold black eye had grown ardent, and he had left his insinuating smile at home. He saluted Rowland however with his usual expressiveness.

"You have more than once done me the honour to invite me to call upon you," he said. "I am ashamed of my long delay and I can only say to you frankly that my time this winter has not been my own." Rowland assented, ungrudgingly, fumbled for the Italian correlative of the adage " Better late than never," begged him to be seated, and offered him a cigar. The Cavaliere sniffed imperceptibly the fragrant weed, and then declared that if his kind host would allow him he would reserve it for consumption at another time. He apparently desired to intimate that the solemnity of his errand left him no breath for idle smoke-puffings. "I must confess," he observed, "that even now I come on business not of my own—or my own at least only in a secondary sense. I have been dispatched as an ambassador—an envoy extraordinary I may say—by my dear friend Mrs. Light."

" If I can in any way be of service to Mrs. Light, I shall be happy," Rowland said.

" Well then, dear sir, Casa Light is in commotion. The signora is in trouble—in terrible trouble." For a moment Rowland expected to hear that the signora's trouble was of a nature that a loan of five thousand francs would assuage. But the Cavaliere continued—" Miss Light has committed a great crime; she has plunged a dagger into the heart of her mother."

" A dagger ! " cried Rowland.

The Cavaliere patted the air an instant with his finger-tips. "I speak figuratively. She has broken off her marriage."

" Broken it off ? "

" Short ! She has turned the Prince from the door." And the Cavaliere, when he had made this announcement, folded his arms and bent upon Rowland his intense inscrutable gaze. It seemed to Rowland that he detected in the polished depths of it a fantastic gleam of irony or of triumph ; but superficially at least Giacosa did nothing to discredit his character as a sympathetic representative of Mrs. Light's affliction.

Rowland heard his news with a kind of fierce disgust ; it seemed the sinister counterpart of Christina's preternatural mildness at Madame Grandoni's assembly. She had been too plausible to be honest. Without being able to trace the connection, he yet instinctively associated her present rebellion with her meeting with Mary Garland. If she had not seen Mary, she would have let things stand. It was monstrous to suppose that she could have sacrificed

so brilliant a fortune to a mere movement of jealousy, to a
refined impulse of feminine devilry, to a desire to frighten
poor Mary from her security by again appearing in the
field. Yet Rowland remembered his first impression of
her; she was "dangerous," and she had measured in each
direction the perturbing effect of her rupture. She was
smiling her sweetest smile at it! For half an hour Rowland simply detested her—he longed to denounce her to
her face. Of course, all he could say to Giacosa was that
he was extremely sorry. "But I am not surprised," he
added.

"You are not surprised?"

"With Miss Light everything is possible. Isn't that
true?"

Another ripple seemed to play for an instant in the
current of the old man's irony, but he made no answer.
"It was a magnificent marriage," he said at last. "I do
not respect many people, but I respect Prince Casamassima."

"I should judge him indeed to be a very honourable
young man," said Rowland.

"Eh, young as he is, he is made of the old stuff. And
now perhaps he's blowing his brains out. He is the last
of his house; it's a great house. But Miss Light will
have put an end to it!"

"Is that the view she takes of it?"

This time unmistakably the Cavaliere smiled, but still
in that very out-of-the-way place. "You have observed
Miss Light with attention," he said, "and this brings me
to my errand. Mrs. Light has a high opinion of your
wisdom, of your kindness, and she has reason to believe
you have great influence with her daughter."

"I—with her daughter? Not a grain!"

"That is possibly your modesty. Mrs. Light believes
that something may yet be done and that Christina will
listen to you. She begs you to come and see her before
it is too late."

"But all this, my dear Cavaliere, is none of my business,"
Rowland objected. "I can't possibly in such a matter take
the responsibility of advising Miss Light."

The Cavaliere fixed his eyes for a moment on the floor,
in brief, but intense reflection. Then looking up,

"Unfortunately," he said, "she has no man near her whom she respects; she has no father!"

"And such a finished fool of a mother!" Rowland gave himself the satisfaction of exclaiming.

The Cavaliere was so pale that he could not easily have turned paler; yet it seemed for a moment that his dead complexion blanched. "Eh, signore, such as she is, the mother appeals to you. A very handsome woman—dishevelled, in tears, in despair, in dishabille!" Rowland reflected a moment, not on the attractions of Mrs. Light under the circumstances indicated by the Cavaliere, but on the satisfaction he should take in accusing Christina to her face of having struck a cruel blow.

"I must add," said the Cavaliere, "that Mrs. Light desires also to speak to you on the subject of Mr. Hudson."

"She considers Mr. Hudson connected with this step of her daughter's?"

"Intimately. He must be got out of Rome."

"Mrs. Light then must get an order from the Pope to remove him. It's not in my power."

The Cavaliere assented deferentially. "Mrs. Light is equally helpless. She would leave Rome to-morrow, but Christina would not budge. An order from the Pope would do nothing. A bull in council would do nothing."

"She is a remarkable young lady!" said Rowland, with bitterness.

But the Cavaliere rose and responded coldly, "She has a great spirit." And it seemed to Rowland that her great spirit, for mysterious reasons, gave him more pleasure than the distressing use she made of it gave him pain. He was on the point of charging him with his inconsistency, when Giacosa went on—"But if the marriage can be saved, it must be saved. It's a beautiful marriage. It *will* be saved."

"Notwithstanding Miss Light's great spirit to the contrary?"

"Miss Light, notwithstanding her great spirit, will call Prince Casamassima back."

"Heaven grant it!" said Rowland.

I don't know," said the Cavaliere, solemnly, "that Heaven will have much to do with it."

Rowland gave him a questioning look, but he laid his finger on his lips. And with Rowland's promise to present himself on the morrow at Casa Light, he shortly afterwards departed. He left Rowland revolving many things: Christina's magnanimity, Christina's perversity, Roderick's contingent fortune, Mary Garland's certain trouble, and the Cavaliere's own fine ambiguities.

Rowland's promise to the Cavaliere obliged him to disengage himself from an excursion which he had arranged with the two ladies from Northampton. Before going to Casa Light he repaired in person to Mrs. Hudson's hotel to make his excuses.

He found Roderick's mother sitting with tearful eyes, staring at an open note that lay in her lap. At the window sat Mary Garland, who turned upon him as he came in, a gaze both anxious and familiar. Mrs. Hudson quickly rose and came to him holding out the note.

"In pity's name what is the matter with my boy? If he is ill, I entreat you to take me to him!"

"He is not ill, to my knowledge," said Rowland. "What have you there?"

"A note—a dreadful note. He tells us we are not to see him for a week. If I could only go to his room! But I am afraid, I am afraid!"

"I imagine there is no need of going to his room. What is the occasion, may I ask, of his note?"

"He was to have gone with us on this drive to—what is the place?—to Cervara. You know it was arranged yesterday morning. In the evening he was to have dined with us. But he never came, and this morning arrives this awful thing. Oh, dear, I'm so excited! Would you mind reading it?"

Rowland took the note and glanced at its half-dozen lines. "I cannot go to Cervara," they ran; "I have something else to do. This will occupy me perhaps a week, and you will not see me. Don't miss me—learn not to miss me. R. H."

"Why, it means," Rowland explained, "that he has taken up a piece of work, and that it is all-absorbing. That's very good news." This explanation was not sincere; but he had not the courage not to offer it as a stopgap. But he found he needed all his courage to support it, for Mary had left her place and approached him, formidably unsatisfied.

"He does not work in the evening," said Mrs. Hudson. "Can't he come for five minutes? Why does he write such a cruel cold note to his poor mother—to poor Mary? What have we done that he acts so strangely? It's this wicked, infectious, heathenish place!" And the poor lady's suppressed mistrust of the Eternal City broke out passionately. "Oh, dear Mr. Mallet," she went on, "I am sure he has the fever, and he's already delirious!"

"I am very sure it's not that," said Mary softly.

She was still looking at Rowland; his eyes met hers and his own glance wandered away. This made him angry, and to carry off his confusion he pretended to be looking meditatively at the floor. After all, what had *he* to be ashamed of? For a moment he was on the point of making a clean breast of it, of crying out, "Good ladies, I abdicate; I can't help you!" But he checked himself; he felt so impatient to have his three words with Christina. He grasped his hat.

"I will see what it is!" he cried. And then he was glad he had not abdicated, for as he turned away he glanced again at Mary, and saw that, though her eyes were full of trouble, they were not hard and accusing, but charged with appealing friendship.

He went straight to Roderick's apartment, deeming this, at an early hour, the safest place to seek him. He found him in his sitting-room, which had been closely darkened to keep out the heat. The carpets and rugs had been removed, the floor of speckled concrete was bare, and lightly sprinkled with water. Here and there, over it, certain strongly odorous flowers had been scattered. Roderick was lying on his divan in a white dressing-gown, staring up at the frescoed ceiling. The room was deliciously cool, and filled with the moist sweet fragrance of the circumjacent roses and violets. All this seemed highly fantastic, and yet Rowland hardly felt surprised.

"Your mother was greatly alarmed at your note," he said, "and I came to satisfy myself that, as I believed, you are not ill."

Roderick lay motionless except that he slightly turned his head towards his friend. He was smelling a large white rose, which he continued to present to his nose. In the darkness of the room he looked exceedingly pale, but his handsome eyes had an extraordinary brilliancy. He let them rest for some time on Rowland, lying there like a Bhuddist in an intellectual swoon, whose perception should be slowly ebbing back to temporal matters. "Oh, I am not ill," he said at last. "I have never been better."

"Your note nevertheless and your absence have very naturally alarmed your mother. I advise you to go to her directly and reassure her."

"Go to her? Going to her would be worse than staying away. Staying away at present is a kindness." And he inhaled deeply his huge rose, looking up over it at Rowland. "My presence in fact would be indecent."

"Indecent? Pray explain."

"Why, you see, as regards Mary Garland. I am divinely happy! Doesn't it strike you? You ought to agree with me. You wish me to spare her feelings; I spare them by staying away. Last night I heard something——"

"I heard it too," said Rowland with brevity. "And it's in honour of this piece of news that you have taken to your bed in this fashion?"

"Extremes meet! I can't get up for joy."

"May I inquire how you heard your joyous news?—from Miss Light herself?"

"By no means. It was brought me by her maid, who is in my service as well."

"Casamassima's loss then is to a certainty your own gain?"

"I don't talk about certainties. I don't want to be arrogant, I don't want to offend the immortal gods. I am keeping very quiet, but I can't help being happy. I shall wait a while; I shall bide my time."

"And then?"

"And then that incomparable girl will confess to me that when she threw overboard her prince she remembered that I adore her!"

"I feel bound to tell you," was in the course of a moment Rowland's response to this speech, "that I am now on my way to Mrs. Light's."

"I congratulate you, I envy you!" Roderick murmured imperturbably.

"Mrs. Light has sent for me to remonstrate with her daughter, with whom she has taken it into her head that I have an influence. I don't know to what extent I shall remonstrate, but I give you notice I shall not speak in your interest."

Roderick looked at him for a moment with a lazy radiance in his eyes. "Pray don't!" he simply answered.

"You deserve I should tell her you are a very shabby fellow."

"My dear Rowland, the comfort with you is that I can trust you. You are incapable of doing anything disloyal."

"You mean to lie here then, smelling your roses and nursing your visions and leaving your mother and Miss Garland to eat their hearts out?"

"Can I go and flaunt my felicity in their faces? Wait till I get used to it a trifle. I have done them a villainous wrong, but I can at least forbear to add insult to injury. I may be an arrant fool, but for the moment I have taken it into my head to be prodigiously pleased. I shouldn't be able to conceal it; my pleasure would offend them; so I lock myself up as a dangerous character."

"Well, I can only hope that your pleasure may never grow less or your danger greater!"

Roderick closed his eyes again and sniffed at his rose. "God's will be done!"

On this Rowland left him and repaired directly to Mrs. Light's. This afflicted lady hurried forward to meet him. Since the Cavaliere's visit to Rowland she had taken a reef, as the saying is, in her distress, but she was evidently still in high agitation, and she clutched Rowland by his two hands as if in the shipwreck of her hopes he were her single floating spar. Rowland greatly pitied her, for there is something respectable in passionate grief, even in a very bad cause; and as pity is akin to love he felt rather more tolerant of her fantastic pretensions than he had done hitherto.

"Speak to her, plead with her, command her!" she cried, pressing and shaking his hands. "She'll not heed *us*, no more than if we were a pair of running fountains. Perhaps she will listen to you; she always liked you."

"She always disliked me," said Rowland. "But that

doesn't matter now. I have come here simply because you sent for me—not because I can help you. I can't advise your daughter."

"Oh cruel, deadly man! You *must* advise her; you sha'n't leave this house till you have advised her!" the poor woman passionately retorted. "Look at me in my misery and refuse to help me! You needn't be afraid, I know I'm a fright, I haven't an idea what I have on. If this goes on she and I may both as well turn scarecrows. If ever a woman was desperate, frantic, heart-broken, such a woman speaks to you now! I can't begin to tell you. To have nourished a serpent, sir, all these years! to have lavished one's self upon a viper that turns and stings her own poor mother! To have toiled and prayed, to have pushed and struggled, to have eaten the bread of bitterness and gone through fire and water—and at the end of all things to find myself at this pass! It can't be, it's too cruel, such things don't happen, the Lord don't allow it. I'm a religious woman, sir, and the Lord knows all about me. With His own hand He had given me his reward! I would have lain down in the dust and let her walk over me; I would have given her the eyes out of my head if she had taken a fancy to them. No, she's a cruel, wicked, heartless, unnatural girl! I speak to you, Mr. Mallet, in my dire distress, as to my *only* friend. There isn't a creature here that I can look to—not one of them all that I have faith in. But I always admired *you*. I said to Christina the first time I saw you that you were a perfect gentleman, and very different from some! Come, don't disappoint me now! I feel so terribly alone, you see; I feel what a nasty hard heartless world it is that has come and devoured my dinners and danced to my fiddles, and yet that hasn't a word to throw to me in my agony! Oh, the money alone that I have put into this thing would melt the heart of a Turk!"

During this frenzied outbreak Rowland had had time to look round the room and to see the Cavaliere sitting in a corner, like a major-domo on the divan of an ante-chamber, pale, rigid, inscrutable.

"I have it at heart to tell you," Rowland said, "that if you consider my friend Hudson—"

Mrs. Light gave a toss of her head and hands. "Oh,

it's not that! She told me last night to bother her no
longer with Hudson. Hudson forsooth! She didn't care
a button for Hudson. I almost wish she did; then perhaps
one might understand it. But she doesn't care for anything in the wide world except to do her own hard wicked
will and to crush me and shame me with her cruelty."

"Ah, then," said Rowland, "I am as much at sea as
you, and my presence here is an impertinence. I should
like to say three words to Miss Light on my own account.
But I must wholly decline to talk to her about Prince
Casamassima. This is simply impossible."

Mrs. Light burst into angry tears. " Because the poor
boy is a prince, eh? because he's of a great family and has
an income of millions, eh? That's why you grudge him
and hate him. I knew there were vulgar people of that
way of feeling, but I didn't expect it of *you*. Make an
effort, Mr. Mallet; rise to the occasion; forgive the poor
fellow his advantages. Be just, be reasonable! It's not
his fault, and it's not mine. He's the best, the kindest
young man in the world, and the most correct and moral
and virtuous! If he were standing here in rags I would
say it all the same. The man first—the money afterwards:
that was always my motto—ask the Cavaliere. What do
you take me for? Do you suppose I would give Christina
to a *vicious* person? do you suppose I would sacrifice my
precious child, little comfort as I have in her, to a man
against whose character a syllable could be breathed?
Casamassima is only too good, he's a saint of saints, he's
stupidly good! There isn't such another in the length
and breadth of Europe. What he has been through in
this house not a common peasant would endure. Christina
has treated him as you wouldn't treat a dog. He has
been insulted, outraged, persecuted! He has been driven
hither and thither till he didn't know where he was. He
has stood there where you stand—there, with his name
and his millions and his devotion—as white as your handkerchief, with hot tears in his eyes, and me ready to go
down on my knees to him and say, ' My own sweet Prince,
I could kiss the ground you tread on, but it isn't decent
that I should allow you to enter my house and expose
yourself to these horrors again.' And he would come
back, and he would come back, and go through it all again,

and take all that was given him, and only want the girl
the more! I was his confidant; I know everything He
used to beg my own forgiveness for Christina. What do
you say to that? I seized him once and kissed him, I did!
To find that and to find all the rest with it, and to believe
that it was a gift straight from the pitying angels of
Heaven, and then to see it dashed away before your eyes
and to stand here helpless—oh, it's a fate I hope you may
ever be spared!"

"It would seem then that in the interest of Prince
Casamassima himself I ought to refuse to interfere," said
Rowland.

Mrs. Light looked at him hard, slowly drying her eyes.
The intensity of her grief and anger gave her a kind of
majesty, and Rowland for the moment felt ashamed of the
somewhat grim humour of his observation.

"Very good, sir," she said. "I am sorry your heart is
not so tender as your conscience. My compliments to
your conscience! It must give you great happiness.
Heaven help me! Since you fail us we are indeed driven
to the wall. But I have fought my own battles before
and I have never lost courage; and I don't see why I
should break down now. Cavaliere, come here!"

Giacosa rose at her summons and advanced with his
usual deferential alacrity. He shook hands with Rowland
in silence.

"Mr. Mallet refuses to say a word," Mrs. Light went
on. "Time presses, every moment is precious. Heaven
knows what that poor boy may be doing. If at this
moment a clever woman should get hold of him she
might be as ugly as she could! It's horrible to think
of it."

The Cavaliere fixed his eyes on Rowland, and his look,
which the night before had been singular, was now most
extraordinary in its mixture of fine anxiety—an anxiety
which seemed to plead against the young man's reluctance
—and mocking exultation.

Suddenly and vaguely Rowland felt the presence of a
new element in the drama that was going on before him.
He looked from the Cavaliere to Mrs. Light, whose eyes
were now quite dry and were fixed in stony hardness on
the floor.

"If you could bring yourself," the Cavaliere said, in a low, soft, tenderly-urgent voice, "to address a few words of solemn remonstrance to Miss Light you would perhaps do more for us than you know. You would save several persons a great deal of pain. The dear signora first, and then Christina herself. Christina in particular. Me too I might take the liberty to add!"

There was to Rowland something acutely touching in this humble petition. He had always felt a sort of imaginative tenderness for poor little unexplained Giacosa, and these words seemed a supreme manifestation of the mysterious obliquity of his life. All of a sudden as he watched the Cavaliere something occurred to him; it was something very odd and it stayed his glance suddenly from again turning to Mrs. Light. His idea embarrassed him, and to carry off his embarrasment, he repeated that it was folly to suppose that *his* words would have any weight with Christina.

The Cavaliere stepped forward and laid two fingers on Rowland's breast. "Do you wish to know the truth? You are the only man whose words she remembers."

Rowland was going from surprise to surprise. "I will say what I can!" he said. By this time he had ventured to glance at Mrs. Light. She was looking at him askance, as if upon this she were suddenly mistrusting his motives.

"If you fail," she said sharply, "we have something else! But please to lose no time."

She had hardly spoken when the sound of a short sharp growl caused the company to turn. Christina's fleecy poodle stood in the middle of the great drawing-room with his muzzle lowered, in pompous defiance of the three conspirators against the comfort of his mistress. This young lady's claims for him seemed justified; he was an animal of amazing shrewdness. He had preceded Christina as a sort of vanguard of defence, and she now slowly advanced from a neighbouring room.

"You will be so good as to listen to Mr. Mallet," her mother said in a terrible voice, "and to reflect carefully on what he says. I suppose you will admit that *he* is disinterested. In half an hour you shall hear from me again!" And passing her hand through the Cavaliere's arm she swept rapidly out of the room.

Christina looked hard at Rowland, but offered him no greeting. She was very pale, and strangely enough it at first seemed to Rowland that her beauty was in eclipse. But he very soon perceived that it had only changed its character, and that if it was a trifle less brilliant than usual it was admirably touching and noble. The clouded light of her eyes, the magnificent gravity of her features, the conscious erectness of her head, might have belonged to a deposed sovereign or a condemned martyr. "Why have you come here at this time?" she asked.

"Your mother sent for me in pressing terms, and I was very glad to have an opportunity to speak to you."

"Have you come to help me or to persecute me?"

"I have as little power to do one as I have desire to do the other. I came in great part to ask you a question. First, is your decision irrevocable?"

Christina's two hands had been hanging clasped in front of her; she separated them and flung them apart by an admirable gesture.

"Would you have done this if you had not seen Mary Garland?"

She looked at him with quickened attention; then suddenly, "This is interesting!" she cried. "Let us have it out." And she flung herself into a chair and pointed to another.

"You don't answer my question," Rowland said.

"You have no right that I know of to ask it. But it's a very clever one; so clever that it deserves an answer. Very likely I should not."

"Last night when I said that to myself I was extremely angry."

"Oh dear, and you are not angry now?"

"I am less angry."

"How very tiresome! But you can say something at least."

"If I were to say what is uppermost in my mind I should say that face to face with you it is never possible to condemn you."

"*Perchè?*"

"You know, yourself! But I can at least say now what I felt last night. It seemed to me that you had consciously cruelly dealt a blow at that poor girl. Do you understand?"

"Wait a moment!" And with her eyes fixed on him she inclined her head on one side meditatively. Then a cold brilliant smile covered her face, and she made a gesture of negation. "I see your train of reasoning, but it's quite wrong. I meant no harm to Miss Garland; I should be extremely sorry to make her suffer. Tell me you believe that."

This was said with ineffable candour. Rowland heard himself answering, "I believe it!"

"And yet in a sense your supposition was true," Christina continued. "I took into my head, as I told you, to be greatly struck with the *fiancée*, and I frankly confess I was jealous of her. What I envied her was simply her character! I said to myself, 'She in my place wouldn't marry Casamassima.' I could not help saying it, and I said it so often that I found a kind of inspiration in it. I hated the idea of being worse than she—of doing something that she would not do. I might be bad by nature, but I needn't be by intention. The end of it all was that I found it impossible not to tell the Prince that I was his very humble servant, but that decidedly I could not marry him."

"Are you sure it was only of Miss Garland's character that you were jealous, not of—not of—"

"Speak out, I beg you. We are talking philosophy!"

"Not of her affection for her cousin?"

"*Sure* is a good deal to ask. Still, I think I may say it! There are two reasons; one, at least, I can tell you: her affection has not a shadow's weight with Mr. Hudson! Why then should one feel it?"

"And what is the other reason?"

"Excuse me; that is my own affair."

Rowland was puzzled, baffled, charmed, inspired. "I have promised your mother," he presently went on, "to say something in favour of Prince Casamassima."

She shook her head sadly. "Prince Casamassima needs nothing that you can say for him. He is a magnificent *parti*. I know it perfectly."

"You know also of the extreme affliction of your mother?"

"Her affliction is demonstrative. She has been abusing me for the last twenty-four hours as if I were the vilest of

the vile." To see Christina sit there in the purity of her
beauty and say this, might have made one bow one's head
with a kind of awe. "I have failed of respect to her at
other times, but I have not done so now. Since we are
talking philosophy," she pursued, with a gentle smile, " I
may say it's a simple matter! I don't love that excellent
Prince. It's very true however that making up one's mind
that one doesn't love a Prince is rather a complicated
operation! I spoke just now of inspiration. The inspiration has been great, but—I frankly confess it—the decision
has been hard. Shall I tell you?" she demanded, with
sudden ardour; "will you understand me? It was on the
one side the world, the splendid, beautiful, powerful, interesting world. I know what that is; I have tasted of the
cup, I know its sweetness. Ah, if I chose, if I should
let myself go, if I should fling everything to the winds,
the world and I would be famous friends! I know its
merits and I think without vanity it would see mine. You
should see some fine things! I should like to be a princess,
and I think I should be a very good one; I would play
my part well. I am fond of luxury, I am fond of a great
society, I am fond of being looked at. I am corrupt, cor-
rupting, corruption! Ah, what a pity that couldn't be
too! Mercy of Heaven!" There was a passionate tremor
in her voice; she covered her face with her hands and sat
motionless. Rowland saw that an intense agitation, hitherto
successfully repressed, underlay the exquisite archness of
her manner and he could easily believe that her battle
had been fierce. She rose quickly and turned away, walked
a few paces and stopped. In a moment she was facing him
again with tears in her eyes and a flush in her cheeks.
" But you needn't think I am afraid!" she said. "I have
chosen, and I shall hold to it. I have something here,
here, *here!*" and she patted her heart. "It's my own. I
shall not part with it. Is it what you call an ideal? I don't
know; I don't care! It is brighter than the Casamassima
diamonds!"

"You say that certain things are your own affair,"
Rowland presently rejoined; "but I must nevertheless
make an attempt to learn what all this means—what it
promises for my friend Hudson. Is there any hope for
him?"

'This is a point I can't discuss with you minutely. I like him very much."

"Would you marry him if he were to ask you?"

"He has asked me."

"And if he asks again?"

"I shall marry no one just now."

"Roderick," said Rowland, "has great hopes."

"Does he know of my rupture with the Prince?"

"He is making a great holiday of it."

Christina pulled her poodle towards her and began to smooth his silky fleece. "I like him very much," she repeated; "much more than I used to. Since you told me all that about him at St. Cecilia's I have felt a great friendship for him. There is something very fine about him; he is not afraid of anything. He is not afraid of failure; he is not afraid of ruin or death."

"Poor fellow!" said Rowland, bitterly; "he is inconveniently picturesque."

"Picturesque, yes; that's what he is. I am very sorry for him."

"Your mother told me just now that you had said that you didn't care a button for him."

"Very likely! I meant as a lover. One doesn't want a lover one pities, and one doesn't want—of all things in the world—a picturesque husband! I should like Mr. Hudson as something else. I wish he were my brother, so that he could never talk to me of marriage. Then I could adore him. I would nurse him, I would wait on him and save him all disagreeable rubs and shocks. I am much stronger than he, and I would stand between him and the world. Indeed with Mr. Hudson for my brother I should be willing to live and die an old maid!"

"Have you ever told him all this?"

"I suppose so; I have told him five hundred things! If it will please you I will tell him again."

"Oh, Heaven forbid!" cried poor Rowland with a groan.

He was lingering there, weighing his sympathy against his irritation and feeling it sink in the scale, when the curtain of a distant doorway was lifted and Mrs. Light passed across the room. She stopped half-way and gave our interlocutors a flushed and menacing look. It found apparently little to reassure her, and she moved away with a passionate toss of her drapery. Rowland thought with horror of the sinister compulsion to which the young girl was apparently still to be subjected. In this ethereal flight of her moral nature there was a certain painful effort and tension of wing; but it was none the less piteous to imagine her being rudely jerked down to the base earth. She would need all her magnanimity for her own contest, and it seemed gross to make farther demands upon it on Roderick's behalf.

Rowland took up his hat. "You asked a while ago if I had come to help you," he said. "If I knew how I might help you I should be particularly glad."

She stood silent a moment, reflecting. Then at last looking up, "You remember your promising six months ago to tell me what you should finally think of me? I should like you to tell me now."

He could hardly help smiling. Madame Grandoni had insisted on the fact that Christina was an actress, and this little speech seemed a glimpse of the cothurnus. She had played her great scene, she had made her point, and now she had her eye at the hole in the curtain and she was watching the house! But she blushed as she perceived his smile, and her blush, which was beautiful, made her fault venial.

"You are an excellent girl!" he said, very positively; and then gave her his hand in farewell.

There was a great chain of rooms in Mrs. Light's apartment, the pride and joy of the hostess on festal evenings, through which the departing visitor passed before reaching the door. In one of the first of these Rowland found himself waylaid and arrested by the distracted mistress of the house.

"Well, well?" she cried seizing his arm. "Has she listened you—have you moved her?"

"In Heaven's name, dear madam," Rowland begged, "leave the poor girl alone! She is behaving very well!"

"Behaving very well? Is that all you have to tell me? I don't believe you said a proper word to her. You are conspiring together to kill me!"

Rowland tried to soothe her, to remonstrate, to persuade her that it was equally cruel and unwise to try to force matters. But she answered him only with harsh lamentations and imprecations, and ended by telling him that her daughter was her own property and that his interference was insolent and scandalous. Her disappointment seemed really to have blighted her wits, and his only possible rejoinder was to take a summary departure.

A moment later he came upon the Cavaliere, who was sitting with his elbows on his knees and his head in his hands, so buried in thought that Rowland had to call him before he roused himself. Giacosa looked at him a moment keenly, and then gave an interrogative shake of the head.

Rowland gave a shake negative, to which the Cavaliere responded by a long melancholy sigh. "But her mother is determined to put on the screw," said Rowland.

"It seems that it must be!"

"Do you consider that it must be?"

"I don't differ with Mrs. Light!"

"It will be a great cruelty!"

The Cavaliere gave a tragic shrug. "Eh! it isn't an easy world."

"You should do nothing to make it harder then."

"What will you have? It's a magnificent marriage."

"You disappoint me, Cavaliere," said Rowland. "I imagined you appreciated the great elevation of Christina's attitude. She doesn't love the Prince; she has let the matter stand or fall by that."

The old man grasped him by the hand and stood a moment with averted eyes. At last, looking at him, he held up two fingers.

"I have two hearts," he said; "one for myself, one for the world. This one is furious with the blessed *ragazza* —the other is enchanted with her! One suffers horribly at what the other does."

"I don't understand double people, Cavaliere," Rowland said, "and I don't pretend to understand you. But I have guessed you are going to play some secret card."

"That card is Mrs. Light's, not mine," said the Cavaliere.

"It's a menace, at any rate?"

"The sword of Damocles! It hangs by a hair. Christina is to be given ten minutes to recant, under penalty of feeling it fall. On the blade there is something written—in strange characters. Don't scratch your head ; you will not make it out."

" I think I have guessed it," said Rowland after a comprehensive silence. The Cavaliere looked at him blankly but intently, and Rowland added, "Though there are some signs indeed I don't understand.'

" Puzzle them out at your leisure," said the Cavaliere, shaking his hand. " I hear Mrs. Light ; I must go to my post. I wish you were a Catholic; I would beg you to step into the first church you come to and pray for us the next half-hour.

" For ' us ' ? For whom ? "

" For all of us. At any rate remember this—I delight in the Christina ! "

Rowland heard the rustle of Mrs. Light's dress; he turned away, and the Cavaliere went as he said to his post. Rowland for the next couple of days kept thinking of the sword of Damocles.

XXI.

Of Roderick meanwhile he saw nothing ; but he immediately went to Mrs. Hudson and assured her that her son was in even exceptionally good health and spirits. After this he called again on the two ladies from North-ampton, but as Roderick's absence continued, he was able to be neither comforting nor comforted. Mary's apprehensive face seemed to him an image of his own state of mind. He was deeply depressed, he felt that there was a storm in the air, and he wished it would come and wash away their troubles. On the afternoon of the third day he went into Saint Peter's, his frequent resort whenever the outer world was disagreeable. From a heart-ache to a Roman rain there were few contrarieties the great church did not help him to forget. He had wandered there for half an hour when he came upon a short figure lurking in the shadow of one of the piers. He saw it was that of an artist hastily transferring to his sketch-book a memento of some fleeting variation in the scenery of the basilica; and in a moment he perceived that the artist was little Sam Singleton.

Singleton pocketed his sketch-book with a guilty air, as if it cost his modesty a pang to be detected in this greedy culture of opportunity. Rowland always enjoyed meeting him; talking with him in these days was as good as a wayside gush of clear cold water on a long hot walk. There was perhaps no drinking-vessel, and you had to apply your lips to some informal conduit; but the result was always a sense of extreme moral refreshment. On this occasion he mentally blessed the ingenuous little artist, and heard presently with regret that he was to leave Rome on the morrow. Singleton had come to bid farewell to Saint Peter's, and he was gathering a few last impressions. He had earned a pocketful of money and he was meaning to take a summer's holiday; going to Switzerland, to Germany, to Paris. In the autumn he was to return home; his family—composed as Rowland knew of a father who was cashier in a bank and five unmarried sisters, one of whom gave lyceum-lectures on woman's rights, the whole resident at Buffalo, New York—had been writing him peremptory letters and appealing to him as a son, brother, and fellow-citizen. He would have been grateful for another year in Rome, but he submitted to destiny the more patiently that he had laid up treasure which in Buffalo would seem infinite. They talked some time; Rowland hoped they might meet in Switzerland and take a walk or two together. Singleton seemed to feel that Buffalo had marked him for her own; he was afraid he should not see Rome again for many a year.

"So you expect to live at Buffalo?" Rowland inquired, looking down the splendid avenue of the nave.

"Well, it will depend upon the views—upon the attitude —of my family," Singleton replied. "Oh I think I shall get on; I think it can be done. If I find it can be done I shall really be quite proud of it; as an artist of course I mean, you know. Do you know I have some nine hundred sketches? I shall live in my portfolio. And so long as one is not in Rome, pray what does it matter where one is?

But how I shall envy all you Romans—you and Mr.
Gloriani—and Mr. Hudson especially."

"Don't envy Hudson; he has nothing to envy."

Singleton chuckled at what he considered a harmless
jest. "Yes, he's going to be the great man of our time!
And I say, Mr. Mallet, isn't it a mighty comfort that it's
we who have turned him out?"

"Between ourselves," murmured Rowland, "he has
disappointed me."

Singleton stared open-mouthed. "Dear me, what did
you expect?"

"Verily," said Rowland to himself, "what did I
expect?"

"I confess," cried Singleton, "I can't judge him ra-
tionally. He fascinates me; he's the sort of man one
makes one's hero of."

"Strictly speaking he is not a hero," Rowland remarked.

Singleton looked intensely grave, and with almost tearful
eyes, "Is there anything amiss—anything out of the way
about him?" he timidly asked. Then as Rowland hesitated to reply he quickly added, "Please, if there is, don't
tell me! I want to know no evil of him, and I think I
should hardly believe it. In my memories of this Roman
artist life he will be the central figure. He will stand
there in radiant relief, as beautiful and unspotted as one
of his own statues!"

"Amen!" said Rowland gravely. He remembered
afresh that the sea is inhabited by big fishes and little, and
that the latter often find their way down the throats of
the former. Singleton was going to spend the afternoon
in taking last looks at certain other places, and Rowland
offered to join him on his sentimental circuit. But as they
were preparing to leave the church he heard himself
suddenly addressed from behind. Turning he beheld a
young woman whom he immediately recognised as Madame
Grandoni's maid. Her mistress was present, she said, and
begged to confer with him before he departed.

This summons obliged Rowland to separate from Singleton, to whom he bade farewell. He followed the messenger,
and presently found Madame Grandoni occupying a liberal
area on the steps of the tribune, behind the great altar,

where, spreading a shawl on the polished red marble, she had comfortably seated herself. He suspected that she had something especial to impart, and she lost no time in bringing forth her treasure.

"Don't shout very loud," she said, "remember that we are in church; there's a limit to the noise one may make even in Saint Peter's. Christina Light was married this morning to Prince Casamassima."

Rowland did not shout at all; he gave a deep short murmur. "Married—this morning?"

"Married this morning, at seven o'clock, *le plus tranquillement du monde*, before three or four persons. The young couple left Rome an hour afterwards."

For some moments this seemed to him really terrible; the dark little drama of which he had caught a glimpse had played itself out. He had believed that Christina would resist; that she had succumbed was a proof that the pressure had been cruel. Rowland's imagination followed her forth with an irresistible tremor into the world towards which she was rolling away with her unappreciated husband and her stifled ideal; but it must be confessed that if the first impulse of his compassion was for Christina, the second was for Prince Casamassima. Madame Grandoni acknowledged an extreme curiosity as to the secret springs of these strange doings—Casamassima's sudden dismissal, his still more sudden recall, the hurried private marriage. "Listen," said Rowland presently, "and I will tell you something." And he related in detail his last visit to Mrs. Light and his talk with this lady, with Christina and with the Cavaliere.

"Good," she said; "it's all very curious. But it's a riddle, and I only half guess it."

"Well," said Rowland, "I desire to harm no one; but certain suppositions have taken shape in my mind which serve as the answers to two or three riddles."

"It is very true," Madame Grandoni replied, "that the Cavaliere, as he stands, has always needed to be explained."

"He is explained by the hypothesis that three-and-twenty years ago, at Ancona, Mrs. Light had a lover."

"I see. Ancona was dull, Mrs. Light was lively, and —three-and-twenty years ago, perhaps—the Cavaliere was

fascinating. Doubtless it would be fairer to say that he
was fascinated. Poor Giacosa!"

"He has had his compensation," Rowland said. "He
has been passionately fond of Christina."

"Naturally. But has Christina never wondered why?"

"If she had been near guessing, her mother's shabby
treatment of him would have put her off the scent. Mrs.
Light's conscience has apparently told her that she could
expiate an hour's too great kindness by twenty years' contempt. So she kept her secret. But what is the profit of
having a secret unless you can make some use of it? The
day at last came when she could turn hers to account;
she could let the skeleton out of the closet and create
a panic."

"I don't understand."

"Neither do I, morally," said Rowland. "I only conceive that there was a horrible fabulous scene. The poor
Cavaliere stood outside, at the door, white as a corpse and
as dumb. The mother and daughter had it out together.
Mrs. Light burnt her ships. When she came out she had
three lines of writing in her daughter's hand, which the
Cavaliere was despatched with to the Prince. They overtook the young man in time, and when he reappeared he
was delighted to dispense with farther waiting. I don't
know what he thought of the look in his bride's face; but
that is how I roughly reconstruct history."

"Christina was forced to decide then that she could not
afford not to be a princess?"

"She had to knock under to a revelation—to humiliation.
She was assured that it was not for her to make conditions,
but to thank her stars that there were none made for her.
If she persisted, she might find it coming to pass that
there would be conditions, and the formal rupture—the
rupture that the world would hear of and pry into—would
then proceed from the Prince and not from her."

"That's all nonsense!" said Madame Grandoni. "What
would the world care?"

"It is nonsense to us, yes; but not to the proudest girl
in the world, deeply wounded in her pride and not stopping
to calculate probabilities, but muffling her shame with an
almost sensuous relief in a splendour that stood within her
grasp and would cover everything. Is it not possible that

the late Mr. Light had made an outbreak before witnesses who are still living?—that the child's coming
into the world was in itself a scandal? Say Light had
quarrelled with his wife and was virtually separated from
her."

"Certainly her marriage now," said Madame Grandoni,
less analytically, "has the advantage that it takes her
away from her dear parents!"

This lady's farther comments upon the event are not
immediately pertinent to our history; there were some
other comments of which Rowland had a deeply oppressive
foreboding. He called on the evening of the morrow upon
Mrs. Hudson, and found Roderick with the two ladies.
Their companion had apparently but lately entered, and
Rowland afterwards learned that it was his first appearance
since the writing of the note which had so distressed his
mother. He had flung himself upon a sofa, where he sat
with his chin upon his breast, staring before him with a
sinister spark in his eye. He fixed his gaze on Rowland,
but gave him no greeting. He had evidently been saying
something to startle his companions; Mrs. Hudson had
gone and seated herself, timidly and imploringly, on the
edge of the sofa, trying to take his hand. Mary was
applying herself to a piece of needlework with conscious
intentness.

Mrs. Hudson gave Rowland on his entrance a touching
look of gratitude. "Oh, we have such blessed news!" she
said. "Roderick is ready to leave Rome."

"It's not blessed news; it's cursed news!" cried
Roderick.

"Oh, but we are very glad, my son, and I am sure you
will be when you get away. You are looking most dreadfully thin; isn't he, Mr. Mallet? It's plain enough you
need a change. I am sure we will go wherever you like.
Where should you like to go?"

Roderick turned his head slowly and looked at her. He
had let her take his hand, which she pressed tenderly
between her own. He gazed at her for some time in
silence. "Poor mother!" he said at last, very incon-
clusively.

"My own dear son!" murmured Mrs. Hudson in all the
innocence of her trust.

"I don't care a straw where you go! I don't care a straw for anything!"

"Oh, my dear boy, you must not say that before all of us here—before Mary, before Mr. Mallet!"

"Mary—Mr. Mallet?" Roderick repeated, almost savagely. He released himself from the clasp of his mother's hand and turned away, leaning his elbows on his knees and holding his head in his hands. There was a silence; Rowland said nothing, because he was watching the girl. "Why should I stand on ceremony with Mary and Mr. Mallet?" Roderick presently added. "Mary pretends to believe I am a fine fellow, and if she believes it as she ought, nothing I can say will alter her opinion. Mallet knows I am a hopeless humbug; so I needn't mince my words with him."

"Ah, my dear, don't use such dreadful language!" said Mrs. Hudson. "Aren't we all devoted to you, and proud of you, and waiting only to hear what you want, so that we may do it?"

Roderick got up and began to walk about the room; he was evidently perfectly reckless. Rowland observed with anxiety that Mrs. Hudson, who did not know on what delicate ground she was treading, was disposed to chide him endearingly, as a mere expression of tenderness. He foresaw that she would bring down the hovering thunderbolt on her head.

"In God's name," Roderick cried, "don't remind me of my obligations! It's intolerable to me, and I don't believe it's pleasant to Mallet. I know they are tremendous—I know I shall never repay them. I am bankrupt! Do you know what that means?"

The poor lady sat staring in dismay, and Rowland angrily interfered. "Don't talk such stuff to your mother!" he cried. "Don't you see you are frightening her?"

"Frightening her? she may as well be frightened first as last. Do I frighten you, mother?"

"Oh, Roderick, what do you mean?" whimpered the poor lady. "Mr. Mallet, what does he mean?"

"I mean that I am an angry, savage, disappointed, miserable man!" Roderick went on. "I mean that I can't do a stroke of work nor think a profitable thought! I mean that I am in a state of helpless rage and grief and shame! Helpless, helpless—that's what it is. You can't help me, poor mother—not with kisses nor tears nor prayers! Mary can't help me—not for all the honour she does me nor all the big books on art that she pores over. Mallet can't help me—not with all his money nor all his good example nor all his friendship, which I am so immensely well aware of : not with all it multiplied a thousand times and repeated to all eternity! I thought you would help me, you and Mary; that's why I sent for you. But you can't, don't think it! The sooner you give up the idea the better for you. Give up being proud of me too; there's nothing left of me to be proud of! A year ago I was a mighty fine fellow; but do you know what has become of me now? I have gone to the devil!"

There was something in the ring of Roderick's voice, as he uttered these words, which sent them home with convincing force.

He was not talking for effect, or the mere personal pleasure of extravagant and paradoxical utterance, as had often enough been the case ere this; he was not even talking viciously or ill-humouredly. He was talking passionately, desperately, sincerely, from an irresistible need to throw off the oppressive burden of his mother's confidence. His cruel eloquence brought the poor lady to her feet, and she stood there with clasped hands, petrified and voiceless. Mary Garland quickly left her place, came straight to Roderick and laid her hand on his arm, looking at him with all her tormented heart in her eyes. He made no movement to disengage himself; he simply shook his head several times in dogged negation of her healing powers. Rowland had been living for the past month in such intolerable expectancy of disaster that now that the ice was broken and the fatal plunge taken his foremost feeling was almost elation. But in a moment his conservative instincts corrected it.

"I really don't perceive," he said, "the profit of your talking in just this way at just this time. Don't you see how you are making your mother suffer?"

"Do I enjoy it myself?" cried Roderick. "Is the suffering all on your side and theirs? Do I look as if I were happy and were stirring you up with a stick for

my amusement? Here we all are in the same boat; we
might as well understand each other! These women
must know that I am not to be counted on. That sounds
remarkably cool, no doubt, and I certainly don't deny your
right to be disgusted with me."

"Will you keep what you have got to say till another
time," said Mary, "and let me hear it alone?"

"Oh, I will let you hear it as often as you please; but
what's the use of keeping it? I am in the humour now;
it won't keep! It's a very simple matter—it isn't worth
keeping. I am a failure, that's all; I am not a first-rate
man. I am second-rate, tenth-rate, anything you please.
After that it's all one!"

Mary turned away and buried her face in her hands;
but Roderick, struck apparently in some unwonted fashion
with her gesture, drew her towards him again and went on
in a somewhat different tone. "It's hardly worth while
we should have any private talk about this, Mary," he
said. "The thing would be comfortable for neither of us.
It's better after all that it be said once for all and dismissed. There are things I can't talk to you about. Can
I, at least? You are such a curious creature!"

"I can imagine nothing you shouldn't talk to me about,"
said Mary.

"You are not afraid?" he demanded sharply, looking
at her.

She turned away abruptly, with lowered eyes, hesitating
a moment. "Anything you think I should hear, I will
hear," she said. And then she returned to her place at
the window and took up her work.

"I have had a great blow," said Roderick. "I was a
great ass, but it doesn't make the blow any easier to
bear."

"Mr. Mallet, tell me what Roderick means!" said Mrs.
Hudson, who had found her voice, in a tone more peremptory than Rowland had ever heard her use.

"He ought to have told you before," said Roderick.
"Really, Rowland, if you will allow me to say so, you
ought! You could have given a much better account of
all this than I myself; better especially in that it would
have been more lenient to me. You ought to have let
them down gently; it would have saved them a great deal

of pain. But you always want to keep things so quiet! Allow me to say that it's very weak of you."

"Speaking too well of you is a fault that's easily mended!" said Rowland with a laugh.

"Oh, what is it, sir; what is it?" groaned Mrs. Hudson insistently.

"It's what Roderick says. He's a failure!"

Mary Garland, on hearing this declaration, gave Rowland a single glance and then rose, laid down her work and walked rapidly out of the room. Mrs. Hudson tossed her head and timidly bristled. "This from *you*, Mr. Mallet!" she said with an injured air which Rowland found harrowing.

But Roderick, most characteristically, did not in the least resent his friend's assertion; he sent him, on the contrary, one of those large, clear looks of his which seemed to express a stoical pleasure in Rowland's frankness, and which set his companion wondering again, as he had so often done before, at the extraordinary incongruities of his temperament. "My dear mother," Roderick said, "if you had had eyes that were not blinded by this sad maternal vanity you would have seen all this for yourself; you would have seen that I am anything but prosperous."

"Is it anything about money?" cried Mrs. Hudson. "Oh, do write to Mr. Striker!"

"Money?" said Roderick. "I have not a cent of money; I am bankrupt!"

"Oh, Mr. Mallet, how could you let him?" asked Mrs. Hudson terribly.

"Everything I have is at his service," said Rowland, feeling ill.

"Of course Mr. Mallet will help you, my son!" cried the poor lady eagerly.

"Oh, leave Mr. Mallet alone!" said Roderick. "I have squeezed him dry; it's not my fault if he has anything left!"

"Roderick, what have you done with all your money?" his mother demanded.

"Thrown it away! It was no such great amount. I have done nothing this winter."

"You have done nothing?"

"I have done no work! Why in the world didn't you guess it and spare me all this? Couldn't you see I was idle, distracted, debauched?"

"Debauched, my dear son?" Mrs. Hudson repeated.

"That's over for the present! But couldn't you see—couldn't Mary see—that I was in a damnably bad way?"

"I have no doubt Miss Garland saw," said Rowland.

"Mary has said nothing!" cried Mrs. Hudson.

"Oh, she's a fine creature!" Rowland said.

"Have you done anything that will hurt poor Mary?" Mrs. Hudson asked.

"I have only been thinking night and day of another woman!"

Mrs. Hudson dropped helplessly into her seat again. "Oh, dear, dear, hadn't we better go home?"

"Not to get out of *her* way!" Roderick said. "She has started on a career of her own, and she doesn't care a straw for me. My head was filled with her; I could think of nothing else; I would have sacrificed everything to her —you, Mary, Mallet, my work, my fortune, my future, my honour! I was in a fine state, eh? I don't pretend to be giving you good news; but I am telling the simple, literal truth, so that you may know why I have gone to the dogs. She pretended to care greatly for all this, and to be willing to make any sacrifice in return; she had a magnificent chance, for she was being forced into a mercenary marriage with a man she detested. She led me to believe that she would send her prince about his business and keep herself free and sacred and pure for me. This was a great honour, and you may believe that I valued it. It turned my head, and I lived only to see my happiness come to pass. She did everything to encourage me to hope it would; everything that her infernal coquetry and falsity could suggest."

"Oh, I say, this is too much!" Rowland broke out.

"Do you defend her?" Roderick cried, with a renewal of his passion. "Do you pretend to say that she gave me no hopes?" He had been speaking with growing bitterness, quite losing sight of his mother's pain and bewilderment in the passionate joy of publishing his wrongs. Since he was hurt he must cry out; since he was in pain he must scatter his pain abroad. Of his never thinking of others save as they figured in his own game, this extra-

ordinary insensibility to the injurious effects of his eloquence
was a capital example; the more so as the motive of his
eloquence was never an appeal for sympathy or compassion
—things to which he seemed perfectly indifferent and of
which he could make no use. The great and characteristic
point with him was the perfect exclusiveness of his emotions.
He never saw himself as part of a whole; only as the
clear-cut, sharp-edged, isolated individual, rejoicing or
raging, as the case might be, but needing in any case
absolutely to affirm himself. All this to Rowland was
ancient history, but his perception of it stirred within
him afresh at the sight of Roderick's sense of having been
betrayed. That *he*, under the circumstances, was hardly
the person to raise the cry of treason, was a point to which
at his leisure Rowland was of course capable of rendering
impartial justice; but Roderick's present desperation was
so peremptory that it imposed itself on one's sympathies.
"Do you pretend to say," he went on, "that she didn't
lead me along to the very edge of fulfilment and stupefy
me with all that she suffered me to believe, all that she
solemnly promised? It amused her to do it, and she knew
perfectly well what she really meant. She never meant to
be sincere; she never dreamed she could be. She's a
ravenous flirt, and why a flirt is a flirt is more than I can
tell you. I can't understand playing with those matters;
for me they are serious, whether I take them up or lay
them down. I don't see what's in your head, Rowland,
to attempt to defend that woman; you were the first to
cry out against her! You told me she was dangerous, and
I pooh-poohed you. You were right; you are always
right. She is as cold and false and heartless as she
is beautiful, and she has sold her heartless beauty to the
highest bidder. I hope he knows what he gets!"

"Oh, my son," cried Mrs. Hudson, plaintively, "how
could you ever care for such a dreadful creature?"

"It would take long to tell you, dear mother!"

Rowland's lately-deepened sympathy and compassion for
Christina was still throbbing in his mind, and he felt
that, in loyalty to it, he must say a word for her. "You
believed in her too much at first," he declared, "and you
believe in her too little now."

Roderick looked at him with eyes almost lurid. "She's

an angel then after all?—that's what you want to prove!"
he cried. "That's consoling for me who have lost her!
You are always right I say; but my dear fellow, in mercy
be wrong for once!"

"Oh yes, Mr. Mallet, be merciful!" said Mrs. Hudson
in a tone which for all its gentleness made Rowland stare.
The poor fellow's stare covered a great deal of concentrated
wonder and apprehension—a presentiment of what a small,
sweet, feeble, elderly lady might be capable of in the way
of suddenly generated animosity. There was no space
in Mrs. Hudson's tiny maternal mind for complications of
feeling, and one emotion existed only by turning another
over flat and perching on top of it. She was evidently not
following Roderick at all in his dusky aberrations. Sitting
without, in dismay, she only saw that all was darkness
and trouble, and as Roderick's glory had now quite out-
stripped her powers of imagination and lifted him beyond
her jurisdiction, so that he had become a thing too precious
and sacred for blame, she found it infinitely comfortable
to lay the burden of their common affliction upon Rowland's
broad shoulders. Had he not promised to make them all
rich and happy? And this was the end of it! Rowland
felt as if his trials were only beginning. "Hadn't you
better forget all this, my dear?" Mrs. Hudson said to
her son. "Hadn't you better just quietly attend to your
work?"

"Work, madam?" cried Roderick. "My work's over.
I can't work—I haven't worked all winter. If I were fit
for anything, this tremendous slap in the face would have
been just the thing to cure me of my apathy. But there's
a perfect vacuum here!" And he tapped his forehead.
"It's bigger than ever; it grows bigger every hour!"

"I am sure you have made a beautiful likeness of your
poor little mother," said Mrs. Hudson coaxingly.

"I had done nothing before, and I have done nothing
since! I quarrelled with an excellent man the other day
from mere exasperation of my nerves, and threw away five
thousand dollars!"

"Threw away—five thousand dollars!" Roderick had
been wandering among formidable abstractions and allusions too dark to penetrate. But here was a concrete fact,
lucidly stated, and poor Mrs. Hudson for a moment looked

it in the face. She repeated her son's words a third time with a gasping murmur and then suddenly she burst into tears. Roderick went to her, sat down beside her, put his arm round her, fixed his eyes coldly on the floor and waited for her to weep herself out. She leaned her head on his shoulder and sobbed broken-heartedly. She said not a word, she made no attempt to scold; but the desolation of her tears was overwhelming. It lasted some time—too long for Rowland's courage. He had stood silent, wishing simply to appear very respectful; but the elation that was mentioned a while since had utterly ebbed and he found his situation intolerable. He was reduced to the vulgar expedient of leaving the room.

The next day, while he was at home, the servant brought him the card of a visitor. He read with surprise the name of Mrs. Hudson and hurried forward to meet her. He found her in his sitting-room, leaning on the arm of her son and looking very pale, her eyes red with weeping and her lips tightly compressed. Her advent puzzled him, and it was not for some time that he began to understand the motive of it. Roderick's countenance threw no light upon it; but Roderick's luminous visage had never had any power of projecting its radiance. He had not been in Rowland's rooms for several weeks, and he immediately began to look at those of his own works that adorned them. He gave himself up to independent contemplation. Mrs. Hudson had evidently armed herself with dignity, and so far as she might she meant to be impressive. Her success however may be measured by the fact that Rowland's whole attention centred in the fear of seeing her begin to weep. She told him that she had come to him for practical advice; she took leave to remind him that she was a stranger in the land. Where were they to go, please? What where they to do? Rowland glanced at Roderick, but Roderick had his back turned and with his head on one side, like a tourist in a church, was gazing at his splendid ' Adam.'

"Roderick says he doesn't know, he doesn't care," Mrs. Hudson said; "he leaves it entirely to you."

Many another man, in Rowland's place, would have greeted this information with an irate and sarcastic laugh, and told his visitors that he thanked them infinitely for their confidence, but that really as things stood now they must settle these little matters between themselves ; many another man might have so comported himself, even if, like Rowland, he had been in love with Mary Garland and pressingly conscious that her destiny was also part of the question. But Rowland swallowed all hilarity and all sarcasm, and entered into Mrs. Hudson's dilemma. His wits, however, were but indifferently at his command ; they were dulled by his sense of the singular change that had taken place in the attitude of this bewildered woman. Her visit was evidently intended as a formal reminder of forgotten vows. Mrs. Hudson was doubtless too sincerely humble a person to suppose that if he had had the wicked levity to break faith with her, her imponderable presence would operate as a chastisement. But by some diminutive logical process of her own she had convinced herself that she had been weakly trustful, and that she had suffered Rowland to think too meanly not only of her understanding but of her social consequence. A visit in her best gown would have an admonitory effect as regards both of these attributes ; it would cancel some favours received and show him that she was not incapable of grasping the theory, at least, of retribution ! These were the reflections of a very shy woman, who, determining for once in her life to hold up her head, was actually flying it like a kite.

"You know we have very little money to spend," she said as Rowland remained silent. "Roderick tells me that he has debts and nothing at all to pay them with. He says I must write to Mr. Striker to sell my house for what it will bring and send me out the money. When the money comes I must give it to him. I am sure I don't know ; I never heard of anything so dreadful ! My house is all I have. But that is all Roderick will say. We must be very economical."

Before this speech was finished Mrs. Hudson's voice had begun to quaver softly, and her face, which had no capacity for the expression of a privileged consciousness, to look as humbly appealing as before. Rowland turned to Roderick and spoke like a schoolmaster. "Come away from those statues and sit down here and listen to me ! "

Roderick started, but obeyed with the most graceful docility, choosing a stiff-backed antique chair.

"What do you propose to your mother to do?" Rowland asked.

"Propose?" said Roderick absently. "Oh, I propose nothing."

The tone, the glance, the gesture with which this was said were horribly irritating, and for an instant an imprecation rose to Rowland's lips. But he had checked it, and he was afterwards glad he had done so. "You must do something," he said. "Choose, select, decide!"

"My dear Rowland, how you talk!" Roderick cried. "The very point of the matter is that I can't do anything. I will do as I'm told, but I don't call that doing. We must leave Rome, I suppose, though I don't see why. We have got no money, and you have to pay money on the railroads."

Mrs. Hudson surreptitiously wrung her hands. "Listen to him, please!" she cried. "Not leave Rome, when we have staid here later than any respectable family ever did before! It's this dreadful place that has made us so unhappy. Roderick's so fearfully relaxed!"

"It's very true that I'm relaxed!" said Roderick serenely. "If I had not come to Rome I shouldn't have risen, and if I had not risen I shouldn't have fallen."

"Fallen—fallen!" murmured Mrs. Hudson. "Just hear him!"

"I will do anything you say, Rowland," Roderick added. "I will do anything you want. I have not been unkind to my mother—have I, mother? I was unkind yesterday, without meaning it; for after all, you know, all that had to be said. Murder will out, and my little troubles can't be hidden. But we talked it over and made it up, didn't we? It seemed to me we did. Let Rowland decide it, mother; whatever he suggests will be the right thing." And Roderick, who had hardly removed his eyes from his statue, got up again and went back to look at it.

Mrs. Hudson fixed her eyes upon the floor in silence. There was not a trace in Roderick's face or in his voice of the bitterness of his emotion of the day before and not a hint of his having the lightest weight upon his conscience. He looked at Rowland with his frank and radiant eye as if there had never been a difference of opinion between them; as if each had ever been for both, unalterably, and both for each.

Rowland had received a few days before a letter from a lady of his acquaintance, a worthy Scotswoman domiciled in a villa upon one of the olive-covered hills near Florence. She held her apartments in the villa upon a long lease, and she enjoyed for a sum not worth mentioning the possession of an extraordinary number of noble, stone-floored rooms, with ceilings vaulted and frescoed, and barred windows commanding the loveliest view in the world. She was a needy and thrifty spinster, who never hesitated to declare that the lovely view was all very well, but that for her own part she lived in the villa for cheapness, and that if she had a clear three hundred pounds a year she would go and really enjoy life near her sister, a baronet's lady at Glasgow. She was now proposing to make a visit to that delectable city, and she desired to turn an honest penny by sub-letting for a few weeks her historic Italian chambers. The terms on which she occupied them enabled her to ask a rent almost jocosely small, and she begged Rowland to do what she called a little genteel advertising for her. Would he say a good word for her rooms to his numerous friends in Rome? He said a good word for them now to Mrs. Hudson, and told her in dollars and cents how cheap a summer's lodging she might secure. He dwelt upon the fact that she would strike a truce with *tables-d'hôte* and have a cook of her own, amenable possibly to instruction in the Northampton mysteries. He had touched a tender chord; Mrs. Hudson became almost cheerful. Her sentiments upon the *table-d'hôte* system and upon foreign household habits generally were remarkable, and if we had space for it would repay analysis; and the idea of reclaiming a lost soul to culinary orthodoxy quite lightened the burden of her depression. While Rowland set forth his case Roderick slowly walked through the rooms with his hands in his pockets. Rowland waited for him to manifest an interest in their discussion, but he had no attention for his friend's pictures. Rowland was a practical man; he possessed conspicuously what is called the sense of detail. He entered into Mrs. Hudson's position minutely, and told her exactly why it seemed good that she should remove immediately to the Florentine villa. She received his advice with great frigidity, looking hard at the floor and sighing, like a person well on her guard against an optimism which might be but an escape from penalties. But she had nothing better to propose, and Rowland received her permission to write to his friend that she would take the rooms.

Roderick assented to this decision without either sighs or smiles. "A Florentine villa is a good thing!" he said. "I am at your service."

"I am sure I hope you will recover your tone there," moaned his mother, gathering her shawl together.

Roderick laid one hand on her arm and with the other pointed to Rowland's statues. "This is my tone just now. Once upon a time I did those things, and they are devilish good!"

Mrs. Hudson gazed at them vaguely, and Rowland said, "That's a capital tone!"

"They are atrociously good!" said Roderick.

Rowland solemnly shrugged his shoulders; it seemed to him that he had nothing more to say. But as the others were going, a last light pulsation of the sense of undischarged duty led him to address to Roderick a few words of parting advice. "You will find the Villa Pandolfini very delightful, very comfortable," he said. "You ought to be very contented there. Whether you work or whether you do what you are doing now, it's a place for an artist to be happy in. I hope you will work."

"I hope I may!" said Roderick, with a magnificent smile.

"When we meet again try and have something to show me."

"When we meet again? Where the deuce are *you* going?" Roderick demanded.

"Oh, I hardly know; over the Alps."

"Over the Alps! You are going to leave me?"

Rowland had certainly meant to leave him, but his resolution was not proof against this single ejaculation. He glanced at Mrs. Hudson, and saw that her eyebrows were lifted and her lips parted in delicate reprehension. She seemed to accuse him of a craven shirking of trouble, to demand of him to repair his cruel havoc in her life by a solemn renewal of zeal. But Roderick's expectations

were the oddest! Such as they were, Rowland asked
himself why he shouldn't make a bargain with them.
"You want me to go with you?" he asked.

"If you don't go, I won't—that's all! How in the
world shall I get through the next six months without
you?"

"How will you get through them with me? That's the
question."

"I don't pretend to say; the future is a dead blank.
But without you it's not a blank—it's certain damnation!"

"Mercy, mercy!" murmured Mrs. Hudson.

Rowland made an effort to turn this precious symptom
of a positive desire to account. "If I go with you, will
you try to work?"

Roderick up to this moment had been looking as unper-
turbed as if the deep agitation of the day before were a
thing of the remote past. But at these words his face
changed formidably; he flushed and scowled and all his
passion returned. "Try to work!" he cried. "Try—try!
work—work! In God's name don't talk that way, or
you'll drive me mad! Do you suppose I am trying *not* to
work? Do you suppose I stand rotting here for the fun
of it? Don't you suppose I would try to work for myself
before I tried for you?"

"Mr. Mallet," cried Mrs. Hudson piteously, "will you
leave me alone with *this*?"

Rowland turned to her and informed her gently that he
would go with her to Florence. After he had taken this
engagement he thought not at all of the pain of his position
as mediator between the mother's resentful grief and the
son's incurable weakness; he drank deep, only, of the
satisfaction of not separating from Mary Garland. If the
future was a blank to Roderick it was hardly less so to
himself. He had at moments a sharp foreboding of im-
pending calamity. He paid it no especial deference, but
it made him feel indisposed to take the future into his
account. On his going to take leave of Madame Grandoni,
this lady asked when he would come back to Rome, and
he answered that he would return either never or for ever.
When she asked him what he meant, he said he really
couldn't tell her, and he parted from her with much

genuine emotion; the more so doubtless that she blessed him in a quite loving maternal fashion and told him she honestly believed him to be the best fellow in the world.

XXII.

THE Villa Pandolfini stood directly upon a small grass-grown piazza, on the top of a hill which sloped straight from one of the gates of Florence. It offered to the outer world a long rather low façade, coloured a dull, dark yellow and pierced with windows of various sizes, no one of which save those on the ground floor was on the same level with any other. Within, it had a great cool grey cortile, with high light arches around it, heavily-corniced doors of majestic altitude opening out of it, and a beautiful mediæval well on one side of it. Mrs. Hudson's rooms opened into a small garden supported on immense substructions which were planted on the farther side of the hill as it sloped steeply away. This garden was a charming place. Its southern wall was curtained with a screen of orange-blossoms, a dozen fig-trees here and there offered you their large-leaved shade, and over the low parapet the soft grave Tuscan landscape kept you company. The rooms themselves were as high as chapels and as cool as royal sepulchres. Silence, peace and security seemed to abide in the ancient house and make it an ideal refuge for unsuccessful lives. Mrs. Hudson had a stunted brown-faced Maddalena who wore a crimson handkerchief passed over her coarse black locks and tied under her sharp pertinacious chin, and a smile which was as brilliant as a prolonged flash of light-ning. She smiled at everything in life, especially the things that displeased her and that kept her talent for mendacity in healthy exercise. A glance, a word, a motion was sufficient to make her show her teeth at you like a cheerful she-wolf. This inexpugnable smile constituted her whole vocabulary in her dealings with her melancholy mistress to whom she had been bequeathed by the late

occupant of the apartment and who, to Rowland's satisfaction, promised to be diverted from her maternal sorrows
by the still deeper perplexities of Maddalena's theory of
roasting, sweeping and bed-making.

Rowland took rooms at a villa a trifle nearer Florence,
whence in the summer mornings he had five minutes' walk
in the sharp black shadow-strip projected by winding
flower-topped walls to join his friends. The life at the
Villa Pandolfini, when it had fairly defined itself, was
tranquil and monotonous, but it might .have borrowed
from exquisite circumstance an absorbing charm. If a
sensible shadow rested upon it, this was because it had an
inherent vice; it feigned a light-heartedness which it very
scantily felt. Roderick had lost no time in giving the
full measure of his uncompromising chagrin, and as he
was the central figure of the little group, as he held its
heart-strings all in his own hand, it reflected faithfully the
eclipse of his genius. No one had ventured upon the cheerful
commonplace of saying that the change of air and of scene
would restore his spirits; this would have had, under the
circumstances, altogether too silly a sound. The change in
question had done nothing of the sort, and his companions
had at least the comfort of their perspicacity. An essential
spring had dried up within him, and there was no visible
spiritual law for making it flow again. He was rarely
violent, he expressed little of the irritation and *ennui* that
he must have constantly felt; it was as if he believed that
a spiritual miracle for his redemption was just barely possible and was therefore worth waiting for. The most that
one could do however was to wait grimly and doggedly,
suppressing an imprecation as from time to time one looked
at one's watch. An attitude of positive urbanity towards
life was not to be expected; it was doing one's duty to
hold one's tongue and keep one's hands off one's own wind-
pipe and other people's. Roderick had long silences, fits of
profound lethargy, almost of stupefaction. He used to sit
in the garden by the hour, with his head thrown back, his
legs outstretched, his hands in his pockets and his eyes
fastened upon the blinding summer sky. He would gather
a dozen books about him, tumble them out on the ground,
take one into his lap, and leave it with the pages unturned.
These moods would alternate with hours of extreme restless-

ness during which he mysteriously absented himself. He bore the heat of the Italian summer like a salamander, and used to start off at high noon for·long walks over the hills. He often went down into Florence, rambled through the close dim streets, and lounged away mornings in the churches and galleries. On many of these occasions Rowland bore him company, for they were the times when he was most like his former self. Before Michael Angelo's statues and the pictures of the early Tuscans he quite forgot his own infelicities and picked up the thread of his old æsthetic loquacity. He found in Florence some of his Roman friends and went down in the evening to meet them. More than once he asked Mary Garland to go with him into the town, where he showed her the things he most cared for. He had some sculptor's clay brought up to the villa and deposited in a room suitable for his work ; but when this had been done he turned the key in the door and the clay never was touched. His eye was heavy and his hand cold, and his mother put up a secret prayer that he might be induced to see a doctor. But on a certain occasion, when her prayer became articulate, he had a great outburst of anger, and begged her to know once for all that his health was better than it had ever been. On the whole, and most of the time, he was a sad spectacle ; he looked so hopelessly idle. If he was not querulous and bitter it was because he had taken an extraordinary vow not to be ; a vow heroic for him, a vow which those who knew him well had the tenderness to appreciate. Talking with him was like skating on thin ice, and his companions had a constant mental vision of spots designated " dangerous."

This was a difficult time for Rowland ; he said to himself that he would endure it to the end, but that he must never try it again. Mrs. Hudson divided her time between looking askance at her son, with her hands tightly clasped about her pocket-handkerchief, as if she were wringing it dry of the last hour's tears, and turning her eyes much more directly upon Rowland, in the mutest, the feeblest, the most intolerable reproachfulness. She never phrased her accusations, but he felt that in the unillumined void of the poor lady's mind they loomed up like vaguely-outlined monsters. Her demeanour caused him the acutest suffering, and if at the outset of his experiment he had seen, how dimly soever, one of those plaintive eye-beams in the opposite scale, the brilliancy of Roderick's promises would have counted for little. These punctual messengers made their way to the softest spot in his conscience and kept it chronically aching. If Mrs. Hudson had been voluble and vulgar he would have borne even a less valid persecution with greater fortitude. But somehow, neat and noiseless and dismally lady-like as she sat there, keeping her grievance green with her soft-dropping tears, her displeasure conveyed an overwhelming imputation of brutality. He felt like a reckless trustee who has speculated with the widow's mite, and is haunted with the reflection of ruin that he sees in her tearful eyes. He did everything conceivable to be polite to Mrs. Hudson and to treat her with distinguished deference. Perhaps his exasperated nerves made him overshoot the mark, and rendered his civilities too grimly perfunctory. She seemed capable of believing that he was trying to make a fool of her ; she would have thought him cruelly recreant if he had suddenly turned his back, and yet she gave him no visible credit for his constancy. Women are said by some authorities to be cruel ; I know not how true this is, but it may at least be pertinent to remark that Mrs. Hudson was intensely feminine. It often seemed to Rowland that he had too decidedly forfeited his freedom, and that there was something grotesque in a man of his age being put into a corner.

But Mary Garland had helped him before, and she helped him now—helped him not less than he had assured himself she would when he found himself drifting to Florence. Yet her help was rendered as unconsciously and indirectly as before ; he had made no apologies and she had offered to remit no penalties. After that distressing scene in Rome which had immediately preceded their departure, it was of course impossible that there should not be on the girl's part some frankness of allusion to Roderick's sad condition. She had been present, the reader will remember, during only half of his uncompromising confession of his errors, and Rowland had not seen her confronted with any absolute proof of Rowland's passion for Christina Light. But he knew that she knew far

too much for her happiness; Roderick had told him, shortly
after their settlement at the Villa Pandolfini, that he had
had a "tremendous talk" with his cousin. Rowland asked
no questions about it; he preferred not to know what had
passed between them. If their interview had been purely
painful he wished to ignore it for Mary's sake; and if it
had sown the seeds of reconciliation he wished to close his
eyes to it for his own—for the sake of that unshaped idea,
for ever dismissed and yet for ever present, which hovered
in the background of his consciousness with a hanging
head and yet an unshamed glance, and whose lightest
motions were an effectual bribe to patience. Had there
been a formal rupture? Rowland wondered, yet without
asking; and he thought it very possible that if there had
not been, it was because Roderick had so completely bidden
farewell to forms. It hardly mattered, however, for if
Mary of her own movement had withdrawn her hand, her
heart had by no means recovered its liberty. It was very
certain to Rowland's mind that if she had given him up
she had by no means ceased to care for him passionately,
and that to exhaust her charity for his weaknesses Roderick
would have as the phrase is a long row to hoe. She spoke
of Roderick as she might have done of a person suffering
from a serious malady which demanded much tenderness;
but if Rowland had found it possible to accuse her of
dishonesty he would have said now that she believed
appreciably less than she pretended in her victim's being
an involuntary patient. There are women whose love is
care-taking and patronising, and who attach themselves to
those persons of the other sex in whom the manly grain
is soft and submissive. It did not in the least please
Rowland to believe that Mary Garland was one of these,
for he held that such women were only males in petticoats,
and he was convinced that this young lady's nature was
typically girlish. That she was a very different woman
from Christina Light did not at all prove that she was a
less considerable one, and if the Princess Casamassima had
gone up into a high place to publish her disrelish of a
man who lacked the virile will, it was very certain that
Mary was not a person to put up at any point with what
might be called the Princess's leavings. It was Christina's
constant practice to remind you of the complexity of her

character, of the subtlety of her mind, of her troublous faculty of seeing everything in a dozen different lights. Mary had never pretended not to be simple; but Rowland had a theory that she had really a more multitudinous sense of human things, a more delicate imagination and a finer instinct of character. She did you the honours of her mind with a grace far less regal, but was not that faculty of quite as remarkable a construction? If in poor Christina's strangely commingled nature there was circle within circle and depth beneath depth, it was to be believed that the object of Rowland's preference, though she did not amuse herself with dropping stones into her soul and waiting to hear them fall, laid quite as many sources of spiritual life under contribution. She had believed Roderick was a fine fellow when she bade him farewell beneath the Northampton elms, and this belief, to her young, strenuous, concentrated imagination, had meant many things. If it was to grow cold, it would be because disenchantment had become total and won the battle at each successive point.

Even in her face and carriage she had something of the preoccupied and wearied look of a person who is watching at a sick-bed; Roderick's broken fortunes, his dead ambitions were a cruel burden to the heart of a girl who had believed that he possessed "genius," and who supposed that genius was to one's spiritual economy what a large bank account was to one's domestic. And yet with Mary Rowland never tasted, as with Mrs. Hudson, of that acrid under-current—that impertinent implication that he had defrauded her of happiness. Was this justice in the girl, or was it mercy? The answer would have been difficult, for she had almost let Rowland feel before leaving Rome that she liked him well enough to forgive him an injury. It was partly, Rowland fancied, that there were occasional lapses, deep and sweet, in her sense of injury. When on arriving at Florence she saw the place Rowland had brought them to in their trouble, she had given him a look and said a few words to him that had seemed not only a remission of guilt but a positive reward. This happened in the court of the villa—the large grey quadrangle, overstretched, from edge to edge of the red-tiled roof, by the deep Italian sky. Mary had felt on the spot the sovereign charm of the place; it was reflected in her intelligent eyes, and

Rowland immediately accused himself of not having done the villa justice. Mary fell in love on the spot with Florence, and used to look down wistfully at the towered city from their terraced garden. Roderick having now no pretext for not being her cicerone, Rowland was no longer at liberty, as he had been in Rome, to propose frequent excursions to her. Roderick's own invitations however were not frequent, and Rowland more than once ventured to introduce her to a gallery or a church. These expeditions were not so blissful to his sense as the rambles they had taken together in Rome, for his companion only half surrendered herself to her enjoyment, and seemed to have but a divided attention at her command. Often, when she had begun with looking intently at a picture, her silence after an interval made him turn and glance at her. He usually found that if she was looking at the picture still she was not seeing it. Her eyes were fixed, but her thoughts were wandering, and an image more vivid than any that Raphael or Titian had drawn had superposed itself upon the canvas. She asked fewer questions than before, and seemed to have lost heart for consulting guide books and encyclopædias. From time to time however she uttered a deep full murmur of gratification. Florence in midsummer was perfectly void of travellers, and the dense little city gave forth its æsthetic aroma with a larger frankness, as the nightingale sings when the listeners have departed. The churches were deliciously cool, but the grey streets were stifling, and the great dove-tailed polygons of pavement were hot to the lingering tread. Rowland, who suffered from a high temperature, would have found all this uncomfortable in solitude ; but Florence had never charmed him so completely as during these midsummer strolls with his preoccupied companion. One evening they had arranged to go on the morrow to the Academy. Mary kept her appointment, but as soon as she appeared Rowland saw that something painful had befallen her. She was doing her best to look at her ease, but her face bore the marks of tears. Rowland told her that he was afraid she was ill, and that if she preferred to give up the visit to Florence he would submit with what grace he might. She hesitated a moment, and then said she preferred to adhere to their plan.

" I am not well," she presently added, " but it's a moral
malady, and in such cases I consider your company an
assistance."

" But if I am to be your doctor," said Rowland, " you
must tell me how your illness came about."

" I can tell you very little. It came about with Mrs.
Hudson being unjust to me—for the first time in her life.
And now I am already better ! "

I mention this incident because it confirmed an impression of Rowland's from which he had derived a certain
consolation. He knew that Mrs. Hudson considered her
son's ill-regulated passion for Christina Light a very regret-
table affair, but he suspected that her manifest compassion
had been all for Roderick, and not in the least for her
companion. She was fond of the young girl, but she had
valued her primarily during the last two years as a kind
of assistant priestess at Roderick's shrine. Roderick had
paid her the compliment of asking her to become his wife,
but that poor Mary had any rights in consequence, Mrs.
Hudson was quite incapable of perceiving. Her sentiment
on the subject was of course not rigidly formulated, but she
was unprepared to regard her companion in the least as a
victim. Roderick was very unhappy; that was enough,
and Mary's duty was to join her patience and her prayers
to those of a disinterested parent. Roderick might fall
in love with whom he pleased; no doubt that women trained
in the mysterious Roman arts were only too proud and too
happy to make it easy for him; and it was very presuming
in a plain second cousin to feel any personal resentment.
Mrs. Hudson's philosophy was of too narrow a scope to
suggest that a mother may forgive where a mistress cannot,
and she thought it a charge upon her own mortgaged
charity that Mary should not accommodate herself to the
position of a handmaid without wages. She was ready to
hold her breath so that Roderick might sigh at his ease,
and she was capable of seeing her young kinswoman gasp
for air without a tremor of compassion. Mary now
apparently had given some intimation of her belief that
if constancy is the flower of devotion, reciprocity is the
guarantee of constancy, and Mrs. Hudson had denounced
this as a very arrogant doctrine. That Mary had found it
hard to reason with Mrs. Hudson, that she suffered deeply

from the elder lady's moral parsimony, and that in short he had companionship in misfortune—all this made Rowland find a certain luxury in his discomfort.

The party at Villa Pandolfini used to sit in the garden in the evenings, which Rowland almost always spent with them. Their entertainment was in the heavily perfumed air, in the dim, far starlight, in the crenelated tower of a neighbouring villa, which loomed vaguely above them through the warm darkness, and in such conversation as depressing reflections permitted. Roderick, clad always in white, roamed about like a restless ghost, silent for the most part, but making from time to time a brief observation characterised by the most fantastic cynicism. Roderick's contributions to the conversation were indeed always so fantastic that though half the time they wearied him unspeakably Rowland made an effort to treat them humorously. With Rowland alone Roderick talked a great deal more—often about the things that had formerly interested him. He talked as well as ever or even better; but his talk always ended in a torrent of groans and curses. When this current set in Rowland straightway turned his back and stopped his ears, and Roderick now witnessed these movements with perfect indifference. When the latter was absent from the star-lit circle in the garden, as often happened, Rowland knew nothing of his whereabouts; he supposed him to be in Florence, but he never learned what he did there. All this was not enlivening; yet with an even, muffled tread the days followed each other and brought the month of August to a close. One particular evening at this time was enchanting; there was a perfect moon, looking so extraordinarily large that it made everything its light fell upon seem small; the heat was tempered by a soft west wind, and the wind was laden with the odours of the early harvest. The hills, the vale of the Arno, the shrunken river, the domes of Florence, were not so much lighted as obscured by the dense moonshine. Rowland had found the two ladies alone at the villa, and he had sat with them for an hour. He felt hushed by the solemn splendour of the scene, but he risked the remark that whatever life might yet have in store for either of them this was a night that they would never forget.

"It's a night to remember when one is dying!" Mary Garland exclaimed.

"Oh, Mary, how can you!" murmured Mrs. Hudson, to whom this savoured of profanity, and to whose shrinking sense indeed the accumulated loveliness of the hour seemed to have something shameless and defiant.

They were silent after this for some time, but at last Rowland addressed certain idle words to the young girl. She made no reply, and he turned to look at her. She was sitting motionless, with her head pressed to Mrs. Hudson's shoulder, and the latter lady was gazing at him through the silvered dusk with a look which gave a sort of spectral solemnity to the sad weak meaning of her eyes. She had the air for the moment of a little old malevolent fairy. Mary, Rowland perceived in an instant, was not absolutely motionless; a tremor passed through her figure. She was crying, or on the point of crying, and she could not trust herself to speak. Rowland left his place and wandered to another part of the garden, wondering at the motive of her sudden tears. Of women's weeping in general he had a sovereign dread, but this somehow gave him a certain pleasure. When he returned to his place Mary had raised her head and brushed away her grief. She came away from Mrs. Hudson, and they stood for a short time leaning against the parapet.

"It seems to you very strange, I suppose," said Rowland, "that there should be any trouble in such a world as this."

"I used to think," she answered, "that if any trouble came to me I should bear it like a stoic. But that was at home, where things don't speak to us of enjoyment as they do here. Here it is such a mixture; one doesn't know what to choose, what to believe. Beauty stands there—beauty such as this night and this place and all this sad strange summer, have been so full of—and it penetrates to one's soul and lodges there and keeps saying that man was not made to suffer but to enjoy. This place has undermined my stoicism, but—shall I tell you? I feel as if I were saying something sinful—I love it!"

"If it is sinful, I absolve you—in so far as I have power. We are made both to suffer and to enjoy, I suppose. As you say, it's a mixture! Just now and here, it seems a peculiarly strange one. But we must take things in turn."

His words had a singular aptness, for he had hardly uttered them when Roderick came out from the house, evidently in his darkest mood. He stood for a moment gazing hard at the view.

"It's a very beautiful night, my son," said his mother, going to him timidly and touching his arm.

He passed his hand through his hair and let it stay there, clasping his thick locks. "Beautiful?" he cried; "of course it's beautiful! Everything is beautiful; every-thing is insolent, defiant, atrocious with beauty. Nothing is ugly but me—me and my poor dead brain!"

"Oh my dearest son," pleaded poor Mrs. Hudson, "don't you feel any better?"

Roderick made no immediate answer; but at last he spoke in a different voice. "I came expressly to tell you that you needn't trouble yourselves any longer to wait for something to turn up. Nothing *will* turn up! It's all over! I said when I came here I would give it a chance. I have given it a chance. Haven't I, eh? Haven't I, Rowland? It's no use; the thing's a failure! Do with me now what you please. I recommend you to set me up there at the end of the garden and shoot me."

"I feel strongly inclined," said Rowland, gravely, "to go and get my revolver."

"Oh, mercy on us, what language!" cried Mrs. Hudson.

"Why not?" Roderick went on. "This would be a lovely night for it, and I should be a lucky fellow to be buried in this garden. But bury me alive if you prefer. Take me back to Northampton."

"Roderick, will you really come?" cried his mother.

"Oh yes, I'll go! I might as well be there as anywhere —reverting to idiocy and living upon alms. I can do nothing with all this; perhaps I should really like North-ampton. If I am to vegetate for the rest of my days, I can do it there better than here."

"Oh, come home, come home," Mrs. Hudson said, "and we shall all be safe and quiet and happy. My dearest son, come home with your poor little mother!"

"Let us go then—quickly!"

Mrs. Hudson flung herself upon his neck for gratitude. "We will go to-morrow!" she cried. "The Lord is very good to me!"

Mary Garland said nothing to this; but she looked at Rowland, and her eyes seemed to contain a kind of alarmed appeal. Rowland observed it with exultation, but even without it he would have broken into an eager protest.

"Are you serious, Roderick?" he demanded.

"Serious? of course not! How can a man with a crack in his brain be serious? how can a d—d fool reason? But I am not jesting, either; I can no more make jokes than utter oracles!"

"Are you willing to go home?"

"Willing? God forbid! I am simply amenable to force; if my mother chooses to take me I won't resist. I can't! I have come to that!"

"Let me resist then," said Rowland. "Go home in this state? I can't stand by and see it."

It may have been true that Roderick had lost his sense of humour, but he scratched his head with a gesture that was almost comical in its effect. "You are a queer fellow! I should think I would disgust you horribly."

"Stay another year," Rowland simply said.

"Doing nothing?"

"You shall do something. I am responsible for your doing something."

"To whom are you responsible?"

Rowland, before replying, glanced at Mary Garland, and his glance made her speak quickly. "Not to me!"

"I am responsible to myself," Rowland declared.

"My poor dear fellow!" said Roderick.

"Oh, Mr. Mallet, aren't you satisfied?" cried Mrs. Hudson, in the tone in which Niobe may have addressed the avenging archers after she had seen her eldest-born fall. "It's out of all nature keeping him here. When our poor hearts are broken, surely our own dear native land is the place for us. Do leave us to ourselves. sir!"

This just failed of being a dismissal in form, and Rowland made a note of it. Roderick was silent for some moments; then suddenly he covered his face with his two hands. "Take me at least out of this terrible Italy," he

cried, " where everything mocks and reproaches and torments and eludes me ! Take me out of this land of
impossible beauty and put me in the midst of ugliness.
Set me down where nature is coarse and flat, and men and
manners are vulgar. There must be something awfully
ugly in Germany. Pack me off there ! "

Rowland answered that if he wished to leave Italy the
thing might be arranged ; he would think it over and
submit a proposal on the morrow. He suggested to Mrs.
Hudson in consequence that she should spend the autumn
in Switzerland, where she would find a fine tonic climate,
plenty of fresh milk, and several very inexpensive *pensions.*
Switzerland of course was not ugly, but one could not have
everything !

Mrs. Hudson neither thanked him nor assented ; but she
wept and packed her trunks. Rowland had a theory, after
the scene which led to these preparations, that Mary was
weary of waiting for Roderick to come to his senses, that
the faith which had borne him company on the tortuous
march he was leading it, had begun to believe it had gone
far enough. This theory was not vitiated by something
she said to him on the day before that on which Mrs.
Hudson had arranged to leave Florence.

" Cousin Sarah, the other evening," she said, " asked you
to leave us to ourselves. I think she hardly knew what
she was saying, and I hope you have not taken offence."

" By no means ; but I honestly believe that my leaving
you would contribute greatly to Mrs. Hudson's comfort.
I can be your hidden providence you know ; I can watch
you at a distance and come upon the scene at critical
moments."

The girl looked for a moment at the ground ; and then,
with sudden earnestness, " I want you to come with us ! "
she said.

It need hardly be added that after this Rowland went
with them.

XXIII.

Rowland had a very friendly memory of a little mountain-inn, accessible with moderate trouble from Lucerne, where he had once spent a blissful ten days. He had at that time been trudging, knapsack on back, over half Switzerland, and not being a particularly light weight on his legs it was no shame to him to confess that he was mortally tired. The inn of which I speak presented striking analogies with a cow-stable; but in spite of this circumstance it was crowded with hungry tourists. It stood in a high shallow valley, with flower-strewn Alpine meadows sloping down to it from the base of certain rugged rocks whose outlines were grotesque against the evening sky. Rowland had seen grander places in Switzerland that pleased him less, and whenever afterwards he wished to think of Alpine opportunities at their best he recalled this grassy concave among the higher ridges, and the August days he spent there, resting deliciously at his length in the lea of a sun-warmed boulder, with the light cool air stirring about his temples, the wafted odours of the pines in his nostrils, the tinkle of the cattle-bells in his ears, the vast progression of the mountain-shadows before his eyes, and a volume of Wordsworth in his pocket. His face, on the Swiss hill-sides, had been scorched to a brilliant hue, and his bed was a pallet in a loft, which he shared with a German botanist of colossal stature—every inch of him quaking at an open window. These had been drawbacks to felicity, but Rowland hardly cared whether or how he was lodged, for he spent the livelong day under the sky, on the crest of a slope that looked at the Jungfrau. He remembered all this on leaving Florence with his friends, and he reflected that, as the midseason was over, accommodations would be more ample and charges more modest. He communicated with his old friend the landlord, and while September was yet young his companions established themselves under his guidance in the grassy valley.

He had crossed the Saint Gothard Pass with them, in

the same vehicle. During the journey from Florence, and especially during this portion of it, the cloud that hung over the little party had been almost dissipated, and they had looked at each other, in the close intimacy of the train and the posting-carriage, without either retributive or argumentative glances. It was impossible not to enjoy the magnificent scenery of the Apennines and the Italian Alps, and there was a tacit agreement among the travellers to abstain from sombre allusions. The effect of this delicate compact seemed excellent; it ensured them a week's intellectual sunshine. Roderick sat and gazed out of the window with a fascinated stare and with a perfect docility of attitude. He concerned himself not a particle about the itinerary or about any of the wayside arrangements; he took no trouble and he gave none. He assented to everything that was proposed, talked very little, and led for a week a perfectly contemplative life. His mother rarely removed her eyes from him; and if a while before this would greatly have irritated him, he now seemed perfectly unconscious of her observation and profoundly indifferent to anything that might befall him. They spent a couple of days on the Lake of Como, at an hotel with white porticoes smothered in oleander and myrtle, and terrace-steps leading down to little boats with striped awnings. They agreed it was the earthly paradise, and they passed the mornings strolling through the cedarn alleys of classic villas, and the evenings floating in the moonlight in a circle of outlined mountains, to the music of silver-trickling oars. One day, in the afternoon, the two young men took a long stroll together. They followed the winding footway that led towards Como, close to the lake-side, past the gates of villas and the walls of vineyards, through little hamlets propped on a dozen arches, and bathing their feet and their pendant tatters, the grey-green ripple; past frescoed walls and crumbling campaniles and grassy village piazzas and the mouth of soft ravines that wound upward through belts of swinging vine and vaporous olive and splendid chestnut, to high ledges where white chapels gleamed amid the paler boskage, and bare cliff-surfaces, with their blistered lips, drank in the liquid light. It all was consummately picturesque; it was the Italy that we know from the steel engravings in old keepsakes and

annuals, from the vignettes on music-sheets and the drop-
curtains at theatres; an Italy that we can never confess
ourselves—in spite of our own changes and of Italy's—
that we have ceased to believe. Rowland and Roderick
turned aside from the little paved footway that clambered
and dipped and wound and doubled beside the lake,
and stretched themselves idly beneath a fig-tree on a
grassy promontory. Rowland had never known anything so divinely soothing as the dreamy softness of
that early autumn afternoon. The iridescent mountains
shut him in; the little waves beneath him fretted the
white pebbles at the laziest intervals; the festooned vines
above him swayed just visibly in the all but motionless
air.

Roderick lay observing it all with his arms thrown back
and his hands under his head. "This suits me," he said;
"I could be happy here and forget everything. Why not
stay here for ever?" He kept his position for a long time
and seemed lost in his thoughts. Rowland spoke to him,
but he made vague answers; at last he closed his eyes.
It seemed to Rowland also a place to stay in for ever; a
place for perfect oblivion of the disagreeable. Suddenly
Roderick turned over on his face and buried it in his
arms. There had been something passionate in his movement; but Rowland was nevertheless surprised when he at
last jerked himself back into a sitting posture, to perceive
the trace of tears in his eyes. Roderick turned to his
friend, stretching his two hands out towards the lake and
mountains, and shaking them with an eloquent gesture, as
if his heart had been too full for utterance.

"Pity me my friend; pity me!" he presently cried.
"Look at this lovely world and think what it must be
to be dead to it!"

"Dead?" said Rowland.

"Dead, dead; dead and buried! Buried in an open
grave, where you lie staring up at the sailing clouds,
smelling the waving flowers and hearing all nature live
and grow above you! That's the way I feel!"

"I am glad to hear it," said Rowland. "Death of that
sort is very near to resurrection."

"It's too horrible," Roderick went on; "it has all come
over me here! If I were not ashamed I could shed a

bushel of tears. For one hour of what I *have* been I would give up anything I may be!"

"Never mind what you have been; be something better!"

"I shall never be anything again; it's no use talking! But I don't know what secret spring has been touched since I have lain here. Something in my heart seems suddenly to open and let in a flood of beauty and desire. I know what I have lost, and I think it horrible! Mind you, I know it, I feel it! Remember that hereafter. Don't say that he was stupefied and senseless; that his perception was dulled and his aspiration dead. Say that he trembled in every nerve with a sense of the beauty and sweetness of life; that he rebelled and protested and struggled; that he was buried alive, with his eyes open and his heart beating to madness; that he clung to every blade of grass and every wayside thorn as he passed; that it was the most pitiful spectacle you ever beheld; that it was a scandal, an outrage, a murder!"

"Good heavens man, are you insane?" Rowland cried.

"I have never been saner. I don't want to be bad company, and in this beautiful spot, at this delightful hour, it seems an outrage to break the charm. But I am bidding farewell to Italy, to beauty, to honour, to life! I only want to assure you that I know what I lose. I know it in every pulse of my heart! Here, where these things are all loveliest, I take leave of them. Good-bye, charming world!"

During their passage of the Saint Gothard Roderick absented himself much of the time from the carriage, and rambled far in advance, along the zigzags of the road. He displayed an extraordinary activity; his light weight and slender figure made him an excellent pedestrian, and his friends frequently saw him skirting the edge of plunging chasms, loosening the stones on long steep slopes or lifting himself against the sky from the top of rocky pinnacles. Mary Garland walked a great deal, but she remained near the carriage to be with Mrs. Hudson. Rowland remained near it to be with Mrs. Hudson's companion. He trudged by her side up that magnificent ascent from Italy, and found himself regretting that the Alps were so low and that their trudging was not to last a week. She was exhilarated; she liked to walk; in the way of mountains, until within the last few weeks, she had seen nothing greater than Mount Holyoke, and she found that the Alps amply justified their reputation. Rowland knew that she loved natural things, but he was struck afresh with the vivacity of her observation of them, and with her knowledge of plants and rocks. At that season the wild flowers had mostly departed, but a few of them lingered, and Mary never failed to espy them in their outlying corners. They interested her greatly; she was charmed when they were old friends and charmed even more when they were new. She displayed a very light foot in going in quest of them and had soon covered the front seat of the carriage with a tangle of strange vegetation. Rowland of course, was alert in her service, and he gathered for her several botanical specimens which at first seemed inaccessible. One of these indeed had at first appeared easier of capture than his attempt attested, and he had paused a moment at the base of the little peak on which it grew, measuring the risk of farther pursuit. Suddenly as he stood there he remembered Roderick's defiance of danger and of Christina Light, at the Coliseum, and he was seized with a strong desire to test the courage of his own companion. She had just scrambled up a grassy slope near him, and had seen that the flower was out of reach. As he prepared to approach it she called to him eagerly to stop; the thing was impossible! Poor Rowland, whose passion had been terribly underfed, enjoyed immensely the thought of having her care for three minutes what should become of him. He was the least brutal of men, but for a moment he was perfectly indifferent to her suffering.

"I can get the flower," he called to her. "Will you trust me?"

"I don't want it; I would rather not have it!" she cried.

"Will you trust me?" he repeated looking at her.

She looked at him and then at the flower; he wondered whether she would shriek and swoon as Christina had done. "I wish it were something better!" she said simply; and then stood watching him while he began to clamber. Rowland was not a trained acrobat and his enterprise was difficult; but he kept his wits about him, made the most of narrow foot-holds and coigns of vantage, and at last secured his prize. He managed to stick it into his button-hole and then he contrived to descend. There was more than one chance for an ugly fall, but he evaded them all. It was doubtless not gracefully done, but it was done, and that was all he had proposed to himself. He was red in the face when he offered Mary the flower, and she was visibly pale. She had watched him without moving. All this had passed without the knowledge of Mrs. Hudson, who was dozing beneath the hood of the carriage. Mary's eyes did not perhaps display that ardent admiration which was formerly conferred by the queen of beauty at a tournament; but they expressed something in which Rowland found his reward. "Why did you do that?" she asked gravely.

He hesitated. He felt that it was physically possible to say, "Because I love you!" but it was not morally possible. He lowered his pitch and answered simply, "Because I wanted to do something for you."

"Suppose you had fallen?"

"I believed I should not fall. And you believed it I think."

"I believed nothing. I simply trusted you, as you asked me."

"*Quod erat demonstrandum!*" cried Rowland. "I think you know Latin."

When our four friends were established in what I have called their grassy valley there was a good deal of scrambling over slopes both grassy and stony, a good deal of flower-plucking on narrow ledges, a great many long walks and, thanks to the tonic mountain air, not a little exhilaration. Mrs. Hudson was obliged to intermit her suspicions of the deleterious atmosphere of the Old World and to acknowledge the superior purity of the breezes of Engelthal. She was certainly more placid than she had been in Italy; having always lived in the country she had missed in Rome and Florence that social solitude mitigated by bushes and rocks which is so dear to the true New England temperament. The little unpainted inn at Engelthal, with its plank partitions, its milk-pans standing in the sun, its "help," in the form of angular young women of the country-side, reminded her of places of summer sojourn in her native land; and the beautiful historic chambers of the Villa Pandolfini passed from her memory without a regret and without having in the least modified her ideal of a satisfactory habitation. Roderick had changed his sky, but he had not changed his mind; his humour was still that of which he had given Rowland a glimpse in that sharp outbreak on the Lake of Como. He kept his despair to himself and he went doggedly about the ordinary business of life; but it was easy to see that his spirit was mortally heavy and that he lived and moved and talked simply from the force of habit. In that sad half-hour among the Italian olives there had been such a fierce sincerity in his tone that Rowland began to abdicate the critical attitude. He began to feel that it was perfectly idle to appeal to his comrade's will; there was no will left; its place was a mocking vacancy. This view of the case indeed was occasionally contravened by certain indications on Roderick's part of the surviving faculty of resistance to disagreeable obligation : one might still have said, if one had been disposed to be didactic at any hazard, that there was a method in his madness, that his moral energy had its sleeping and its waking hours, and that in an attractive cause it was capable of rising with the dawn. But on the other hand, pleasure in this case was quite at one with effort; evidently the greatest bliss in life for Roderick would have been an inspiration. And then it was impossible not to feel tenderly to a despair which had so ceased to be aggressive—not to forgive much apathy to a temper which had turned its rough side inward. Roderick said frankly that Switzerland made him less miserable than Italy, and the Alps seemed less to mock at his idle hands than the Apennines. He indulged in long rambles, generally alone, and was very fond of climbing into dizzy places where no sound could overtake him, and there, flinging himself on the never-trodden moss, of pulling his hat over his eyes and lounging away the hours in perfect immobility. Rowland sometimes walked with him; though Roderick never invited him he seemed properly grateful for his society. Rowland now made it a rule to treat him as a perfectly sane man, to assume that all things were well with him, and never to allude to the prosperity he had parted with or to the work he was not doing. He would have still said, had you questioned him, that Roderick's condition was only a lugubrious interlude. It might last yet for many a weary hour; but it was a long lane that had no turning. Rowland's interest in Mary's relations with her cousin was still a very lively one, and perplexed as he was on all sides he found nothing penetrable here. After their arrival at Engelthal, Roderick appeared to care for the young girl's society rather more than he had done hitherto, and of this revival of ardour Rowland could not fail to make a note. They sat together and strolled together, and she often read aloud to him. One day on their coming to lunch, after he had been lying half the morning at her feet, in the shadow of a rock, Rowland asked him what she had been reading.

"I don't know," Roderick said, "I don't heed the sense." Mary heard this, and Rowland looked at her. She looked at Roderick sharply and with a little blush. "I listen to Mary," Roderick continued, "for the sake of her voice. It's stupefyingly sweet!" At this Mary's blush deepened, and she looked away.

Rowland, in Florence, as we know, had suffered his imagination to wander in the direction of certain conjectures which the reader may deem unflattering to her constancy. He had asked himself whether her faith in Roderick had not languished, and that demand of hers which had brought about his own departure for Switzerland had seemed almost equivalent to a confession that she needed his help to be constant. Rowland was essentially a modest man, and he did not risk the supposition that Mary had contrasted him with Roderick to his own advantage; but he had a certain consciousness of duty resolutely done which allowed itself to fancy at moments that it might be not unnaturally rewarded by the bestowal of such stray grains of enthusiasm as had crumbled away from her estimate of his companion. If some day she had declared in a sudden burst of passion that she was completely disillusioned and that she gave up her recreant lover, Rowland's expectation would have gone halfway to meet her. And certainly if her passion had taken this course no generous critic would utterly condemn her. She had been neglected, ignored, forsaken, treated with a contempt which no girl of a fine temper could endure. There were girls, indeed, whose

fineness, like that of Burd Helen in the ballad, lay in
clinging to the man of their love through thick and thin
and in bowing their head to all hard usage. This attitude
had often an exquisite beauty of its own, but Rowland
thought that he had solid reason to believe it never could
be Mary Garland's. She was not a passive creature; she
was not soft and meek and grateful for chance bounties.
With all her reserve of manner she was proud and eager;
she asked much and she wanted what she asked; she
believed in fine things and she never could long persuade
herself that fine things missed were as beautiful as fine
things achieved. Once Rowland passed an angry day. He
had dreamed—it was the most insubstantial of dreams—
that she had given him the right to believe that she looked
to him to transmute her discontent. And yet here she
was throwing herself back into Roderick's arms at his
lightest overture, and betraying his own half fearful, half
shameful hopes! Rowland declared to himself that his
position was detestable and that all the philosophy he could
bring to bear upon it would make it neither honourable
nor comfortable. He would go away and make an end of
it. He did not go away; he simply took a long walk,
stayed away from the inn all day, and on his return found
Mary sitting out in the moonlight with Roderick.

Rowland, communing with himself during the restless
ramble in question, had determined that he would at last
cease to observe, to heed or to care for what these two
young persons might do or might not do together. Nevertheless some three days afterwards, the opportunity presenting itself, he deliberately broached the subject with
Roderick. He knew this was inconsistent and faint-hearted;
it was an indulgence to the fingers that itched to handle
forbidden fruit. But he said to himself that it was really
more logical to return to the question than to drop it, for
they had formerly discussed these mysteries very sharply.
Was it not perfectly reasonable that he should wish to
know the sequel of the situation which Roderick had then
delineated? Roderick had made him promises, and it was
to be expected that he should wish to ascertain how the
promises had been kept. Rowland could not say to himself
that if the promises had been extorted for Mary's sake, his
present attention to them was equally disinterested; and

so he had to admit that he was indeed faint-hearted. He may perhaps be deemed too rigid a casuist, but I have repeated more than once that he was solidly burdened with a conscience.

"I imagine," he said to Roderick, "that you are not sorry at present to have allowed yourself to be dissuaded from putting an end to your affair with your cousin."

Roderick eyed him with the vague and absent look which had lately become habitual to his face and repeated—"Dissuaded?"

"Don't you remember that in Rome you wished to break off your engagement, and that I urged you to hold to it, though it seemed to hang by so slender a thread? I wished you to see what would come of it. If I am not mistaken you are now reconciled to it."

"Oh yes," said Roderick, "I remember what you said; you made it a kind of personal favour to yourself that I should remain faithful. I consented, but afterwards, when I thought of it, your attitude greatly amused me. Had it ever been seen before?—a man asking another man to gratify him by *not* suspending his attentions to a pretty girl!"

"It was as selfish as anything else," said Rowland. "One man puts his selfishness into one thing, and one into another. It would have been a great bore to me to see your cousin in low spirits."

"But you liked her—you admired her, eh? So you intimated."

"I admire her extremely."

"It was your originality then—to do you justice you have a great deal of a certain sort—to wish her happiness secured in just that fashion. Many a man would have liked better himself to make the woman he admired happy, and would have welcomed her low spirits as an opening for sympathy. You were very incongruous about it."

"So be it!" said Rowland. "The question is, Are you not glad I was incongruous? Are you not finding that you do care for your cousin after all?"

"I don't pretend to say. When she arrived in Rome I found I didn't care for her, and I honestly proposed that we should have no humbug about it. If you on the contrary thought there was something to be gained by having

a little humbug I was willing to try it! I don't see that
the situation is really changed. Mary is all that she ever
was—more than all. But I don't care for her! I don't
care for anything, and I don't find myself inspired to make
an exception in her favour. The only difference is that I
don't care now whether I care for her or not. Of course
marrying such a useless lout as I am is out of the
question for any woman, and I should pay Mary a poor
compliment to assume that she is in a hurry to celebrate
our nuptials."

"Oh you'll do—you're in love!" said Rowland, not very
logically. It must be confessed at any cost that this assertion was made for the sole purpose of hearing Roderick
deny it.

But it quite failed of its aim. Roderick gave a liberal
shrug of his shoulders and an irresponsible toss of his head.
"Call it what you please! I am past caring for the names
of things."

Rowland had not only been illogical, he had also been
slightly disingenuous. He did not believe that his companion was in love; he had argued the false to learn the
true. The truth was that Roderick was again in some
degree under a charm and that he found a healing virtue
in the company of a woman of tact. He had said shortly
before that her voice was sweet to his ear; and this was a
happy sign. If her voice was sweet it was probably that
her glance was not amiss, that her touch had a quiet magic,
and that her whole personal presence had learned the art of
not being irritating. So Rowland reasoned, and invested
Mary Garland with the subtlest merits.

It was true that she herself helped him little to definite
conclusions and that he remained in puzzled doubt as to
whether these happy touches were still a matter of the
heart or had become simply a matter of the conscience.
He watched for signs that she took a pleasure in Roderick's
favour again; but it seemed to him that she was on her
guard against interpreting it too largely. It was now her
turn—he fancied that he sometimes gathered from certain
nameless indications of glance and tone and gesture—it was
now her turn to be indifferent, to care for other things.
Again and again Rowland asked himself what these things
were that she might be supposed to care for, to the injury of

ideal constancy; and again, having designated them, he divided them into two portions. One was that larger experience in general which had come to her with her arrival in Europe; the vague sense, borne in upon her imagination, that there were more things one might do with one's life than youth and ignorance and Northampton had dreamt of; the revision of old pledges in the light of new emotions. The other was the experience in especial of Rowland's—what? Here Rowland always paused, in perfect sincerity, to measure afresh his possible claim to the young girl's regard. What might he call it? It had been more than civility and yet it had been less than devotion. It had spoken of a desire to serve, but it had said nothing of a hope of reward. Nevertheless Rowland's fancy hovered about the idea that it was recompensable, and his reflections ended in a reverie which perhaps did not define it, but at least on each occasion added a little to its volume. Since Mary had asked him as a sort of favour to herself to come with them to Switzerland, he thought it possible she might let him know whether he seemed to have done her a service. The days passed without her doing so, and at last Rowland walked away to an isolated eminence some five miles from the inn and murmured to the silent rocks that she was ungrateful. Listening nature appeared not to contradict him, so that on the morrow he asked the young girl with a touch of melancholy malice whether it struck her that his deflection from his other plan had been attended with brilliant results.

"Why, we are delighted that you are with us!" she answered.

He was anything but satisfied with this; it seemed to imply that she had forgotten that she had formally asked him to come. He reminded her of her request and recalled the place and time. "That evening on the terrace, late, after Mrs. Hudson had gone to bed and Roderick being absent."

She perfectly remembered, but the memory seemed to trouble her. "I am afraid your kindness has been a great charge upon you," she said. "You wanted very much to do something else."

"I wanted above all things to oblige you, and I made no sacrifice. But if I had made an immense one it would be more than made up to me by any assurance that I have helped Roderick into a better condition."

She was silent a moment, and then, "Why do you ask me?" she said. "You are able to judge quite as well as I."

Rowland blushed; he desired to justify himself in the most veracious manner. "The truth is," he said, "that I am afraid I care only in the second place for Roderick's holding up his head. What I care for in the first place is *your* happiness."

"I don't know why that should be," she answered. "I have certainly done nothing to make you so much my friend. If you were to tell me you intended to leave us to-morrow, I am afraid that I should not venture to ask you to stay. But whether you go or stay, let us not talk of Roderick!"

"But that," said Rowland, "does not answer my question. *Is* he better?"

"No!" she said, and turned away.

He was careful not to tell her that he intended to leave them.

XXIV.

ONE day shortly after this as the two young men sat at the inn-door watching the sunset, which on that evening was very rich and clear, Rowland made an attempt to sound his companion's present sentiment touching Christina Light. "I wonder where she is," he said, "and what sort of a life she is leading her prince."

Roderick at first made no response. He was watching a figure on the summit of some distant rocks opposite to them. The figure was apparently descending into the valley, and in relief against the crimson screen of the western sky it looked gigantic. "Christina Light?" Roderick at last repeated, as if arousing himself from a reverie. "Where she is? It's extraordinary how little I care!"

" Have you completely got over it ? "

To this Roderick made no direct reply; he sat brooding a while. " She's a humbug ! " he presently exclaimed.

" Possibly ! " said Rowland.   " But I have known worse ones."

" She disappointed me ! " Roderick continued in the same tone.

" Had she really given you up ? "

" Oh, don't remind me ! " Roderick cried.   " Why the devil should I think of it ?   It was only three months ago, but it seems like ten years."   His friend said nothing more, and after a while he went on of his own accord.   " I believed there was a future in it all !   She pleased me—pleased me ; and when an artist—such as I was—is pleased, you know ! "   And he paused again.   " You never saw her as I did ; you never heard her in her great moments.   But there is no use talking about that !   At first she wouldn't regard me seriously ; she chaffed me and made light of me. But at last I forced her to admit I was a great man.   Think of that, sir !   Christina Light called me a great man.   A great man was what she was looking for, and we agreed to find our happiness for life in each other.   To please me she promised not to marry till I should give her leave.   I was not in a marrying way myself, but it was damnation to think of another man possessing her.   To spare my sensibilities she promised to turn off her prince, and the idea of her doing so made me as happy as to see a perfect statue shaping itself in the block.   You have seen how she kept her promise !   When I learned it, it was as if the statue had suddenly cracked and turned hideous.   She died for me, like that ! "   And he snapped his fingers. " Was it wounded vanity, disappointed desire, betrayed confidence ?   I am sure I don't know ; you will certainly have some good name for it."

" The poor girl did the best she could," said Rowland.

" If that was her best, so much the worse for her !   I have hardly thought of her these two months, but I have not forgiven her."

" Well, you may believe that you are avenged.   I can't think of her as happy."

" I don't pity her ! " said Roderick.   Then he relapsed into silence, and the two sat watching the colossal figure

as it made its way downward along the jagged silhouette
of the rocks. " Who is this mighty man," cried Roderick
at last, " and what is he coming down upon us for ? We
are small people here, and we can't undertake to keep
company with giants."

" Wait till we meet him on our own level," said Rowland,
" and perhaps he will not overtop us."

" He's like me," Roderick rejoined ; " for ten minutes he
will have passed for a great man ! " At this moment the
figure sank beneath the horizon-line and became invisible
in the uncertain light. Suddenly Roderick said, " I should
like to see her once more—simply to look at her."

" I would not advise it," said Rowland.

" It was her beauty that did it ! " Roderick went on.
" It was all her beauty ; in comparison, the rest was
nothing. What befooled me was to think of it as my own
property ! And I had made it mine—no one else had
studied it as I had, no one else understood it. What does
that stick of a Casamassima know about it at this hour ?
I should like to see it just once more ; it's the only thing
in the world of which I can say so."

" I would not advise it," Rowland repeated.

" That's right, my dear fellow," said Roderick ; " don't
advise ! That's no use now."

The dusk meanwhile had thickened, and they had not
perceived a figure approaching them across the open space
in front of the house. Suddenly it stepped into the circle
of light projected from the door and windows, and they
beheld little Sam Singleton stopping to stare at them. He
was the giant whom they had seen descending along the
rocks. When this was made apparent Roderick was
seized with a fit of intense hilarity—it was the first time
he had laughed in three months. Singleton, who carried
a knapsack and walking-staff, received from Rowland the
friendliest welcome. He was in the serenest possible
humour, and if in the way of luggage his knapsack contained nothing but a comb and a second shirt, he produced
from it a dozen admirable sketches. He had been trudging over half Switzerland and making everywhere the most
vivid pictorial notes. They were mostly in a box at
Interlaken, and in gratitude for Rowland's appreciation
he presently telegraphed for his box, which according to

the excellent Swiss method was punctually delivered by post. The nights were cold, and our friends, with three or four other chance sojourners, sat in-doors over a fire of great logs. Even with Roderick sitting moodily in the outer shadow they made a sympathetic little circle, and they turned over Singleton's drawings, while he perched in the chimney-corner, blushing and explaining, with his feet on the rounds of the chair. He had been pedestrianising for six weeks, and he was glad to rest a while at Engelthal. It was an economic repose however, for he sallied forth every morning with his sketching tools on his back, in search of material for new studies. Roderick's hilarity, after the first evening, had subsided, and he watched the little painter's serene activity with a gravity that was almost portentous. Singleton, who was not in the secret of his personal misfortunes, still treated him with timid frankness as the rising star of American art. Roderick had said to Rowland at first that Singleton reminded him of some curious little insect with a remarkable mechanical instinct in its *antennæ;* but as the days went by it was apparent that the modest landscapist's unflagging industry grew to have an oppressive meaning for him. It pointed a moral, and Roderick used to sit and con the moral as he saw it figured in Singleton's bent back, on the hot hill-sides, protruding from beneath his white umbrella. One day he wandered up a long slope and overtook him as he sat at work; Singleton related the incident afterwards to Rowland, who, after giving him in Rome a hint of Roderick's aberrations, had strictly kept his own counsel.

"Are you *always* like this?" said Roderick, in almost sepulchral accents.

"Like this?" repeated Singleton, blinking confusedly, with an alarmed conscience.

"You remind me of a watch that never runs down. If one listens hard one hears you always—tic-tic, tic-tic."

"Oh, I see," said Singleton, beaming ingenuously. "I am very equable."

"You are very equable, yes. And do you find it pleasant to be equable?"

Singleton turned and smiled more brightly, while he sucked the water from his camel's-hair brush. Then, with

a quickened sense of his indebtedness to a Providence that
had endowed him with intrinsic facilities, "Oh, delightful!"
he exclaimed.

Roderick stood looking at him a moment. "Damnation!"
he said at last solemnly, and turned his back.

Later in the week Rowland and Roderick took a long
walk. They had walked before in a dozen different direc-
tions, but they had not yet crossed a charming little wooded
pass which shut in their valley on one side and descended
into the vale of Engelberg. In coming from Lucerne they
had approached their inn by this path, and feeling that
they knew it had hitherto neglected it in favour of un-
trodden ways. But at last the list of these was exhausted,
and Rowland proposed the walk to Engelberg as a novelty.
The place is half bleak and half pastoral; a huge white
monastery rises abruptly from the green floor of the valley
and complicates its picturesqueness with an element rare
in Swiss scenery. Hard by is a group of chalets and inns,
with the usual appurtenances of a prosperous Swiss resort
—lean brown guides in baggy homespun, lounging under
carved wooden galleries, stacks of alpenstocks in every
doorway, sun-scorched Englishmen without shirt-collars.
Our two friends sat a while at the door of an inn, discussing a pint of wine, and then Roderick, who was indefatigable, announced his intention of climbing to a certain
rocky pinnacle which overhung the valley and, according
to the testimony of one of the guides, commanded a view
of the Lake of Lucerne. To go and come back was only
a matter of an hour, but Rowland, with the prospect of
his homeward trudge before him, confessed to a preference
for lounging on his bench or, at most, strolling a trifle
farther and taking a look at the monastery. Roderick
went off alone, and his companion after a while bent his
steps to the monasterial church. It was remarkable, like
most of the churches of Catholic Switzerland, for a hideous
style of devotional ornament; but it had a certain cold
and musty picturesqueness, and Rowland lingered there
with some tenderness for Alpine piety. While he was
near the high-altar some people came in at the west door;
but he did not notice them, and was presently engaged in
deciphering a curious old German epitaph on one of the
mural tablets. At last he turned away, wondering whether

its syntax or its theology were the more uncomfortable, and, to his infinite surprise, found himself confronted with Prince and Princess Casamassima.

The surprise on Christina's part, for an instant, was equal, and at first she seemed disposed to turn away without letting it give place to a greeting. The Prince however saluted gravely, and then Christina in silence put out her hand. Rowland immediately asked whether they were saying at Engelberg. but Christina only looked at him without speaking. The Prince answered his questions, and related that they had been making a month's tour in Switzerland, that at Lucerne his wife had been somewhat obstinately indisposed, and that the physician had recommended a week's trial of the tonic air and goat's milk of Engelberg. The scenery, said the Prince, was stupendous, but the life was terribly sad—and they had three days more! It was a blessing, he urbanely added, to see a good Roman face.

Christina's attitude, her solemn silence and her penetrating gaze, seemed to Rowland at first to savour of affectation; but he presently perceived that she was deeply agitated and was afraid of betraying herself. "Do let us leave this hideous edifice," she said; "there are things here that set one's teeth on edge." They moved slowly to the door, and when they stood outside, in the sunny coolness of the valley, she turned to Rowland and said, "I am extremely glad to see you." Then she glanced about her and observed against the wall of the church an old stone seat. She looked at Prince Casamassima a moment, and he smiled more intensely, Rowland thought, than the occasion demanded. "I wish to sit here," she said, "and speak to this old acquaintance—alone."

"At your pleasure, dear friend," said the Prince.

The tone of each was measured, to Rowland's ear; but that of Christina was dry and that of her husband was splendidly urbane. Rowland remembered that the Cavaliere had told him that Mrs. Light's candidate was a prince indeed, and our friend wondered how he relished a peremptory accent. Casamassima was an Italian of the undemonstrative type, but Rowland nevertheless divined that, like other princes before him, he had made the acquaintance of the thing called compromise. "Shall I come back?" he asked, with the same smile.

"In half an hour," said Christina.

In the clear outer light, Rowland's first impression of her was that she was more beautiful than ever. And yet in three months she could hardly have changed; the change was in Rowland's own vision of her, which that last interview on the eve of her marriage had made unprecedentedly tender.

"How came you here?" she asked. "Are you staying in this place?"

"I am staying at Engelthal, some ten miles away; I walked over."

"Are you alone?"

"I am with Roderick Hudson."

"Is he here with you?"

"He went half an hour ago to climb a rock for a view."

"And his mother and—and the *promessa*—where are they?"

"They also are at Engelthal."

"What do you do there?"

"What do *you* do here?" said Rowland, smiling.

"I count the minutes till my week is over. I hate mountains; they depress me to death. I am sure Miss Garland likes them."

"She is very fond of them, I believe."

"You believe—don't you know? But I have given up trying to imitate Miss Garland," said Christina.

"You surely need imitate no one."

"Don't say that," she said, gravely. "So you have walked ten miles this morning? And you are to walk back again?"

"Back again to dinner."

"And Mr. Hudson too?"

"Mr. Hudson especially. He is a great walker."

"You men are happy!" Christina cried. "I believe I should enjoy the mountains if I could do such things. It is sitting still and having them scowl down at you! Prince Casamassima never walks. He only goes on a mule. He was carried up the Faulhorn in a palanquin."

"In a palanquin?" said Rowland.

"In one of those machines—a *chaise à porteurs*—like a woman."

Rowland received this information in silence; it was equally unbecoming to be either amused or shocked.

"Is Mr. Hudson to join you again? Will he come here?" Christina asked.

"I shall soon begin to expect him." ·

"What shall you do when you leave Switzerland?" Christina continued. "Shall you go back to Rome?"

"I rather doubt it. My plans are very uncertain."

"They depend upon Mr. Hudson, eh?"

"In a great measure."

"I want you to tell me about him. Is he still in that perverse state of mind that afflicted you so much?"

Rowland looked at her mistrustfully, without answering. He was indisposed, instinctively, to tell her that Roderick was unhappy; it was possible she might offer to try to cure him. She immediately perceived his hesitation.

"I see no reason why we should not be frank," she said. "I should think we were excellently placed for that sort of thing. You remember that formerly I cared very little what I said, don't you? Well, I care absolutely not at all now. I say what I please, I do what I please! How did Mr. Hudson receive the news of my marriage?"

"Very badly," said Rowland.

"With rage and reproaches?" And as Rowland hesitated again—"With silent contempt?"

"I can tell you but little. He spoke to me on the subject, but I stopped him. I told him it was none of his business nor of mine."

"That was an excellent answer!" said Christina softly. "Yet it was a little your business, after those sublime protestations I treated you to. I was really very fine that morning, eh?"

"You do yourself injustice," said Rowland. "I should be at liberty now to believe you were insincere."

"What does it matter now whether I was insincere or not? I can't conceive of anything mattering less. I *was* very fine—isn't it true?"

"You know what I think of you," said Rowland. And for fear of being forced to betray his suspicion of the cause of her change he took refuge in a commonplace. "I hope your mother is well."

"My mother is in the enjoyment of superb health, and

may be seen every evening at the Casino at the Baths of
Lucca confiding to every new-comer that she has married
her daughter to a pearl of a prince.''

Rowland was anxious for news of Mrs. Light's companion, and the natural course was frankly to inquire
about him. "And the Cavaliere Giacosa is well?" he
asked.

Christina hesitated, but she betrayed no other embarrassment. "The Cavaliere Giacosa has retired to his native
city of Ancona, upon a pension, for the rest of his natural
life. He is a very good old man!"

"I have a great regard for him," said Rowland gravely,
at the same time that he privately wondered whether
the Cavaliere's pension was paid by Prince Casamassima
for services rendered in connection with his marriage.
"And what do you do," he continued, "on leaving this
place?"

"We go to Italy—we go to Naples." She rose and
stood silent for a moment, looking down the valley. The
figure of Prince Casamassima appeared in the distance,
balancing his white umbrella. As her eyes rested upon it
Rowland imagined that he saw something deeper in the
strange expression which had lurked in her face while he
talked to her. At first he had been dazzled by her blooming beauty, to which the lapse of weeks had only added
splendour; then he had seen a heavier ray in the light of
her eye—a sinister intimation of sadness and bitterness.
It was the outward mark of her sacrificed ideal. Her eyes
grew cold as she looked at her husband, and when after
a moment she turned them upon Rowland they struck him
as intensely tragical. He felt a singular mixture of
sympathy and dread; he wished to give her a proof of
friendship, and yet it seemed to him that she had now
turned her face in a direction where friendship was power-
less to interpose. She half read his feelings apparently
and she gave a beautiful sad smile. "I hope we may
never meet again!" she said. And as Rowland gave her
a protesting look—"You have seen me at my best. I
wish to tell you solemnly, I *was* sincere! I know appearances are against me," she went on quickly. "There is a
great deal I can't tell you. Perhaps you have guessed it;
I care very little. You know at any rate I did my best.

It wouldn't serve; I was beaten and broken; they were stronger than I. Now it's another affair!"

"It seems to me you have a large °chance for happiness yet," said Rowland vaguely.

"Happiness? I mean to cultivate rapture; I mean to go in for bliss ineffable! You remember I told you that I was in part the world's and the devil's. Now they have taken me all. It was their choice; may they never repent!"

"I shall hear of you," said Rowland.

"You will hear of me. And whatever you do hear, remember this: I *was* sincere!"

Prince Casamassima had approached, and Rowland looked at him with a good deal of simple compassion as a part of that "world" against which Christina had launched her mysterious menace. It was obvious that he was a good fellow and that he could not in the nature of things be a positively bad husband; but his distinguished inoffensiveness only deepened the infelicity of Christina's situation by depriving her defiant attitude of the sanction of relative justice. So long as she had been free to choose she had esteemed him; but from the moment she was forced to marry him she had detested him. Rowland read in the young man's elastic Italian mask a profound consciousness of all this; and as he found there also a record of other curious things—of pride, of temper, of bigotry, of an immense heritage of more or less aggressive traditions—he reflected that the matrimonial conjunction of his two companions might be sufficiently prolific in incident.

"You are going to Naples?" Rowland said to the Prince by of way conversation.

"We are going to Paris," Christina interposed slowly and softly. "We are going to London. We are going to Vienna. We are going to St. Petersburg."

Prince Casamassima dropped his eyes and fretted the earth with the point of his umbrella. While he engaged Rowland's attention Christina turned away. When Rowland glanced at her again he saw a change pass over her face; she was observing something that was concealed from his own eyes by the angle of the church wall. In a moment Roderick stepped into sight.

He stopped short, astonished; his face and figure were
jaded, his garments dusty. He looked at Christina from
head to foot, and then, slowly, his cheek flushed and his
eye expanded. Christina returned his gaze, and for some
moments there was a singular silence. "You don't look
well!" Christina said at last.

Roderick answered nothing; he only looked and looked,
as if she had been a statue. "You are no less beautiful!"
he presently cried.

She turned away with a smile and stood a while gazing
down the valley; Roderick stared at Prince Casamassima.
Christina then put out her hand to Rowland. "Farewell,"
she said. "If you are near me in future, don't try to see
me!" And then after a pause, in a lower tone—"I *was*
sincere!" She addressed herself again to Roderick and
asked him some commonplace about his walk. But he said
nothing; he only looked at her. Rowland at first had
expected an outbreak of reproach, but it was evident that
the danger was every moment diminishing. He was forgetting everything but her beauty, and as she stood there
and let him feast upon it Rowland was sure that she knew
it. "I won't say farewell to you," she said; "we shall
meet again!" And she moved gravely away. Prince
Casamassima took leave courteously of Rowland; upon
Roderick he bestowed a bow of exaggerated civility.
Roderick appeared not to see it; he was watching Christina as she passed over the grass. His eyes followed her
until she reached the door of her inn. Here she stopped
and looked back at him.

XXV.

ON the homeward walk that evening Roderick preserved
an ominous silence, and early on the morrow, saying nothing
of his intentions, he started off alone; Rowland saw him
striding with light elastic steps along the rugged path to
Engelberg. He was absent all day and gave no account of

himself on his return. He said he was deadly tired, and he went to bed early. When he had left the room Mary Garland drew near to Rowland.

"I wish to ask you a question," she said. "What happened to Roderick yesterday at Engelberg?"

"You have discovered that something happened?"

"I am sure of it. Was it something painful?"

"I don't know how at the present moment he judges it. He met the Princess Casamassima."

"Thank you!" said Mary simply, and turned away.

The conversation had been brief, but like many small things it furnished Rowland with food for reflection. When one is looking for symptoms one easily finds them. This was the first time Mary Garland had asked Rowland a question which it was in Roderick's power to answer, the first time she had frankly betrayed Roderick's reticence. Rowland ventured to think it marked an era.

The next morning was sultry, and the air, usually so fresh at those altitudes, was oppressively heavy. Rowland lounged on the grass a while, near Singleton, who was at work under his white umbrella within view of the house; and then in quest of coolness he wandered away to the rocky ridge whence you looked across at the Jungfrau. To-day however the white summits were invisible; their heads were muffled in sullen clouds and the valleys beneath them curtained in dun-coloured mist. Rowland had a book in his pocket and he took it out and opened it. But his page remained unturned; his own thoughts were more absorbing. His interview with Christina Light had made a great impression upon him, and he was haunted with the memory of her almost blameless bitterness and of all that was tragic and fatal in her latest transformation. These things were immensely appealing, and Rowland thought with infinite impatience of Roderick's having again become acquainted with them. It required little imagination to apprehend that the young sculptor's condition had also appealed to Christina. His consummate indifference, his supreme defiance, would make him a magnificent trophy, and Christina had announced with sufficient distinctness that she had said good-bye to scruples. It was her fancy at present to treat the world as a garden of pleasure, and if hitherto she had played with Roderick's passion on its stem, there

was little doubt that now she would pluck it with an
unfaltering hand and drain it of its acrid sweetness. And
why the deuce need Roderick have gone marching back
to destruction? Rowland's meditations, even when they
began in rancour, often brought him comfort; but on this
occasion they ushered in a quite peculiar quality of unrest.
He felt conscious of a sudden collapse in his moral energy;
a current that had been flowing for two years with liquid
strength seemed at last to pause and stagnate. Rowland
looked away at the sallow vapours on the mountains; their
dreariness had an analogy with the stale residuum of his
own generosity. At last he had arrived at the uttermost
limit of the deference a sane man might pay to other
people's folly; nay, rather, he had transgressed it; he had
been befooled on a gigantic scale. He turned to his book
and tried to woo back patience, but it gave him cold
comfort and he tossed it angrily away. He pulled his
hat over his eyes and tried to wonder dispassionately
whether atmospheric conditions had not something to do
with his ill-humour. He remained some time in this
attitude, but was finally aroused from it by a singular
sense that although he had heard nothing some one had
approached him. He looked up and saw Roderick standing
before him on the turf. His mood made the spectacle unwelcome, and for a moment he felt like speaking roughly.
Roderick stood looking at him with an expression of
countenance which had of late become rare. There was
an unfamiliar spark in his eye and a certain imperious
alertness in his carriage. Confirmed habit, with Rowland,
came speedily to the front. "What is it now?" he asked
himself, and invited Roderick to sit down. Roderick had
evidently something particular to say, and if he remained
silent for a time it was not because he was ashamed of it.

"I should like you to do me a favour," he said at last.
"Lend me some money."

"How much do you wish?" Rowland asked.

"Say a thousand francs."

Rowland hesitated a moment. "I don't wish to be
indiscreet, but may I ask you what you propose to do
with a thousand francs?"

"To go to Interlaken."

"And why are you going to Interlaken?"

Roderick replied without a shadow of wavering, "Because that woman is to be there."

Rowland burst out laughing, but Roderick remained serenely grave. "You have forgiven her then?" said Rowland.

."Not a bit of it!"

"I don't understand."

"Neither do I. I only know that she is incomparably beautiful, and that she has waked me up amazingly. Besides, she asked me to come."

"She asked you?"

"Yesterday, in so many words."

"Ah, the shameless jade!"

"Exactly. I am willing to take her for that."

"Why in the name of common sense did you go back to her?"

"Why did I find her standing there like a goddess who had just stepped out of her cloud? Why did I look at her? Before I knew where I was, the spell was wrought."

Rowland, who had been sitting erect, threw himself back on the grass and lay for some time staring up at the sky. At last, raising himself, "Are you perfectly serious?" he asked.

"Deadly serious."

"Your idea is to remain at Interlaken some time?"

"Indefinitely!" said Roderick; and it seemed to his companion that the tone in which he said this made it immensely well worth hearing.

"And your mother and cousin meanwhile are to remain here? It will soon be getting very cold, you know."

"It doesn't seem much like it to-day."

"Very true; but to-day is a day by itself."

"There is nothing to prevent their going back to Lucerne. I depend upon your taking charge of them."

At this moment Rowland reclined upon the grass again; and again after reflection he faced his friend. "How would you express," he asked, "the character of the profit that you expect to derive from your excursion?"

"I see no need of expressing it. The proof of the pudding is in the eating! The case is simply this. I desire immensely to be near Christina Light, and it is such a huge refreshment to find myself again desiring something, that

I propose to drift with the current. As I say, she has waked me up, and it is possible that something may come of it. She makes me feel as if I were alive again. This sort of thing," and he glanced down at the inn, " I call death ! "

" That I am very grateful to hear. You really feel as if you might do something ? "

"Don't ask too much. I only know that she makes my heart beat, makes me see visions."

" You feel encouraged ? "

" I feel excited."

" You are really looking better."

" I am glad to hear it. Now that I have answered your questions, please to give me the money."

Rowland shook his head. " For that purpose I can't ! "

" You can't ? "

" It's impossible. Your plan is pure folly. I can't help you in it."

Roderick flushed a little, and his eye expanded. " I will borrow what money I can then from Mary ! " This was not viciously said ; it had simply the ring of passionate resolution.

Instantly it brought Rowland to terms. He took a bunch of keys from his pocket and tossed it upon the grass. "The little brass one opens my dressing-case," he said. " You will find money in it."

Roderick let the keys lie ; something seemed to have struck him ; he looked askance at his friend. " You are awfully considerate of Mary ! "

" You certainly are not. Your proposal is an outrage."

" Very likely. It's proof the more of my desire."

" If you have so much steam on then, use it for something else ! You say you are awake again. I am delighted ; only be so in the best sense. Isn't it very plain ? If you have the energy to desire, you have also the energy to reason and to judge. If you can care to go, you can also care to stay, and staying being the more profitable course, the inspiration, on that side, for a man who has his self-confidence to win back again, should be greater."

Roderick plainly did not relish this simple logic, and his eye grew angry as he listened to its echo. " Oh, the devil ! " he cried.

But Rowland gave him more of it. "Do you believe that hanging about Christina Light will do you any good? Do you believe it won't? In either case you should keep away from her. If it won't it's your duty; and if it will you can get on without it."

"Do me good?" cried Roderick. "What do I want of 'good'—what should I do with 'good'? I want what she gives me, call it by what name you will. I want to ask no questions, but to take what comes and let it fill the impossible hours! But I didn't come to discuss the matter."

"I have not the least desire to discuss it," said Rowland. "I simply protest."

Roderick meditated a moment. "I have never yet thought twice about accepting any favour of you," he said at last; "but this one sticks in my throat."

"It is not a favour; I lend you the money only under compulsion."

"Well then, I will take it only under compulsion!" Roderick exclaimed. And he sprang up abruptly and marched away.

His words were ambiguous; Rowland lay on the grass wondering what they meant. Half an hour had not elapsed before Roderick reappeared, heated with rapid walking and wiping his forehead. He flung himself down and looked at his friend with an eye which expressed something purer than bravado and yet baser than conviction.

"I have done my best!" he said. "My mother is out of money; she is expecting next week some circular notes from London. She had only ten francs in her pocket. Mary Garland gave me every sou she possessed in the world. It makes exactly thirty-four francs. That's not enough."

"You asked Mary Garland?" cried Rowland.

"I asked her."

"And told her your purpose?"

"I named no names. But she knew!"

"What did she say?"

"Not a syllable. She simply emptied her purse."

Rowland turned over and buried his face in his arms. He felt a movement of irrepressible elation, and he barely stifled a cry of joy. Now, surely, Roderick had shattered

the last link in the chain that bound Mary to him, and
after this she would be free! . . . . When he turned
about again, Roderick was still sitting there, and he had
not touched the keys which lay on the grass.

"I don't know what is the matter with me," said
Roderick, "but I have an insurmountable aversion to
taking your money."

"The matter, I suppose, is that you have a grain of
wisdom left."

"No, it's not that. It's a kind of brute instinct. I
find it extremely provoking!" He sat there for some
time with his head in his hands and his eyes on the
ground. His lips were compressed, and he was evidently,
in fact, in a state of high disgust. "You have succeeded
in making this thing uncommonly unpleasant!" he exclaimed.

"I am sorry," said Rowland, "but I can't see it in any
other way."

"That I believe, and I resent the range of your vision
pretending to be the limit of my action. You can't feel
for me or judge for me, and there are certain things you
know nothing about. I have suffered, sir!" Roderick
went on, with increasing emphasis and with the ring of
his fine old Virginian pomposity in his tone. "I have
suffered damnable torments. Have I been such a placid,
contented, comfortable man this last six months that when
I find a chance to forget my misery I should take such
pains not to profit by it? You ask too much, for a man
who himself has no occasion to play the hero. I don't say
that invidiously; it's your disposition and you can't help it.
But decidedly there are certain things you know nothing
about."

Rowland listened to this outbreak with open eyes, and
Roderick, if he had been less intent upon his own eloquence,
would probably have perceived that he turned pale. "These
things—what are they?" Rowland asked.

"They are women, principally, and what relates to
women. Women for you, by what I can make out, mean
nothing. You have no imagination—no sensibility, nothing
to be touched!"

"That's a serious charge," said Rowland gravely.

"I don't make it without proof!"

" And what is your proof ? "

Roderick hesitated a moment. " The way you treated Christina Light. I call that grossly obtuse."

" Obtuse ? " Rowland repeated frowning.

" Thick-skinned, beneath your good fortune."

" My good fortune ? "

" There it is—it's all news to you ! You had pleased her. I don't say she was dying of love for you, but she took a fancy to you."

" We will let this pass ! " said Rowland, after a silence.

" Oh, I don't insist. I have only her own word for it."

" Her own word ? "

" You noticed, at least, I suppose, that she was not afraid to speak ! I never repeated it, not because I was jealous, but because I was curious to see how long your ignorance would last if it were left to itself."

" I frankly confess it would have lasted for ever. And yet I don't consider that my insensibility is proved."

" Oh, don't say that," cried Roderick, " or I shall begin to suspect—what I must do you the justice to say that I never have suspected—that you too have a grain of conceit ! Upon my word when I think of all this, your protest, as you call it, against my following Christina Light seems to me thoroughly offensive. There is something monstrous in a man's pretending to lay down the law to a sort of emotion with which he is quite unacquainted—in his asking a fellow to give up a lovely woman for conscience' sake when *he* has never had the impulse to strike a blow for one for passion's ! "

" Oh, oh ! " cried Rowland.

" It's very easy to exclaim," Roderick went on ; " but you must remember that there are such things as nerves and senses and imagination and a restless demon within that may sleep sometimes for a day, or for six months, but that sooner or later wakes up and thumps at your ribs till you listen to him ! If you can't understand it, take it on trust and let a poor visionary devil live his life as he can ! "

Roderick's words seemed at first to Rowland like something heard in a dream ; it was impossible they had been actually spoken—so supreme an expression were they of the insolence of egotism. Reality was never so consistent

as that! But Roderick sat there balancing his beautiful
head, and the echoes of his strident accent still lingered
along the half-muffled mountain-side. Rowland suddenly
felt that the cup of his chagrin was full to overflowing,
and his long-gathered bitterness surged into the simple
wholesome passion of anger for wasted kindness. But
he spoke without violence, and Roderick was probably at
first far from measuring the force that lay beneath his
words.

"You are incredibly ungrateful," he said. "You are
talking arrogant nonsense. What do you know about my
senses and my imagination? How do you know whether
I have loved or suffered? If I have held my tongue and
not troubled you with my complaints, you find it the most
natural thing in the world to put an ignoble construction
on my silence! I loved quite as well as you; indeed I
think I may say rather better. I have been constant. I
have been willing to give more than I received. I have
not forsaken one mistress because I thought another more
beautiful, nor given up the other and believed all manner
of evil about her because I had not my way with her.
I have been a good friend to Christina Light, and it seems
to me my friendship does her quite as much honour as
your love!"

"Your love—your suffering—your silence—your friendship!" cried Roderick. "I declare I don't understand!"

"I dare say not. You are not used to understanding
such things—you are not used to hearing me talk of my
feelings. You are altogether too much taken up with
your own. Be as much so as you please; I have always
respected your right. Only when I have kept myself in
durance on purpose to leave you an open field, don't by
way of thanking me, come and call me an idiot."

"Oh, you claim then that you have made sacrifices?"

"Several! You have never suspected it?"

"If I had do you suppose I would have allowed it?"
cried Roderick.

"They were the sacrifices of friendship and they were
easily made; only I don't enjoy having them thrown back
in my teeth."

This was under the circumstances a sufficiently generous
speech; but Roderick was not in the humour to take it

generously, "Come, be more definite," he said. "Let me know where it is the shoe has pinched."

Rowland frowned; if Roderick would not take generosity he should have full justice. "It's a perpetual sacrifice to live with a transcendent egotist!"

"I am an egotist?" cried Roderick.

"Did it never occur to you?"

"An egotist to whom you have made perpetual sacrifices?" He repeated the words in a singular tone; a tone that denoted neither exactly indignation nor incredulity, but (strange as it may seem) a sudden violent curiosity for news about himself.

"You are selfish," said Rowland; "you think only of yourself and believe only in yourself. You regard other people only as they play into your own hands. You have always been very frank about it, and the things seemed so mixed up with the temper of your genius and the very structure of your mind that often one was willing to take the evil with the good and to be thankful that considering your great talent you were no worse. But if one believed in you as I have done one paid a tax on one's faith!"

Roderick leaned his elbows on his knees, clasped his hands together and crossed them shadewise over his eyes. In this attitude for a moment he sat looking coldly at his friend. "So I have made you very uncomfortable?" he went on.

"Extremely so."

"I have been eager, grasping, obstinate, vain, ungrateful, indifferent, cruel?"

"I have accused you mentally of all these things—with the exception of vanity."

"You have often hated me?"

"Never. I should have parted company with you before coming to that."

"But you have wanted to part company, to bid me go on my way and be hanged?"

"Repeatedly. Then I have had patience and forgiven you."

"Forgiven me, eh? Suffering all the while?"

"Yes, you may call it suffering."

"Why did you never tell me all this before?"

"Because my affection was always stronger than my

resentment ; because I preferred to err on the side of kindness because I had myself in a measure launched .you in the world and thrown you among temptations; and because nothing short of your unwarrantable aggression just now could have made me say these painful things."

Roderick picked up a blade of long grass and began to bite it; Rowland was puzzled by his expression and manner. They seemed strangely cynical; there was something revolting in his deepening calmness. "I must have been hideous," Roderick presently resumed.

"I am not talking for your entertainment," said Rowland.

"Of course not. For my edification!" As Roderick said these words there was not a ray of warmth in his brilliant eye.

"I have spoken for my own relief," Rowland went on, "and so that you need never again go so utterly astray as you have done this morning."

"It has been a terrible mistake then?" What his tone expressed was not wilful mockery, but a kind of persistent irresponsibility which Rowland found equally exasperating. He answered nothing. "And all this time," Roderick continued, "you have been in love? Tell me the woman."

Rowland felt an immense desire to give him a visible palpable pang. "Her name is Mary Garland," he said.

Apparently he succeeded. The surprise was great; Roderick coloured as he had never done. "Mary Garland? Heaven forgive us!"

Rowland observed the "us;" Roderick threw himself back on the turf. The latter lay for some time staring at the sky. At last he sprang to his feet and Rowland rose also, rejoicing keenly, it must be confessed, in his companion's confusion.

"For how long has this been?" Roderick demanded.

"Since I first knew her."

"Two years! And you have never told her?"

"Never."

"You have told no one?"

"You are the first person."

"Why have you been silent?"

"Because of your engagement."

"But you have done your best to keep that up."

" That's another matter ! "

" It's very strange ! " said Roderick presently. " It's like something in a novel."

" We needn't expatiate on it," said Rowland "All I wished to do was to rebut your charge that I am an abnormal being."

But still Roderick pondered. " All these months, while I was going my way ! I wish you had mentioned it."

" I acted as was necessary, and that's the end of it."

" You have a very high opinion of her ? "

" The highest."

" I remember now your occasionally expressing it and my being struck with it. But I never dreamed you were in love with her. It's a pity she doesn't care for you ! "

Rowland had made his point and he had no wish to prolong the conversation ; but he had a desire to hear more of this and he remained silent.

" You hope, I suppose, that some day she may ? " Roderick asked.

" I shouldn't have offered to say so ; but since you ask me, I do."

" I don't believe it. She idolises me, and if she never were to see me again she would idolise my memory."

This might be vivid insight and it might be profound fatuity. Rowland turned away ; he could not trust himself to speak.

" My indifference, my neglect of her, must have seemed to you horrible. Altogether I must have appeared simply hideous."

" Do you really care," Rowland asked, " what you appeared ? "

" Certainly. I have been damnably stupid. Isn't an artist supposed to be a man of perceptions ? I am hugely disgusted."

" Well, you understand now, and we can start afresh."

" And yet," said Roderick, " though you have suffered, in a degree, I don't believe you have suffered so much as some other men would have done."

" Very likely not. In such matters quantitative analysis is difficult."

Roderick picked up his stick and stood looking at the ground. " Nevertheless, I must have seemed hideous,"

he repeated—"hideous." He turned away frowning, and
Rowland offered no contradiction.

They were both silent for some time, and at last
Roderick gave a heavy sigh and began to walk away.
"Where are you going?" Rowland then asked.

"Oh, I don't care! To walk; you have given me
something to think of." This seemed a salutary impulse,
and yet Rowland felt a nameless perplexity. "To have
been so stupid damns me more than anything!" Roderick
went on. "Certainly I can shut up shop now."

Rowland felt in no smiling humour, and yet in spite
of himself he could almost have smiled at the very consistency of the fellow. It was egotism still—æsthetic disgust at the graceless contour of his conduct, but never a hint
of simple sorrow for the pain he had given. Rowland let him
go, and for some moments stood watching him. Suddenly
Rowland became conscious of a singular and most illogical
impulse—a desire to stop him, to have another word with
him—not to lose sight of him. He called him and Roderick
turned. "I should like to go with you," said Rowland.

"I am fit only to be alone. I am damned!"

"You had better not think of it at all," Rowland cried,
"than think in that way."

"There is only one way. I have been hideous!" And
he broke off and marched away with his long elastic step,
swinging his stick. Rowland watched him, and at the end
of a moment called to him. Roderick stopped and looked
at him in silence, and then abruptly turned and disappeared
below the crest of a hill.

XXVI.

ROWLAND passed the remainder of the day as best he
could. He was half exasperated, half depressed; he had
an insufferable feeling of having been placed in the wrong
in spite of his excellent cause. Roderick did not come
home to lunch; but of this, with his passion for brooding

away the hours on far-off mountain sides, he had almost made a habit. Mrs. Hudson appeared at the noonday repast with a face which showed that Roderick's demand for money had unsealed the fountains of her distress. Little Singleton consumed an enormous and well-earned meal. Mary Garland, Rowland observed, had not contributed her scanty assistance to her kinsman's pursuit of the Princess Casamassima without an effort. The effort was visible in her pale face and her silence; she looked so ill that when they left the table Rowland felt almost bound to remark upon it. They had come out upon the grass in front of the inn.

"I have a headache," she said. And then suddenly, looking about at the menacing sky and motionless air, "It's this horrible day!"

Rowland that afternoon tried to write a letter to his cousin Cecilia, but his head and his heart were alike heavy, and he traced upon the paper but a single line. "I believe there is such a thing as being too reasonable. But when once the habit is formed, what is one to do?" He had occasion to use his keys and he felt for them in his pockets; they were missing, and he remembered that he had left them lying on the hill-top where he had had his talk with Roderick. He went forth in search of them and found them where he had thrown them. He flung himself down in the same place again; he felt indisposed to walk. He was conscious that his mood had greatly changed since the morning; his extraordinary acute sense of his rights had been replaced by the familiar chronic sense of his duties. Only, his duties now seemed impracticable; he turned over and buried his face in his arms. He lay so a long time, thinking of many things; the sum of them all was that Roderick had beaten him. At last he was startled by an extraordinary sound; it took him a moment to perceive that it was a portentous growl of thunder. He aroused himself and saw that the whole face of the sky had altered. The clouds that had hung motionless all day were moving from their stations, and getting into position for a battle. The wind was rising, the turbid vapours were growing dark and thick. It was a striking spectacle, but Rowland judged best to observe it briefly, as a storm was evidently imminent. He took his way down to the inn and found

Singleton still at his post, profiting by the last of the rapid-failing light to finish his study, and yet at the same time taking rapid notes of the actual condition of the clouds.

" We are going to have a most interesting storm ! " the little painter gleefully cried. " I should like awfully to *do* it."

Rowland adjured him to pack up his tools and decamp, and repaired to the house. The air by this time had become tremendously dark, and the thunder was incessant and deafening; in the midst of it the lightning flashed and vanished, like the treble shrilling upon the bass. The inn-keeper and his servants had crowded to the doorway and were looking at the scene with faces which seemed a proof that it was unprecedented. As Rowland approached, the group divided to let some one pass within, and Mrs. Hudson came forth, as white as a corpse and trembling in every limb.

" My boy, my boy, where is my boy ? " she cried. " Mr. Mallet, why are you here without him ? Bring him to me ! "

" Has no one seen Mr. Hudson ? " Rowland asked of the others. " Has he not returned ? "

Each one shook his head and looked grave, and Rowland attempted to reassure Mrs. Hudson by saying that of course he had taken refuge in a chalet.

" Go and find him, go and find him ! " she cried, insanely. " Don't stand there and talk, or I shall drop dead ! " It was now as dark as evening, and Rowland could just distinguish the figure of Singleton scampering homeward with his box and easel. " And where is Mary ? " Mrs. Hudson went on ; " what in mercy's name has become of her ? Mr. Mallet, why did you ever bring us here ? "

There came a prodigious flash of lightning, and the limitless tumult about them turned clearer than mid-summer noonday. The brightness lasted long enough to enable Rowland to see a woman's figure on the top of an eminence near the house. It was Mary Garland, questioning the lurid darkness for Roderick. Rowland sprang out to interrupt her vigil, but in a moment he met her coming back. He seized her hand and hurried her to the house, where, as soon as she stepped into the covered gallery, Mrs. Hudson fell upon her with frantic lamentations.

" Did you see anything—nothing ? " she cried. " Tell Mr. Mallet he must go and find him, with some men, some lights, some wrappings. Go, go, go, sir ! In mercy, go ! "

Rowland was extremely perturbed by the poor lady's vociferous folly, for he deemed her anxiety superfluous. He had offered his suggestion with sincerity ; nothing was more probable than that Roderick had found shelter in a herdsman's cabin. These were numerous on the neighbouring mountains, and the storm had given fair warning of its approach, Mary stood there very pale, saying nothing, only looking at him. He expected that she would try to soothe her cousin. " *Could* you find him ? " she suddenly asked. " Would it be of use ? "

The question seemed to him a flash intenser than the lightning that was raking in the sky before them. It shattered his dream that he weighed in the scale ! But before he could answer, the full fury of the storm was upon them ; the rain descended in sounding torrents. Every one fell back into the house. There had been no time to light lamps, and in the little uncarpeted parlour, in the unnatural darkness, Rowland felt Mary's hand upon his arm. For a moment it had an eloquent pressure ; it seemed to be a retractation of her senseless challenge, an assurance that she believed, for Roderick, what he believed. But nevertheless, thought Rowland, the cry had come, her heart had spoken ; her first impulse had been to sacrifice him. He had been uncertain before ; here at least was the comfort of certainty !

It must be confessed however that the certainty in question did little to enliven the gloom of that formidable evening. There was a noisy crowd about him in the room —noisy even with the accompaniment of the continual thunder-peals ; lodgers and servants, chattering, shuffling, bustling, annoying him equally by making too light of the tempest and by vociferating their alarm. In the disorder it was some time before a lamp was lighted, and the first thing he saw as it was swung from the ceiling was the white face of Mrs. Hudson who was being carried out of the room in a swoon by two stout maid-servants, with Mary Garland forcing a passage. He rendered what help he could, but when they laid the poor woman on her bed Mary motioned him away.

"I think you make her worse," she said.

Rowland went to his own room. The partitions in Swiss mountain-inns are thin, and from time to time he heard Mrs. Hudson moaning three doors off. Considering its great fury the storm took long to expend itself; it was upwards of three hours before the thunder ceased. But even then the rain continued to fall heavily, and the night, which had come on, was impenetrably black. This lasted till near midnight. Rowland thought of Mary Garland's question in the porch, but he thought even more that, although the fetid interior of a high-nestling chalet may offer a convenient refuge from an Alpine tempest, there was no possible music in the universe so sweet as the sound of Roderick's voice. At midnight, through his dripping window-pane, he saw a star, and he immediately went down stairs and out into the gallery. The rain had ceased, the cloud-masses were dissevered here and there, and several stars were visible. In a few minutes he heard a step behind him, and, turning, saw Mary Garland. He asked about Mrs. Hudson and learned that she was sleeping, exhausted by her fruitless lamentations. Mary kept scanning the darkness, but she said nothing to cast doubt on Roderick's having found a refuge. Rowland noticed it. "This also have I guaranteed!" he said to himself. There was something that Mary wished to learn and a question presently revealed it. "What made him start on a long walk so suddenly?" she asked. "I saw him at eleven o'clock, and then he meant to go to Engelberg and sleep."

"On his way to Interlaken!" Rowland said.

"Yes," she answered under cover of the darkness.

"We had some talk," said Rowland, "and he seemed, for the day, to have given up Interlaken."

"Did you dissuade him?"

"Not exactly. We discussed another question, which for the time superseded his plan."

Mary was silent. Then—"May I ask whether your discussion was violent?" she said.

"I am afraid it was agreeable to neither of us."

"And Roderick left you in—in irritation?"

"I offered him my company on his walk. He declined it."

Mary paced slowly to the end of the gallery and then came back. "If he had gone to Engelberg," she said, "he would have reached the hotel before the storm began."

Rowland felt a sudden explosion of ferocity. "Oh, if you like," he cried, "he can start for Interlaken as soon as he comes back!"

But she did not even notice his anger. "Will he come back early?" she went on.

"We may suppose so."

"He will know how anxious we are and he will start with the first light," said Mary.

Rowland was on the point of declaring that Roderick's readiness to throw himself into the feelings of others made this extremely probable; but he checked himself and said simply, "I expect him at sunrise."

Mary bent her eyes once more upon the irresponsive darkness, and then in silence went into the house. Rowland, it must be averred, in spite of his resolution not to be nervous, found no sleep that night. When the early dawn began to tremble in the east he came forth again into the open air. The storm had completely cleared the atmosphere and the day gave promise of cloudless splendour. Rowland watched the early sun-shafts slowly reaching higher, and remembered that if Roderick did not come back to breakfast there were two things to be taken into account. One was the heaviness of the soil on the mountain-sides, saturated with the rain, which would make him walk slowly; the other was the fact that, speaking without irony, he was not remarkable for throwing himself into the sentiments of others. Breakfast at the inn was early, and by breakfast-time Roderick had not reappeared. Then Rowland admitted that he was nervous. Neither Mrs. Hudson nor her companion had left their apartment; Rowland had a mental vision of the two women sitting there looking at each other and listening; he had no desire to see them more closely. There were a couple of men who hung about the inn as guides for going up the Titlis; Rowland sent each of them forth in a different direction to ask for news of Roderick at every chalet door within a morning's walk. Then he called Sam Singleton, whose peregrinations had made him an excellent mountaineer and whose zeal and sympathy were now unbounded, and the two started together on a journey of research. By the time they had lost sight of the inn Rowland was obliged to confess that decidedly Roderick had had time to come back.

He wandered about for several hours, but he found only the sunny stillness of the mountain-sides. Before long he parted company with Singleton, who to his suggestion that separation would multiply their powers, assented with a silent frightened look which reflected too vividly his own rapidly-dawning thought. The day was magnificent; the sun was everywhere; the storm had lashed the lower slopes into a deeper flush of autumnal colour, and the snow-peaks reared themselves against the near horizon in shining blocks and incisive peaks. Rowland made his way to several chalets, but most of them were empty. He thumped at their low foul doors with a kind of nervous savage anger; he challenged the stupid silence to tell him something about his friend. Some of these places had evidently not been open for months. The silence everywhere was horrible; it seemed to mock at his impatience and to be a conscious symbol of calamity. In the midst of it, at the door of one of the cabins, quite alone, sat a hideous *crétin* who grinned at Rowland over his goitre when, hardly knowing what he did, he questioned him. This creature's family was scattered on the mountain-sides; he could give Rowland no help to find them. Rowland climbed into many awkward places, and skirted intently and peeringly many an ugly chasm and steep-dropping ledge. But the sun, as I have said, was everywhere; it illumined the deep places over which, not knowing where to turn next, he halted and lingered, and showed him nothing but the stony Alpine void—nothing so human even as death. At noon he paused in his quest and sat down on a stone; the conviction was pressing upon him that the worst that was now possible was true. He stopped looking; he was afraid to go on. He sat there for an hour, sick to the depths of his soul. Without his knowing why, several things, chiefly trivial, that had happened during the last two years and that he had quite forgotten, became vividly present to his mind. He was aroused at last by the sound of a stone dislodged near by, which rattled down the mountain. In a moment, on a steep rocky slope opposite to him, he beheld a figure

cautiously descending—a figure which was not Roderick.
It was Singleton, who had seen him and began to beckon
to him.

"Come down—come down!" cried the painter, steadily
making his own way down. Rowland saw that as he
moved, and even as he selected his foothold and watched
his steps, he was looking at something at the bottom of
the cliff. This was a great rugged wall which sloped back-
ward from the perpendicular, and the descent, though
difficult, was with care sufficiently practicable.

"What do you see?" cried Rowland.

Singleton stopped, looked across at him and seemed to
hesitate; then, "Come down—come down!" he simply
repeated.

Rowland's course was also a deep descent, and he
attacked it so precipitately that he afterwards marvelled
he had not broken his neck. It was a ten minutes' head-
long scramble. Half-way down he saw something that
made him dizzy; he saw what Singleton had seen. In the
gorge below them a vague white mass lay tumbled upon
the stones. He let himself go, blindly, fiercely. Singleton
had reached the rocky bottom of the ravine before him,
and had bounded forward and fallen upon his knees.
Rowland overtook him and his own legs bent under him.
The thing that yesterday was his friend lay before him as
the chance of the last breath had left it, and out of it
Roderick's face stared upward open-eyed at the sky.

He had fallen from a great height, but he was singularly
little disfigured. The rain had spent its torrents upon
him, and his clothes and hair were as wet as if the billows
of the ocean had flung him upon the strand. An attempt
to move him would show some hideous fracture, some
horrible physical dishonour, but what Rowland saw on
first looking at him was only a strangely serene expression of life. The eyes were those of a dead man, but in
a short time, when Rowland had closed them, the whole
face seemed to awake. The rain had washed away all
blood; it was as if Violence, having done her work, had
stolen away in shame. Roderick's face might have shamed
her; it looked admirably handsome.

"He was a beautiful fellow!" said Singleton.

They looked up through their horror at the cliff from

which he had apparently fallen, and which lifted its blank and stony face above him, with no care now but to drink the sunshine on which his eyes were closed ; and then Rowland had an immense outbreak of pity and anguish. At last they spoke of carrying him back to the inn. " There must be three or four men," Rowland said, " and they must be brought here quickly. I have not the least idea where we are."

" We are at about three hours' walk from home," said Singleton. " I will go for help ; I can find my way."

" Remember whom you will have to face ! " said Rowland.

" I remember," the excellent fellow answered. " There was nothing I could ever do for him in life ; I will do what I can now."

He went off, and Rowland stayed there alone. He watched for seven long hours, and his vigil was for ever memorable. The most rational of men was for an hour the most passionate. He reviled himself with transcendent bitterness, he accused himself of cruelty and injustice, he would have lain down there in Roderick's place to unsay the words that had yesterday driven him forth on his lonely ramble. Roderick had been fond of saying that there are such things as necessary follies, and Rowland was now proving it. At last he grew almost used to the dumb exultation of the cliff above him, and he tried to understand what had happened. Not that it helped him ; before the absoluteness of the fact one hypothesis after another lost its interest. Roderick's passionate walk had carried him farther and higher than he knew ; he had outstayed supposably the first menace of the storm and perhaps even found a defiant entertainment in watching it. Perhaps he had simply lost himself. The tempest had overtaken him and when he tried to return it was too late. He had attempted to descend the cliff in the darkness, he had made the inevitable slip, and whether he had fallen fifty feet or three hundred little mattered now. The condition of his body indicated the shorter fall. Now that all was over Rowland understood how exclusively, for two years, Roderick had filled his life. His occupation was gone.

Singleton came back with four men—one of them the landlord of the inn. They had formed a sort of rude bier of the frame of a *chaise à porteurs*, and by taking a very round-about course homeward were able to follow a tolerably level path and carry their burden with a certain decency. To Rowland it seemed as if the little procession would never reach the inn ; but as they drew near it he would have given his right hand for a longer delay. The people of the hotel came forward to meet them in a little silent solemn convoy. In the doorway, clinging together, appeared the two bereaved women. Mrs. Hudson tottered forward with outstretched hands and the expression of a blind person ; but before she reached her son Mary Garland had rushed past her and, in the face of the staring, pitying, awe-stricken crowd, had flung herself with the magnificent movement of one whose rights were supreme and with a loud tremendous cry, upon the senseless vestige of her love.

That cry still lives in Rowland's ears. It interposes persistently against the reflection that when he sometimes —very rarely—sees her, she is unreservedly kind to him ; against the memory that during the dreary journey back to America, made of course with his assistance, there was a great frankness in her gratitude, a great gratitude in her frankness. Mary Garland lives with Mrs. Hudson, at Northampton, where Rowland visits his cousin Cecilia more frequently than of old. When he calls upon Mary he never sees Mrs. Hudson. Cecilia, who having her shrewd impression that he comes to see the young lady at the other house as much as to see herself, does not feel obliged to seem unduly flattered, calls him whenever he reappears the most restless of mortals. But he always says to her in answer, "No, I assure you I am the most patient !"

THE END.